Silver Search

An *ISCFleet* Novel

The second book
in the
Preeminent War
Series

Rock Whitehouse

In God We Trust.

(All others we monitor.)

Unofficial Army Security Agency/Air Force Security Service motto.

Authors Note

Thanks for picking up *Silver Search*. This is the second book the in three-volume *Preeminent War* series, which began with *Silver Enigma* and will finish with *Silver Victory*.

In this part, we pick up where *Silver Enigma* left off, with Carol and David together (*finally!*) at Fleet HQ, and Joanne Henderson's *Intrepid* out dispensing the first set of 'Sentinel' surveillance drones to watch for the enemy. The mystery at Beta Hydri (d) 'Big Blue' awaits the return of *Antares*, while David is set to begin a hopeful new chapter in his career with Dan Smith on *Columbia*.

Silver Search will answer some questions left open in *Silver Enigma,* and will hopefully leave you with even more interesting questions by the end.

Some readers have noted the use of military terms and acronyms in *Silver Enigma*. I have provided a list of the acronyms and terms at the back of the book.

Anytime one is trying to tell a multi-threaded story like this one, the cast of characters can grow fairly large. To help with that, there's also a list of significant characters at the back of the book.

Both lists can also be found at www.iscfleet.com/bonus-material.

I've also had questions about the stars in the story. Beta Hydri, GL 674, and the rest are all actual stars, depicted in their actual positions. A lot of them are red dwarfs, because, well, there are a lot of red dwarfs around. It's the most populous type of star in the galaxy.

I hope you will find this 'a very good sequel' to *Silver Enigma*, as one beta-reader described it.

As always, I'm interested in your questions and comments, so shoot me an email at rock@iscfleet.com.

Rock Whitehouse
September, 2019

"As I have reported, Admired Third Kiker, once the cohorts were lost, we had not the resources to assert our natural authority."

"So, Hess Tse Sim, you were indeed defeated by a single mystery vessel?"

"Yes, Admired Third, that is ultimately true. We did, however, destroy it as well."

"And what have you learned from this?" Jaf asked, retaking control.

"They are very advanced, Respected Second. A drive like ours, similar communications, and weapons we must respect."

"Respect?" cried Ashil Kiker. "We are the Preeminent. We *take* respect. We *command* worship. We do not *give* it."

Hess Tse Sim did not respond. Perhaps he may have given the wrong response.

"The decision is made, Hess Tse Sim. Your discipline shall be here and now."

"I accept the judgement of the Council, Respected Second." He closed his eyes and bowed his head, his large clawed hands covering his eyes in the traditional position of submission. A rebuke was forthcoming, he knew, perhaps a demotion, but certainly no dishonor.

They seized him with enthusiasm, their sharp teeth and claws tearing the flesh from his bones. The Second was favored with his organs. The rest consumed him quickly, but his cries lasted longer than most, as he had proved to be an inferior instance, and they chose not to be merciful.

The head was left as a prize for The First. He would allow it to mature on his food shelf for several rotations, and once the scent was fully ripe and the contents tenderized, he would consume it.

Intrepid
GL 832
Monday, July 25. 2078, 0845 UTC

An ISC Fleet ship's hangar deck was a large and complex structure. To preserve the internal ship atmosphere, incoming shuttles first arrived in a docking airlock not much bigger than the shuttle itself. Once inside the ShuttleLock, the outer doors would close and the inside of the airlock would be re-pressurized. The inner doors then opened and the shuttle moved into the large internal hangar.

Today, *Intrepid*'s shuttle would be used to launch the first Sentinel surveillance drone. The Sentinel was a new invention from FleetIntel that could watch a star system continuously, permitting the Fleet's limited and valuable ship resources to be used elsewhere. On this long trip, Intrepid would release the first six at their assigned stars.

Lieutenant Natalie Hayden, *Intrepid's* Weapons Maintenance Officer, was moving all around the hangar, hovering, more or less, as her techs took the first

Sentinel off its shipping cradle and loaded it on a transport cart. Once on the cart, they used the same portable lift to pick a Radioisotope Thermoelectric Generator (RTG) power supply off its pallet and move it to the back end of the Sentinel. *Intrepid's* Intel Chief, Warrant Officer Ben Price, was already there, and together with the Weapons crew, he and Hayden slid the RTG into place and secured the six latches that held it on the probe.

"Hey, Lieutenant Hayden," Ben called, "maybe we should sign it?"

Natalie looked at him blankly. "Sign it?"

"Yeah, like they used to sign bombs. Let's just get a marker and get the launch crew to sign on the inside of that last access door."

Hayden remained skeptical. "No one will ever see it, Price."

"Maybe not. But it would be fun for the crew, right?" The Chief heard this and piped in that he thought it would be a good idea.

"Should we ask Captain Henderson?" Price asked.

"Is there the slightest chance she'd say no?" Natalie responded, her inner mischievous streak starting to warm up to the idea.

"Yes."

"Then hell no we're not asking her." She pulled a marker from her sleeve pocket and handed it to the most junior member of the Weapons crew. They each signed their names, Price and Hayden last. Price ran the initial system checks from his NetComp and pronounced it ready. They carefully moved the cart into the shuttle, then clamped the cart to the floor. When Hayden took the shuttle out and reversed the gravity in the cargo bay, it wouldn't pay to have the cart leave with the Sentinel. Once the shuttle was in position outside, she would remove the straps holding the probe down before opening the cargo doors.

They came out of FTL an hour later close to the desired orbit. In a couple hours, the ship was right where it needed to be, and it was time to put the Sentinel overboard. Price headed forward to the Intel section where he would perform the post-launch checkout. Hayden reread her deployment procedure and settled into the shuttle cockpit. She slipped on a headset and powered up the shuttle. In a few seconds, the shuttle reported itself ready for duty, and she could select the comms channel they had agreed on beforehand.

"Jesse, this is Nat," she called.

"We hear you, Natalie," Jesse Woodward, the Communications Officer, responded in his low baritone. They often kidded him about his disc jockey delivery. "Price, are you up?"

"I'm here, Lieutenant Woodward. We're ready in Intel."

Hayden closed the shuttle cockpit door, and the Weapons crew moved the shuttle in and closed the inner door. She could see the lock status on her panel, so once the inner door reported closed, she began venting the ShuttleLock.

"Opening outer door," she said as she commanded the action. In a few seconds, the door was open, and with one touch of the control stick, she moved the shuttle out of *Intrepid*. As she did, the red dwarf star, about half the size of the Sun, flooded the cockpit with its yellow-orange light. The windows auto-tinted, but there was a limit to how dark they could get. It was still pretty bright inside, and she quickly found her red filter sunglasses and slapped them on.

Hayden moved the shuttle out about a kilometer, a tiny distance in astronomical terms but far enough that the two-meter-long laser communications scope on top of *Intrepid* could see the Sentinel. She set the shuttle to hold its position.

"OK, I'm going back to unstrap it." She took off her headset and slipped off her safety harness. It was a tight turn to get from the left seat to the cargo bay access door, and she needed to be careful not to bang her head on the top of the bay entry. Once through the door, she removed the straps holding the Sentinel to the cart and secured them underneath. She made her way back to the cockpit, double checking that she had closed the access door correctly. Retaking the left seat, she buckled herself back in and slipped the communications headset back on.

"OK, it's unstrapped," she said, reaching for the cargo door open control. "Opening the doors now." She heard the whistle of the cargo atmosphere leaving, then the quiet hum of the door mechanism. Doors open, she reached for the cargo bay's G-floor control.

"Here goes." She moved the control from plus-one to minus-point-one. As she did, the Sentinel slowly rose from the secured cart and moved out of the open cargo doors. She watched it on the cargo bay video monitor.

"It's out, Price."

Price commanded the laser comm system to connect to the Sentinel. As the status indicators lit up, he let the others know. "Connection is made," he reported. "Starting checkout sequence." His first task was to command the Sentinel to find its three navigation stars. It took several minutes for it to determine its orientation and swing into the correct position. Finally, the Sentinel reported itself ready.

"OK Lieutenant Hayden, it's good to go. Only twenty minutes, less than I expected."

"Fine, returning." The shuttle moved back into the ship through the ShuttleLock. As Hayden stepped out, Ben Price was entering the hangar from forward.

"Looks good so far, " he said. "I didn't see any problems, did you?"

Hayden shook her head. "No, nothing. Went smooth."

She walked towards the hangar's forward passage entry, Price in step with her. "Lunch?"

Hayden smiled and nodded her agreement, and they headed to the wardroom together.

August 2078

ISC Fleet HQ Intel Section
Ft. Eustis, VA
Tuesday, August 2, 2078, 0830 EDT

David and Carol enjoyed their free Sunday together, having spent Saturday evening at the Harris' cookout. After brunch at the Bachelor Officers' Quarters (BOQ), they spent much of the afternoon walking the post, their desire for real air and sunshine still not nearly satisfied. Later, they got off the post for dinner in town. In a quiet back corner booth, they talked about how natural it felt, how easy it was for them to be together. This, they knew, is where they had both been heading all along. But this respite from the war was only for that one day, and they recognized how fortunate it was that they had even that much time. When Monday came, the war would be back in the front of their minds, and there would be work waiting for both of them.

David spent Monday in a borrowed Intel workroom reviewing the scan data from the battle *Sigma* had fought with the enemy at GL 876, correlating it with his own written report. The Flight Data Recorder (FDR) didn't lie, so if he found a discrepancy between his own recollections in his report and the FDR dump, he knew the dump wasn't wrong. It was hard to see that his memory of the timing and sequence of events might not be perfect, but it clearly wasn't, so he worked most of the day getting it all to line up in a narrative that he could live with. He felt he owed it to his lost shipmates to be as clear and accurate as he could be.

Carol sat with Kathy Stewart, whom she found to be a delightful work partner, to prioritize the list of academic candidates for the return mission to Beta Hydri. It was hard; some candidates looked good initially but did not seem to have the required personality. If you were not a demonstrated team player, you went to the bottom of the list, maybe lower. Younger was better, but not to the point that it meant inexperience. Regular fieldwork was a definite plus, as this was to be a hands-on expedition. They considered gender and nationality irrelevant, except that they had to be a citizen of an ISC-treaty country.

Tuesday morning found David and Carol walking to work together from the BOQ. It was a warm, rainy day and they were glad for the covered walkway stretching from their quarters to Fleet HQ. She was planning to sit in on his presentation to FleetIntel on behalf of *Antares*, as would Terri Michael. Jack Ballard, who would normally attend any briefing in FleetIntel, was busy with mission planning. Later in the morning, David would meet with Frances Wilson and a mysterious FPI engineer known only as 'Lloyd.' As they entered the Intel Section, David caught sight of Terri Michael for the first time since he'd returned. He walked directly to her; his hand extended.

"Good morning, ma'am."

"Hello, Powell, it's good to see you again." She took his hand and shook it firmly.

"I just wanted to tell you again, in person this time, how grateful I am to you."

Terri smiled and leaned her head towards Carol. "Truthfully, it was your partner Carol here who did it. I just delivered the message to CINC."

"Still, without you, it would not have happened, and I want you to know how much I appreciate it."

Terri nodded, then put her hand on his shoulder. "Congratulations, Powell, you earned it."

Ron Harris had entered in the middle of this discussion. "So, now that we're all so happy and appreciated can we, like, get some work done?"

They moved on into the conference room.

"*Lieutenant* Powell—has a nice ring to it, wouldn't you say?" Harris said, playing along just a little.

David smiled broadly. "It does, sir!"

"So, *Lieutenant* Powell, tell us what your thoughts are on the tracking."

"Well, sir, the scan data is in the report. The first Type I came out of FTL almost behind us—a bearing of 170 degrees. And then it just hung there. I had several conversations with John Sanders, and he was very apprehensive as well." David paused to take a breath.

"Go on, David," Terri Michael prompted.

"Yes, ma'am. So, after an hour, Commander Davis decides to strike, and just as he does, the next Type I appears, also just pacing us."

Carol leaned forward, "The data shows that these ships kept a constant position and range. They could not possibly have done that without knowing exactly where *Sigma* was and her course."

David nodded. "Yes, clearly. One of the most disconcerting things for me was the accuracy. Sanders said that they were holding a constant position within the accuracy of our sensors' abilities to measure it."

"So, tell me about your conversation with Ensign Farley."

David slumped back a little, remembering Leah, then regained himself.

"Well, sir, she called me —I think it was after the second set of hits. This isn't in the audio on the FDR. She was back in the Comms Equipment area, and she and Jeff Shaw were looking at something. She was talking about periodic fluctuations, and then she was cut off by the next strike."

"Well," Terri Michael began, thinking about what she could remember of SLIP system operations, "this was after a SLIP message was sent, right?"

6

David nodded.

"Normal procedure after a message is sent is to check the receiver status. Sometimes a SLIP transmission can sort of bleed over onto the receiver and knock it out of alignment."

David's face brightened. "So maybe they saw something on the SLIP receiver status display?"

"That's what I'm thinking, yes."

Harris looked back at David. "That's interesting. You'll be meeting with Frances Wilson and Lloyd later on to discuss that part in more detail."

"Yes, sir, I understand."

"I've listened to the Bridge audio," Harris said, changing the subject, "and it bears out what you're describing. I heard several officers express their concerns, and Davis just held his position. I don't think I really understand it."

"It's hard to think about, Admiral, because Commander Davis was always very good to me, and to the crew in general. It seems like he just maybe overplayed his hand a little?"

"Well, this hand cost us a lot of lives," Terri responded. "And a ship. Len was infuriated by the attack on Inor —swore he'd make them pay ten times over. That worried me, but it never occurred to me that he'd take this kind of chance."

Harris agreed. "Even Linda Rodriguez, who was as forward-leaning and aggressive as anyone I know, can be heard more or less asking him what the hell he's doing. He didn't like it."

"If I may," Carol began, "this is a lesson for all of us. This enemy isn't going to be easy. We've had some wins, but they aren't going to just let us light them up whenever we encounter them. Look at what happened to *Columbia* —they just got out in time because Commander Reynolds had the sense to run like hell when he needed to."

"So, what are you saying, Carol?" David asked.

"I guess I'm saying if they do something unexpected, something, well, weird, like this was, you don't wait. You run, and come back for another day." Carol's tone was plain, a matter of fact, saying something she felt was clear on its face.

"Most commanders are not going to like that advice, Lieutenant Hansen," Harris pointed out.

Carol shrugged. "Perhaps not, but isn't that what this situation is telling us?"

"Could be, Carol, could well be. But on the other hand, we can't just bug out whenever something looks a little strange."

"Well, Commander, for what it's worth, on *Sigma*'s bridge everyone except Commander Davis knew we should have gotten the hell out of there after like five minutes of that bugger hanging out on our tail." David looked around the table before continuing. "I know it's a command decision, and for sure it's a judgment call that can't be reduced to an equation, but we need to let our commanders know what happened here so they can adjust their thinking when something like this happens again."

"I agree, Lieutenant Powell, and I'll draft an advisory for the fleet along the lines of your thinking."

"Yes, sir. I apologize if I spoke out of turn, sir, but it was strange and avoidable, and people died." The stress and regret were plain on David's face.

Ron Harris leaned forward, looking first at one, then the other. "Listen, both of you. I will tell you if you're out of line. I take no offense at sincere, well-founded opinions strongly expressed. It helps to know that this isn't a casual thought, as you said, a rule that can't be expressed in an equation."

"Yes, sir. Thank you, sir." They started to get up when David spoke again. "One more thing, Admiral, after the SLIP was hit, they never fired at us again. Abe Jackson picked that up. I was too busy shooting to notice."

"I saw that in your report," Harris said. "Do you draw the same obvious conclusion that I do?"

"I do, sir. For me, that fact alone is conclusive evidence. All by itself it seals the case that they were using the SLIP to track us."

Harris nodded his agreement. "Yes, David, I agree with you. It seems awfully definitive." Harris leaned back in his chair, thinking. "I will include that in the notice to the fleet." He looked at his watch and leaned forward again, ready to stand up. "Thanks, David. I really appreciate you spending a little time with me."

They all stood and left the office. It was almost time for David's meeting with Frances and Lloyd, and Carol still had work to do on the academics list with Kathy Stewart. Harris and Terri Michael went back to his office and drafted an update to the fleet.

```
PRIORITY 207808021400UTC
TO: ALLFLEET
FROM: FLEETINTEL
SUBJECT: SLIP

TOP SECRET
ANALYSIS OF SIGMA ENGAGEMENT DATA AND DEBRIEF OF SURVIVORS
LEAVES FLEETINTEL WITH STRONG BELIEF THAT ENEMY HAS DEVELOPED
A METHOD OF TRACKING FLEET SHIPS USING THE SLIP SYSTEM.
EXACT EXPLOITATION TECHNIQUE UNDER INVESTIGATION.
SHIPS WHICH ENCOUNTER CONSTANT BEARING/DISTANCE
BEHAVIOR BY ENEMY VESSELS SHOULD CONSIDER IMMEDIATE RETIREMENT
AND SHOULD SHUT DOWN SLIP SYSTEM UNTIL CLEAR.
WE WILL PROVIDE MORE SPECIFIC INFORMATION/GUIDANCE AS IT BECOMES
AVAILABLE.

HARRIS
END
```

ISC Fleet HQ Intel Section
Ft. Eustis, VA
Tuesday, August 2, 2078, 1000 EDT

Lloyd waited uncomfortably in Frances' office. The old leather armchair in the corner was soft enough, but the topic on the table made him nervous. Finally, the new Fleet guy, Powell, knocked on the door frame and came in. Frances made the introductions, and afterwards Lloyd looked at him closely. Pleasant looking, nothing special, average height and build. Something intense in the eyes, though. Lloyd could not miss that. And something more in his bearing, something hard and determined about him. Kelly Peterson, sitting next to Powell, seemed relaxed and in control. She, like a lot of the Intel people he had met, seemed to know how to keep their knowledge and expertise just under the surface. They seemed so normal, like regular people, until you got them into a conversation and then they'd kick your intellectual ass without breaking a sweat.

Frances started the discussion. "So, Lieutenant Powell, Lloyd here is the authority on the SLIP system."

"Authority? Forstmann and I invented it!" Even as he was saying it, Lloyd wondered why he suddenly felt so defensive, and felt such a need to make sure everyone knew he was the expert in the room.

Frances gave him a puzzled glance and then continued. "Yes, we know that, Lloyd." She turned back to Powell.

"So, David, can you tell Lloyd and me what Ensign Farley told you?" Powell nodded, taking a second to gather his thoughts, then spoke directly to Lloyd.

"I only know part of what was happening. Leah was killed in the middle of the conversation."

Lloyd's eyebrows went up, and he shifted in his chair. One thing this Powell was, for sure, was tough. It couldn't be easy to talk about a conversation with a shipmate that was terminated by her death.

"Piecing the conversation together afterwards, we think her chief tech had pointed out something on the SLIP receiver status display. He was with her. She was telling me about 'periodic fluctuations' when the missile hit."

"That's it?" Lloyd asked, disappointed.

"That's all I heard."

"But you think they were tracking you with it?"

"Yes, well, Leah did, anyhow. Before she mentioned the fluctuations, she said she thought they were tracking us with the SLIP receiver and that they could do it from FTL."

Lloyd looked over at Frances. "Not much to go on."

Frances nodded her understanding. "True, but Farley was the Communications officer. She knew the SLIP system as well as anyone on the ship. If she thought the enemy was tracking with it, we should give that a lot of weight."

"Shit," Kelly Peterson said, suddenly sitting upright in her seat. Three sets of eyes went to her.

"Shit!" she repeated, louder this time. "Periodic fluctuations! Frances, remember that low-level signal we couldn't figure out? The thirty-five-second one?" Frances' eyes widened with recognition.

David looked from one to the other. "Care to share?"

Kelly looked over at Frances, who nodded her agreement.

"We've been copying a wide spectrum of SLIP transmissions trying to find the enemy."

"And doing TDOA?" he asked, and Lloyd's head snapped over to Powell. "You understand that?"

Powell looked back at him. "It's an introductory exercise in the first level Intel school. Time Difference of Arrival is a classic communications intelligence technique."

Lloyd just looked back at him, baffled, as he continued.

"Mrs. Wilson, just so I understand, you've been monitoring enemy communications?"

Frances leaned forward in her chair, her elbows on the desk. "We've been trying to, David. We've copied a few signals that we can locate, but it's not like we're copying all their traffic."

"Yet," Kelly added.

David took a moment to absorb what he'd just heard.

"OK, so tell me about this 35-second repeating signal."

"Only Tranquility copied it —,"

"*Only* Tranquility?" he interrupted. "How many of these scanners are out there?"

Again, Frances nodded her assent to Kelly. "Four. Here, Inor, Kapteyn, and Tranquility."

David looked at Kelly, then back to Frances. "You've all been pretty busy, eh? Good work. So, Kelly, Tranquility copied this thing?"

"Yes. There were three instances, ninety minutes each, where they saw this repeating signal. No one else saw it."

"When did this happen?"

"June 26, early morning UTC."

David looked at her. "June 26th?"

"Yes," Kelly answered, unsure where David was going with this.

"Tranquility, is, what, maybe ten, eleven hours from GL 876 by SLIP?"

They all looked at David, but no one spoke.

"Seems like you copied them tracking us," David finally said, breaking an uncomfortable silence.

"Oh my God..." Frances said quietly.

David looked over at Lloyd. "So, Mister SLIP inventor, any ideas?"

Lloyd shifted uneasily in his chair, feeling the spotlight focused on him. "No, not offhand. We didn't understand this signal at all before."

David held his eyes on Lloyd. "Well, it's just a thought, but could you reproduce this and see what our SLIP units do with it?"

Lloyd was unhappy with this exchange already, and now it was getting worse. "I'll need to think about that. Let me get back in the lab and see."

Frances looked from Lloyd to David and back. "I think that would be a good start."

"I agree, Mrs. Wilson," David said, "but make sure the signal strength is low. We don't want to tip the enemy that we're on to how they're tracking us."

Lloyd nodded, got out of his chair, and left the room. He was frustrated that he didn't know the answers to the questions he was being asked, and he was suddenly very afraid his brainchild might have a flaw that had already cost dozens of lives. But the only recourse for him now was to get back in the lab and figure it out. Whatever the answer was, he knew he had to find it.

Kelly sat for a moment, then turned to David, sad.

"I'm sorry, David. We didn't have any idea what this signal was."

He smiled grimly. "Kelly, there was nothing you could have done even if you did. The fight was already over before the signal even got to Tranquility II."

She nodded and stood to go back to her own desk.

David waited for her to be gone and then looked directly at Frances.

"Can he do it?"

Frances shrugged. "He did help invent the thing. I guess if anyone can figure this out, it's Forstmann and him."

"Kind of an odd duck, you know? He reacts pretty obviously when he hears something he doesn't know."

"Yes, I've noticed that."

"Yeah, it's like he's surprised that someone would know something he doesn't. That bothers me."

"Well, I don't think it's conceit, I just think he hasn't encountered that many people at his level, and he's surprised when he does."

"His level is pretty high, for sure. I just hope it's high enough."

"Amen to that."

David stood and left Frances' office, carrying new anxiety about whether they would really be able to solve this puzzle. He hoped, but he also doubted.

Bachelor Officers' Quarters
Ft. Eustis, VA
Wednesday, August 3, 2078, 0715 EDT

David was having breakfast when his phone buzzed with a message. He planned another day hanging around FleetIntel, but today he didn't have anything specific to do. He liked talking to Evans, and Ann Cooper, and Frances, too. *Columbia* was still more than a week away, and he welcomed the time to adjust to a new role and get up to speed on what FleetIntel was thinking. He was also planning for another evening with Carol. Her extended presence on the surface was an unexpected gift for both of them. But *Antares* would be pulling out soon, and David knew they would be gone for a long time. Today she would also be in FleetIntel, working with James George and Ron Harris to make the final calls on which academic experts they should approach to go to Beta Hydri with them.

David was also writing a lot of letters. He was the senior survivor of *Sigma's* near-fatal battle; as such, it fell to him to communicate with the families of the crew members that died. Some he knew very well, like John Sanders, but others in the ranks he really knew almost nothing about. Still, he did his best to convey what had happened and that the crewmember had performed well in hard circumstances.

This all came back into sharp focus as he read his message.

```
SLIP PERSONAL 207808020930UTC
TO: FLEET/LT DAVID POWELL
FROM: SIGMA/SLT MARGARET WHITE
SUBJECT: REMAINS

DAVID:
I WANTED TO LET YOU KNOW THAT THE SEARCH OF SIGMA WAS COMPLETED 7/28.
WE HAVE IDENTIFIED FIFTY-ONE SETS OF REMAINS ON BOARD.
I WILL SEND A FULL LIST TO FLEETPERS BUT WANTED YOU TO KNOW THAT
LISA BRIGGS WAS AMONG THOSE IDENTIFIED. ONLY TECHNICIAN PAULA JOHNSON
WAS FOUND ON THE BRIDGE.
THE REMAINS WILL STAY IN FROZEN STORAGE AND WILL BE SENT BACK
ON THE FIRST AVAILABLE VESSEL.
SORRY TO HAVE TO REPORT SUCH NEWS BUT THIS IS WHAT WE BOTH DO.

WARMEST REGARDS,
PEG

END
```

He looked away, saddened by this reminder of that day on *Sigma*. Carol looked at him as she sat down across the table, the obvious question on her face. He handed the phone over to her to read.

"Oh, God, David, I am so sorry."

"Yeah, it's still hard to think about."

"I know."

"But at least some of them will be coming back. And, as Lieutenant White says, this is part of what we do." David leaned back, setting his coffee carefully back down on the table.

"What's she like?" Carol asked between bites, "I've never met her."

"Crazy tall and thin, like six foot three or something. Very smart, very nice. She said I had set the record for the shortest time in grade as an ensign ever."

Carol laughed. "I bet you did, now that you say that!"

"That's how she introduced herself. You'd like her."

"I think I would."

"All business, though, once we got back out to *Sigma*. She took command, switched into engineer mode, and off she went."

"A pro."

"Right, exactly."

"Still, reading between the lines, I hear kindness in her voice. She didn't have to send this."

David nodded, picking up his coffee as he thought about it. "True. "

"Too bad about Lisa."

"Briggs was very good to me, Carol. She tried to draw me out, get me involved with stuff around the wardroom. I thought maybe she was hoping for something more."

Carol waited for him to continue, when he didn't, she prompted him. "But?"

"But Lisa was a great person. You knew her: smart, attractive, thoughtful. I liked her a lot, but it could never go beyond that for me. I couldn't let her believe otherwise."

"The way you talk about her makes me think of Marty."

"Sure, I get that. He was a good guy, a good friend to you, just as she was to me."

Carol set down her fork and looked David in the eye. "It's only been a few days, David, but you know I'm here for you, right?" She reached across to take his hand. "We can talk about *Sigma*, or Davis, or whatever else, if you need to."

"I know, Carol, I do. I'm doing pretty good so far, but thanks."

"You had a nightmare last night."

He nodded sheepishly. "Yes. It was the same one I've had a few times. I see the missiles coming right at us and I'm screaming at Leah to go tell Briggs to duck." He looked over at Carol. "It's stupid, I know. Childish, even."

"I don't think so. I think you're just trying to work through the loss of so many people you knew and cared about."

"Sure, maybe."

13

"You did everything you could. You know that, right?"

"I did everything I could think of at the time, sure. Maybe I could have done something better, I don't know."

As he spoke, she could hear his inner self second-guessing decisions made weeks ago, decisions that could not now be changed. "You weren't in command. Davis was."

"I know."

"Right. Don't forget that." Carol looked at him for a moment. "Have I said this morning that I love you?"

He smiled. "Sure. Just a second ago."

"OK, just checking." Carol thought a second and then changed the subject. "Have you seen your Grandmother?"

"Grandma Virginia? No, not in person. I had a video call with her yesterday."

"I bet she was glad to hear from you."

"She was. It's just her and me now. She was really upset about *Sigma*."

"No doubt. Did you tell her about us?"

"Oh sure. She was really happy about it. She remembers you well."

"Nice. You should go see her."

"Don't think I'll have time. I'll video call her again before I go."

Carol nodded her understanding and they passed the rest of breakfast in silence, as Carol went back to thinking about candidate academics, while David was still seeing the lost faces he would always remember.

FPI Development Lab
Outside Lewistown, Montana
Wednesday, August 4, 2078, 0715 MDT

In an FPI workshop fifty feet below the top of a small granite outcrop, Lloyd sat alone with his boss and mentor Randy Forstmann. They sat on opposite sides of a steel work table, each looking intently at the SLIP system design drawings on their tablets. Lloyd had returned from ISC HQ late Monday, and they had spent all day Tuesday reviewing the signal data that the Tranquility site had reported. The evidence for enemy tracking via SLIP was compelling, but they struggled to identify the actual method, and knowing the depth of their own understanding, it was disconcerting to both of them that the answer wasn't immediately apparent.

The polished internal components of a SLIP emitter/receiver lay scattered on the table between them. Finally, Forstmann looked up.

"They said that *Sigma* was not fired on after the SLIP system was taken out."

"Yes, I know that," Lloyd said, annoyed.

"Do we know if the strike on *Sigma*'s SLIP system removed the external apparatus from the ship?" Lloyd looked up at him, not understanding. Forstmann continued. "We've been thinking about this as an internal problem with the emitter, but what if it's a resonance within the external hardware instead? If the apparatus was damaged, that might explain how they were unable to find her once it was hit." Lloyd thought about that as he looked through the reports FleetIntel had provided him.

"It doesn't say," he answered. Randy Forstmann pulled out his phone and called Ron Harris, asking him if they were aware of whether the SLIP had been damaged or not. The conversation was short.

"He'll check with Powell, and if he doesn't know, he can check with the repair crew."

"But that's two days!"

"Yes, it is."

Forstmann got up and walked to the other end of the room where a SLIP emitter sat on the floor. It was a sphere perhaps a meter in diameter, painted a dull black to blend in with the stealth coating of the ship. It was titanium, mostly, only a few millimeters thick, with a secret blend of other trace elements. They'd spent almost a year deriving the best alloy for this strange process. Forstmann himself was surprised it worked, as he considered the initial theory that Lloyd had proposed very unlikely to succeed. But he also thought it would be a critical technology if it did and so he funded the effort. And, it had paid off. As he stood there considering what might be the root of this problem, his phone rang. It was Harris. After another short conversation, he hung up and turned to Lloyd.

"Powell can't say. There was a lot of damage to *Sigma*, but he doesn't really know if they hit the apparatus or not. They're going to ask the repair supervisor to check and let them know."

"So, two days, at least," Lloyd responded with disgust.

"Right."

Lloyd, clearly frustrated, put down his tablet and crossed his arms. "We know the channel, or, we think we do —what if we just tried it ourselves?"

Randy sat back down at the table. "I was thinking along those lines myself. If our theory is that the receiver is somehow resonating, then we'd need a low-power emitter to send the pulses and then a second set to try to detect the resonances."

"We have most of what we need here, I think," said Lloyd. "We'll need to get the team up to speed."

Forstmann reached for his phone, starting the cascade of phone calls and electronic messages that would bring twenty or more of the best physical science and engineering minds down on this small town.

The last call was to the Calvert Hotel for rooms.

Intrepid
L143-23
Friday, August 5, 2078, 1015 UTC

Natalie Hayden knocked on the edge of the Chief Intel Officer's open door. Ben looked up, then stood as she came in, closed the door, and sat down.

"Jesus Christ, Ben, stop acting like I'm your superior," she said with disgust.

"Well, *Lieutenant* Hayden, that's kinda what you are."

She shrugged. "Yeah, well, let's not do that in private, OK? "

"Sure." He closed what he was looking at and leaned forward on his elbows. "So, what's on your mind?"

"Tell me about Henderson."

Ben made a frustrated face. "What, you, too? I got harassed the day I set foot on this ship about her. I'm sick of it. I —"

"No, Ben," she said, cutting off his objections. "I understand that part. You were friends, I get that. Just tell me more about her."

It took Ben a few seconds to calm down and switch his response to the question Natalie was really asking.

"So, what's *your* impression so far?" he asked.

"She wants to look tough, a hard-ass, all business. But I wonder if that's how she really is."

Ben nodded. "Well, she is the Captain, and she has to keep the crew at a distance to do her job."

"True, but I just wonder what's behind it."

"She's plenty smart, but grounded, practical. She's all about getting the job done, whatever that means, in the best way she can find. She's not that complicated."

"What about her personal life? Married?"

Ben frowned, wondering how much he should say, finally deciding public information was as far as he would go.

"I can't say too much on that. After all, we talked a lot about things not meant to be shared. She's been divorced for a long time, but I'm not going beyond that. Don't let that get around."

"OK, understood."

Ben had some questions of his own. "So, is our boss The Great Senior Lieutenant Kirkland still pissed at me for, like, breathing?"

"He misses your predecessor. They were really close—maybe too close—and it was a shock when Craig got booted off to make room for you."

"Any advice?"

"Yes, Captain."

She smiled. "Seems to me I recall some annoying Warrant constantly telling me to check my assumptions back when I was in Plans."

Ben nodded. "Yes, ma'am, I recall him as well. Guess I should take my own advice?"

"Yeah, and don't forget Pournelle."

Ben smiled as he noticed the puzzled look on Natalie's face. "Ah yes, *the relentless application of logic...*"

Joanne turned and headed back to the Bridge.

"Pournelle?" Natalie asked.

"Yeah, the writer. He had a saying that he kept repeating, more or less that all problems could be solved by the relentless application of logic."

"Didn't Sherlock say something like that?" she asked as she pulled off yet another inspection panel. "Something about once you remove the impossible whatever is left must be true?"

"Yeah, that's close," Ben responded absentmindedly as he flipped through the plans on his NetComp. He stopped and looked up at the Weapons Chief Tech.

"Say Chief, you did this section on the RTG before you put it on, right?" The chief looked over at one of the young techs.

"Patrick?" he asked.

"Yes. At least, I think so..."

His hesitation produced an ugly scowl on the Chief Tech. "You told me you did the procedure, Patrick. Did you or did you not follow the plan?"

The frightened look on Dion Patrick's nineteen-year-old face was all Ben needed to see.

"OK, Chief, I'll disconnect the RTG lines and we can re-check." As Ben half-crawled into the Sentinel to disconnect the lines between the power supply and the probe, he could hear the Chief giving Technician Patrick some pithy and explicit advice to remember the next time he had a critical task to complete. As Ben pulled back out of the opening, he saw Natalie's pained expression, clearly embarrassed that one of her crew had apparently screwed up. Ben flipped open the small control panel so he and Natalie could check the settings. They looked up at each other in surprise.

"Switches look right to me," Ben said, handing the NetComp over to Natalie.

"Yeah, looks right."

The Chief and his young Tech also looked at the controls and agreed they were as specified.

"Except the power ready light is out," Natalie observed. She turned to Patrick. "Last step is to verify the light is on. Was it?"

"Yes, Lieutenant, it was on."

Ben looked hard at the young man, then went back to his NetComp.

"You're sure?" she asked again.

"I am sure, ma'am. It was on." Natalie looked at Ben, who was still staring at the troubleshooting chart.

"OK, Patrick, go open panel six and press the reset." It took a few seconds for the young man to get the right panel open and perform the reset.

"Done, sir."

"OK, I'll recycle the switches here and see what happens." It had been expedient to use the off-the-shelf RTG unit, but the flip side of that choice was the complexity in configuring it to run the Sentinel, something it was not designed to do. Ben went over the settings with the young tech and the RTG came online as expected. Ben reached back inside and restored the power and control connections.

The Sentinel came to life.

"OK, so?" Natalie asked.

"Beats the hell outta me, Lieutenant."

"Can we trust the damned thing?"

Ben shrugged. "Let's give it a few hours before we release it. If there's anything really wrong, we should see it in that time."

Joanne Henderson was not happy about the delay, but she understood Ben's reasoning. She trusted him well enough that if he had asked for another whole day, she'd have agreed to it. He was well aware of her confidence in him, and equally aware that he had to respect that part of their relationship and never ask for more than was really necessary.

Hansen Family Farm
Near Lancaster, Ohio
Thursday, August 5, 2078, 0930 EDT

It had been several months since Carol was last home. She'd spent several days there recuperating just after they returned from Inor. With the trip to Beta Hydri on the horizon, it would be some time before she had another chance. She'd hardly finished asking before Terri Michael ordered her off the ship with two days off.

Early the next morning Carol packed a small bag and headed for the subcar station just a block from the BOQ. After thirty years of effort, the build-out of the nationwide subterranean transportation system, nicknamed the 'subcar,' was probably 80% complete. The ability to provide simple, on-demand services without the traveler needing to own a vehicle was a major factor in its acceptance by the general public. It was efficient, far safer than surface automobiles, and while public, the cars were small, and travel was still private. As she approached, the subcar station doors opened, and she stepped into the elevator. Fifty feet later, she stepped out onto the platform where a car was already waiting. She slipped into the well-padded front seat, closed the door, and inserted her Fleet ID card into the slot on the panel.

"Good morning, Lieutenant Hansen. Your destination, please?"

"The farm."

After a moment the route was calculated and cleared by the system control center.

"Ready," the car reported.

"Depart."

The car moved silently away from the station. Carol decided not to pull out her NetComp to work, or listen to music, or watch a movie. She just settled back in the seat, closed her eyes, and tried to visualize the farm as she remembered it. There was only the slightest sensation of speed as the car sped along on magnetic rails through the carefully bored and smoothed tunnels, the rails powered by the heat of the planet below. She felt the slight deceleration as she approached a main junction in the tunnel network. The car swung gently left and soon settled into the next segment of the trip. A moment of acceleration and all was silent again. Two hours later she was at the station near home and her mother was waiting.

Now happily dressed in her oldest jeans and work boots, topped with a well-worn SFU t-shirt and wide-brimmed hat, she sat on the white rail fence overlooking a sunny paddock, squinting out at the older man in front of her, leading his horse in exercise. He was shorter and heavier than she recalled, but with the same lively eyes that radiated laugh lines. But they weren't just laugh lines. They were built one by one, day by day, by early rising and late retiring, days spent in the hot sun and bitter cold of the farm. There was a lot of automation now, but even with the latest equipment, there was still a need for the farmer to be present, to see with his own eyes what the instruments told him, to walk the corn or bean or soy fields himself. There really was no substitute for the experienced, learned eye of the man, or woman, whose name was on the gate.

Her mother Laura stood outside the fence next to her, leaning against the top rail, a generous cowboy hat shading her graying hair and face now almost as lined as her husband's.

Carol's father completed the last lap with Sirius, then let him free and walked back to the fence.

"You know, Carol, I still don't get it," he said with a shake of his head.

"Fleet?"

"Yes, Fleet. With your grades, you could have done anything you want. Maybe something, you know, safer. Something a little closer to home."

"Ols! Now, don't you push her!" her mother called to him.

Carol smiled slightly, inclining her head. "But Dad, I *am* doing *exactly* what I want."

He looked her in the eye for a long moment. "I worry, Carol. I worry every night."

"I know you do." She looked down, rocking her legs back and forth as she sat on the top rail, then raised her head again. "I can't tell you not to. But just know that I am where I *want* to be."

Her father nodded reluctantly. "I suppose..."

"No *'spose* about it!" she said brightly, quoting him back to himself. That made him smile a little.

"Ols, this was her choice. She's done well, and we don't need to second guess the girl!"

"I worry, Carol," he repeated, ignoring his wife for the moment, looking down and kicking at the ground under the fence where some weeds had chosen to cluster. "This war..." His voice faded with an almost audible shrug.

Carol looked at him sympathetically. "I didn't count on a war, either, Dad. I didn't. But someone has to do this, and assuming I'm as smart as you think, maybe I'm the one who needs to do it."

She had him there, he knew.

Carol's mother had been injured on the farm when Carol was in sixth grade, and she recovered enough for 'normal' activities, but farm work was anything but normal. So, Carol picked up her share of the work, putting in hours before and after school, skipping extra-curricular luxuries like sports or band. Her parents lightened the load best they could, and made sure there was time for Friday night football games and the occasional school dance. Certainly, there was no shortage of escorts for her, and Ols Hansen found himself amused at the intimidation Carol imbued in them.

He felt a little of that now as he considered the grown woman in front of him. He saw very clearly the reflection of the woman he'd married thirty years before in her face, her inner strength. He smiled inwardly, grateful that she favored her mother and not himself.

Carol treated them to lunch at the little clapboard diner down the road, where neighbors and several old friends had somehow heard she was in town. In the afternoon, there was work to be done, and she felt a surprising joy in hauling feed and walking the corn with him. There was a quiet satisfaction in doing real work again, something with actual, tangible results. The stalls had been dirty. Now they were clean, and she had done that.

Chores complete, they saddled their horses — Sirius, Rigel, and Capella — and took a slow walk around the path that encircled the farm. At the rear of the property was a small pond, and they dismounted there to sit on the bank and let the horses have a drink.

Her father leaned back on his elbows and looked over at his daughter.

"So, Powell?"

"Yes, David. You met him a couple times up at the U."

"I remember. Decent enough looking fella, as I recall. Polite as hell."

Carol laughed. "They're polite in hell?"

"Carol!" her mother pretended to scold, laughing along.

Carol's tone changed, suddenly serious. "Yes, he's well mannered. And smart. Even better, he loves your daughter with everything he is."

Ols took off his oversized hat to swat a fly, then plunked it back on his head.

"And does my daughter love him back?"

"With everything *she* is."

Ols nodded. "Good, very good."

Carol pulled him up off the ground and hugged him hard, like a small child might.

"So, am I gonna get any grandchildren out of this deal?" she heard her mother ask from behind her. She turned to Laura, smiling.

"Someday, yeah, probably."

"Good. That would be nice," her father said. There was a wistfulness in his voice that she hadn't heard before.

"I love you, Dad."

"I know you do, girl, I know. I love you, too. You're as good a daughter as any man could hope to pray for."

"But?"

"But nothing. Well, maybe, but I still worry."

"It's OK, Daddy, really."

They retrieved their reins and remounted the horses to complete their walk. Her mother pulled up next to her.

"So, Weapons Officer still?"

"Yeah, it's really nice to be the one doing the shooting!"

"That's my girl!" came Ols's voice from behind.

Late in the day, Laura had a typically enormous farm dinner ready for them. They laughed their way through the meal with stories of the farm, the school, long lost boyfriends, neighborhood intrigue, and a few instances of wayward livestock. Carol had never forgotten what a chef her mother was, and she ate until she couldn't chew anymore.

They spent a quiet evening on the screen porch as she told them about her shipmates, more about Inor, and much more about David. She couldn't tell them about Beta Hydri, although she desperately wanted to. That would have to wait. She did tell them she'd be gone for a long time. Her mother, despite her confidence in Carol, fretted about that and Carol did her best to reassure her. They sat quietly on the porch long after Ols had bid them good night. As the sky turned black and Vega and Altair became obvious in the sky, they walked out into the open, enjoying the relatively cool, clear night.

"I don't know where in the sky to look for you," Laura said finally, the catch in her voice carrying more worry than she had let on to her husband.

"Well, you can't see where we're going from here, Mom. So, just pick a star and pray for us, OK?"

Laura nodded sadly, holding back her tears as she took her daughter's arm as they looked at the stars.

"Where is Inoria?"

"You can't see it now. It'll be low in the south in the winter. It's south and west of Orion, just northwest of Rigel. Some catalogs call it 'Keid.'"

"And this new star so far away?"

"Like I said, you can't see it from here, so let's just say it's way down south and let it go at that, OK?"

"OK."

They stood arm in arm for a long time, looking up, enjoying the clear night.

"I love you, Momma. Whatever might happen to me out there, know that."

"I know, I know."

The next morning, they were up early, Carol picking up some of her old chores as if she had never been away. After a sweaty morning around the barn, they had lunch on the porch. Later that day Ols and Laura took her to the subcar station at the state road junction. She hugged them both tightly, then spent the whole trip back to Fort Eustis happier for her parents than she could ever remember. They were still as solid as she remembered, funny and loving in a way that reminded her of a movie. But unlike some old 'B' movie, this was all real, all true. They loved each other and the farm and everything that came with all of it. They had everything they needed to be happy, right where they were.

Except, she had to admit, grandchildren. For that, they'd just have to wait a while longer.

The desert near Palmyra
The Reformed Syrian Republic
Monday, August 8, 2078, Midmorning Local Time (0835 UTC)

Professor Gabrielle Este got up from her knees to take a long drink from her water bottle. It wasn't close to noon yet at this dig site, and the place already felt like a convection oven. As she stood, sweat ran off her dark eyebrows and stung her green eyes. Her long dark hair was pulled back, and as she ran her deeply tanned hands along the side of her head, she could feel the sandy grit sticking to it.

She and her team had not entirely given up on retrieving something meaningful from the chaos caused by the insanity of the first quarter of the century. The idea that in modern times such willful ignorance, such extreme ideological vanity, could even exist, let alone cause such needless damage to priceless and irreplaceable places, still galled her. The destruction might be irrecoverable, but she wasn't ready to give in to that, at least not quite yet. She was about to pick up her trowel and return to her task when her phone buzzed. Pulling it from a pocket in her desert shorts, she saw no picture, only a number and a text identification of 'Fleet HQ.' She may have been in the desert a lot lately, but she wasn't living under a rock, so she knew what the Fleet was, and with a war on she had heard of several scientists in a variety of disciplines who had been asked to provide Fleet their expertise. But, an archeologist? That seemed unlikely. She hit the 'Who is this?' button on her phone and put it back in her pocket. A minute later it buzzed to tell her she had a message. *How am I supposed to get any work done?* She thought to herself. She dropped the trowel, again, and yanked the phone back out. There was a video message. *Video?* She hit play, if only to see who was calling and what the heck they wanted. She saw a handsome, sandy-haired man, maybe 35, a star on each collar. He looked earnestly, directly, at her.

"Doctor Este, my name is Ron Harris, and I am Chief of Intelligence for ISC Fleet. You are probably aware that we have been asking for a lot of help from academics lately, and we've been gratified by their willingness to lend us a hand. I have a new problem, a serious problem, where I think we could use your knowledge and experience. If you're willing, please call back and we can discuss getting you a briefing. Thanks for taking the call." She looked at the frozen face left at the end of the recording and decided she liked him. His pitch was brief, unrehearsed, direct and to the point. He was smart, she thought, and honest. She called back.

"Good morning Doctor Este. Thanks for responding so quickly."

"Well, Admiral Harris, calls from Fleet Intelligence don't come every day. What can you tell me?"

Harris looked away for a second, thinking, then looked back at her.

"Not that much. It's very far away, as you might guess. I can tell you, it's a place that's very disturbing to all of us, and we really want to understand better what happened. That's about all I can say in the open."

"That's not much to go on."

"I know, it really isn't. But that's all I can give you right now." He was sympathetic but firm, as if he realized her predicament but was constrained to do much about it.

She was surprised at how willing she found herself to consider this. But, if a one-star admiral found something 'disturbing,' that really might be an interesting challenge. Or, she reminded herself, it might be horrifying beyond belief.

"So, what do I need to do? What's the next step?"

"You'll have to sign a nondisclosure. Whether you agree to help or not, I can't brief you if you don't agree to keep it confidential."

"OK, let's assume I'll sign. What then?"

"Well, I can pick you up wherever you are and bring you here. We can be anywhere on the planet in an hour." OK, now she was *really* intrigued.

"In an hour? Just how anxious are you to get an archeologist on this?"

Again, he looked away, then back. "Doctor Este I needed you a month ago, I just didn't know it yet. I will send a shuttle for you this minute if you're willing to come."

"What about my work here? I'm working from grants and they're expecting some kind of results."

"Current grants will be repaid, and we'll see that you have funding to return and continue your work there, for at least a few years."

She sat back on her legs, and it was her turn to look away to think. "OK, I'll come. I will send you my location shortly. Be here in two hours."

"As you wish, Doctor. Thanks."

She smiled and clicked off the connection. She left the now-forgotten trowel where it was and walked back to the ragged tent city the dig team lived in. Once there, she sent her location to Harris. She explained to the leader of the excavation project that she had been called by Fleet and would have to leave immediately.

"I may be back," she told him, "but I should at least hear what they have to say."

Her desert dig clothing fashion closely reflected her desert dig lifestyle: hot, boring, and monotonous. So, packing to leave didn't take long. A few pairs of khaki slacks and shorts, some long-sleeved t-shirts, a decent supply of socks and underwear, an extra pair of dig shoes. That was it. Shortly after she had completed her packing she heard, or maybe felt, the Fleet shuttle arriving just outside their irregular collection of tents. She walked to the edge, facing the shuttle, and waited for something to happen. Shortly a door, o*r, do they call it a hatch?* she wondered to herself, opened, and a figure came out, looked around briefly before spotting her, and set off in her direction. There was something familiar about this person, like she knew her or had seen her before. *That's odd,* she thought, *I don't know anyone in — wait — is that Hansen?*

The figure walked directly to her, shoved her large sunglasses to the top of her head, and reached out her hand.

"Good afternoon, Doctor Este, I'm —"

"Carol freaking Hansen," Este interrupted.

"Well, I don't use *that* middle name very much, but yeah, that's me. It's a pleasure to meet you." Hansen smiled, her head inclined slightly, understanding her fame, unwanted as it was, and what that did to people she met for the first time. They shook hands, and Hansen picked up Gabrielle's bag.

"Shall we?" she asked, indicating the shuttle. As they walked, Gabrielle looked at Carol carefully, taking in the uniform, assessing the actual woman against what she had read and seen. Hansen walked upright and at a brisk pace, despite the bag, and they chatted about the weather at the site. *So ungodly hot* they agreed. Walking on Carol's right Gabrielle could see a round ship's crest with '*Antares*' at the top on her right sleeve, she'd also seen the American flag on the left.

"So where am I going?"

"*Antares* is right above us. You'll meet with Admiral Harris and some others there."

Gabrielle stopped short. "Above us?"

Carol stopped and looked over at her. "More or less, yeah. A couple thousand miles above us."

When Gabrielle didn't move, Carol continued, the humor clear in her voice. "So, I take it he didn't mention a ride into space?"

Gabrielle shook her head.

Carol waited a moment, then said: "I can hold your hand if it'll help."

Gabrielle looked at her, laughed, and continued on towards the shuttle. "I think I can handle it. Just surprised, But, thanks for the offer, Lieutenant."

"Call me Carol."

"Gabrielle, more usually, Gabe."

Carol looked at her in surprise. Gabe was a funny nickname for a woman, but a particularly incongruous for one as delicate in appearance as Gabrielle Este. She was obviously tough underneath, Carol knew, but her slight build and thin face made her look like anything but the hardened desert researcher she was.

"OK, Gabe it is."

Antares
Earth Orbit
Monday, August 8. 2078, 1500 UTC

The ride up to *Antares* was short, less than an hour, and smooth. Gabrielle and Carol sat together in the back of the shuttle and made small talk about Ohio and how funny it seemed that Gabrielle was at Ohio State and Carol had grown up in Lancaster. So close, but so far apart. Gabrielle was older by a decade, having done her undergrad in her home state of Iowa then completed her Ph.D. work at Arizona State before settling into post-doc research and teaching in Columbus. She had spent perhaps eight summers working in the field, be it Egypt, Iraq, Syria, or elsewhere. Wherever she went, it was always hot and dusty, and Gabrielle would be home for a week before she really felt clean again and there was no grit under her feet in the shower.

The shuttle docked at a forward attachment point on *Antares*. Carol guided her down the long passageways, finally turning into the Intel section. There stood Ron Harris, who smiled and reached out a hand to her.

"Welcome, Doctor Este. Thanks so much for coming."

"My pleasure, Admiral. Hard to back down when Carol Hansen is picking you up."

Harris smiled, a wry, slightly conspiratorial grin. "Well, we use what advantages we have, you know? Actually, she asked to do it."

"Sir!" Carol objected, "That was our secret."

Gabrielle turned to Carol, hands out as if to ask 'what gives?'.

"I read your bio. I wanted to meet you, and we could really use your help. And, yeah, I know I have a famous face and name, not that I like it much, but I thought you might feel more comfortable coming with me than with, say, this knucklehead."

She indicated her XO, James George, who looked at her with mock offense.

"Keep that up Hansen, and you'll be famous for your court-martial."

Harris decided it was time to move on. "If you comedians are done, can we get back to work?" He turned to George. "Where is Cordero?"

"Just arrived, sir. Be here shortly."

Gabrielle looked surprised. "Greg Cordero? The lost language guy?"

Harris nodded. "That's him."

Gabrielle moved into the conference room and sat near the far end. "I knew him at Arizona State. Really smart guy. I've read all his books. You guys must really have yourselves in a fix."

The Fleet personnel all looked at one another. *She's about to find out* they all thought together.

Greg Cordero appeared in due course, and he and Gabrielle greeted each other warmly. Cordero was tall and quite thin, with dark hair and eyes and complexion that matched his Latin roots. He had a bright, quick smile and animated features. Carol liked him immediately, as did Harris. This was someone they could work with.

28

Harris handed the academics a tablet with the nondisclosure statement. They each read it, signed, and handed it back.

"You're aboard *Antares* because about a month ago this ship found what we call a blue dot, an Earth-like planet." He paused to take a breath. "On that planet, we found evidence of what we think is a genocide by our enemy."

Carol picked the narrative up from there, her tone even but carrying the gravity, the ghastly details of what they had seen. "We found evidence of the eradication of a modern, spacefaring society, something like the 1970's level of technology. It appears they put up a determined resistance to the enemy but were eventually over-come."

"What kind of creatures are we talking about?" Greg asked. "Somehow I'm not thinking slime molds or tube worms."

"There are a lot of skeletons around, Doctor Cordero, which we will study later. Meantime, we found some images in structures that seem to be residences." She flipped through her tablet and then showed Este and Cordero the same striking image she and Jack Ballard had shown CINC: a being that looked something like a cross between a simian and some kind of feline. It had patterned fur that was white and brown with areas of black, but the most shocking feature of the image was how the multi-colored human-looking eyes looked out from the image with obvious intelligence.

Gabrielle thought to herself. *It's a portrait, pure and simple. This, what — Person? Animal? Creature? — sat down and had its picture taken just like my great-grandparents once did.* She was enthralled.

"Beautiful..." Gabrielle said quietly.

Harris nodded. "Indeed. There are more images like that on the planet."

"You said 'genocide.' They're all dead?" Cordero asked.

"Yes," Harris answered, "as far as we know, they're all dead."

"Why do you believe the killers were the same as the Inor attackers?" Este asked.

"There is evidence of an RFG attack similar to what was seen at Inor. We don't think that's a coincidence."

"Any idea how long they've been dead?" Cordero asked.

"Based on the overgrowth, something more than twenty years. We're still work-ing on that, and we were hoping you might be able to help us with that assessment as well. "

Gabrielle leaned forward to join the conversation, "What other kinds of tech-nology did they have? Radio? Computers?"

"Radio, yes, and radar, we think. They had photography as we've already shown you. They had artificial satellites, maybe for weather forecasting or other types of scientific purposes. Yes, we're pretty sure there are computers somewhere, but we didn't really have time to identify any."

"Weapons?"

"The picture there is less clear, as if that's possible. We're not sure what weapons the enemy was using. We didn't have much time before we were ordered to return."

Este looked over at Cordero. "I think they were doing pretty well for amateurs, don't you think, Greg?"

Cordero smiled and looked over at Harris.

"This is very good initial work, Admiral. Plenty of facts and some good initial theories. Well done."

Carol picked back up where she left off, showing them the outside of a structure.

"We spent a couple Sols, which, by the way, are forty-seven-plus hours long on Big Blue, to get lots of drone imagery of buildings in the largest city. On the way back we had some time to study the images. If you look at the buildings, there are markings of two types. One is a set of seven symbols that appear in a variety of orders, the other is a group of forty or so, so far, that also seem to be in different orders in different contexts. Our somewhat uninformed theory is that the seven are numbers and the others are some kind of alphabet, but we really don't know."

"*Sols*?" Greg asked.

"We call a solar day on Big Blue a 'Sol' to keep it separate from our concept of a twenty-four hour 'day.' Sols are sequentially numbered – there aren't weeks or months – from when we first arrived at the planet. We'll arrive about Sol 63, I think."

"And, *Big Blue*?" Gabrielle asked.

Carol shrugged. "Every place needs a name, Gabe. Seemed appropriate at the time."

Harris leaned forward on the table. "These symbols are part of why you're here. We need to know what this says and if it has any relevance to what they were fighting."

"What is the planet like? How long were you down there?" Cordero asked.

"The initial evaluation was by overhead observation followed by close-up drone photography. They were there about ten days."

"Yeah, we had to come back for the SLUGs." James George said, sounding a little annoyed, to Harris' clear displeasure.

"Slugs?" Cordero asked. After a short silence, Harris gave his best in-for-a-penny-in-for-a-pound shrug and nodded to George.

"It's a radiologically-sanitized breathing system. It sterilizes the air coming in so the outside environment can't infect you, and sterilizes your exhaled air so you can't infect the outside environment, either. Since you're not carrying oxygen tanks, you can stay a long time."

"So why 'SLUG'?" Este asked.

"The five-kilogram slug of Cobalt-60 inside needs a bit of lead shielding. So, it's heavy, maybe twenty-five kilos. We're taking twenty back with us."

"So, Admiral," Este asked, "with the SLUGs, we can get on the ground?"

Harris leaned forward. "Yes. And that's what I am really asking you to do. Get down there, help us find out what we can about this society, and about this enemy."

"What else can you tell me about the planet?"

Carol spoke up. "Nice place, if you ask me. The area this society lived in was fairly warm, something like Arizona in the spring or fall. They don't have seasons like ours because the planet's inclination is small, only a few degrees. There are three smallish continents — think Australia — and the rest is ocean, better than 90%, actually."

"That's a lot of water. Is the climate damp? Are there ice caps?"

"It is a lot of water, although we don't know how deep the ocean is. The climate where they lived is moderately dry. They lived along the coastline between the sea and a mountain range. It reminded me of southern California. There are sizeable ice caps north and south, as one would expect based on the small inclination."

"Have you done any environmental testing? Bacteria, viruses, radioactivity?"

"We brought back soil samples. They tested negative for pathogens initially, but a second set is now at CDC. Radioactivity is nominal - maybe a bit more than here but nothing to be concerned about."

Greg was looking at the pictures of the symbols they had seen. Ballard had organized samples of each set, showing the consistency of each individual symbol and samples of the collections as seen at Beta Hydri. He looked at Harris.

"Do we have any detailed photographs of the skeletons? The hands, in particular."

Carol smiled slightly. "We do. Three fingers and something like a thumb on each hand. The feet, oddly enough, have something that looks like six toes."

Cordero nodded thoughtfully, his gaze off into the distance. "I think you may be right on the numbers, but I would have expected six characters or eight, not seven."

"And the rest?" Harris asked, hopefully.

Cordero sighed and leaned back in his chair, looking at the ceiling. "Well, there's no Herodotus to lean on and no Rosetta Stone to be found. You can't work out an unknown language in a total vacuum. But I've been working on an automated decipherment program that we can try." He leaned forward again, his expression serious as he thought more deeply about the problem in front of him, "But, they're modern. They have writing. That should mean books, other kinds of markings, you know, normal stuff like traffic signs, building names, personal names. We'll just have to see what we can find."

Carol looked at Harris, who nodded, then back at Cordero. "So, you're in?" she asked.

Cordero smiled. "Oh yeah, I'm in. Gabe?"

Este wasn't smiling. She looked across at Cordero, then to Harris. "Yes, I'll come. What I see here is horrible, and I mean, Holocaust horrible. Someone has to document it, understand it, stop it. I'm in, Admiral."

"Thanks. How much time do you need to be ready to leave?"

"I only have desert clothes with me. I'll need to get back to Columbus, get unpacked and repacked and then I'll be ready."

"So?"

"A couple days tops."

"Great, Greg?"

"I guess I have to ask — how long will we be gone, and, if you can tell me, where the hell are we going?"

"You're going to Beta Hydri, which is 24 light years to the south of us. So, that's 48 days round trip —"

"You can do a light-year *per day?*" Gabrielle asked, incredulous.

"Yeah, sometimes a little more, but that's what we plan for," James George replied.

"The other issue," Ron said, "Is that we will be making a stop at Inor before we go to Beta Hydri."

"Why?" Este asked.

"We're taking the new ambassador. Also, there is an event there that the Inori have requested Commander Michael, Lieutenant Hansen, and any other *Liberty* crew to attend."

"An *event?*" Este asked.

"It's the dedication of a memorial to the *Liberty* the Inori have built. You'll attend as well. It might actually be good for you to experience Inor before you get to Beta Hydri. Have either of you been there?"

"Uh, today's my first time off the planet," Greg paused, smiling. "Wow, that sounds strange."

"I understand!" Ron responded. "You're looking at sixty days travel plus three weeks on the planet. So, I guess it's around Beta Hydri in eighty days."

There were groans all around.

"Boss, did you make that up yourself or did Meredith feed you that just for our amusement?" Kathy Stewart asked. Up to now, she'd been sitting, silently watching the back-and-forth with the academics, and taking notes.

"Stewart, I will have you know I write all my own material."

32

"It shows," she deadpanned. Gabrielle looked across at Carol.

"Are they always like this?"

"No, Gabe, today is actually better than most."

"CAROL!" they yelled at her, laughing.

Cordero looked around. "You know, I wasn't sure about jumping in with the military on this, I just wasn't sure I would fit in."

"And?" Ron asked.

"This is serious work you're asking us to do, but I am glad to see that you don't take yourselves too seriously."

"Make no mistake, Doctor Cordero," Kathy said, the humor gone from her voice, "The Admiral is in command here, and we do as he says. But he's smart enough to give and take a joke and still get everything done."

"I see."

"But when it's time to buckle down, believe me, we will."

"Thank you, Ms. —"

"Stewart, but Kathy will do fine."

"Thank you. And please, make it Greg, not Doctor or, worse, Doctor Cordero."

"So, Greg," Ron asked, "how much time will you need?"

"About like Gabe, I guess, just time to get the condo closed up and pack."

"OK, it's about 1600 UTC now, so that's about 10 AM in Arizona, noon in Columbus. We can shuttle you both back down today," he stopped to think. "Then how about we pick you up Friday morning? I'll send you the time and place."

That was acceptable to both, and Carol walked them to the shuttle port. She reached out her hand to each of them in turn.

"Good to meet both of you. I don't know if I'll be coming down for you, but if not, I will see you when you get back up."

They boarded the shuttle and, in a few minutes, they were gone.

FPI Development Lab
Outside Lewistown, Montana
Tuesday, August 9, 2078, 0925 MDT

Lloyd called Frances Wilson from his Montana workshop. He'd been up nearly nonstop since the rest of his team had arrived five days earlier, pausing only for short naps when he was feeling stumped. They tried several configurations, finally managing to produce something superficially similar to what they believed was the enemy tracking signal. The word from Peg White at Tranquility II was that the SLIP emitter was intact. That surprised them. It was another day and night before they finally had some results.

"Mrs. Wilson, I have some news."

Lloyd's voice was unusually quiet, she thought, sounding exhausted, maybe even depressed.

"Good news, I hope?"

"We've reproduced the tracking."

"Really! That is good news, isn't it?"

"Yes, I guess."

"Lloyd, is there something more to this you're not telling me?"

"Other than it's all my fault, no."

"OK, Lloyd, let's set that aside for now. Just tell me what you've learned."

"There's a small interconnect between the receiving side and the emitter, which has to be there since they share the hardware. This signal — this goddamn snake-ass piece of shit, I'm not sure I know how to say this — burrows across that port and is amplified slightly in the emitter side before being echoed back out."

"Can it be fixed?"

"Yes, it can. There's a software fix we can install to shut down the emitter's action when it's not actually transmitting."

"So, Lloyd, does this account for all the behaviors? The tracking? The fact that they couldn't track once the SLIP electronics were hit?" Lloyd sat back in his chair, now feeling the exhaustion that had been accumulating in his body for days.

"Yes, Mrs. Wilson. If the emitter electronics are off, the amplification can't happen, and the signal doesn't get echoed. That's mostly what the software fix does — kills off part of the apparatus when it's not transmitting."

"So, Lloyd, what exactly makes this your fault?" she asked, trying to soften the guilt he was obviously feeling.

"I designed this system — I built that cross-over to get around another problem that would have made it more expensive to produce."

"Seems like reasonable engineering to me — you could not have known that it might be exploited in this way, could you?"

"Maybe not, but if I'd done it differently, you know, maybe..."

Frances let the silence run a few seconds, which felt like a lifetime to Lloyd.

"The important part, Lloyd, is that you were able to find how they were doing it and how we turn it off. That's what you should be focusing on."

"I suppose."

Frances was unaccustomed to this contrite version of Lloyd, who was normally confident almost to the point of conceit.

"Lloyd, get some sleep. This is a huge win for us; try to focus on that."

Lloyd found himself a little surprised at her response. She was so hard on him most of the time, he'd expected a lecture.

"How soon can you get us the software fix?"

"It's already in testing. We should be able to send it to Fleet tomorrow or the next day. That part is out of my hands."

"That's just fine, thanks, Lloyd. Now go get some rest, and I want to see you here next Monday." She hung up the phone and walked to Harris' office. The door was open, and she dropped herself into his guest chair.

"Lloyd found the tracking issue."

Harris' eyes brightened. "Really? Wow, that is good news."

Frances nodded in response. "It is, but he sounds very different, almost broken."

Ron sat back in his chair, thinking. "He's just solved one of our biggest mysteries and probably saved hundreds of lives. He might have won the war for us. What's his problem?"

"He thinks the problem is his fault — an engineering choice that backfired."

"Well, he could not have known how the enemy would use this, could he?"

"No, I don't see how he could."

"I guess I don't get it then, but he's pretty cocky so maybe having a mistake shoved in his face, publicly, is hard for him to process. What's the fix?"

"They have a software fix for the SLIP control system. Lloyd says we should have it in a couple days."

"Software?" Harris asked, surprised.

"Yes. Seems there is a crossover between receiver and emitter that somehow gets amplified at just the right frequencies. Turn off the emitter power and the problem goes away."

"Interesting. Thanks, Frances. We'll get an update out to the Fleet later today."

She rose and went back to her own space, wondering whether her secret favorite annoying-but-brilliant engineer had taken a hit he would not recover from. She hoped not. They would likely need him again.

ISC Fleet HQ, Intel Section
Ft. Eustis, VA
Wednesday, August 10, 2078, 0830 EDT

A short, balding man arrived at the Intel front desk, appearing slightly confused as he looked over his glasses to examine the card in his hand.

"I'm looking for an Admiral Harris?"

Roger Cox looked up from the desk. "Sir, the Admiral is not available. May I ask what this is about?"

"I had a call from him yesterday about a project. I'm Joe Bowles."

Roger stood, unconsciously at attention. "Yes, Colonel Bowles. The Admiral told me you might be coming in."

The man on the opposite side of the desk looked up at Roger. "I haven't been called 'Colonel' in ten years, Ensign."

"Well, sir, I know the Admiral would like to speak to you."

"You just said he wasn't available."

Roger nodded as he worked his phone. "Indeed, sir, he isn't here. But I can set up a secure video conference with him." Roger put the phone to his ear. "Sir, it's Cox. Colonel Bowles is here."

Roger hung up after a short conversation.

"And where is the good Admiral Harris?"

Roger smiled slightly. "Elsewhere, sir. I'm not really —"

"Supposed to tell me? I understand."

Roger led the older man to a small conference room, where he was joined by Elias Peña, Rich Evans, and Ann Cooper.

"This is a lot of brass for one old fart," Bowles commented as he looked around while they set up the conference with Harris.

"You're not just any old fart, sir," Evans responded with a grin as Harris appeared on the screen.

"Thank you, Doctor Bowles, for coming in. I have a problem I could use your help with, sir. If you're willing to consider it, Commander Peña has a nondisclosure for you to sign."

"Admiral, I'm just a long-retired, near-sighted old Army pathologist. I'm not seeing what I can contribute to this enormous interstellar war we're all stuck in."

"Well, sir, if you're willing to hear me out I think this would be an interesting project for you."

Bowles looked at Harris for a few seconds, shrugged, and signed on the tablet Peña had placed in front of him.

"Show him the pictures, Elias." Peña flipped to the drone images of the battlefield.

"These are —"

"Skeletons."

"Yes, sir."

"How long ago?"

"We're not sure, Doctor Bowles. We were hoping —"

"I'd answer that for you."

Harris, now interrupted twice, waited for just a beat before responding.

"Exactly, Doctor Bowles. Your work with the dating of military remains is precisely the kind of expertise we need."

"That's not all I know how to do, Admiral."

"Yes, sir, I know. Commander Peña has read your book. Your approach to understanding battlefields will be important to our work."

"OK, so, how far is this place?"

"You'll be gone for almost three months."

Bowles looked directly at Harris's image on the screen. "That's a long time to be away from my grandchildren, Admiral."

"Yes, it is."

"So, why me?"

Elias, who had been the lead in picking Bowles, took over for Harris. "You've done some interesting work deciphering military movement and outcomes based on the dating and positioning of remains. You know how to manage this like the archeological site it is."

Bowles gave up a small smile. "Don't stop now, Commander, it's working."

"I just had one major question, sir."

"Oh?"

"Yes. If it's necessary, can we do Carbon 14 dating on another planet."

The older man leaned back in his chair, crossed his arms, and looked at them. "If this is an Earth-like planet around a Sun-like star, there's no reason to think that nitrogen in the atmosphere would not be converted to Carbon-14 just as it is here."

Ann leaned forward on the table. "That sounds hopeful."

"It is. We would need to verify that with contemporary living tissue. Based on the pictures there is plenty of plant growth — I assume those are plants, I mean, they're green and all — which we could use to establish a baseline."

Bowles lost ten years on his face as he talked, and his whole bearing changed, his back became straight, and his head came up to look directly at what he clearly now considered his new students. He looked over at Ann.

"*Three months.*"

"Yes, sir. With 21 days, more or less, on the planet."

He nodded slowly, thinking about his decision. "What else do I need to know?"

Elias responded, "If you need to go to the surface, you will require training on what we call a 'SLUG.' It's like scuba gear for an alien planet, but it's heavy, and you'd be wearing an isolation suit as well."

"I'm pushing sixty, son, but I walk three miles a day, cut my own grass, trim my own trees. I think I can do it."

"There will be an archeologist and an ancient language expert going as well."

"Who?"

"The archeologist is Gabrielle Este. She's done a lot of work piecing together shattered historical monuments in the Middle East. The linguist is Greg Cordero. His research on one-sided translations is right on target."

Bowles looked again at the photograph. "Am I looking at our enemy or another victim?"

"Another victim. We've documented the same kind of attack here that occurred at Inor."

"You've shown me skeletons but nothing alive."

Harris spoke for the group. "Far as we know, sir, they're all dead."

"You're taking a linguist. There is something to read?"

Evans answered. "So far, just markings on buildings, nothing in much detail. They're at a 1970s level of tech, so we believe there will be libraries or knowledge repositories of some kind that he can exploit."

Bowles nodded his understanding. "When would we leave?"

"Plan is to leave on the 23rd of this month. There will be a brief stop at Inor, then on to Beta Hydri."

"Twelve days. Not much time."

"Yes, we understand that, sir."

"What about security? Is the enemy likely to bother us while we're there?"

"We think that's unlikely," Harris answered, "But, we're taking three squads of Marines along just in case."

"I was thinking more along the lines of a cruiser."

"You'll be going on *Antares*, sir."

Bowles showed some surprise at that.

"Commander Michael will be responsible for our safety should the enemy make the mistake of showing up."

"That's the ship with the *Liberty* survivors, is it not?"

"It is sir," Ann answered. "As I recall, there's about sixteen of them in the crew."

Bowles sat up straight, as if he had come to his decision. "I saw her speech when they got back from Inor. She's a fine officer. OK, I'll go."

The formerly retired Army pathologist took a subcar back up to rural Maryland, with a promise to be back at Fleet HQ, ready to depart, by the 22nd.

Fleet Shuttle Facility
Ft. Eustis, VA
Monday, August 15, 2078, 0700 UTC

The Fleet shuttle was waiting for David at 0300. The Shuttle Terminal was closed at this hour, but the gates were chained open for those few unlucky enough to travel before it opened at 0500.

Carol rode with him from the BOQ, a short, silent ride. The evening before they had a private send-off dinner in town at the same Chinese place as on their first Sunday night together. For David, it felt like a lifetime ago, but it was just two weeks earlier. He hauled his duffel out of the Jeep and stood for a moment breathing in the warm, muggy night. The lights of the Fort and those up and down the

James River reminded him of stars. Looking up, he could see a few real stars shining dimly through the thin mist in the air. The usual night sounds of crickets and the occasional bullfrog quietly accompanied their goodbyes. They both looked across the pad at the waiting shuttle. Carol held him very tight, then looked in his eyes.

"I love you," she said quietly.

"And I love you," he responded, then looked over at the shuttle and back to her face. There wasn't much light, and the shadows falling across her face made her look very different somehow. He looked at her for what felt like a long time. Then, at last, it was time to go.

"We're going to have a long life together, Carol. I know it. I can feel it. But, meanwhile—"

"Meanwhile, we fight," she finished. He held her briefly one last time, hoisted the duffel and stepped off for the shuttle. He didn't look back. Carol watched him leave, leaning against the Jeep with her arms around herself as in an embrace.

David was a little afraid that if he dared to look back, he might not be able to go, and that would not do. The shuttle crew checked his ID, took his bag and then he walked up the three steps and disappeared.

Carol turned and climbed back into the Jeep. The driver was a long-retired US Navy chief petty officer, far too old now to serve in the Fleet, but he felt far too young to just sit idly on the sidelines. So, he volunteered at the BOQ, managing to become porter, chauffeur, concierge, and privy counselor to the young officers as they passed through. He loved them all in his faux gruff way, and they adored him in return. He'd been down to the shuttle pad in the middle of the night many times, watching variations of this same sad drama unfold.

"You want to wait, Lieutenant?" he asked kindly.

Carol shook her head. "No, let's go."

"As you say, ma'am." He pulled the vehicle off the shuttle pad parking area and started back for the BOQ. Carol rode in silence, knowing there would be no more sleep tonight.

The shuttle lifted off for the two-hour trip up to *Columbia* as Carol walked dejectedly into her room and dropped into her desk chair. She pulled out her new notebook — a real paper notebook, not an app — and began to write: *And now, you're gone. And now, the really hard part begins. That future you see seems very far away.* As tears came, she found she could write no more.

They knew their assignments would be taking both of them back out into deep space, where their ships would likely be under electromagnetic radiation (EMR) restrictions. That meant there would be few chances to exchange personal SLIP messages. So, instead, they decided to keep journals that they could exchange the next time they were together. It was a throwback idea, for sure, but somehow holding a real pen to real paper connected them to their emotions more deeply and clearly than typing or dictating ever could.

David was the only passenger on the shuttle. He slumped down in a seat in the back, feeling his life surgically bifurcated: half his future was at the end of this ride, the other half he'd just left behind on the surface.

The shuttle docked with *Columbia* and the pilot came back to David. "Well, Lieutenant Powell, we're here. Good luck to you, sir."

David rose, thanked the pilot, then pulled his duffel out of the webbed storage in the back of the shuttle and walked to the airlock. He looked at his NetLink, suddenly realizing that by coming from EDT to UTC, he'd just lost four hours. It was still early morning in Virginia, but the work day was well underway on *Columbia*.

As he passed through the inner door onto a brightly lit *Columbia* passageway, there was a young Marine and a blond Senior Lieutenant minding access to the ship.

"Good morning. Lieutenant David Powell reporting."

Without checking the access list on her tablet, she replied, "Good morning, Lieutenant Powell."

She extended her hand and gave him a firm, sincere handshake.

"Melinda Hughes. Welcome aboard."

"Thanks very much."

"Captain Smith has requested that you see him in his regular office immediately."

David felt a little uncertain. Dan Smith was a former classmate, his one-time best friend, but he had hoped to come aboard quietly. "Is there a problem, Lieutenant?"

She shook her head. "Not that I am aware of, but he was very clear that you see him right away. I'll get someone to put your gear in your quarters. You're in with Lieutenant Murphy, the Logistics department head. The compartment number will be on your NetComp."

"Thanks."

Dan Smith's ship, just a destroyer, was still enormous by Earth standards. Including the Forstmann Drive module at the aft end of the ship, *Columbia* was a good three hundred meters long. Her livable spaces consisted of individual modules, three meters high and wide, and nine meters long. Sometimes the ship felt like a giant worm or some primitive multi-cellular life-form. Walking through the passages, which were themselves modules, one was aware of the seams and the hatches and doors that set each module apart. The paint scheme was originally a typical military grey, but now an occasional blue or cream or green gave the ship some visual variety. *Columbia* wasn't new anymore, and while she was certainly clean and spaceworthy, she was beginning to show the wear of war in space with her crew. There were nicks and scratches and dents here and there in her passages where something had been dragged or dropped or knocked over, either by accident or in one of the fights she had seen. Like most of her crew, she wasn't old or weak, but neither was she as beautiful and perfect as she had once been. She reflected their pain, their losses, their victories. She was a fighter, and so were they.

During his work with FleetIntel, David had put his spare time waiting for *Columbia* to good use, studying her general layout, weapons, and surveillance resources. He had no trouble finding the Captain's office from the port airlock. In the outer office a young acne-faced, redheaded crewman was typing at a workstation. He stood as David entered.

"At ease, please. I'm Lieutenant Powell."

"Yes, sir, one moment."

As the young man picked up the phone it struck David as amusing that a ship captain's office in the late 21st century would look so much like what he had seen in books and movies of a hundred or more years earlier. People in authority still need a gatekeeper, and typing still worked because it was silent and private. Dictation into voice recognition was fine when you were alone, but put a half dozen people in a room, and it became an unbearable babble. Thought-control dictation was a cool idea but in practice was not as useful as hoped. Too many random thoughts got into the product. One could have a random, even socially inappropriate, thought while typing and it didn't come out. Thought dictation was just a little too accurate for most users' comfort.

The inner office door opened and Dan Smith stepped out.

"Come in Lieutenant Powell." He turned to the crewman, "Parker, no calls, please."

They moved into his office and Smith closed the door. It was a small place, a desk bolted to one wall and a couple of uncomfortable steel chairs. Funny how space in space was always at a premium. David stood at attention.

"Lieutenant David Powell reporting, as ordered, sir," he said impersonally.

"Yeah, well, screw you, David!" he said, laughing as he extended his hand across the desk. "I am really glad to see you."

"Good to see you, too, Dan. I'm sorry it's been so long."

They sat.

Dan looked at him, his expression stern. "I have to ask — what the hell happened to you? You sent one message that Friday night and then you're gone, vanished." David sat still, silent. "Did you think we weren't concerned about you? Did you not get our messages?"

David looked off to his left, not really looking at anything, rather looking back into his past, into the painful period after his father's suicide. There had been no funeral, no visitation, no opportunity for family and friends to comfort the survivors. His mother had forbidden it, along with any discussion of the how's and why's of what happened. Eventually, David was sure, the isolation of her denial was part of what killed her.

"I got your messages, Dan, all of them. I didn't reply because I wasn't going to be part of that anymore."

Dan kept at it. "We were not just classmates, David, we were best friends. What am I to make of you just walking away from all of us?"

Feeling again the pain of loss, David responded as evenly as he could. "I knew right away I would not graduate. I knew I would have to fulfill my obligation later, and not with a commission. I stayed away because I thought a clean break would be the best for all concerned."

"Well, just this once, you were full of shit. We missed you, we wanted to help you, and you were nowhere to be found."

"Yes, I know. I am sorry now to have cut you off, all of you, but at the time I thought it was best to just put the University behind me and deal with what I had to do. It was too hard to still be connected to that dream."

Smith nodded gently. "OK David, I won't say I understand, but I see that you did what you thought you had to do. But know this — it really hurt all of us — Carol, Larry Covington, Joe Scheck, the whole group of us. Your absence left a void. We were not the same after that."

"Yes, I see that. I am sorry. I missed all of you guys. Larry and Joe were such an odd couple."

"What? A tall shaved-head black Baptist and a short, bearded Jew as best friends? It's almost a cliché." Dan could see the softening in David. "Look, I know what it cost you to withdraw, then to watch Carol — all of us — walk the stage and get what you had craved your whole life. I get that." Dan shifted in his chair. "You earned it, David, but you didn't get it."

David, who had been looking at the floor, raised his head.

"But now I have it."

"Indeed, you do. And Carol, too. But I need to know, David, are you ready to be who you're supposed to be now?"

"I think I am, yes. Ever since that day on *Sigma*, I've felt like myself again."

"Good. So how is my Carol?"

"She is as wonderful as ever," David replied, recalling the last couple weeks.

"Someday you should ask her about our night in the bar at Kapteyn before the *Otbara* search," Dan said, smiling.

"Kapteyn?"

"Yeah, she got pretty emotional, and a little drunk. Girl killed almost a whole pizza and most of a bottle of wine all by herself."

"Carol?"

"Yeah, it was a surprise to me, too. But she figured out what she really wanted."

"Oh, what was that?"

"You."

David finally smiled. "I guess I owe you some thanks as well."

"Maybe, but it was mostly me helping her find her own way. It must have been hard to leave her."

"It was. But we both know what this is all about."

"Yes. Meanwhile..."

"Meanwhile, we fight." David interrupted him.

"Meanwhile, we fight," Dan answered.

Dan Smith straightened up in his chair. He was the Captain again.

"So, tell me about this tracking."

"Seems they found a connection between the SLIP receiver and emitter. A signal of just the right type will cross that connection and be amplified. Turn off the emitter, and it won't happen."

"So, we would see this signal in the receiver status?"

"Right. Part of the software fix they're sending adds an alarm to the Comm workstation on the Bridge if it detects that signal. That happens even if the emitter power is off."

"OK, well, we pay a penalty for powering off the emitter, since it will take a couple minutes for it to come up and align itself before we can transmit. Until we get the fix, I suppose we could put a watch on the status display."

"You could, sure. Boring work, though."

"It would be, for sure. I'll think about it. Meantime, Lieutenant Powell, you're Deputy Chief of the Intel Section. Senior Lieutenant Gurgen Khachaturian is Chief. He's pretty good but I expect you will make him better. At some point, Katch will get promoted out of here and I figure you'll take his place unless Fleet-Intel grabs you first. Learn the admin stuff along with the operations. Your intel experience on *Sigma* will help. The staff will respect that."

"Yes, Captain."

"The Nav Officer will get you on the rotation for Conn certification. On my ship, everybody flies, nobody just rides. So, Maz Dawes will be looking for you to get a schedule set. He's tough but very competent. The XO is Maz's classmate, Alona Melville."

Smith paused before continuing, thinking about exactly how to say what was on his mind,

"David, I need you to be yourself here. I need the whole cynical, analytic, insightful, ruthlessly anti-stupid David Powell in my Intel section. I can't manage with anything less."

"I will do what I can to be as difficult as possible, sir." Now, David was actually grinning.

"That's better. We're still old friends, and in private that's what we'll be."

"But you are the Captain here, and I respect that."

"I knew you would. And don't forget, you have a wedding to attend next June at the Fleet resort."

"Oh, so, Linda finally said yes?" David's eyebrows came up as he smiled his best snarky smile.

"OK, pal, that's fine. Go ahead and make fun of your commander's love life. Now, I see you really are back after all." Dan's laugh faded as his tone turned serious again, "Your day to command will come, David. A little delayed, maybe, but it will come. And don't be too impressed with these oak leaves," Dan said, pointing to his collar. "I think these are mostly a convenience for Fleet. I put you in with Jim Murphy, the Logistics section head. Good guy, same rank, about the same age. He's been on board for a while now and he happens to not have a room-mate. I think you'll get along."

"I am sure we'll do fine."

"Are you working on the Senior Lieutenant exam yet?"

"No."

"Get on it. You'll get points for *Sigma*."

"Yes, sir, I will try."

"OK, mister always-first-in-his-class, you 'try.' That's it for now — see you at dinner." They stood and shook hands.

"Thank you, sir."

David opened the door, nodded to crewman Parker, and moved on out of the captain's office. He had a cabin to find and a new life to immerse himself in. It had not seemed a comfortable fit at first, something like too-new shoes giving him blisters, but now he was starting to feel what he had always hungered for. That this was a place he *belonged*; this was where he could use his formidable gifts to their fullest. His nervousness now gone, he forgot his previous angst about walking like an officer and found that he was just walking like himself, which he was starting to realize was really the same thing after all.

Antares
Earth Orbit
Monday, August 22, 2078, 0930 UTC

Carol Hansen, Weapons Maintenance Officer Jon Swenson, and Maintenance Officer Ensign Miguel Anthony spent the days after David left with *Columbia* prepping *Antares* for the arrival of the three dozen Marines that would accompany them to Beta Hydri. CINC was rightfully concerned about the security of the ground teams and tripled their usual complement. Marine Captain Wayne Barnes came aboard about halfway through the process and pitched right in.

The Marines' bunks were three levels down from the main deck that included the Bridge, ship's offices, Intel work area, and the entrance to the hangar. This was normally unused storage space, but they managed a typical barracks setup, and Ensign Anthony wrangled a plumbing detail to create shower and toilet facilities on that same level. Whatever he asked Terri Michael to ask Ops for, he seemed to get. *Good to be a priority for the brass,* he thought. They set up a firing range on the next level down, the lowest usable deck in the ship.

Antares' small armory could never handle so many weapons, so part of the firing range level was set up for weapons and ammunition storage. It was a strange departure for the Fleet, which generally carried only minimal personal firepower, but they all worked to meet the Marines' needs.

Friday morning, a Fleet Shuttle arrived with the Marines. Carol and Miguel were there to welcome them and direct them to their quarters. The first Marine to come through the hatch was a face very familiar to Carol from the dark hours of the enemy attack on Inoria.

"Jackson!" Carol exclaimed.

"Good morning Lieutenant Hansen! It's good to see you again, ma'am!" he replied. Carol took notice of his new sergeant's stripes, pulling him aside as the others continued to come aboard.

"So, I see the promotion virus got to you, too?"

"Yes, ma'am, I guess so. I have the First Squad."

"How are the others? Lochner? Dobo?"

"Both Corporals, now, Lieutenant. They're not on this junket, but I saw them a week ago, and they said to say hello to you."

"Great! Tell them hello back from me."

Jackson nodded, then pointed in the direction of the down ladder.

"I best be getting back to the squad, ma'am."

"Of course. We'll be seeing you later, Leon."

"Yes, Lieutenant, I expect so." Smiling, he stepped off and hustled down the ladder to the Marines' level with the rest of his squad.

"Inor?" Anthony asked her once Jackson had disappeared.

"Yes. He was one of the Marines that I found in the city. He doesn't realize it, but he's a big part of why I got promoted. All I had to do was ask and he did everything I needed."

"Sounds like a good Marine."

"Yeah, not much question about that."

Once the last of the three squads made their way down the ladder, Carol headed back forward to check the status of her weapons. It would soon be time to leave.

ISC Fleet HQ Intel Section
Fort Eustis, VA
Monday, August 22, 2078, 0930 EDT (1330 UTC)

First thing Monday morning, Ron Harris set up an unscheduled meeting of his core group for 0930. As they filed in ninety minutes later, there was a new face in the room. She wore the gold oak leaves of a Lieutenant Commander. She was thin, with blond hair pulled back from her severe, angular face. Her bearing radiated toughness and distance. As they sat, Ron introduced her.

"This is Doctor Susan Scranton. She's just finished the academic officer assimilation school. She will be standing up the Exobiology group. CINC wants us to figure out who, or what, we're up against. Doctor Scranton is tasked with accomplishing that goal."

"But we haven't found a single thing yet to support that work," Elias Peña pointed out.

"We will," she said, her voice hard and determined. "Eventually, we will."

"What about the Beta Hydri culture?" Kelly Peterson asked.

"That's not a priority for Doctor Scranton, Kelly, but we can consult with her if we have a specific question."

"I see," she responded.

There was a slightly too-long quiet in the room.

"Staff?" Peña finally asked.

Scranton looked at him, well, *through* him, and replied. "I will be looking for a small staff of biologists and techs for a lab, but not many."

Harris looked around the table. "I know there's been a lot of change around here lately. It's necessary. I know you all know that."

"What is the doctor cleared for, sir?" Roger Cox asked.

"Everything. She'll be a regular at our status meetings."

Kelly Peterson looked across at Scranton. "Well, welcome Commander Scranton. If there is anything any of us can do to help you, please just ask."

Scranton looked across the table at the young woman. "I will be making my requests through Admiral Harris and I will expect you to follow through on what he approves." *Here, have a bucket of ice water from me,* she seemed to say. Harris looked at Scranton for a second, then turned back to his analysts.

"*Antares* leaves today, so I will be gone for a while. Meantime, let's get moving on what we already have to work on." He turned to Ann Cooper. "Ann, please pull together a briefing on our current projects — TDOA, Sentinels, the SLIP issue, and the Beta Hydri find and bring Doctor Scranton up to speed on what we're doing."

"Yes, sir," she replied evenly.

"Admiral, I don't see that I need —"

"You need to know what's going on, Doctor, in order to contribute to these gatherings," he replied, firmly. "Ann, can you have that ready by tomorrow?"

"Yes, sir. I can combine and edit what we already have into a presentation for Doctor Scranton. Should take maybe two hours."

"OK, fine," there was a pause. "I'll be leaving shortly for *Antares*, as will Kathy. Commander Peña will be in charge in my absence."

"Good luck, sir," Rich Evans said.

"Thanks, Rich, I appreciate it. One more thing: Doctor Scranton has proposed a mission to GL 876."

"The *Sigma* battle site?" Rich asked, surprised.

"Yes. Since it appears from *Sigma*'s sensor data that the enemy left without deorbiting, it's possible we will be able to locate remains."

"Sounds like a long shot," Roger Cox commented quietly.

"Long doesn't begin to cover it," Ann added.

Scranton sat, arms crossed, glaring at the speakers. "I am in charge of this effort, and if I think it's necessary, it's necessary."

Harris looked at her. "We believe in the free exchange of information here, Doctor, and we don't permit isolated silos of control."

"But, Admiral —"

"But nothing, Commander," Harris cut her off. She sat silent as he turned to his deputy.

"Elias, her trip to GL 876 is approved if she decides it's worthwhile. I thought maybe we should ask Ops to give us *Columbia*. Having Powell handy might be helpful."

"Might be hard for him to go back there, sir." Ann offered.

Harris shook his head. "Maybe, Ann, but my impression of him says he can handle it."

"Very tough underneath," Frances Wilson said. "Just like Hansen."

"Carol Hansen?" Scranton asked.

Kathy smiled as she replied. "Yes, Commander. She and Powell are, well, close."

"She is leaving today?" Scranton asked, either oblivious or ignoring the implications about David Powell.

"Yes, *Antares* leaves tonight for Beta Hydri, by way of Inor. Did you need to see her for some reason?" Harris asked. Scranton looked at Harris and then seemed to pull back as if she had almost revealed something she didn't really want known.

"No, never mind. Just curious." Ron Harris doubted there was much idle curiosity anywhere in Susan Scranton, but he let it pass.

"Anything else?"

After the status meeting, Ron went back to his office with Elias Peña, verified the contents of his safe — really just the *Liberty* FDR and a few personnel documents — handed him the keys and left. He caught a ride home to say goodbye to Meredith and his three young girls. Girls who were, he realized, not so young as they used to be. The first on the stressful cusp of teen-hood, the last blowing her teachers away in first grade. The middle one quietly excelling at everything she touched. *So much like their mother*, he thought. The goodbye hugs and kisses complete, he reluctantly tossed his bag in the waiting Jeep and headed for the shuttle pad. It would be a long trip, and the sooner it started, the sooner he'd get back home, where he most wanted to be.

Antares
Earth Orbit
Monday, August 22, 2078, 1930 UTC

Terri Michael sat at the head of the crowded wardroom table, with Ron Harris on her right and Marine Captain Wayne Barnes on her left. As they finished dinner and turned in their dishes, she drew a tall diet soda for herself and started the discussion.

"Well, this is quite the crowd! Again, let me welcome all of you to *Antares*. I think we're all anxious to get back to Beta Hydri. I wanted us to have a chance to talk over the schedule."

"It's going to be a long trip," James George offered.

"Yes, it is. As you all already know, we're making a stop at Inor before we go to Beta Hydri. There are two reasons for this. First, there is a memorial that the Inori have erected to the *Liberty* crew lost there. We have sixteen of the twenty-six survivors here on *Antares*, and those folks will be attending. Also, we'll be carrying the new Terran Ambassador, Carter Calhoun, and three of his staff."

"I get that we're going, Captain," Greg Cordero asked. "But I thought the exploration of Beta Hydri was our highest priority?"

"Well, it is, and I resisted this assignment. But, ISC feels that other than stationing a ship in orbit, the Inori have been somewhat neglected over the last six months. And, it is appropriate that as many *Liberty* survivors attend this memorial's dedication as possible, and we're the largest group available."

"Still seems like an unnecessary distraction."

"I can see why you'd say that. But I think you will find it interesting." She looked around the table. "I think all of you should see this as the opportunity that it is. The Inori have a complex, very alien culture, but you will find yourselves welcome and comfortable there."

Gabrielle had a different feeling about it. "I, for one, am happy to be going. I've heard so much about them and their city that I'm looking forward to seeing it for myself."

Cordero leaned over to her and said, "Teacher's pet!" in his best stage-whisper.

Gabrielle poked him gently in the ribs. "Troublemaker."

Terri turned away from their friendly combat to look at Harris. "Admiral?"

"Not much to add to what you've already said, Commander. Just that despite my over-inflated rank, I want to reiterate that Commander Michael is the Captain here and I am just her humble passenger."

"More precisely," Terri responded, "the Admiral is in charge of the ground exploration, while I'm responsible for the ship." She turned to Captain Barnes.

"Wayne, can you go over the training schedule?"

"Yes, ma'am. The trip to Inor will give us additional time, which I actually think is good. We'll be doing SLUG training daily, which includes Doctor Bowles, Doctor Cordero —"

"Greg!" Cordero interrupted.

"OK, Greg, and Doctor Este —"

"Gabe!" Este interrupted. Barnes smiled, shook his head, and continued.

"OK, OK — I get it, I do. It's just habit!" He laughed a little at himself, then continued. "Along with the academics, we'll be training ship personnel that will be going to the surface." He looked down at his tablet. "So, Doctor Soto, Ballard, Hansen, Lewis, Swenson, George, several Intel techs." Looking around the table, he received nods of understanding in response.

"Weapons training. Fleet personnel should qualify on the 2K7X fleet standard rifle and be ready to carry one to the surface."

Terri looked around the table. "Any objections?"

"Could I qualify?" Greg Cordero asked. Barnes looked at Terri Michael, who looked over at Harris.

"What are you thinking, Greg?" Harris asked.

"Well, Admiral, I am about as unmilitary as they come, as should be clear to everyone by now, but if we get into some kind of shit, I'd prefer to be able to contribute beyond rolling myself into the smallest possible ball."

"OK with me," Ron Harris answered. "Gabe?" Este looked at Cordero, her arms crossed. Then she looked back at Harris.

"I had not thought about that at all. But, yeah, if we get into trouble, I'd rather be able to shoot back than just watch."

"Doctor Bowles?"

"I think I'll pass on the 2K7X, Admiral." Bowles smiled as he continued, "I've always found it best to leave the gunslinging to the gunslingers."

"OK, then," Barnes continued, "We'll set up the academics with Sergeant Jackson. He has experience doing initial 2K7X instruction." He paused to take a sip of coffee. "Back to the schedule — SLUG training will be in the hangar. We'll start with two hours AM and PM, then expand it after a week or so. One session for those new to the units and a second session for Fleet personnel that have already seen them. The Marines have been training on them for a couple weeks already, so we'll continue that in the early morning every day."

"You're going to be a busy man, Captain Barnes," XO James George observed.

Barnes smiled. "A busy Marine is a happy Marine, sir. The more we work them on what they need to be able to do, the better they'll be."

"Any other questions?"

"How long to Inor?" Joe Bowles asked.

Navigator Alex Williams leaned forward. "Fifteen and a half days, more or less. We do just a little over a light year per day."

"And from there to Beta Hydri?"

"Twenty-four and a half days."

"Thanks, Lieutenant Williams. Long time."

"So, let's get going, right?" George added with a smile.

"Yes, let's get going," Barnes answered.

"Agreed. The Ambassador is due aboard at 2015. As soon as his shuttle is off, we'll get moving."

"Anything else?" Michael asked again. When there were no more questions, she concluded the meeting. "OK, that's all for now. We'll have a status meeting here every morning at 1000. Good evening, everyone."

Terri Michael rose, and the officers rose as one with her. They filed out to their quarters or whatever duty they might have yet to do that night. The excited chatter of anticipation died slowly as they left, some of it flowing out into the passageway.

As a group, they were ready to go, intensely curious about what really happened on the surface of Big Blue. They were going to get the chance to find out, and they felt very fortunate for that opportunity.

Intrepid
GL 674
Thursday, August 24, 2078, 0930 UTC

Intrepid came out of FTL about half an astronomical unit (about 75 million kilometers) from GL 674, a red dwarf about a third the size of the Sun. Back in March, Kieran Barker's *Dunkirk* task force had encountered and destroyed an enemy ship here, and both Captain Joanne Henderson and Intel Chief Warrant Officer Ben Price were not surprised to find that system on the Sentinel list. As Ben and Natalie went through their now-familiar ballet of deploying the Sentinel, the Bridge Surveillance position lit up.

"Enemy object detected, Captain!" Marco Gonzales called out. Joanne stepped down from the Command position to see what they had found. It took a few minutes for the techs to reorient the large visual telescope and get a high-resolution image of the object.

"Looks like a Sigma Sphere, ma'am. Spectrum matches." *Sigma*'s fateful encounter with a spherical enemy object was now well known throughout the Fleet, and the spectrum and size had been added to their target criteria.

"Sure does, Lieutenant. Where is it?"

"Close by. It's about thirty degrees to our left, same distance from the star. We're still working on the precise orbit."

Jim Kirkland came over from the Weapons position. "You thinking about hitting it, Captain?"

Henderson shook her head. "No. This whole mission is about speed and stealth. We'll drop our Sentinel and move on."

"Shouldn't we call this in? Intel will be interested."

"Again, no. We'll tell them when we get back."

"But, Captain —"

"But nothing, Lieutenant Kirkland," she cut him off abruptly. Her stern expression met his for a second, then more evenly she continued "We're playing the long game here, Lieutenant, strategic, not tactical. If it were just us, then yeah, I would happily smoke that little piece of shit. As it is, we stick to the script we've been given. Understood?"

"Yes, Captain." Kirkland moved back to his Weapons station, disappointed.

"Lieutenant Gonzales, make sure you get good imagery and get the orbit defined, right?"

"Yes, Captain."

"If you need a few more hours to do that, let me know."

"Yes, Captain." Henderson left Alonzo Bass with the Conn and walked back to the hangar. There, she found Ben Price in a typical position — underneath and half inside the Sentinel, swearing.

"Good morning, Mr. Price!"

"Hello, Captain. Forgive me if I don't get up."

Natalie Hayden, standing just outside the Sentinel, laughed.

"Problems?"

"Not really, ma'am," Natalie answered. "Just the usual hook-ups and status checking. What was the alarm?"

"There's a Sigma Sphere here."

"Really?" came Ben's voice from inside the Sentinel. "Planning to swat it?"

"Nope."

"Good call." He clambered out from underneath the probe, closing the access panel and standing up. "OK, it's ready."

Henderson nodded, then pulled Ben and Natalie away from the techs working on the Sentinel.

"The Sphere is about thirty degrees away, Ben. Should we drop it here or would you want to move it somewhere else?"

Ben shrugged. "Not much choice there, Captain. The orientation stars are pre-defined, so we need to drop it in the orbit that FleetIntel has specified."

"Ugh, right."

Natalie looked at her Captain with a glint in her eye. "I'd love to have seen us crush that sphere, ma'am."

"Next time, Lieutenant Hayden; next time, we will."

"Anything else, Captain?"

"No, carry on." Joanne turned and headed back to the Bridge. Natalie got her techs started on the loading process. In an hour or two they'd be outside deploying the Sentinel. Then, on to whatever star was next.

Antares
En Route Inor
Monday, August 29, 2078, 0700 UTC

The Marines, under the watchful eye of Captain Barnes, worked out with the SLUGs daily. After a few days, they began working Gabrielle, Joe, and Greg with them as well. The routine was simple, really: Put it on, take a brisk walk around the hangar for a half hour, sit ten, back up to walk, sit, walk — on and on it went. They had almost 40 days' travel time, and they planned to use that time wisely. Gabrielle, already fit from her time in the desert, adjusted well after her initial problems balancing something that weighed more than a third of her own mass. For Greg, it was more like a long wade through thigh-deep water. He could carry the thing, but keeping it up for a half-hour was difficult. He woke up every morning with his whole body sore to the touch. Joe Bowles was in very good shape for a man of his age and did not have quite the conditioning curve that Greg did. Still, he was weary of it by the end of each day, too.

"Joe," Greg asked at breakfast a couple days into the training, "How is it that you're in such better shape than I am?"

"Well, Greg, I was an Army officer for thirty years. I was not a warrior, per se, just a battlefield surgeon and then, later, a pathologist." Joe set down his coffee.

"But I never wanted to dishonor the uniform by becoming soft. I frequently had to deal with officers who kept themselves in the highest state of conditioning you can imagine. I couldn't be some marshmallow rear-area lame-ass excuse for an officer."

"And you've kept that up?"

"Some, yes. I'm not as disciplined as I once was, but I keep busy."

The Marines supervising the training were impressed by the academics, if only for their stubborn refusal to quit and their impressive vocabulary of swear words. Cordero taught them to cuss in Aztec, which made them laugh and broke the monotony. Bowles amused himself and the Marines by describing, step by nauseating step, the worst autopsies he'd ever done. After a week of training, the Marines decided they'd be glad to step out on Big Blue with them.

Jack Ballard and Carol and the rest of the officers had worked with dummy SLUGs in University training scenarios, so they were familiar with them and the heat and weight of carrying one. Still, they worked out daily to get back into shape. The Intel techs had only a brief, perfunctory exposure to them in training and they had more trouble with it. Two were washed out by Barnes because they just couldn't tolerate the confinement in the apparatus.

"It's no shame," he said, "Not everyone can do this." The techs didn't see it that way, but there was no getting around the fact that they just couldn't use the damn things.

After the first week, they started adding more weight. Big Blue was about nine percent larger than the Earth, which meant a corresponding increase in surface gravity.

The qualification on the 2K7X Infantry Attack Weapon also went well. The 2K7X was a complex system internally, but once learned, was fairly easy to use. It had both direct-fire medium-caliber cartridges and a guided smart cartridge. Leon Jackson explained both to the academics.

"The direct fire round is accurate to 2000 meters. It has a kick, for sure. It's a big bullet, and there's no way to avoid Professor Newton." He set down the long, heavy-looking cartridge and picked up a blunt-nosed larger cartridge.

"Now, the guided smart round only works out to like 750 meters. But, if you put the laser on the target, and you hear the tone in your earpiece, it will go out and kill that target. Doesn't matter what the target does, the Golf Sierra will hit it center mass."

Leon worked them out on low-load training cartridges for both options, and they did well enough, Gabrielle turning out to be the better marksman. When asked how the professors were doing, Leon answered carefully, "Well, they're more likely to kill what's in front of them than behind them. That's good enough."

Late that night, Carol took down her journal and wrote about her day.

Dear David,

Well, I qualified. I guess I shouldn't be surprised — we both did it back at the U — but I was still pretty happy when Leon Jackson signed me off. I hope we don't need them, but if we do, I can hit what I aim at.

Kinda like you, maybe? HA!

It's only been two weeks, you know? It's hard when I think of that. There's so much more ahead than there is behind. So much more to happen.

We'll be at Inor soon for the delivery of the ambassador and the memorial dedication. Not sure how I feel about that — half of me is anxious to see it and half of me is dreading it. Doesn't much matter in the end, since both halves of me have to go. (Did you like that line? I did.)

I hope all is well with Dan on Columbia. I'm sure he busted you pretty good when you got there, but he thinks the world of you. You'll do great.

Oh, yeah, and I think the world of you, too.

Hope to see you sooner than I think.

—Carol

ISC HQ FleetIntel Section
Ft. Eustis, VA
Monday, August 29, 2078, 1105 EDT (1505 UTC)

The argument in Ron Harris' office had been going on for several minutes. Even with the door closed, most of the staff could make out what was happening. Susan Scranton's impatience, some staff thought *impertinence*, had earned her another session with Elias Peña.

"I don't see—"

"Then learn to see, Commander. We work together here, and that has proven to be the right approach."

"It's a waste of my time."

"It isn't. Doctor Scranton, your qualifications do not extend to excusing yourself from the overall operation of the FleetIntel section. We expect your participation in all aspects of our work where you can contribute." Peña stared at her, throttling back his anger. "And that means areas where you might not realize you can contribute. You're new to the Fleet, Doctor Scranton, and you've been granted a higher rank than is typical based on your education and expertise. But that rank carries obligations. Admiral Harris and I had a discussion about this before he left, and you can consider my words as his."

She sat quietly for a moment. "I work best alone, Commander. I piss people off, I know, but keeping my focus on the problem in front of me has always worked in the past."

"I understand that thinking, Doctor, perhaps better than you realize. But here, we work together, and that includes you. I need you in the status meetings like the rest of the staff. You might be surprised what they can contribute to your work, too."

Her expression made it clear how dubious she thought that idea was. She chose not to respond directly, but instead took the opportunity to change the subject.

"About that; After looking at the *Sigma* data in more detail, I've decided it's worth going back to GL 876 to look for remains."

"Well, Admiral Harris approved that already. You're sure there's something there to find?"

"I can't be positive, but it's quite possible. We have so little information on these creatures that I think it's worth the effort to see if we can figure out what they are."

"I wonder about that, Doctor," Peña said in a more collegial tone. "Even if you find a complete body, assuming there is a body somewhat like ours, what will that tell you?"

Scranton tried very hard not to roll her eyes. She needed Peña's buy-in, even if he had no idea what he was talking about. She tried to answer respectfully.

"Their bodies, just like ours, are the result of their evolution on whatever planet they come from. Their anatomy is the outward manifestation of that evolution."

"So, you think you can sort of reverse-engineer their environment and general capabilities from their remains?"

She looked up in surprise. "Well, yes. I didn't expect you to understand that."

"See, Doctor, we're not so clueless after all."

She had no response to that, but her face reflected the frustration that seemed to animate most of her conversations with the Intel personnel.

"I work better alone," she said flatly, as if there were no other possible options.

"Get over it," Peña said in a tone that sounded very much like an order. Softening a little, he asked, "How much time do you need to prepare to leave?"

"The gear just arrived, so I need forty-eight hours to check it and repack."

"I will call Operations and see when we can get you out there. Meantime, go ahead and get prepared assuming you're leaving in three days."

She nodded in response. Peña looked at her for a long second, considering what to say to crack through her stone outer wall.

Finally, he just said, "Dismissed."

Scranton looked at Peña for a second before standing up and leaving the office. She walked back to her own workspace at the back of the section. Elias picked up his phone and dialed the Operations Section.

"Good morning, Mark, Elias Peña here. Doctor Scranton has decided to go back to GL 876. I think Cook and Harris agreed that *Columbia* would be the best choice."

There was a delay as LDCR Mark Rhodes checked on *Columbia's* status. "She's almost to GJ 3618," he said, "From there it will be about twelve days to Kapteyn."

"And a day more to get Dr. Scranton there from here," Peña commented.

"Right. We have one of the new Fleet Shuttles available, so that might work. How much gear does she have?"

"A few hundred kilos. It just came in a couple days ago."

"OK, so no problem there. When can she be ready?"

"She says forty-eight hours."

"OK, so, that's mid-day Wednesday. How about 8 AM our time on Thursday?"

"I'll tell her. That puts her at Kapteyn on September 13th?"

"Right. I'll issue an order for *Columbia* to be there on the 13th as well. It will cut short their check of GJ 3618, but this is a higher priority."

"Thanks, Mark. I will tell her."

"Glad to help, Elias." They hung up, and Peña walked back to Scranton's workspace. She looked up cautiously from the carton she was unpacking as if expecting another lecture on collegial discourse.

"We have a Fleet Shuttle assigned to leave for Kapteyn 8 AM local time Thursday. You'll need to get your equipment down there by Wednesday afternoon. Does that work for you?"

She looked surprised. "Yes."

"OK, then, consider it done. It's almost twelve days to Kapteyn, so prepare yourself for a long trip in a small space with strangers."

She smiled a little. "You make that sound like something unpleasant. Strangers tend to leave me alone."

"Unlike your new colleagues?" Peña asked with just a touch of humor.

"Something like that, yes."

Peña just shook his head in frustration as he left her to her task and walked back to his office.

Over in Operations, Mark Rhodes verified with Admiral Cook that *Columbia* was still the choice for this mission and got her explicit authorization for the orders he was about to release.

```
ROUTINE 207808291600UTC
TO: COLUMBIA
CC: FLEETINTEL
FROM: FLEETOPS

PROCEED TO KAPTEYN STATION ARRIVING ON OR ABOUT 207809131200 UTC
TO PICKUP FLEETINTEL LDCR SUSAN SCRANTON MD AND EQUIPMENT.
WHEN READY PROCEED TO GL 876 AS DIRECTED.

END
```

Columbia
GJ 3618
Tuesday, August 30, 2078, 0700 UTC

David responded to the call from the Bridge, hustling forward with Katch to see what the captain was calling about. Dan showed him the message they had just received from Fleet Operations. Dan looked from one of his Intel experts to the other. "Any clue what this is about?"

"No," Katch answered.

David stiffened as he read the message himself. "The *Sigma* battle site? What are they thinking?" he asked no one in particular.

Looking again at the message, Dan had an idea. "Whatever happened to the sphere you hit?"

"No clue, Captain. We lost track of it when the Type I's started showing up. It might still be there."

Alona Melville joined the conversation. "We're supposed to be at Kapteyn on the 13th. That gives us three more days here if we want it."

Dan nodded. "Correct." He turned back to Katch and David. "How is the survey going?"

Katch answered, "Lieutenant Hughes would be better to ask, but I'd say we're maybe twenty-five percent complete."

"OK, we'll do what we can in the next seventy-two hours and then we're leaving."

"Yes, sir,"

As they turned to leave Dan spoke again. "David?"

"Sir?"

"They're sending us back to where you lost a lot of friends, David. Damn near got killed yourself. Is this going to be a problem?"

David looked Dan Smith in the eye. "None, sir. Whatever it takes to kill the bastards is fine with me."

"Very well."

As Katch headed back to the Intel section, David hung back. "Thanks for asking, Captain, but really, I'm good."

"Understood."

As David left the Bridge, Alona Melville sat down next to Dan in the command position.

"Think he's as over it as he sounds?"

"Oh, yeah. He's fine."

"I hope you're right," she said quietly, a question mark floating in her tone.

"You'll see, Alona. You'll see."

Melville got back up and left the Bridge, but her words echoed in Dan Smith's head. He really was confident his old friend was good to go on this project. Despite his gentle exterior, David had always had a tough streak, and when it came to this enemy, Dan felt sure he'd be ready.

Later that night, David wrote in his journal.

Hi Carol —

Well you just won't believe this one.

We're heading off to Kapteyn to pick up some doctor and heading back to GL 876. That's all I know but it has to be some weird intel snoop project.

Things are going OK here. Dan is the greatest, as I know you know. The Intel boss, Katch, is first rate.

I'm in a good place here, Carol, and I feel like I finally belong. Not like when I'm with you, mind you. Because that's, well, different. But hear me say again, I love you. Hear me say again, I'll always want to be beside you.

All we have to do is survive our planet's first interstellar war.

No sweat, right?

-D

September 2078

Fleet HQ Shuttle Pad
Ft. Eustis, VA
Thursday, September 1, 2078, 0745 EDT

Susan Scranton arrived early, dragging a small bag behind her. Her fleet-issue duffel was already in her locker on board. She looked carefully at the vessel she would be residing in for the next dozen days. It had no scratches or dents in its angular, flat black exterior. It was a new, large fleet shuttle, over thirty meters long. The split hatch was open, the lower half doubling as stairs.

She had spent most of the afternoon before supervising the pad crew as they loaded her equipment into the cargo hold. In the end, she reluctantly admitted to the loadmaster that the equipment was indeed secure and unlikely to suffer damage in transit. The balance of the load for this trip was tools and supplies for the repair shop at Kapteyn.

This morning there would be just three passengers to accompany the crew of four. The nominal capacity of the shuttle was twenty, so this trip would allow plenty of personal space, something Scranton was relieved to learn. She walked up the stairs where a female Warrant Officer greeted her.

"Good morning, Doctor Scranton."

"Hello," was her noncommittal answer. Scranton looked around at the interior. *Functional* was the best description, but she understood functional and didn't care much for luxury. The twenty seat/bed positions were arranged in ten rows of two across. Each had a media viewer for either personal or onboard entertainment. Screens could be lowered from the overhead for privacy, but, in truth, it was going to feel like a very long camping trip in a tent. She hated camping. In the back of the cabin, she could see the small kitchen, and two tables for meals.

Her greeter gave her a moment to look around, then continued her welcome speech. "We're very light on passengers this trip, Commander, so there are plenty of seats. The forward two rows are for the crew, so pick whatever you like behind that." She reached into a pocket and handed Scranton a keycard. "Your duffel is in locker number 10."

She nodded silently in response.

"You listed no dietary restrictions, ma'am, is that correct?" Scranton looked back at the officer.

"That's correct. I have no restrictions. But I don't eat much anyway."

"We'll have regular meals on schedule: breakfast starts at 0600, lunch at noon, dinner at 1800."

"I see."

"Anything else you need to know, Commander?"

"No, that will be all." She walked to the last row of seats. "I'll take one of these."

"If I may, being closer to the kitchen and the showers is actually less desirable. It will be quieter farther forward."

Scranton walked forward, selecting a spot one row removed from the crew. Scranton opened her bag and started stowing her NetComp, books, and other small items in the storage bins of the seat unit. The Warrant left her, walked forward to the open cockpit door, slipped in, and closed it behind her.

"So, Cardenas," the shuttle commander asked, "How's our first guest?"

"Cold, Lieutenant Small, cold as an asteroid's ass."

Janine Small looked back at her. "Now, now, let's not be judgmental."

"Or sexist!" said the second-in-command, Ensign Chad Compton.

"With respect, screw you both. This one is going to be a pain in the ass."

Janine Small shrugged. "I'm not so sure. I talked to FleetIntel, and they said she's a real loner, but not one to make a lot of demands."

"I hope you're right. But I plan to spend as much time up here as possible, as far away from that woman as possible."

"Well, Ms. Cardenas, we'll all take our turns up here and back there, and we'll just make the best of it, right?"

"Yes, ma'am. If you say so." Cardenas slipped back out of the cockpit to return to her orientation duties.

"You worried?" Compton asked his commander.

"Nah, not really. She's a serious academic. I don't know exactly what's in the cargo, but there's a shitload of crates back there, so, she's not exactly going to Kapteyn on holiday. Most likely the Doctor will bury her face in her books, and we'll only see her at meals, if then."

Compton nodded his agreement, and they went back to the more immediate business of the departure checklist.

Antares
At Inor
Wednesday, September 7, 2078, 1730 UTC

Carter Calhoun was a Southern gentleman in the best sense of the word. Of average height, thin and athletic in his appearance, he'd been asked by the United Nations to take over the diplomatic responsibilities at Inor. Sidney Johnston had been relieved not long after the *Liberty* crew returned home, and for the ensuing six months, the Second Secretary had been managing Terran affairs. The UN had strongly considered choosing someone other than another American. But, as the

Deputy US Ambassador, Calhoun had made a solid reputation for himself as a smart, flexible thinker, and someone whose word was reliable, so they decided he'd do.

Senior Lieutenant Jack Ballard drew shuttle duty that day, bringing the new ambassador and the rest of the visiting party to the surface. Carol sat right seat in the cockpit, stealing an early preview of the city of Inoria as they descended from *Antares*. As they disembarked into a bright, pleasant day, Carol flashed back to the day she had stepped off *Liberty*'s shuttle with Marty Baker. She let herself have that feeling for a few seconds, then pulled herself back to the present as Gabrielle touched her arm.

"What do I do?"

Greg stood close by, also looking apprehensive as he viewed the receiving line.

"Just go down the line. They'll each welcome you. You say 'I am welcomed' and shake their hands."

"What? 'I am welcomed'?"

"The Inori expect a response in the same manner as the prompt. You don't just give them a generic 'thanks.'"

"How am I supposed to shake their hands? They're enormous!"

Carol smiled. "Yeah, they are, but their palms are surprisingly soft. The Inori are used to new humans, so just go with it and you'll be fine."

After the Ambassador and Terri Michael went down the line, Carol followed Gabrielle and Greg.

Ron Harris elected to stay aboard *Antares*, and there was to be no mention that he was here or who exactly these additional people were. The Inori wouldn't ask, and Harris wanted to keep this mission as quiet as possible. Joe Bowles also skipped the Inoria trip. He didn't give any reasons, just "No, thanks."

Unlike *Liberty*'s earlier visit, Terri Michael made sure *Antares* was fully staffed, ready to respond to any event that might happen while she was on the surface. The new Unity Class destroyer *Aquarius* was also on station, taking its turn watching the system. There was plenty of firepower overhead this time, and so no there was need to worry while on the surface.

Standing on the shuttle pad, which was on a small hill east of the city proper, Carol could see construction in progress at several places in the city. She was glad that the tall towers destroyed on that ugly day were on their way back up.

The Inori provided transport for the Ambassador and his entourage, a typical open-sided tour bus. Carol and Jack jumped in the back row, away from the senior personalities. As they moved down the gentle grade and into the city, Carol saw that the city had been completely cleared of debris. When she left back in February, the cleanup had barely started, and Inori building materials were scattered everywhere. This day, the city was clean again, and the streets busy with Inori moving

61

about their business. A high degree of normalcy had returned, and Carol thought that was encouraging.

The loud, breezy transport stopped at the Terran embassy. The building itself had escaped unscathed in the attack, but the street and several nearby structures had been severely damaged. Today, those broken structures were gone, new construction taking their place. The elaborate 'Fountain of Earth' the Inori had constructed in front of the embassy had also been repaired, and water now flowed properly out of the North Pole, meandered through the oceans, and dripped off the Antarctic as intended.

As the now-empty transport pulled away, Carol looked past the repaired fountain to the memorial across the street. It was a flat stone structure, a half meter thick, three meters high and two meters wide, rising from the center of a large open area paved in fine stone. As she and Jack crossed the street, she saw that at the top there was writing in Inori, but down the left side, there was a list of names, in English, with 'Captain Dean Carpenter' at the top.

An Inori guide came to stand with them. "All Inori, Carol Hansen, all Inori shall remember what your shipmates did for us on that day. We are most grateful."

Carol could only nod in response, and after a moment the Inori moved away.

On the right side of the stone slab was a list written in the Inori language, which she took to be translations of those same names. About halfway down the list, she saw the name she was looking for, *Ensign Martin Baker*. Jack stood just behind her, reading the list. He could see which name her eyes rested on.

"I never knew him."

Carol reached out and touched the name, then spoke without turning around. "I didn't either, really, until we were on *Liberty*. He was good company. I'm sure he thought of himself as just a regular guy; plain, reliable, no drama, no problems."

"But?"

"But, men like that aren't really all that ordinary. And I was fresh out of a relationship with someone who wasn't that way at all. But Marty was happy just hanging out. He called himself my sidekick, like Batman and Robin or something. But I knew all along he was searching for someone for himself."

"You seem to have a knack at collecting regular guys as sidekicks."

She turned and slipped an arm around him. "Oh, Jack, I couldn't have made it through the whole *Sigma* thing without your support. I know that."

"I didn't mean it as something negative, Carol. You must realize how people respond to you, how they feel around you."

"I don't think about it, no. I can't, Jack. To actually believe you're somehow 'something special' is the start of a road to conceit that I never want to travel. If you and Marty are just regular guys, I guess I'm just a regular girl."

She'd given the perfect answer, Jack realized, and he wasn't going to pursue that thought any further. She was unusually both self-aware and sensitive to the feelings of those around her. Her openness was part of the magnet that drew others to her. Her genuine caring for her peers, her crew, and others she encountered was something remarkable to watch, Jack knew. He'd seen it. He'd experienced it. Perhaps her most engaging trait was that there was no artifice to her, nothing false or feigned. It was all genuine, all just who she was down to her core, and he realized she had no idea how unique and admirable she really was. He felt slightly jealous of David Powell for a moment, then reminded himself that she was completely genuine in that commitment, too.

He shook off his analysis of Carol Hansen. "We have an hour before the ceremony. Shall we have a look around?"

"Yes."

She released him, and they started walking northeast, retracing some of her route with Marty. Rorina was high in the sky on this clear, warm day, and Carol and Jack wore their Inor-specific sunglasses to filter the light down to something their eyes could tolerate. While the city again looked beautiful overall, scars could still be seen here and there — patches in the masonry that would eventually fade to match. Large scaffolds wrapped around the taller structures being rebuilt. They went up step by step: steel forms were placed, then filled, then removed after the concrete-equivalent core set. Then, the external and internal coverings were added, a hard masonry layer with those iridescent inclusions that made Inoria so 'otherworldly,' as humans often described it, frequently without noticing the irony in the sentiment.

It was a long, slow process, and Carol could see that the reconstruction of Inoria would take years. Watching it also told her something about how old Inoria was, how it must have gradually developed from smaller roots. The Inori were content in their place, with what Ino had provided for them, and how their society prospered in Ino's world. They mourned the lost, but they persisted with life and with the job of rebuilding. In the Inori, she saw peace, quiet determination, and caring for each other that she didn't frequently observe back home.

Humans could learn a lot from the Inori.

Carol and Jack arrived back at the embassy as the ceremony was about to start. She joined the line of *Liberty* veterans on the left. A line of Inori stood to the right, many showing white scars from wounds received during the attack, the color stark against their sandy-colored skin. The young Builder that Terri had carried to the beach was there, and he thanked her with a small gift of Inori pottery. He didn't speak English, so the interpreter explained that the characters on the cup included his name and an expression of his gratitude.

The Inori council was present, and they spoke effusively of the humans' help, both during and after the attack. They welcomed the new ambassador warmly, with no mention of the uncomfortable time when they didn't have one. Carol stood next to Warrant Officer Denise Long, whose experience the day of the attack was nightmarish. Her two friends and two guides were killed beside her in the first moments of the attack, while she was left standing, untouched. Carol slipped an arm in Denise's when she seemed to be faltering a little, and with Carol's help, she managed to get through the ninety minutes of diplomatic and emotional discourse.

As the ceremony ended, Long looked up at Carol, "I was such a coward," she said with thick disgust in her voice.

Terri Michael heard that and moved swiftly to her side. "You were unarmed, alone, with death falling all around you. The Fleet never prepared you for that, Denise. Don't criticize yourself for being normal."

"With respect, Captain, by that definition neither you nor Lieutenant Hansen is 'normal.' I needed to be more like you that day, and I wasn't."

"You can't change the past, Ms. Long," Jack said, having joined the conversation. "You can only go forward from here."

"Perhaps." She was clearly not convinced. She left the small group alone, walking in the general direction of the shuttle pad, away from the embassy and away from where her friends had died.

Another survivor, a senior reactor tech who worked with Long regularly, saw her leave and came to Terri.

"You want I should go with her, ma'am?"

"What do you think? You probably know her better than I do."

"Well, ma'am, I think she believes she deserves to be alone. She talks about that day from time to time, Captain, and she's not too happy with herself."

"So?"

"So, I'm going, ma'am. She shouldn't be alone."

"Good. Carry on."

"Yes, Captain."

The man trotted the fifty meters or so to where Denise Long was walking away. He fell in stride beside her, and they continued on together.

Antares
Enroute Beta Hydri
Monday, September 12, 2078, 0530 UTC

Greg Cordero dragged his sore butt out of his bunk and partly walked, mostly limped, to the toilet. The necessities dealt with, he switched on the light over his wash basin and cleaned up well enough to be presentable at breakfast. He had signed on to this trip as an expert in language reconstruction, not a pack horse or marathon runner. But the physical work was necessary, and he found that even while his muscles ached to the bone, it sharpened his thinking and supported his excitement as he contemplated the task ahead.

The Marines running Greg and Gabrielle and Joe Bowles around the hangar knew what they were doing, and while it hurt like hell at the moment, he enjoyed the workouts. And honestly, the Marines were fun once you got to know them and let them know you. Now dressed, he made his way to the wardroom, which at 0545 was already half full and alive with conversation. He gathered his breakfast and a large cup of coffee and sat with some young officers. A female warrant officer from Engineering greeted him in between bites and asked him about how he would manage to translate the Big Blue language.

"So," she continued, "with all these symbols, how can you work that out? Seems awfully hard to me."

Greg thought before responding. "It works by association and context, and as we gather more samples, it weighs the strength of those associations, and disassociations, to build a multi-dimensional graph of the relationships among words." He looked across at her, realized she was following so far, and continued. "That's the easy part, the mechanical part. The hard part is to impose some kind of meaning on the relationships, but once we start to break those down, the algorithm can open up large parts of the data tree to us, and we can begin to see what the language is saying."

"So, are you doing translation, or decryption?"

"That's a good question; the process is actually something of both. Think of those two approaches as running on parallel tracks, passing whatever hints or nuggets they find back and forth, both processes trying to get to a coherent solution."

"So, does this system have a name?"

"'Swadesh,' after a linguist who worked on language families."

"That's an odd name. Sounds like Swedish and swaddle had a baby."

Greg had to smile at that. "Yes, it does. I suppose I could have used his first name, Morris. But, whatever, he came up with a set of universal words that we should look for to find the connections between languages."

"Wasn't Morris a cat or something?"

"Uh, yeah, maybe."

"Well, Doctor Cordero —"

"Greg"

"OK, Greg, I have a degree in physics I thought was hard, but this sounds even worse. Will you be able to speak it?"

Greg snuck a peek at her name. "No. Ms. Long —"

"Denise."

"Probably not. Unless there are recordings or some other sound reference." Again, he paused before continuing. "I might guess that a letter is a vowel or consonant, or what passes for those in the language, but without something to tell me what phoneme or syllable the symbol represents, we'll never speak it."

"Pity."

"It is, I suppose. But if we can manage to extract the meaning, then we can read their literature, learn their names, know what they believed. That is something in itself, don't you think?"

"I suppose," she said, with some finality. "But if you can't *say* their name, what's the point?" She took a final gulp of her tea and got up. "Sorry, but I have a reactor to run."

"And you thought *my* job was hard?"

Long smiled in response and headed out of the wardroom, back to the reactor and her comfort zone. Cordero was less remote than she assumed a Ph.D. would be, and his explanations managed to bring the uninformed along without being condescending. She liked that about him.

Greg was left thinking about her final comment. There really was value, he knew, in being able to extract the meaning from a language without being able to speak it. They could, after all, run it through a translation and read it in English. But, on another level, Long had a point. Poetry is pointless without the sound of the words. Maybe they'd get lucky and find something. He'd been focusing on isolating and identifying the numbers and letters already seen in the drone images. The Fleet people had been right, the seven symbols were almost certainly numbers. He'd provisionally defined them as base-six numbers, 1-6, with a separate symbol for zero. He had also defined the alphabet, with forty-three characters so far. There might be more once they got on the surface.

He thought briefly about Long as he turned in his plate and coffee cup and started for his quarters. She reminded him a little of Gabe: attractive, but tough and very smart. She wore no rings. He then reminded himself that he had just come out of a bad and expensive relationship, and he really didn't need to be complicating his life with a new one just now. He had more than enough work to do as it was, and he'd be well-advised to stick to that.

The officers and academics held several long planning meetings, punctuated with stiff arguments, on where to start and what to prioritize for exploration. The military types argued to explore the battlefield first, while the academics made a forceful case for a more prosaic starting point.

"Put me in the room with the goddamn portrait!" Cordero had thundered at Harris. "I can't tell you why they were willing to die until I understand what they loved. I need to figure out who they are first. Then maybe — *maybe* — I can tell you what they were defending."

Gabrielle put her hand on his shoulder to keep him in his seat, and as he finished, she shook it gently to pull him back.

"But, Greg," Harris responded, sincerely and without offense to the volume of Cordero's feelings, "we need to know about their weapons, what tactics they might use on the ground. We need to get to the battlefield to know that."

As they talked it out, they devised a plan, first outlined by Ballard and Hansen, that laid out a middle ground that both sides could live with. Carol reminded them of the forty-seven-hour-plus day on Big Blue and the futility of working the whole of over twenty-three hours of daylight. They would take advantage of that to split the day into two eight-to-ten-hour exploration shifts, with time between to recover one team and deploy the other. The additional Marines would be useful in providing assistance and security. They could really do both, and she and Jack showed them how.

"This is pretty much what Jack and I did with the drones when we were there before," Carol pointed out. "We split the day because there was no way we were going to be able to work all through the daylight."

As much as Carol loved the portrait and the intelligence of it that touched her heart, she joined the technical team that would investigate the battlefield. Ballard would manage Cordero and Este as they began the search for the roots of Beta Hydri society. They'd start at the portrait house, and see where that led them.

ISC Fleet HQ Intel Section
Ft. Eustis, VA
Tuesday, September 13, 2078, 0815 EDT

Frances Wilson looked up as a notification alert sounded on her workstation, alerting her to a new Time-Difference-Of-Arrival (TDOA) message location solution. She pulled the detailed information side-by-side on her screen as Don Curtis appeared in her doorway.

"Did you see it?"

"Just now."

"Where is it?"

Don walked around to stand behind Frances as she displayed the results. All four operating Sentinels had seen the same message, as had the four permanent monitoring stations. The Sentinels called in on schedule early Sunday, and the FleetIntel computer network crunched out the location.

"It's like one of those early ones we got back in June. Enemy Station is talking again, twenty-five light-years down south."

"When?"

"Uh, based on the intercept times and the location, the process back-calculates the transmission time to last Wednesday, September 7 at 0922 UTC."

"It's short, just two seconds."

"One point nine three, to be precise."

Kristin Hayes, a young former Air Force sergeant recently hired away from NSA, arrived, and joined the conversation. "That's maybe eight or nine from that facility." She sat across from Frances. "But if it was an HQ, wouldn't we expect to see more traffic? Seems like it's awfully quiet."

"We had several hits back in June. Now, it's back on the air. I don't know what any of that means," Don commented.

"What does this do for our location?"

Frances took the results from the eight previous transmissions and asked the computer to combine the data for a more refined location

"OK, computer says 8 hours zero minutes Right Ascension, minus 67 Declination, 25.2 light-years away."

"What's near there?" Kristin asked. Frances opened a new app and plugged in the estimated position of the enemy facility.

"Well, there's GL 687 and... oh shit."

"What?"

"Beta Hydri. Less than twelve light years."

Kristin agreed. "Oh, shit."

They looked at each other for a moment.

"I'll talk to Commander Peña," Frances said. "We may need to think about a recon."

"I was thinking more about *Antares*," Don said quietly.

"Yes, that, too."

Frances left her office and sat down with Elias Peña to brief him on what they had seen.

"This station, now that we've got a solid location, is only twelve light years from Beta Hydri."

"Still, a recon is a pretty big step, Frances," he worried, "Let me think about it."

"Yes, I understand. What about *Antares*?"

"We should let them know, but right now I'm not sure what we can say to them that would be useful."

"If you like, I can discuss that with Kristin and Don and get back to you."

"Sure, that would be fine."

As they were talking, Fiona Collins appeared at Peña's door. He looked up in surprise.

"Captain Collins?"

"Good morning, Commander. Do you have a minute or should I come back?"

Frances got out of her chair. "We're done here, Captain, he's all yours!"

Fiona waited for Frances to leave, then stepped into Peña's office and closed the door behind her.

Elias looked at the closed door and then back at Collins. "What's on your mind, Captain?"

Fiona looked uncomfortable. "Any word from *Intrepid*?"

"I think you know, Captain Collins, they're not calling in."

"I know, but —"

"You're worried for some reason?"

"Actually, I think I might be worried for no reason, but I'm still worried."

Peña nodded his understanding, "Joanne."

"And Ben."

"Well, Captain, I can say this much; the Sentinels are calling in as expected, right on schedule."

"Well, that's something, anyway. Seen any results yet?"

Peña smiled. "Funny you should ask. Frances and I were just discussing the latest intercept. That facility down south?"

"Enemy Station?"

"Correct. Enemy Station sent a message last Wednesday. That makes eight, and with more points of reference, we're getting a progressively better location on it. I was going to come to see you later today. As Frances just pointed out, it's only twelve light-years from Beta Hydri."

"You thinking about paying a visit?"

"Just a little peek, nothing lethal."

Fiona smiled. With her nagging fear about *Intrepid* set to rest for the moment, she could focus better on what Peña was thinking.

"OK, so, let's get with Ops and see what's available."

"That would be fine, Captain, thanks."

"I didn't mean later." She pulled out her phone and pounded out the number for Operations. "Good morning, Commander Rhodes. Does Admiral Cook have some time for me?"

She did, so Fiona and Elias walked down the dark hall and up the two flights to the Operations section, their footsteps on the hard tile floor echoing around them. As they entered, Mark Rhodes waved them on into Cook's office.

"Good morning, Elias. So, what's on your mind, Fiona?"

"Intel feels they've got a good location on Enemy Station."

"Yes?"

Elias nodded. "We'd like a recon, ma'am. Just a look."

"Why the sudden rush?"

"Well, not so sudden, Admiral. We've been discussing it for a while. But, with this latest location, we now know it's awfully close to Beta Hydri. Given what happened there, we feel it's worth checking out."

Patty Cook leaned back in her chair, thinking. Then she leaned forward and called out, "Hey, Rhodes, get your ass in here."

Fiona, surprised by Cook's volume and language, waited for Mark Rhodes to enter the office and sit down. As he did, Fiona realized that his oak leaves had changed color from gold to silver.

"Yes, Admiral?"

"How would *Chaffee* like a field trip?" The whole picture now made sense to Fiona. Rhodes had been promoted to full Commander and was taking command of *Chaffee*.

"Congratulations, Mark."

"Thanks, Captain. Just happened this morning."

Well, at least Fiona hadn't been missing it for long.

Rhodes turned back to Cook.

"Where did you have in mind?"

"Enemy Station."

Rhodes shifted in his chair, surprised. He'd read the intel reports; he already knew what she was talking about and where they thought it was. "That's a long way, Admiral. Almost fifty days round trip."

"It is."

"What exactly is the mission?"

Elias spoke, "Just surveillance. Go find it, image it, see what goes on around it, get back."

"Sounds interesting."

"When do you take command?" Fiona asked.

"Tomorrow."

"Wow, that's quick."

"Yeah, current Captain turned up with osteosarcoma, so they needed to get him back and get someone else aboard. XO is just about due to rotate off."

"And here you were?"

"Something like that, I guess. I think Admiral Cook is just tired of me."

"Yeah, not." Cook looked at her tablet, then back across at the officers seated opposite her. "Commander Rhodes, your last assignment from me is to cut an order for *Chaffee* to recon Enemy Station. Let's send them, that is, *you*, oh, next Wednesday, September 21st. That will give you a chance to settle in and the crew a little off time. Expect a week of surveillance and then right back here."

"As you say, Admiral."

"Thank you all." Cook had a way of telling you she was finished with you without making you feel like you'd been dismissed. Tact, they call it. The three officers rose and left the inner office.

As they left the Operations Section, Elias turned to Fiona.

"Thanks, Captain Collins, I appreciate your help."

"You're welcome, not that you really needed me. Cook would have gone for it."

"She doesn't know me like she does you and Harris."

"Elias, you're doing great. The Senior staff knows it. Just keep it up."

"Thanks, Captain Collins. That means a lot."

They walked the rest of the way back to their sections in silence, then Elias gave the good news to his TDOA team.

Columbia
Kapteyn Station
Tuesday, September 13, 2078, 1150 UTC

Columbia slipped into dock at Kapteyn just before noon. Once she was secure, Dan Smith pulled David aside, and they headed out for *The Corner Bar*. Dan dropped into the same booth where he and Carol had talked several months before.

"Right here, pal, right *here*, is where I saved your ass," Dan said with a laugh, pointing to the table.

"And don't think I don't know it. Or that you'll be reminding me the rest of my life!"

"Maybe not quite that long, we'll see." They ordered pizza but no beers. There was still work to do on board, and Scranton was due at any time. They both knew it would not pay to greet her smelling like a brewery.

"So, when does *Antares* get there?"

"Not for a while, like October 4th or something. They had to go to Inor first. Carol's going to have a lot of work to do out there."

"Yeah, they all will, I think. Did you see the portrait?"

David nodded. "It was in the last Intel update before we left. Amazing thing to see. But I'm more interested in the battlefield."

"Really?"

"Yeah. I'd want to know what they were defending and why. There's something there about what kind of a culture it was, I think."

"And maybe about what kind of enemy we're up against."

"Agreed."

The pizza arrived, and they ate in silence for a few minutes, David thinking about Carol and his other former classmates.

71

"So, is Larry still on *Intrepid*?" he finally asked.

"Yeah, Nav. You know Henderson fired Court, right?"

"Carol told me. She showed me the SLIP he sent her right after Henderson took over."

"Shithead had it coming," Dan said quietly, with no small dose of disgust.

"For sure. Carol tried to help him, but some people, you know, they just don't get it."

"Hard to help someone who already knows everything about everything but actually nothing about anything."

David laughed. "Good description."

"Where are they, anyhow?"

Dan shook his head. "Not here. I can tell you later."

They finished their lunch with talk of other friends and where they were, what had happened, where they might go next. Dan paid the check, and they headed back for the ship.

The hard-looking Lieutenant Commander left the fleet shuttle much as she had arrived, pulling a small case behind her. There was no farewell, goodbye, thanks-for-the-lift, or whatever. She just quickly packed up and left. Ensign Compton watched her leave and then slipped back into the cockpit, where Lieutenant Small and Warrant Officer Cardenas were doing the final post-docking shutdown check-list.

"Ice queen gone?" Cardenas asked sarcastically.

Compton looked at her. "Yes, Cardenas, Commander Scranton has departed. You know, you could show a little respect."

"Militarily, yes, sir, I do. Personally, not so much."

"She was all work the whole trip," Lieutenant Janine Small said without looking up. "I don't know that I ever saw her just sitting or watching a movie or whatever. She worked, she ate, she slept."

"And really, not much sleep the last few days," Compton added.

"She's headed for *Columbia*," Small said thoughtfully. "I need to find Dan Smith."

"Worried she'll burn herself out?"

"Yup."

Cardenas looked from one officer to the others, incredulous. "You're worried about that rude, thoughtless, pain in the ass?"

"Well, sure. She's got a mission to do, Cardenas. Don't forget that shitload of equipment we brought for her." Small ticked off three items on the checklist as she closed a small access panel next to her seat. "Something's up, something significant, and she's in the middle of it. Whatever it is, we all want her to succeed, right?"

She finished the checklist, handed the tablet to Compton, and walked off the shuttle.

As David and Dan turned into the corridor to *Columbia*'s docking port, they found themselves following a thin, blonde Lieutenant Commander. Dan looked across her to see that Mike Clark, his Weapons Maintenance Officer, was minding the access hatch.

Mike saw Dan and David coming, but since they made no effort to overtake the woman, he focused on her instead.

"Good afternoon, Commander," he said pleasantly.

"I need to see Smith," she said bluntly. When Dan didn't respond, Mike figured he was to play along. He had no idea what was up but assumed Dan knew what he was doing.

"And you are?" Mike asked respectfully.

"Scranton. Is this *Columbia* or not? Smith is supposed to be here." Her rough attitude surprised Mike. Most Fleet officers knew to be polite, at least, when speaking to others, whether senior or junior. It was an essential part of Fleet culture.

"Yes, ma'am, this is *Columbia*. It's the Captain that you're looking for?"

"Of course. Where is he?"

Dan finally stepped forward. "Hello, Commander Scranton, I'm Dan Smith." He left off the usual 'glad to meet you' because, well, he wasn't, at least not so far.

She turned to him abruptly, apparently surprised.

"It's *Doctor* Scranton."

In a glance, Dan took in her severe features, the dark circles under dull gray eyes, somewhat hollowed cheeks, the drawn, exhausted expression of her face. *Was it fatigue*, he wondered, *or something else?*

"How may I assist you, Doctor?" he asked her carefully.

"Well, I need to get my equipment off that damn shuttle and over here into your sickbay. I'll need my own place to work, and —"

"Commander Scranton," Dan interrupted her, "we are aware of your requirements, and we're working on them." He looked over at Mike. "Where do we have the Commander assigned, Lieutenant Clark?"

"Second surgeon's quarters, sir, right off the sickbay."

That was exactly what Scranton wanted, but she made no sign of it nor any indication that she appreciated the gesture.

"Good. Let's get a med tech up here to escort the Commander —"

"I can find my way, Mr. Smith." Dan looked at her for several long seconds.

"That's *Captain* Smith, Commander. And I will thank you to treat my officers with the same respect and consideration you yourself deserve." When she didn't respond, he continued. "Do I make myself clear, Commander Scranton?"

"Yes, Captain, you do. I just —"

"Very well, then. You have permission to board and find your quarters. Our ship's physician, Doctor Gerry Knight, is expecting you. Lieutenant Clark will advise when your equipment arrives so you can check its condition before we load it on the ship. Please prepare a briefing on your project for Intel, the XO, and myself. 1400 today."

"Yes, Commander, I should —"

"Proceed, Commander Scranton." She looked at him briefly, started to speak again, then seemed to change her mind. She walked through the airlock and turned in the direction of the sick bay.

"What the hell?" Clark asked. Dan turned to David.

"Go find the shuttle pilot, Lieutenant Small —"

"Janine Small?"

"Yes."

David smiled. "She'll be in the bar."

Mike agreed, "Or crashed in the hotel, yeah."

"And when I find her?"

"Ask her what Scranton was like on the way out."

"You mean other than rude and abusive?" Clark asked.

"I don't think this is just arrogance, Mike. Her whole demeanor is off. She looks like she hasn't slept in weeks. David, go talk to Small."

"Dan!" came a voice from behind him. Dan turned around to see that Janine Small had not waited to be found.

"Holy shit!" she cried in surprise, "It's David freaking Powell!" They shook hands briefly before she turned back to Smith.

"We need to talk."

"Scranton?"

"Yes."

"Good, I was just about to send David bar-hopping to find you."

"Oh, Smith," she said, sliding an arm around him. "You know me all too well!" They walked far enough down the corridor that Clark and Powell could not hear, but the concern was obvious on Janine's face. David decided to get back to his own work and leave the management of one unpleasant lady doctor to the experts.

The three flatbed carts of equipment arrived at 1315. Scranton pronounced them acceptable, and the med techs unloaded them into OR #2.

As the ship's ubiquitous digital clocks clicked over to 1400, David entered the Intel conference room. Katch, Dan Smith, and Alona Melville were already there. David took a second to study Scranton. She carried a spare, hard frame and, if possible, even harder features. She stood at the digital erasable board at the front of the small room and waited. She greeted no one as they entered.

Once David sat down, Dan looked up from his tablet. "We're all here, Commander Scranton. You may proceed."

"Thank you, Captain," she said, in what so far seemed a rare moment of manners. "The purpose of this trip, in short, is to find some enemy remains for DNA and anatomic study."

There was a palpable silence. Smith reacted first. "You want body parts?"

"Yes."

Powell sat back in his chair, trying very hard not to roll his eyes.

She tapped her fingers nervously on her leg for a second.

"Part of our problem with this enemy is our complete lack of information about them. We have no insight into their behavior. They don't signal. They don't demand. They just attack. Maybe if we knew better what they are, we would be better able to cope with them."

Powell leaned forward, "Or, devise better weapons to kill them."

Scranton nodded, "Yes, that too."

Smith looked at her for a moment. "Assuming we can find anything, how will you decide what they are?"

"That's what the equipment I brought with me is for. I have a DNA analyzer with a reference database of species-specific DNA patterns. I also have an electron microscope and some additional small instruments."

Dan paused. "I assume this is a mission where we'll want to avoid contact with living, whole specimens?"

She wasn't quite sure it was a joke. "Yes, Captain, that would be advisable."

There were a few moments of quiet as the ship's officers read the briefing materials she had given them.

"*Sigma* was attacked four months ago," Smith said.

She nodded.

"You don't think the, um, samples, will be degraded?"

"I understand what you mean, but exposed biologic tissue will essentially freeze-dry. We will have to evaluate what we see in that context, of course, but I believe the data will be perfectly valid. It may also be effectively sterilized, but we're less sure of that."

"Sterilized would be good," Powell deadpanned. That earned him another scowl from Scranton.

Katch asked, "So, Commander, are you thinking we'll find these, uh, remains, just floating in space or are we supposed to find the shipwreck itself?"

"I can't say. I think you who have been out here are better equipped to answer that than I am. I just need material to examine."

"Katch, let's have Powell take the lead on this one."

"Fine with me, sir." Katch felt relieved to let someone else deal with this tough doctor, and turned his head to give Powell a joyously evil grin.

"OK, I think we're done here. I want a detailed briefing for the full staff tomorrow morning." They all rose with the captain and filed out of the room.

Scranton was the last one out of the little workroom. She left without another word and headed for the sickbay. She disappeared into the room for the rest of the day, popping up only for one bathroom break. By late afternoon the space began to look more like a lab and less like an operating theater. Boxes of instruments now covered the floor. The techs worked to remove whatever associated OR equipment — anesthesia, infusion, monitors — could be moved. They scrambled to securely stash the masses of sealed supplies now piled on tables all around the main treatment area.

For Susan Scranton, tomorrow would be yet another tedious briefing for people who didn't understand her work. But her mood was gradually changing with the feeling that she was getting closer to her goal. She fought to hide her desperation to find, and kill, this enemy. Her pain was deep and personal, but she dared not share it with the officers around her. She'd rather be respected than pitied, even if it meant offending a few people. All that mattered was getting the answer and putting it to work. For her, everything else was either a distraction or an irrelevancy.

As dinner time approached, XO Alona Melville made her way down to sickbay to see how it was going. She found Scranton leaning over a case on the floor, straining to lift something out.

"Can I offer a hand, Doctor?" Scranton stood up, startled. She was dripping with sweat. The room felt very warm and humid.

"Sure, Lieutenant," she said breathlessly.

"Alona, please."

Scranton just nodded and did not return the offer for a first-name relationship.

Alona ignored it for the moment. "So how do we pick this thing up? Oh, and let's fix the air, OK?"

Alona adjusted the room controls to drop the temperature and humidity. With the two of them, it was fairly easy to lift the DNA sequencer out of the case and place it on a side counter.

"You don't want this on the operating table? There's more space."

"No, I'll do the dissections there. It has an overhead x-ray."

"Ugh. Dissections."

Scranton half-shrugged. "Might sound gross but it's part of the job. Better them than us."

76

Melville nodded agreement. "No argument there. You ready to call it a day? You've been doing hard labor all afternoon."

Scranton looked around, taking stock of her progress. "I can quit now. The sequencer was the last item on my stretch-goal checklist for today."

"Dinner in the wardroom is at 1830. So, you have a little less than an hour."

"Fine. I need a shower and a change of uniform."

"You have a private shower in your quarters. That perk comes with the doctor gig." Scranton looked relieved, the first real emotion Alona had seen from her. One final wipe with the towel and she headed out of the OR, locking the door behind her.

Dan Smith ran his ship 'tight and loose,' meaning, tough and by-the-numbers when it counted but relaxed and less formal when not in combat or on alert. He was a very junior Lieutenant Commander, promoted, he suspected, because he was already here and Fleet was short on available officers. Most of his staff were like him: young and working above their rank and experience. He could not be 'the old man' as the captain, so he kept meal conversation relaxed, open, and free-wheeling. But everyone knew once they left the wardroom who was the captain, and who wasn't. It was an intentionally healthy and interesting place to be. Dan insisted on it.

By dinner time, the word was out among the crew that there was a black mission afoot, having something to do with the sick bay and the mysterious tough-looking doctor they had picked up.

Dinner that night was roast pork with sweet potatoes, green beans, and sauerkraut. After walking the buffet and taking a seat, Scranton looked at the table and then across at Melville. "How do you get this stuff out here?"

Melville looked over at James Murphy, *Columbia's* logistics officer, who answered for her. "It's a really big ship, Commander, comparatively speaking. The volume advantage on a ship like this means we can carry a lot more supplies, in proportion to the size of the crew, than smaller vessels. Vegetables and fruit are flash frozen, and the meats are shrink-wrapped and radio-sterilized. It makes for very long shelf life."

Scranton just shook her head. "That crew on the shuttle —"

"Are having steak tonight." Murphy interrupted.

Smith looked at Murphy in mock surprise and anger.

"Murph, you gave away my steaks?"

"More like sold, sir, and not all of them," he said between bites, "but yeah, your personal stash got hit kinda hard."

Scranton found herself unsure how much of this was banter and how much was real. Across the table, she could see Powell failing to suppress a grin, and next to him Melville wasn't doing much better. Murphy, as head thief and underhanded back-door deal-maker, was a running gag in the wardroom.

"What did you get for them?"

Murphy pointed across the table. "Commander Scranton's stuff." Now the joke was obvious, and Scranton laughed nervously as well.

"Good deal, Murph. We'll need it."

"Yessir, I thought you'd say that."

The truth, of course, was that Smith had arranged for Murphy to treat the shuttle crew to a decent meal. Even the larger Fleet Shuttles had limited space, so 'real' food was at a premium. As Scranton had experienced on the way out, they had had nutritionally correct but fairly dull reconstituted meals. Smith treated them whenever the stores permitted, and the shuttle crews appreciated it.

"Speaking of supplies, Lieutenant Murphy, how is the load-in progressing?"

"Not bad, sir, but not great, either. I had to rotate some stuff forward before we put in the additional food and other supplies for this trip."

"How much longer?"

"I'll need all of tomorrow, boss. Sorry."

"So, how about we plan on departing Friday morning?"

"Yes, sir, that would give me plenty of time. If you can live with that, it will take a little pressure off the crew as well."

"OK then, let's call it 0600 Friday."

"Yes, sir, that works for me, thanks."

By the end of the meal, there was only Scranton and Melville still remaining with Smith in the wardroom.

"Doctor Scranton, you've put in some very tough days. Get some sleep and make it an easy day tomorrow. There will be plenty of time for you to get set up before we get to the *Sigma* engagement site."

She shook her head. "Captain, I need to keep at it until I have the equipment ready. There is so much to do —"

"Commander, I talked to Lieutenant Small. You haven't slept more than a couple hours in days."

Scranton looked hard at him. "I think I am in a far better position than you to determine my fitness to do my job." After a moment she added, "Sir."

Smith inclined his head and softened his tone but not his message. "Really, Commander, it's time to let up a little. I asked you for a full briefing for the officers, but let's make that Thursday morning. Meantime, get some sleep. If you need some help with that, Gerry Knight can give you something."

"But Captain..." she started, then seemed to wilt slightly.

Melville, who had not spoken during this exchange, looked at Scranton.

"Susan, this is your first trip this far out?"

78

Scranton nodded, ignoring or missing Melville's familiarity.

"I have learned the value of pacing myself. The skipper is correct. You need a rest."

"Yes, Lieutenant," she surrendered.

"OK, that's settled," Dan said, relieved. "But remember that the days can get fuzzy out here and it's easy to work more than is really healthy. Do your job but be mindful of yourself as well. You can't complete your task if you're passed out from exhaustion." Smith stood up, motioning the two women to remain seated. "Easy day tomorrow, Commander, then you can do the full mission briefing Thursday morning. I will be in my duty cabin. Good night."

Scranton left shortly afterward, slightly disappointed by her first confrontation with the captain. Maybe he has a point, she conceded quietly. She returned to her quarters, tried to reread some research on cross-species DNA markers and identification without really absorbing anything new, and eventually turned in.

Later that evening, Melville took a walk around the darkened ship, chatting with the on-duty crew. She ended up at the captain's duty cabin. She paused, reconsidering, then knocked.

"Come." As she opened the door, Smith was at his desk reading a personnel file which he closed as she entered.

"Yes, Lieutenant?" She paused again, standing just inside the door of the tiny cabin, which she slid closed behind her. The duty cabin was only intended for the captain to use while underway, so that he or she was only a few seconds from the Bridge. There was a desk with a few shelves built into the wall, a bunk above, and not much else. Calling it 'Spartan' didn't describe it adequately.

"Don't push her too hard, Dan. She's new out here. She'll figure it out."

"I know, Alona, I know. I don't want to bully her. But Small said she had been living on coffee and cereal bars for days. She was worried Scranton wouldn't make it to the station. And, she looked like hell at dinner — just plain exhausted. I had to break the cycle."

Melville nodded agreement. "Yes, this time, I agree. But we can't dictate every officer's work life. She's obviously highly motivated."

Smith leaned forward, his hands on his chin. "More than motivated, I think. There's something else driving her. Something deeper." He thought for a moment. "OK, after tomorrow we'll keep an eye on her but let her find her own way."

Alona looked at him for a few seconds. "Would you have grounded a male officer like that?"

Dan leaned back in his chair, a pained look on his face. "Oh, Alona, you know me better than that. She's right on the cusp of burnout, and this whole mission turns on her personal performance. Her gender was, and is, irrelevant."

Melville nodded and slipped out without saying anything more.

The night passed quietly after that.

Powell spent most of the evening reviewing his college biology. He needed to freshen his understanding of DNA, RNA, mitochondria, and basic cell dynamics. He had no trouble getting to sleep after that.

Smith finished reading Scranton's personnel file, such as it was. BS from Western Michigan, MD from Wisconsin, Ph.D. from Johns Hopkins. She did research on inherited childhood diseases at Mayo until abruptly joining the Fleet just days after the Inor attack. After the academic officer orientation course, she appeared at FleetIntel as a Lieutenant Commander. Pretty common stuff for an expert spook.

Melville watched a movie, then snuck out of her cabin to check on Scranton. After confirming with the night sick bay crew that Scranton was in her quarters, she turned in for the night.

Katch drafted a letter to his wife and son and filed it for transmission when they were off EMR restriction. Then he had a few shots of Jack from his hidden cache and fell asleep on the floor by his bed, fully dressed.

The next morning found Powell back reading up on his biology. He had coffee with Melville in the wardroom, then drew a third cup to take back to his cabin. Susan Scranton wandered into the wardroom as Powell was leaving.

"Feeling better, Doctor Scranton?" he asked.

"I guess," she mumbled. "Ask me again after coffee."

"Yes, ma'am," he said happily as he went back to his books.

Scranton slid into a seat across from Melville and sipped her coffee gently. It was pretty good but really hot.

"Decent coffee. The stuff on the shuttle was crap."

Melville just looked at her. "Like Murph said last night, we have a lot more storage space per crewmember than a shuttle. So, we have a few advantages."

"I don't like being ordered to bed like a child," she finally said. "I am an officer in this Fleet, and I deserve more respect."

"You weren't treated like a child, Doctor Scranton. Both the captain and I felt that you had been running too hard for too long. It's part of our job to look after our crew, including our fellow officers. This is an important mission, Doctor, and you are the one irreplaceable component."

"Irreplaceable? First time I've heard that. Crazy is more commonly used. Nutty bitch, sometimes." she said bitterly.

Melville took it all in but didn't pursue the thread further. "You won't hear that here. Breakfast?"

There was a buffet in the pass-through kitchen window. It was somewhat depleted by earlier visitors, but they were still able to assemble a decent brunch. They sat mostly in silence. Other officers came and went.

Finally, Melville asked, "So how are you going to spend your day off?"

Scranton made a face. "Well, since I can't *work*, I think I'll review the plan for sequence analysis. We need to be able to adapt to what we find, so I was going to try to flow chart out at least some of the possibilities. And I have to prepare the briefing for tomorrow."

Melville nodded her agreement. "Sounds good. I have some good old movies on in my media box if you're interested."

Scranton's look made it plain she had no plans for movies today.

OK, I tried, Alona thought. *At least she'll have a slower day.*

Columbia
Kapteyn Station
Thursday, September 15, 2078, 0830 UTC

Susan Scranton stood at the far end of the wardroom table, the title slide of her presentation 'Project Helix' displayed in the standard fonts and colors the Fleet required. The officers were all in place within a few minutes, coffee mugs in hand. She took a deep breath and began.

"I know much of this will be old news to some of you, but I believe it is necessary that we all have a grasp of our current understanding of exo-biology and how that affects the plans for this mission."

She looked around the room. So far, so good.

"Our first firm evidence of life beyond Earth was from Mars in the early 2030s. We found fossilized bacteria and primitive multicellular organisms similar in appearance to those on the early Earth. There was no DNA, of course, so while this finding was exciting at first, further study led to a less momentous conclusion: One could not tell, really, if these were truly Martian or whether they had been cross-contaminated from Earth."

Powell spoke up. "Or if it was Earth that was cross-contaminated from Mars. We could, really, all be displaced Martian refugees."

"Unlikely," Scranton replied, "since the best research so far indicates that Earth is the origin of its own life. The other thesis based on the Martian organisms, discounting contamination, was that simple life might arise fairly easily given decent conditions. It's possible Mars just wasn't warm and wet long enough for higher forms. We should also recognize, frankly, that we're not done looking and there may yet be surprises in the rocks."

Her next slide read 'Europa Disappointment.'

"The concept that simple life might be easy took quite a hit when we finally got into the ocean under the ice on Europa. Instead of meter-long telepathic electric eels, or an obelisk 1 by 4 by 9, we got nothing. No bacteria, no fish, no deep ocean tube worms, nothing. It was sterile."

"So much for Arthur C. Clarke," Katch commented.

"Enceladus was the second instance of life. It wasn't intelligent beings or even fish, but there was simple life there. It has strange physiology based on the low pH and high concentration of metals in its environment. It looks almost like a moss or a lichen attached to the rocks at the bottom of the ocean. Its DNA has been sequenced, and we don't believe it is a contaminate. The genome is quite different from any terrestrial organism."

Dan set down his coffee. "So, all this is pre-Drive stuff. There was no other life discovered before Inoria?"

Scranton shook her head. "No, Captain, nothing else before Inoria. The Drive, of course, changed the whole calculus. Researchers could get on a ship in Earth orbit and be at Pluto in hours. That kind of access was a pipe dream before the Forstmann Drive. A further disappointment was the terrestrial planet at Proxima Centauri A. It looked very promising from a distance, but it also turned out to be sterile. Clearly, there are factors we don't fully understand. Chance, perhaps. If the planet has just the right conditions and all the right things happen, you get life. Otherwise, just chemistry."

She took a breath before continuing.

"So, let's talk about Inor. There we have a fully developed ecosystem, covering three planets, with higher and lower forms, predators and prey, vegetation, and small animals. "

"How different from us are the Inori other than in physical appearance?" Dr. Knight asked.

"They are quite distinct. They were technologically similar to us when we found them, except for the FTL drive and nuclear power. Their medical and physiological understanding was somewhat behind. They knew about cells and nuclei — general morphology — and that some attributes passed from generation to generation, but had no idea about DNA, RNA, or how proteins are actually built. To be fair, neither did we until the 1950s, which really isn't that long ago in scientific terms." She paused for a breath and another sip of her coffee.

"Their genome is quite different from ours, but we can identify a few common sequences related to metabolic processes, a case of nature solving the same problem the same way in different places. We don't think that's unusual."

"I heard they don't have mitochondria?"

"No, Doctor Knight, they do not. The ATP energy cycle occurs within a different structure in the cell cytoplasm. It does the job of mitochondria but is not encapsulated and does not have its own DNA. It's possible that the presence of mitochondria is a marker for terrestrial organisms. Again, not enough data to say that as a fact, but it seems reasonable."

"Interesting," Knight said quietly.

"Yes, it is. It sets up some interesting questions about identifying and analyzing non-terrestrial species."

Knight continued, seemingly engaged for the first time. "Have we sequenced the genome of any of the other species on Inor?"

"Yes, two species of aquatic animals — fish I guess — were provided and we have that on board as well. To anticipate your next question, no, the Inori and the fish are not closely related. We see some common sequences but no more than we would with humans and salmon."

"So are the Inori reptiles or mammals or what?" asked Jim Murphy.

"They are none of those. They are warm-blooded live-bearers, which would tend to make them mammals, but they have no fur or hair, and they don't give milk. They're obviously not reptiles. If they laid eggs, they'd almost be birds." There was some laughter at that.

Scranton was getting more engaged, and her tone warmed noticeably. "But they are just as intelligent as we are, and have a well-formed culture. They're just different, and we probably shouldn't try to fit them into terrestrial categories."

"So, you like the Inori?" Melville asked.

For the first time since she came aboard, Scranton smiled. A real, warm, genuine expression. Powell almost spilled his coffee.

"No, Lieutenant, I love the Inori. Their culture is complex and somehow quiet and restful. They are thoughtful in ways we are not. They are generous to us and to each other. They are strong without being aggressive. They love their Ino, and they completely believe he loves them. Given where and how they live, that's hard to argue with." After a moment of light, her smile faded, and she was all business again. Powell was sorry to see it go. With that, she was almost human. Without it, he was less sure.

Next slide: Wreckage Location

"Powell, would you please discuss the wreckage?"

"Yes, Commander. First, I looked back into what technical intelligence we have on the enemy, and it seems we've never tried a serious forensic analysis of their ship wreckage." He turned to look at the captain. "It's shocking, sir, really. The first few times we hit them, we were at a disadvantage and bugged out. One time where we did hold the space, the commanding officer described the wreckage as 'fragmentary' and just left. At Inor, most of the wreckage had deorbited and burned up before the relief ships arrived. The rest was likely in the ocean, and we never pressed the Inori to get at it."

"Powell, what about *Sigma*? There must have been shrapnel or other evidence left from the hits she took." asked the Navigator, SLT Maz Dawes.

Katch spoke up. "Yes. They found shrapnel similar in content and design to what was found on Inor — small heavy spheres of common metal, likely mined from an asteroid. It was mostly nickel and iron with some lead and uranium. We don't think that means anything in terms of ship construction."

"What about the explosive?"

Katch shrugged. "That is less clear. Trace element analysis indicates it's something like the Torpex used in torpedoes in the Second World War. There may be other materials as well. Whatever it is, it burns pretty fast and pretty completely."

Powell waited a moment to see that the sidebar was over before continuing.

"So, we don't have any ship mass or construction information to go on. From basic physics, we can expect the wreckage to be in an expanding sphere, more or less, moving in the same direction the vessel was headed when it was destroyed. We know the course and speed from the *Sigma* IR data."

Another pause.

"Those were some big explosions. But lacking knowledge of the construction of the vessel we have unlimited uncertainty about how much inertia was imparted to the departing debris."

Alona Melville rolled her eyes. "Cute."

"Thanks. I worked on that phrase most of last evening. A major part of the uncertainty are those explosions. We assume they were ordinance, but we don't know where they were stored in the vessel, or how the vessel came apart as a result of the blasts. It's quite possible that the ordinance was all external and the ship is somewhat intact, likely riddled with shrapnel holes, but essentially whole. On the other hand, if the explosions reflect stores from deep within the ship, the whole thing might be in very small pieces, and the biologic samples we're interested in could have been consumed in the explosion."

The captain interrupted, "I get that you can't know everything, David. What is FleetIntel's estimate of what's out there?"

"Assuming they haven't invented anything new, FleetIntel made an estimate using a titanium and steel hull similar to ours. The IR data did give a rough estimate of the energy expended. In general, larger pieces should be closer to the center and smaller pieces further out. FleetIntel estimates by now the wreckage is in a sphere about thirty million kilometers in diameter. For reference, at its closest approach, Mars is fifty-six million klicks from Earth. So, a little more than half that distance."

Powell again looked around to make sure they understood the scope of what he was saying.

"Even if the entire ship is on the edge of that sphere, which of course it isn't, we're looking at over a million square kilometers per kilogram of wreckage.

Assuming, of course, that Intel's assessment of a two million metric ton ship is correct."

"Two million metric tons?" Melville asked, incredulous. "A damn aircraft carrier is only a hundred thousand!"

"True, Lieutenant, but enemy ships are two and half times longer than a thousand-foot carrier, and around three times wider as well."

"Still, Powell, that's a helluva lot of mass to be hauling around."

Powell looked back at Commander Scranton, and she rose to continue the briefing.

"So, you have to be wondering what the plan here is," she paused. "Truth is, the plan will unfold dependent on what we find. We will examine the evidence macroscopically, microscopically, and chemically, including DNA. What I do after that depends entirely on what I learn as we go."

Dan Smith looked skeptical. "This is a long way to go, Commander, to make it up on the spot."

"Yes, Captain, it is. But this is science. We will follow the evidence as it unfolds. As we learn new facts, we will adjust our actions to obtain more new facts."

Smith still looked unconvinced, so Scranton pressed on. "Captain I could give you a hundred-page three-dimensional flow chart of what I was going to do, but it would be dead as soon as we learned something we didn't expect. The Chief of Intel believes this is worthwhile. I hope you will, too."

Gerry Knight spoke up, "Captain, I think she's on the right track, and she's giving it to you straight. This is how I would do it. We just have to play each stroke where it lies."

Smith shrugged. "Fine. I will defer to the scientists on this one. What do we know about the enemy, Dr. Scranton?"

"Essentially nothing, sir. No one has ever seen or heard the enemy. Since they struck at Inor with the apparent intent to invade, we can guess that they are more or less like the Inori, and us, in size, type of sensory organs, relative intelligence. But even that is guesswork."

Melville asked, "Shouldn't we assume they are more intelligent than us? They appear more advanced in space travel and weapons, at least."

"More advanced, possibly, but I am not convinced of that. More intelligent, not necessarily. They as a species may have evolved earlier than we did and therefore simply have a head start on us in technological development. They also could have followed a more efficient path through technological progress. As you all know, our own path to technology was far less than linear. We just don't know."

"Or they could be huge-headed brain-eating telepathic grey-skinned monsters with an IQ of a thousand," Lieutenant Mike Clark offered. Scranton tilted her head and smiled slightly.

85

"Unlikely, seems to me. But, yes, possible."

"Lieutenant Clark, you are to cut back on the 1950's sci-fi, OK?" the captain offered. He paused for a moment. Time to get back to business.

"So how hard do you think it will be to find this wreckage?" Scranton asked Melinda Hughes, the Surveillance Officer.

"Well, I think it makes sense that most of the remains will be near the edge of the sphere. I am a little more hopeful than Lieutenant Powell, but his arithmetic is correct: it's a sphere on whose surface we can expect to find one kilo of wreckage every million square kilometers."

"And we're looking for organic samples that won't reflect much radar and probably won't show up on IR," Melville added.

Katch spoke up. "Captain, if I may, we should consider looking for large objects first. If their ship is compartmented in any way similar to ours, it's possible the larger pieces may contain specimens within partial, or even whole, compartments. These will be easier to locate. We should also look for star occultation as an additional search method. It has the advantage of being completely passive."

"And completely luck-dependent!" commented Melville.

Katch nodded and shrugged in response.

"OK. To summarize, we're looking for a sphere thirty million kilometers in diameter moving at thirty thousand kilometers an hour away from us, and somewhere around the edge of that sphere we expect to find a kilo of shit every million square klicks?"

Powell smiled. "Yes sir, but don't forget that we think the sphere is expanding in diameter twelve thousand kilometers every hour."

Dan Smith scowled. "Powell, you're a pain in the ass."

David smiled again. "Indeed, sir, but I am *your* pain in the ass."

"Roger that. I like the occultation idea, Katch. The XO is correct that it will take some luck, but if there are large pieces out there, we might see them earlier that way. Go ahead and work with Lieutenant Hughes to see if she can help you with integrating the optical systems and setting up a watch." Hughes, sitting at the end across from Scranton, nodded acknowledgment.

"Very well, we're adjourned."

David left the wardroom, pausing for Melinda Hughes to exit. She smiled at him as she exited, saying, "My office, say, Saturday, 0930?"

"Done."

Hughes headed forward to her Surveillance Section's spaces while Powell followed Katch back to the Intel work area.

That night David let his feelings out about this project to Carol.

Dear Carol —

OK, the GL 876 project is officially weird. This hard-ass Doctor Scranton wants us to go find enemy body parts for her to dissect.
Nuts, right?
Or, maybe not. After all, she brought a ton of equipment aboard. I'm not at all sure we'll find anything, but we're going anyway.
Melinda Hughes — Surveillance Officer — is really really smart. Love her approach to things. Good sense of humor, too. Getting to know the rest — Mike Clark, XO Alona Melville — better now. I'm feeling more comfortable as the days go on. Dan keeps pushing me to say what I think, so I'll keep doing it until he tells me to stop.
Thought of you often today, more even than usual.
Stay safe.

—D

Columbia
Enroute GL 876
Saturday, September 17, 2078, 0930 UTC

Senior Lieutenant Melinda Hughes entered the Surveillance Section work area and spotted Technical Chief Larry Allen talking to a junior tech. Whatever the tech had done, Chief Allen clearly did not approve. She grabbed Allen by the arm and dragged him, smiling, into her office.

"Got a job for you, Chief."

He accepted her assault with good humor and sat across from her comfortably. Hughes, despite what her pretty face and small size might imply to some, was a tough boss. Still, Allen liked her competence and integrity. Her word was good, and that was Chief Allen's one litmus test for a good officer. She had a decent sense of humor, too, and he believed that she really cared about her staff, of which he was the most senior. He waited while she worked on her tablet for a moment.

"Consider yourself read in on a compartmentalized project." She finally said without looking up.

"You mean Project Meat Market?"

She looked up. "That's the best the crew can do? Meat Market?"

"Well, Lieutenant, you know how it is, some I can't really repeat in polite company."

"Like?"

"Like, I can't really repeat them, ma'am."

She laughed slightly, then went back to her tablet.

"Ever done a star occultation search?"

Katch knocked gently at the open door, and he and David came in. Chief Allen began to stand up.

"Relax, Chief," Katch said, "keep your seat." Allen nodded his acknowledgment and then looked back at Hughes as if expecting an explanation. Katch leaned against the wall by the door.

"I was just asking the Chief about occultation searches," she said, still reading the tablet.

"You read him in?" Katch asked.

"Apparently the word on Project Meat Market is already out."

Katch shook his head and laughed quietly. He looked at Allen. "Meat Market? That's the best you could do?"

"Yes, sir. I already covered that with Lieutenant Hughes."

"Acknowledged," Katch deadpanned. "So, tell me about the occultation search."

"We have software for it, but damned if I know when we last did one." Allen leaned back in his chair, hand rubbing his chin absentmindedly as he thought for a moment. "We should be able to cover it if you're willing to accept some time delay."

Katch stood up straighter. "Time delay?"

"As you all know, the primary function of the external sensors is to look for enemy activity. The second function is to locate the ship in space. If you're willing to wait for the results, the incoming scan data can take its normal immediate route through the primary surveillance and nav functions, then through the occultation logic as an additional data consumer at the end of the line. That way we can get complete coverage 360 by 360."

Katch was intrigued. "How much delay? Seconds? Minutes?"

"Some number of seconds, sir. I don't think it would be as long as a minute. We're only interested in visual data, so that helps, but I would not want to get your hopes up." The chief was now looking at the wall while he thought about the problem. "I am pretty sure we're looking at less than a minute. After we get it up and running, we'll have hard data to refine that estimate."

Katch looked at David, who nodded his agreement. Hughes turned back to Allen.

"OK, get on it."

"When do you want to start?"

"I'll need it when we drop out of FTL at GL 876. So, you have plenty of time."

"Yes ma'am, we'll have it up as soon as we can."

Allen rose and left the office, his mind already three steps down the path to setting up the search. He called over a junior tech and, without telling him exactly why, got him started on the procedure for adding a data consumer to the visual scan stream. Allen then pulled up the occultation processing logic on his console, reminding himself of how it worked. It was fairly simple in concept, but comparing every star on every scan to that same star on subsequent scans took a lot of processor time.

Katch took Allen's seat, and they moved on to their next topic.

"Has he approved radar yet?" Hughes asked.

"Captain's discretion, I guess," David commented.

"You know he's worried about being detected —"

"So am I," Hughes interrupted, cutting Katch off.

"Yeah, me too. So how do we search this big an area with radar without calling attention to ourselves?"

"The Intel alert last March indicated that the enemy likely understands radar. We'll have to be very careful about it."

"Understood. But I have a question for you."

"OK…"

"You heard the briefing, one kilo of junk for every million square clicks of wreckage sphere."

"Right."

"Can we even detect that?"

Hughes leaned back in her chair, then picked up her tablet, looking for a reference. She looked up at David. "No guidance from FleetIntel on this?"

David shook his head. Setting down the tablet, Hughes pulled out a notebook and a pencil.

"The debris sphere is thirty million klicks in diameter?"

Katch nodded. Hughes slapped the pencil down. She could do this calculation in her head, and she didn't like the results at all.

"Christ, that's a hundred light-seconds. I don't believe we can search that with radar." She thought for a moment. "We could use it to look ahead a short distance, maybe to avoid something, but as a general search tool, forget it."

David's shoulders slumped, deflated. "So, this is a fool's errand after all."

Hughes looked up at him with some sympathy. "We'll see. Maybe not."

After Katch and David left, Melinda sat back down and thought about the radar problem for a few moments. She finally concluded that the laws of physics really were in charge, and there was not much she could do about it. She had only so much antenna, only so much power, and therefore only so much ability to see. Two plus two always equals four. Period. It really was a dead end. Too bad.

October 2078

Columbia
GL 876
Sunday, October 2, 2078, 1315 UTC

A few hours after they came out of FTL at GL 876, Lieutenant Commander Dan Smith looked out from his chair on *Columbia*'s bridge across the wide array of consoles and displays in front of him. He thought the bridge design was a little too *Star Trek*, but despite the apparent chaos of colors, text, flashing lights, charts, and graphs visible from his command chair, it was functional. From his slightly-elevated perch, he could see the displays of each ship section, arranged in a semi-circle around him. Beyond and above that row of consoles, there were display screens capable of showing any data stream Dan, or any of the bridge crew, might need to see. Above these displays were the windows, reaching to nearly over his head, and through which now he could see only the inky dark of deep space and the pinpoint diamonds of innumerable stars, all very far away from him. The red dwarf GL 876 was off to his left and slightly behind him as they approached the estimated location of the enemy wreckage.

"Goddamn middle of nowhere," he mumbled to himself.

"Sir?" asked the Conn officer seated next to him, Lieutenant Abbas.

"Never mind."

"Minding never, sir." They shared a small grin over the exchange. Just below and to the right of Smith's position, SLT Melinda Hughes was standing behind the Surveillance position, watching the radar and occultation data streams. She had convinced the captain to run the radar at half power, with longer pulses to increase their detection range. They had been at it for a few hours already with no results. The occultation data stream, or 'blink stream' as they had come to call it, had also shown nothing. David Powell stood just behind Hughes, arms crossed, leaning against the captain's elevated platform. A young Technician 1, Sunil Anand, was running the gear. Her hands paced nervously over the controls, adjusting the displays, checking the settings, never seeming to come to rest. Chief Allen sat next to her.

"It's OK, Anand, you can't make something appear that isn't there," he said reassuringly.

"Yes, Chief. But I am afraid of missing something."

"Are your settings correct for what we're trying to do?"

"Yes, Chief. I just thought —"

Allen interrupted gently, "Then take a moment and see what develops."

She nodded, still nervous.

Powell was watching all this interaction from a few feet away. "Technician Anand, how old are you?"

Without looking away from her screens, she responded, "Nineteen, sir." Hughes turned her head and gave Powell her best 'what the hell was that?' look. Powell just smiled back.

"You're doing fine, Anand. Just remember at nineteen your officers were all still useless college kids," he said, still looking at Hughes. He heard Allen laugh as he continued, "Just keep it up."

Sunil nodded her acknowledgment, again without taking her eyes off the screens in from of her. A few more minutes passed, with Powell motionless in the back, Hughes just behind her watch crew, and Sunil Anand's hands working the displays.

An alert tone sounded, just loud enough to be heard across the bridge.

"Where is it?" Hughes asked.

"Ahead, ma'am, ten degrees above and fifteen to starboard. Range is about fifteen thousand." Anand's fingers were now busier than ever.

"OK get the narrowband dish on it."

"Already moving, Lieutenant."

By now Dan Smith was out of his command chair and standing among the officers behind the Surveillance watch station.

"How big is it?" he asked.

"I can't tell yet, sir." Chief Allen answered.

"Narrowband data coming online now, sir," Anand reported. The middle screen on their workstation started to light up with a radar picture. "Range is sixteen thousand three hundred. It's moving — towards us and slowly up and to the right." The picture began to show an image of twisted metal, but the image had missing parts. The thing seemed to morph in shape from moment to moment.

Allen looked at the image for a few seconds and then worked his controls. The picture blanked and then came back, clear.

"It's tumbling. I needed to get the processor to recognize that. The image should improve." And it did. They could now see the motion of the object, seemingly end-over-end.

The captain stepped forward.

"How big, Chief?" Allen looked over at his young student.

"It's about two meters across, sir," she said.

"Shit," he said quietly. "Any danger of collision with us?"

"No sir, it's already off our course and moving away."

Katch appeared next to the captain, speaking quietly. "Two meters, sir. Two lousy goddamn meters. We could get it in a shuttle cargo compartment."

Smith looked away from the radar data, directly at Katch. "It's tumbling, Katch. You have a death wish not listed in your personnel file?"

"Not at all, sir. Commander, it's a real piece of an enemy ship. It's right there!" Katch said, pointing out the windows above them for emphasis. "I'd like to try."

Smith shook his head. A moment later, he turned his head back over his shoulder. "Conn!" he called to Abbas.

"Sir?"

"XO and Nav to the bridge." Abbas nodded his acknowledgment and picked up the phone at his station. He spoke a few words, then hung it back up.

"Five minutes, Captain," he called back to Smith.

The XO arrived as expected, with the Navigation officer Maz Dawes right behind. Smith pulled his officers into the small open area at the far right of the bridge. He looked directly at Katch.

"How would you do it?" Katch thought for a moment.

"I guess I'd just suck it in. I'd open the cargo doors, they're plenty big enough, and then just engage the Forstmann panels in the cargo bay floor to drag it in."

"That tumble isn't going to magically stop. You'll make a mess of my shuttle, Katch." He walked back to the Surveillance station. "How fast is that thing tumbling?"

Allen worked briefly. "About three RPM, Captain."

Smith walked back to his ad hoc consultants in the corner of the bridge.

"OK, not going to happen."

"But, sir —"

"Big fish, Katch," Dan interrupted, putting a finger in his Intel Chief's chest. "We're after the really big fish, not the little droppings."

"Yes, sir," Katch replied, deflated.

"I understand, Katch, but I'm sticking to the plan."

"Of course, sir."

Dan looked at him for a moment. "We're going to find one of the wrecks, Katch, and when we do, it's gonna be fun."

"I hope so, sir."

"OK, then." Dan turned and walked away, effectively ending the conference.

Katch looked at David. "We could have gotten it."

David shrugged and replied, "Not without denting the shuttle, and, oh yeah, maybe getting yourself killed."

"Still, we could —"

"With respect, Lieutenant Khachaturian, the captain said 'No.' With a capital N. So, we should, maybe, get back to work?"

Katch frowned again, but followed David off the Bridge and back to the Intel work area. Maybe he could get some spectra or something off this object to make it worthwhile.

"You know what this *does* mean, right?" David asked him.

"What?"

"It means we're on the right track. We're barely here, and already there's ship bits around. That's *really* good news."

Antares
Beta Hydri (d) ' Big Blue'
Tuesday, October 4, 2078, 0945 UTC

Terri Michael brought her ship out of FTL about a million kilometers away from Big Blue, about two-and-a-half times the distance from the Earth to the Moon, and well above the plane of the system. From there, they could observe the planet and look for signs of enemy activity. She and Ron Harris had several conversations during the transit about whether the enemy would continue to monitor this system somehow. Neither thought this place could be just left alone, as it made little sense to them to leave this crime scene without a tripwire, Unless, of course, the enemy didn't consider this a crime. That idea came up several times in both their public and private conversations. It troubled them, but it was as yet an unanswerable question.

Harris was sitting next to Terri on the Bridge as the universe came back in focus around them. As usual, Weapons Officer Carol Hansen had the rotaries loaded and ready to deploy. Ryan Lewis had doubled up his Surveillance crew, and Jack Ballard was standing nearby, just in case they saw something unusual. Gabrielle Este stood behind the Weapons station, occasionally chatting with Carol. Joe Bowles stood near Cordero, in front of the Command position, silently observing the process.

The newcomers all gasped at the view out the windows. Big Blue stood bright against the black backdrop of space. Beta Hydri was behind them, so the planet was nearly completely illuminated.

"Welcome, ladies and gentlemen, to Beta Hydri (d), our very own Big Blue," Terri said, smiling.

"Oh my God, Carol, the pictures don't nearly do it justice!"

Carol looked away from her Weapons status display.

"No, Gabe, they don't. It's hard to explain to people that even with high-res 3D images, there's nothing like seeing it with your own eyes."

Greg Cordero leaned his back against the Command position, his eyes also fixed on the blue jewel out the Bridge windows. Even as he admired the beauty of the place, Greg was mulling over how he could break down the alien language.

Terri looked down at Ryan.

"So, Lieutenant Lewis, remind me what time it is down there?"

"It's just after noon on Sol 63, Commander. Dawn on Sol 64 is about 2045 tomorrow."

"Very well. We'll start on the surface on Sol 65, Friday evening our time."

"So, what are we doing for three days?" Cordero asked.

"Watching," Jack Ballard answered. "We're looking for any sign of enemy activity. Later we'll go lower and make some more mapping orbits."

Terri nodded. "Right. We'll stay right here for 24 hours. Then, as Jack says, we'll descend to a low polar orbit and get updated imagery of the place."

"You can't use a Sleuth for that?"

Ryan Lewis turned around. "Resolution is much better from the ship. Larger aperture, much longer focal length. The Sleuth is fine for sniffing around but can't give us the detail we need here."

Bowles was unusually quiet as he absorbed the view. His generally gregarious approach to life was set aside as he processed the reality of being in deep space, at a planet that looked just like home, with a bizarre and violent event to investigate. Harris didn't miss the change.

"So, Doctor Bowles, beautiful, isn't it?"

Bowles nodded. "It is, Admiral, it is. Hard to understand sometimes how these blue beauties get here. There's so much that's just grey and dead."

"Indeed, that's true. Places like this are pretty rare."

"Which makes it that much more of a shame, that out of such beauty rises such evil. It's awful what happened here."

"Agreed. It's an irony I've thought about as well."

The two men stood in front of the command position for several minutes, watching Lewis' techs as they began to catalog the objects around Big Blue. Their first priority was to locate anything resembling the enemy's construction, then, anything new, then, finally, to update the positions of the satellites and other small bodies they had seen before. This process would take most of the first day.

Late that evening, Carol took her journal with her to the Conn. With the Surveillance teams verifying the system, she expected a very quiet shift.

Dear David —

We're at BH, and it looks as beautiful as ever. Even our hard-data scientist draftees agree about that.

It never seems like enough to say I miss you, but I miss you.

I've got plenty of work here to distract me, but know that you're always around me, floating here just behind my eyes. We'll be silent the whole time, so I don't know if you've sent me anything, or where you are, or how you are.

I do know sometime soon we'll be together again, and that is something worth waiting for.

—Carol

As she was finishing her note to David, Greg Cordero strolled onto the Bridge. "So, Carol, I have a question."

She put down her journal and waved him up to sit with her at the Conn position. "Sure. What's on your mind?"

"You all rotate shifts here at the Conn, even when we're FTL, right?"

"Yes."

"Why? Seems like nothing much can happen. Can't the ship fly itself?"

"Well, it is quiet most of the time. And, yes, the Nav system really is flying the ship."

"So, what do you do?"

"I read a lot, study for the next promotion exam, that kind of thing. We watch the Comm station for messages, keep an eye on the Reactor, and pray the Drive doesn't fart and turn us all into cosmic rays."

"Oh, so that's all?"

"Yeah, that about covers it."

"Cosmic rays?"

"Or sub-atomic particles, or drop us into some other universe. No one seems to be quite sure what would happen if it went haywire."

Cordero sat with her for another half-hour, looking out at Big Blue. They chatted off-and-on about life onboard, discussing more small questions he had. Then he headed back to his cabin, slightly amazed at her cool approach to such a dangerous job.

Intrepid
Earth Orbit
Thursday, October 6, 2078, 0900 UTC

Captain Joanne Henderson looked out her Bridge windows at a very welcome sight: Earth. They had been away a long time, and her crew was more than ready for some leave time. Admiral Cook had no immediate plans for *Intrepid*, so she sent up a small relief crew and authorized three weeks of liberty for the whole ship. Natalie Hayden went to the surface on one of the first shuttles, heading back to her small apartment near ISC HQ. Like most of the crew, her first priority was sleep: real, quiet, private, Earth-bound sleep. No ship vibrations or hard footsteps going by her cabin door on metal plate floors.

The crew was mostly off within a day, but today Joanne remained on board, completing some personnel work at the command station. She could be doing this in her duty cabin just behind the Bridge, but then, the Bridge had a much better view of the blue planet below. She planned to leave after the relief Captain came aboard. Meanwhile, with the crew 'ashore' this would be one of the quieter places on the ship.

She sent her after-action report to Operations and FleetIntel by laser. They had successfully deployed all six Sentinels. There were a few recommendations for improvements in them, but the ugly little spy-bots had performed as expected. She included the sighting of a 'Sigma Sphere' at GL 674, something that had left her wondering just how many of those little spheres were out there, and what their purpose was. She could not escape the obvious conclusion that they were reconnaissance drones, just like the Sentinels. If they were, they'd have to call home at some point, and when they did, the Sentinel would hear. She had a nagging fear that the converse was true as well, which might mean trouble. Time would tell.

Tomorrow, Joanne would meet *Aurora*'s Captain Navarro to brief him on the launch process and the changes Natalie and Ben had proposed. *Aurora* would be taking out eight Sentinels, more than doubling the number deployed. She served with Navarro early in her career but had not seen him for some years. She thought it would be interesting to catch up with him.

There were commendations to write, as well. The Fleet didn't give out medals, but performance above the usual standard would count heavily for promotion. She wrote Natalie Hayden's commendation, but she had XO Alonzo Bass write Ben Price's. It probably wasn't necessary, but she felt better about it. Both she and the XO would endorse both documents.

Ben came to her office just before he left for home. After the door closed, there was a long embrace and a few quiet moments before he spoke.

"I am glad, Joanne, really glad, to serve on your ship."

"But?"

"But," he said with a smile, "I really miss our evenings in the bar. I miss the laughing together, the long stream-of-consciousness conversations."

She nodded as she leaned back in her chair. "I know. I do, too. It was a unique time."

"Sometimes I feel like I should have turned this gig down. I should have stayed in Plans, and we would have stayed friends."

"We will never not be friends, Ben. Never. But as you know full well, this ship is my first priority."

"I know, Joanne; I just would not want you to be here feeling alone."

"I'm not. And I'm not staying. Cook is sending a relief captain, so I get some time off, too."

"Good. Plans?"

"Someplace warm."

Ben nodded and started to get up.

"So, dinner with Natalie anytime soon?" Joanne asked with a comic, conspiratorial tone.

"Um, well, tomorrow, yeah." What did Joanne know that he didn't?

"Good. She's wonderful, you know."

"Yeah, I think so, too, but how —"

"What, you think because I'm the Captain I'm suddenly deaf and blind?"

"No, but —"

"The hook is set, Ben, I expect she'll be reeling you in soon."

"Wait, *her* hook is set? I thought *I* was the fisherman in this scenario!"

"Just keep thinking that and this might work out for both of you."

Ben leaned across his Captain's desk and kissed her on the cheek, then turned and headed out of the office. As an officer and a friend, his devotion and trust in her were complete.

On the other hand, Natalie would be meeting him at six-thirty tomorrow, and he hoped that relationship would be headed in an entirely different direction.

ISC Fleet HQ Intel Section
Ft. Eustis, VA
Friday, October 7, 2078, 0930 EDT

Joanne sat in the Intel conference room, on one side of the famous 'Table' that the Intel staff met around. While she waited, she surveyed the condition of the old maple library table which, legend had it, was stolen from the Capitol building late one night. She doubted that story, but the table was surely a tough old salt, covered with stains and nicks but still reporting for duty able-bodied and ready to serve.

Juan Navarro arrived a few minutes after 0930, shook hands with Joanne and took a seat, waiting for the Intel personnel. They made small talk about where they'd been since sharing time as Ensigns on *Vostok*.

Ann Cooper arrived in her usual breezy manner, followed by her Sentinel team, Scott Morgan, and Kelly Peterson.

"Good morning, Captain Henderson, Captain Navarro. Thanks for coming in."

After introductions, Ann let Scott lead the discussion.

"We've made some changes since the Version Zero Sentinels *Intrepid* deployed, so I want to go over those first."

"We had some suggestions?" Henderson asked, wondering if her detailed recommendations had been for naught.

"Yes, Captain Henderson, we actually had a couple of the same ideas and have implemented those already."

"That's encouraging."

"Two major ones, really. First, the configuration data is now on a removable chip; it's basically the same memory chip you'd find on a Sleuth. So, should you have a hardware failure of some kind, as you almost did, Captain Henderson, you can swap the chip to the next unit in line and keep going."

"Excellent. That was something my team suggested."

"The second major change is with the RTG interface. FleetShips has added a control data line so the Sentinel can direct the power-up process and control the RTG itself."

"So, no more panels and switches?"

"No, ma'am, no more long sequences of opening and flipping and closing."

"That's very good."

Ann looked from one Captain to the other.

"We knew this process was going to be awkward at first, but there was a high priority on getting the units out. Now that we had some time to evolve the design, it should be much easier."

Navarro shifted in his seat. "That sounds very good to me. I read Captain Henderson's report, and these are the two items that most concerned me. Anything new about the deployment?"

"No, that remains as is, unless your crew figures out something better."

"Well, we'll manage."

Kelly fired up the flat monitor on the wall. "Now, about your stars…" She got up and moved to the screen.

"Since *Intrepid* left, we have developed information that indicates the enemy likely originates in the deep southern sky. If I had to throw a dart at a star, I'd say Alpha Mensae, but we don't know that yet. We do know that there is a facility about 25 light years out."

"That's a long way, Warrant Officer Peterson."

"It is, sir. But, here's the list for you." The screen lit up with the list of stars, distances, and travel times.

"Eight stars, Captain, almost a hundred days travel time."

"Long trip."

"Yes, Captain, it surely is. But I want you to know these stars are targeted based on a line from that facility to us, here."

"So, if they come sniffing around in this direction, we'll know about it?"

"That's the idea, yes."

"We're dropping the communications blackout for this trip," Ann added. "As we do with regular system visits, we'd like you to report as you leave each star."

"Fine by me. Anything else?"

"No, sir. That's all we had."

As they left FleetIntel, Joanne politely declined Navarro's invitation to lunch. She had a post-mission meeting with Cook, and then she'd be meeting Fiona Collins at *The Drive* for early drinks and a late dinner.

The Drive Pub and Bistro
Newport News, VA
Friday, October 7, 2078, 1830 EDT

This time Ben Price did not avoid the richly paneled dining room at *The Drive*, but rather installed himself in a small booth along the left-hand wall. Natalie arrived shortly after he did, and dropped into the seat across from him just as their young waiter arrived. She ordered a margarita, large, and Ben remained loyal to his Scotch: Dewar's, double, neat.

After the drinks were ordered, Ben looked at her for a moment. She was attractively dressed, carefully made-up, and her hair had clearly been trimmed and styled.

"You look great," he said, careful to sound complimentary but not surprised.

"I better. There's serious time and money in this hair and face tonight."

"Nat, you always look great."

"Price, if you're telling me I wasted my money —"

"No, no, no, you're an even better you than I expected."

"Smartass."

They shared a laugh at the exchange.

Ben caught her eye and held it for a second. "So, Natalie, is it still too early to tell?"

She smiled again, remembering their conversation in his office back in August. "No, Price, it's not. I —" She was interrupted by the arrival of the drinks.

"Dinner?" the waiter asked. Natalie and Ben matched their eyes, and she shook her head slightly.

Ben responded. "Later. I think we'll have a couple rounds first."

As the young waiter left, Ben raised his Scotch.

"So, what shall we drink to?"

She leaned forward, elbows on the table, and raised her glass to his. "How about...*possibilities*?"

Ben smiled in response, and they each took a sip. Natalie took a moment to look around the dining room.

"I've never been in here. Is this where you and Henderson would sit?"

Ben thought he heard a trace of something more in her voice. A residual question, maybe, about his relationship with Joanne?

"Uh, no. We always sat in the last booth in the bar on the other side. It had a great view of the place. Perfect for people watching."

"You mean, as in making snarky private fun of the people around you?"

"I mean exactly that, and Henderson was a master! Collins, too. Good God, we laughed a lot." Ben took another sip, then set down his drink and looked at Natalie. "I'm very glad you're here, Nat."

"Yeah, me, too." She looked at him evenly with a small smile, not letting his eyes leave hers.

"You know what I've been through. I'm...well..."

"Not looking right now?" She was offering him an easy off-ramp, just in case he wasn't ready for her.

Ben paused a moment, wondering how to say what he felt without scaring her away.

"Not looking for anything superficial," he replied, staying right on course.

She looked down at the table and then back up at him. "I don't do superficial, Ben. I don't do *casual*." She squeezed the last word out as if it were an obscenity.

"Good, because I like you very much, Nat. I'd like to see if there could maybe be something more."

"Oh, there is, Ben, there definitely is."

He looked at her for several seconds, studying her face in the faux candlelight and wondering how he could possibly be so lucky as to have fallen into the orbit of this woman. He reached over and touched her hand. She grasped his in return.

"Thanks. But, just for the record, Miss Lieutenant Hayden —"

"Watch the 'Miss' business, buster!"

"For the record, ma'am, I would have been very glad to see you even without the, um, *investments*, you made today. I'll take you just like you were every day on the ship."

"Except the uniform, right? That would be weird."

100

He managed not to laugh, but her deadpan delivery was hard to resist. "Yeah, except for the uniform."

"Well, I needed a trim, and when I mentioned I had a date tonight —"

"This is a date?"

"Hell yes, this is a date!" She looked around for a moment, then turned back to him. "Anyhow, *for the record,* when I told them that, and how long we'd been out, they offered to do a little makeover. I had fun."

They ordered another round, and as this evening's live band began to play, Ben moved over and sat next to her, his flimsy excuse being that he wanted to see the band. They passed on dinner and instead ordered an appetizer each, then cross-grazed through two sets by the band and one more round of drinks. They talked sporadically, sitting very close so they could hear over the music. Eventually, they tired of trying to out-decibel the electronics, paid the check with a generous tip and left.

The sun had set hours before, but it was a warm evening, typical for early October in Virginia. Instead of calling for a ride, they walked along a wide boulevard towards Natalie's apartment. The hooded sidewalk lights gave enough illumination for them to see but didn't shed any extraneous light skyward, so the stars were easily visible. They talked about those stars, about people they had known, how they had felt about Inoria, and what might be happening next for them. They'd just experienced one of the longest trips Fleet had ever done, and now they had only three weeks off before going back out. Somewhere far away, most likely. Somewhere dangerous.

They made plans for lunch the next day at Shield's Tavern up in Williamsburg, a place Natalie loved. They both wanted to get away from the Fleet, to get back out into the 'real world,' as they called it.

They walked arm-in-arm for the last half mile. At Natalie's door, there was an awkward moment as she wondered what to say, or ask, but Ben just drew her close and lightly kissed her goodnight. Once she was safely inside, he turned and headed for his own place about a mile away.

Ben relished the walk home, each step filled with warm memories of the evening just past and the pleasant anticipation of more of the same tomorrow. Opening the door to his apartment, he saw it was still sparsely furnished, but instead of feeling empty because of what he had lost, it now seemed to offer space for something new.

Something new that might be truly beautiful.

Big Blue
Third Town South
Friday, October 7, 2078, 2100 UTC (Just after Sunrise, Sol 65)

The shadows were still long as the shuttle set down on a side-street just off the coastal thoroughfare that ran the entire length of the settlement. They had nick-named that road 'The PCH' on their first visit, its placement and length recalling California's famous oceanside highway.

As Greg had asked, they were delivering him to the house with the portrait he had seen the first day on *Antares*. Gabrielle and Jack Ballard were with him. Carol Hansen was with the technical intelligence team, who would be examining the battlefield later that same Sol.

The hatch opened, and they stepped out into the bright sunshine, white-suited and weighed down by the SLUGs and the higher gravity of Big Blue. Gabrielle and Sergeant Jackson looked around for a few moments as Ballard oriented him-self to the picture on his internal visor. Finally, he pointed to the east and started walking. The Marines took positions on either side and behind, weapons at the ready, heads swiveling, watching for whatever might threaten their charges. They knew the chances of an armed alien encounter were nil. But *Antares* had detected small animals during the first exploration, and an attack by some toothy predator could not be excluded.

As they walked the two hundred meters to the house, Gabrielle looked from side to side, trying to absorb the feel of the place. *It looks so normal*, she thought, *almost like a small town anywhere back home.*

Greg studied the symbols on the buildings, photographing them as he went. After a dozen houses, he stopped and stood in the street, looking around. Gabrielle saw the symbols as well.

"Addresses?" she asked, her voice clear over the comm link.

Greg's suit moved, looking somewhat like a shrug.

"Maybe. I can't believe it could be that simple."

"I guess people will always need a system for identifying places and finding each other —" she started. Greg turned to Ballard.

"Jack, are there street addresses on Inor? I should remember, but I don't."

"Not exactly. There are street names, and they will say something like 'second door east of X street on Y.'"

"So, there is an address, but they express it less specifically than we do?" Ga-brielle asked.

"Yeah, I guess that's close enough."

They resumed walking and came to an intersection with a small road that ran north and south. Gabrielle looked around.

"OK, here we are at the corner of A and B. How do I know where I am?"

They saw nothing that resembled street signs.

The aliens constructed their houses out of dark masonry material. The roofs appeared to be similar to the walls. To the casual observer, the houses were all alike, with roofs which slanted down to the front. The front of the houses had only a door, no windows. As they stood in the intersection, Sergeant Jackson pointed out that the houses were only on the east-west street. The smaller intersecting north-south road had no structures on it.

Gabrielle turned to Greg. "OK, maybe we don't care about which intersection this is? Maybe it's only the street with the houses that matters?"

That earned her another shrug from Greg, who then stepped off to the east.

The narrow hard-packed road felt familiar to Gabrielle. There were trees along the sides, which looked like oversized ferns, or some weird variation of a palm tree, but fuller and not nearly so tall. They didn't seem to have been planted in rows, but clearly, they gave shade to the houses and had been kept off the roads. A few smaller trees were growing haphazardly here and there, probably seeded by themselves after the residents died. Other vegetation seemed to be encroaching on the road, creeping outward from the edges. What would have been lawns back on Earth were covered with a low green cover that reminded Jack of clover.

Finally, Jack Ballard stopped and pointed to a house. "That's it."

Gabrielle and Greg stood on the road, trying to see the whole before getting into the details. They could not tell if the dark color was natural or some kind of paint. They walked around the side and found window openings that seemed to indicate a single floor. In the back, there were tall windows around a small court-yard which was covered by the roof. Jack took them around to the window through which they had photographed the portrait. It was still there, of course. They walked back around to the front. The door just stared back at them.

"So, Jack, how do we get in?"

"Dunno. We just flew the drones around."

Gabrielle suppressed a laugh as she watched Greg and Jack looking at each other. Clearly, each expected the other to know how to open the door.

"OK, guys, you have to be able to open the door, right?" They looked at her as if she was the alien. "So, figure it out. It can't be that hard. We know they had an opposable digit and three fingers. Can't be all that different."

"Yeah unless it's electronic and the power is off," Jack said, disgusted.

"Or voice activated," Greg added, equally annoyed. They pushed and pulled, top, bottom, left, right. Nothing.

It was Este's turn to be annoyed. "You're forgetting that we think this is mid-20th century tech. Electronic doors and voice recognition are probably beyond them at this point."

"Maybe it only opens from the inside?" Sergeant Jackson offered.

"Or, it's locked?" said one of the other Marines. Jack took a step back, trying to see what he might have missed.

"No hinges that we can see — no marks on the ground where it swung out." The door recessed slightly into the wall.

"Pocket door?" Gabrielle offered. Greg tried to slide it left and nothing happened, but when he pushed it right, it moved slightly. They all pushed together, and the door opened about a foot before stopping again. They moved it back-and-forth, and with each cycle, the door moved a little more until finally it gave up and slid fully open. As Jack looked up, he realized there was a cloud of rust and accumulated dirt around them.

"I hope to hell you guys can get that closed again," Gabrielle commented, laughing, as she followed the Marines inside. Jackson and his men searched the building, found no remains and nothing that looked threatening.

"I don't know for sure, Lieutenant Ballard, but it looks safe to us."

Ballard nodded to Jackson, who took his men back outside. He sent two to look 'around the block' while he reexamined the exterior of the house. He had the fourth keep watch on the street.

With the Marines gone, the team started their examination of the house.

"OK, we're in the entrance. The house is deeper than I thought," Gabrielle observed.

"Yeah, the windows look out on the courtyard." There were living spaces to the left and right. Greg went to the left, to the room with the portrait. Jack went to the right, leaving Gabrielle looking out on the courtyard.

"I don't believe it!" they heard Greg say on the comm radio.

"What is it?" Gabrielle asked.

"Come and see for yourself," Greg responded, a wonder in his voice.

Gabrielle entered the room and stopped in her tracks. On the wall opposite the portrait, not visible from the outside, was a bookcase. Shelves of bound volumes covered the entire wall.

"I never expected...to find so much. Who are these people?" Greg walked to the bookcase, excitedly looking up and down the collection. Gabrielle also looked at the shelves and noticed the markings on their edges. She touched Cordero on the shoulder.

"Greg, the shelves are labeled." She looked back at the portrait and saw something else on the wall. She gripped Cordero's shoulder tighter. "It gets better. Look at that." He turned to look where she was pointing.

"Is that a nameplate?" Ballard asked.

"Maybe," Greg answered, looking at the writing. Suddenly the recognition hit him, and his eyes grew wide. Pointing to the first part of the portrait label, he almost shouted: "Gabe, are those the same characters that are on the house?" She looked hard at the wall and then went back outside.

She came back shortly, breathless. "Yes, they are."

"Has to be a name," Cordero spoke in a voice that was almost a whisper.

"Yep."

"It's not supposed to be this easy," Ballard observed.

Cordero stood very still, scanning the shelves, absorbing the size of the library. He pulled out a camera and took a long video of the entire wall, with close-ups of the labels. There were at least fifty volumes, in a variety of sizes.

"Greg, we have to open one," Gabrielle said. She saw a wider shelf at about waist level in the center of the bookcase with no volumes on it. "There is a reading desk."

"OK, but which one?" Jack asked.

When Greg finally spoke, there was a distance in his voice.

"One of my earliest memories as a boy is the largest book on my grandfather's shelf. It was Webster's Unabridged Dictionary — a real printed version. It was like six inches thick, and maybe a hundred years old, and when he took it down, it was like he was opening a sacred text. I loved it when he let me just sit and read it." He closed his eyes, returning in his mind to a small dusty study now very far away. "I can still smell it, feel the pages in my hands, the print under my fingertips. So much knowledge, so many words, just there for the taking." He pointed to the shelf. "Any bets on what the biggest volume here is?"

The volume he indicated sat alone on the middle shelf. He took it down with both hands. The sides of the book were hard, almost like wood. There were characters on the spine but none on the front or back. Slowly, carefully, he opened the cover.

"Wow! Will you look at that?" There was writing on the first page, not printed, but written by hand in the alphabet they had seen all around. The pages were thicker and stiffer than Terran paper.

"A dedication?" Ballard asked. Greg looked at the writing for a long moment, then pointed to the end.

"Same characters as the nameplate," he said, matter of fact. He then opened the second page and found two printed columns of characters. There was a small column on the right with a single grouping, then a larger set of characters to the left. He stopped and stared at it, as did Gabrielle and Jack.

"I think it's a dictionary. Dear God in Heaven, I never thought we'd be this lucky."

Jack turned to leave. "I gotta call this one in." As he walked back outside, he selected the ship's frequency. "*Antares* this is Ballard. Need actual."

"Roger actual, stand by." There was a pause while the Comm techs found Terri Michael and got her on the line.

"Actual," she said.

"Two words, Commander. Library. Dictionary. I think Cordero is in a trance."

A hundred thousand kilometers above, Terri Michael was intrigued. "Roger that. Bag the Webster's and bring it back."

Ballard smiled. "Yeah, I don't think I could get him back without it anyhow."

"Very well, Lieutenant."

He walked back into the house. Cordero was slowly turning pages in the dictionary.

"OK, Doctor, Noah is coming back with us."

Cordero didn't seem to hear. After a few moments, he turned to Ballard and Este.

"Do you understand what this is?" he said with intensity. "This is better than a Rosetta Stone. If this really is a dictionary, their whole language might open up to us. If we can link even ten or twenty words to their meaning, we may be able to bootstrap the rest. Then we can read their books, understand their culture." He ran his gloved fingers down the column of words. They were no longer just collections of symbols to him, devoid of meaning. They were now words, he had but to work them out.

"This is way beyond anything I could have dreamt. I love these people. They are just like us. They practically *are* us."

Behind her isolation suit visor, Gabrielle smiled at his sense of wonder. "Greg, this is great, but we need to keep looking. If there was some kind of picture book, like a child's dictionary..."

"Yes, Gabe, you're right. That would be huge."

They pulled two more large volumes off the shelf. They were full of dense text, but neither of them had any pictures. Finally, Greg pulled a thin book off the lowest shelf and opened it.

"Pay dirt!"

"What?"

"Pictures, Gabe, just like you said." Greg turned a few pages, trying to understand what the book was. The first page had a picture of a person — they couldn't think of any other word — with what looked like a title and a description. The person was lighter-framed than the one in the portrait.

"Is it just me or does that look like a female?" Jack asked.

"Well, it does look thinner than our patriarch over here," Gabe said, pointing to the portrait. "But for all we know the lighter and thinner ones are the males and the more solid ones are the females."

"Or, this could be like Inor where male and female don't really apply."

Greg turned the page and found an image of an animal that looked much like a round-headed goat. It might have been a little smaller than the Earth-bound animal. Again, below the image was what looked like a title and then a block of text which they hoped was the description.

Gabrielle left Jack and Greg to peruse the picture book and went back into the main part of the house. Looking out the windows, she noticed for the first time a stone-rimmed fire pit in the courtyard, with rusty metal remnants of some kind of frame laying across it. From this vantage point, she couldn't tell if there were ashes in the pit or not. She took note of the frame, photographing it for reference, and moved on. She knew what she was looking for: a kitchen, a bedroom, a toilet, probably a bath. But nothing looked familiar. Not that she expected to find flush toilets and fired clay dinnerware, but there should be a place for waste elimination and some kind of food preparation space. The aliens' body layout was similar to humans, so she was expecting recognizable, but likely very different, systems.

She turned with some surprise as she heard Sergeant Jackson reenter the house.

"Doctor Este, ma'am, something outside I'd like to show you." She followed the tall, quiet Marine back outside, where he walked around to the back of the house.

"There's a building over there," he said, pointed to a structure in the middle of the block, "that might be a latrine. There's holes in the floor —"

Gabrielle didn't let the man finish but sprinted, as best she could in an isolation suit and a SLUG and nine percent more weight, the fifty meters or so to the structure. Sure enough, there were paths worn in the masonry on either side of openings in the floor. She could imagine the Beta Hydri people walking in, finding a spot, taking care of business. She clicked her intercom.

"What do you guys think about a communal toilet?"

Jack answered her first. "Sounds gross."

"But *we* have them, Lieutenant Ballard," Jackson reminded him, "in every barracks, every office building."

Gabrielle looked around at the houses. "Jack, we're exactly in the middle of the block. Two streets, six houses on each side of the middle. This, uh, *facility*, would service twenty-four houses."

"Still sounds gross. But Jackson is correct. We do have shared toilets on Earth but not in residential areas."

Gabrielle and Leon Jackson walked out of the toilet house and paused, Gabe looking at the surrounding neighborhood.

"Jackson," Gabrielle said, "We need to look at more houses."

"Well, Doctor, I have three Marines with not much to do. We could crack some doors and take a look around for you."

"I like that idea!" Gabrielle jumped as she heard Jack Ballard's voice said over the comm. She'd forgotten they were all on one link. She turned back to Jackson.

"Start with the houses on either side of this one, then the ones on the opposite street."

"Sure, ma'am."

"You've seen what the inside of this one looks like. I expect the rest to be similar, so let me know if you see something new."

"Will do, Doctor."

As the four Marines went off to explore other houses, Gabrielle went back into where Jack and Greg were working and continued exploring the rest of the residence. After a few minutes, she came back to Ballard.

"So, Jack, what's missing?"

"Dunno. What?"

"There are no bedrooms and no sleeping furniture that I can see. There are chairs, sort of, and tables, again sort of, but nothing flat that looks like a bed."

"That's strange."

"Yeah, maybe they slept sitting up?" she offered.

"Or maybe they didn't sleep at all," Jack said. "The Inori sleep, which made most folks think it was a universal trait of a complex brain."

"No kitchen, either. Don't tell me they didn't eat."

Jack shrugged. "Maybe they didn't eat inside? You saw the fire pit, right?"

"I'm all for a barbeque in the summer, but what did they do when it was cold outside?"

Jack looked at her for a second. "Low axial tilt, Gabe. They don't have seasons like ours."

"What?"

"The planet spins almost upright compared to the plane of the orbit. No tilt, so no seasons. That's also why the polar caps are like twice the size of Earth's. There's no polar summer to melt them down."

"So, no seasons at all?"

"Well, the orbit isn't perfect, but it's almost as perfect as Earth's, about two percent eccentricity. So, there would be some minor variation in how much solar warming they get, but nothing like what we see back home."

"Strange."

"Yeah, it is. Inor is kinda the same, really, but it revolves on its side, and only a small area is habitable."

Gabrielle and Greg looked over the bookshelf and chose two more large volumes to take back, along with the picture book. They took pictures of the books in place and made sure the shelf labels, if that's what they were, appeared in the images. They put the books in sample bags.

Gabrielle searched the house, taking mental note of what she wanted to explore again later. They had spent several hours on the surface by now, and the SLUGs and the gravity were starting to wear on all of them.

With the help of the Marines, they got the door closed and headed back for the shuttle. Cordero took a long look at the house before he left. He was reluctant to go, as if leaving behind a new-found friend.

"Time to go, Doctor Cordero," Leon Jackson said to him. Greg turned to see the Marine waiting for him on the street, nodded sadly, and started walking away.

"A good day, Doctor?"

"Oh, yes, Sergeant, a very good day."

Big Blue
The Battlefield
Saturday, October 8, 1078, 0730 UTC (Midday Sol 65)

James George set the shuttle down on a side-street just off the battlefield. Captain Barnes was the first off, leading his squad out to secure the area before he would permit the others to leave the shuttle. Joe Bowles had convinced *Antares's* physician Marcia Sota to join his expedition. George watched from the cockpit as Barnes' small force scattered. The original site itself was about two hundred meters square, but as they moved about, they found more remains outside the central area.

A young female Marine called back to Barnes. "Captain! There are a lot more under these trees."

Joe Bowles had heard enough. He tapped George on the shoulder.

"Open the goddamn door, Commander. I can't do anything sitting here." James verified that everyone aboard was ready, then reopened the shuttle hatch. Bowles came out at full speed, Carol scrambling to catch up with him, with Marcia Soto right behind.

"Who just called with the new remains?" A smallish white-suited figure about fifty meters away waved at him from under a group of trees.

"Here, Doctor Bowles." Wayne Barnes beat Bowles to the spot by a couple steps. Together they walked around the small grouping, photographing, and correlating them to the open battlefield beyond. Bowles kneeled to look more carefully at the skeletons, then abruptly stood up and looked around.

"We aren't outside the battlefield, Captain. It's all around us."

"Sir?"

"These people aren't defending the field over there," he said, pointing.

Barnes followed Bowles' finger, then turned back to the victims in front of them.

"They're holding a different position?"

"Yes."

The site was bordered on the west by the main north-south road that ran the entire length of the settlement. The wide white sandy beach was a few meters west of that. The ground rose to the east, ending in a five-meter ridge just off the edge of the killing field, with another five-meter rise close behind. They had cut the ridge to permit the road to rise gradually to the east, much as is done for roads on Earth. There were trees along the road and extending to the south in a sparse wood, something less than a forest but denser than a park. They could now see many more skeletons under the canopy of trees, skeletons they could not have seen in the original overhead imagery. Barnes walked a few meters away to look at another group, then back.

"Doctor Bowles?"

"Captain?"

"No kit, sir. No helmets, no body armor, no uniforms; just these little rifles and what looks like ammo cartridges."

"Interesting. That probably says something about the culture. Make sure you mention that to Professor Este." Bowles moved around to face the five skeletons, then knelt down. "Why, my friends, why are you here?"

"They're here to defend something worth defending," Carol said quietly.

"Well, Lieutenant Hansen, I think we already know that," he replied with no small amount of sarcasm. "The question is why are they *here.*" He pointed to the tree for emphasis. "And there, and there..."

Carol let the sarcasm pass. "Yes, Doctor, I see."

Bowles knelt there for a full minute, looking at the bones, and looking past them to what was behind.

"They hit the middle one first — there's a hole burnt right through the front of the skull. The rest are lying on top of him. Then the one on the right, same wound." The officers and Marines around him followed his white-suited finger. "They hit this one on the left in the chest. Look at the charring on the sternum. And the last two took chest shots as well."

Wayne Barnes watched Bowles carefully. "All kill shots, Doctor. They weren't wounded."

"Go to the head of the class, Captain. This is precise, well aimed, lethal work. This is not a ground force we should underestimate. These bastards know what they're doing."

Barnes knelt down to look at their weapons. They all seemed to use the same model. It looked like a small rifle, but the butt design was unfamiliar, and there wasn't an obvious trigger. He pulled a large sample bag from his pack and carefully inserted one. "Looks like a hunting rifle."

"Possibly." Bowles turned to Carol. "Take a couple Marines, Lieutenant, and see what's on that ridge. There were remains up there if I remember the photographs correctly."

"Yes, Doctor, there are," she responded. "I'll see about it."

"Do that. And, Lieutenant?"

"Sir?"

"I was rude before. I get that way sometimes when I'm trying to put a picture together. It's not personal, but I do apologize."

"Thanks for that, Doctor, but I understand."

Barnes sent three Marines to meet Carol on the ridge.

"Anything in particular you want us to look for up here, Doctor Bowles?" Carol asked over the radio.

"I think they came across the ridge and through the road gap. I was hoping there would be some artifacts to support that."

"OK, we're looking." They found spent cartridges from the defenders, but nothing they could not identify. The defenders had all fallen along the road cut and the higher ridge. As they looked further back from the cut and below the crest of the ridge, there was nothing.

"I keep looking for footprints, or some kind of track, anything..." one Marine said to her.

"Yeah, me, too. But it's been a long time since this happened. I doubt we'll find much."

"One more thing, Lieutenant..."

"What?"

"There are no enemy remains, ma'am, none. What does that mean?"

"I wish I knew, corporal. They cleaned up after themselves at Inor, and they've deorbited whole ships into a star to keep from being taken."

"So, you think they took their dead home?"

Carol shrugged, a gesture hard to see under the SLUG and isolation suit, but clear in her voice. "If there were any, yes, I think they picked everything up before they left." Carol clicked on her microphone. "There doesn't seem to be much up here, but next trip we should scrub this area with a metal detector."

"Good thought, Lieutenant," came Bowles' reply. She led her small detail further east, down the far side of the ridge that ended steeply at the battlefield. The Marine came to stand next to her again.

"One more thing, Lieutenant Hansen?"

"Sure."

"They took their own dead back, but they left these people here to rot in the open? How does someone do that?"

"We wouldn't. Even in our worst wars, we got around to burying the dead, whatever side they were on."

"I thought I hated them before, but now..." Carol looked at the young Marine shaking her head at what she was seeing.

"But now it's personal?"

"Yes, ma'am, exactly." Carol nodded her understanding and headed back to the west, towards the main field. As she reached the crest of the ridge, she took in the view. The field before her was green, the ocean a deep emerald in the distance, lighter in the shallows near the shore. It was a calm day, with only small white caps as the waves came lazily ashore just beyond the battlefield.

"You know, Lieutenant, this is kinda a nice place."

"It sure is. Now, if I could just lose those twelve or thirteen pounds I just gained..."

"And drop the SLUGs..."

"It would be fine, just a fine place to be."

They worked their way down the front of the ridge, a slope which was gentle enough for them to side-step down. Marcia Soto was surveying the dead, counting and cataloging the visible wounds. Barnes and Joe Bowles were standing near the center of the field, Bowles drawing on a pad. He looked up as he drew, then pointed to the left.

"I think there's something over there. The enemy split the defenders' lines somewhere along here," he pointed to an area near the road. "But then they continued to try to hold on both sides, the shelter we saw in the drone imagery and something in that direction."

They walked towards the shelter that the circles of skeletons seemed to be defending. As they got closer, Marcia stopped.

"The bodies are getting smaller, Joe."

Bowles nodded. "You're right, Marcia, they are. Shorter and less massive."

"Females? Adolescents?"

"Possibly, but we don't know the gender setup of this species yet, so —" At that moment he came to a smaller skeleton with a fatal head wound like many of the others, and three small and incomplete skeletons laying where the abdomen would have been.

"Shit," Joe cursed with an intense clarity of recognition and anger they had not heard before.

Carol caught up to them and followed their eyes to the remains on the ground. "Oh, my God."

Bowles paused only a moment. "OK, let's keep going. We have a job to do here."

As they approached the shelter, they found more pregnant mothers. They also found small individuals, presumably young. Some were very small, and they agreed those were infants. The mothers were all killed with head or back or chest shots. The children likewise, right down to the infants, whose wounds were so massive as to leave very little bone material behind. They saw weapons that resembled knives near some remains at the entrance to the shelter.

"They fought to the end," Bowles observed sadly.

"With whatever they had," Marcia Soto added.

The shelter had an entrance about two meters wide, while the building itself was around ten meters wide and fifteen deep. Inside they found a nightmarish charnel chaos of bones, dozens laid one on the other. It was impossible to tell how many without a careful excavation, but they ranged from small to tiny.

Barnes and Soto photographed the scene, then turned away, disgusted.

"What now?" Barnes asked after a moment.

Bowles looked around. "I want to see what's over there." He pointed to the south. "The people in the trees are holding the enemy back from something in that direction."

"I don't understand," Marcia said.

"Don't understand what?"

"Well, Joe, why would they run to this place? It's a dead end."

"I don't know yet."

Barnes turned back from his own study of the area. "Maybe they were driven here. This is really shitty ground, what with the ocean at their backs and the enemy on the ridge to the east. Really shitty ground."

"And the enemy split their line as they came through the gap?" Carol asked.

"Seems reasonable," Joe answered. "Let's get over there and see what we can find."

They walked the hundred meters along the PCH to the second structure which looked to be the apex of the second band of defenders under the trees. As they approached, Carol stopped.

"What, Lieutenant?"

"Doctor Bowles, there are no bodies around this place." They all looked again at the small structure, and indeed, it was not surrounded by bones. There were fallen defenders nearby, but nothing around the entrance or within. Like the first shelter they investigated, there were numerous burn marks on the building where enemy fire had hit it. The impacts seemed to have melted some of the masonry and left a dark, singed ring.

Carol stepped carefully inside the entrance and then suddenly stopped. "It's hollow."

"What?"

"The floor, Wayne, it's hollow." She pounded her feet harder, and they could all hear the echo of a void beneath.

"What the hell..."

Carol spun to face the small group standing in the entrance. "Wayne! No bodies. A hollow floor —"

Bowles looked at her skeptically, on hand on his hip. "You think this is an escape route of some kind?"

"I'd love to think that, Doctor Bowles, I really would."

Barnes joined her inside, and together they tried to find the edges of the void beneath the floor.

"OK, we gotta clean out the damn dirt. I don't suppose we brought a broom?"

They hadn't, so they used their feet and hands as both broom and shovel, digging out the accumulated dirt and pushing it out the entrance until they had uncovered a dark metal door. The combination of SLUGs, heavier gravity, and grunt work left them sweating and out of breath, hearts pounding.

"Enough! Take a break, all of you," Soto demanded. "Water!"

Reluctantly, Hansen, Barnes, and two Marines came out of the building and dropped to the ground, each leaning against a tree. They took a deep drink of water from the supply in their isolation suits. After a few minutes, they returned to the building where James George and Joe Bowles were standing on the newly revealed door, discussing what to do next.

"OK, what now?" George asked.

"It's almost certainly a trapdoor of some kind, Commander."

"Even if we can figure out how to open it, should we?"

Barnes knelt down, looking at the edges of the door. "I'd be really worried about a booby trap...but I can't see anything that looks suspicious."

"After all this time, on an alien world, I would not be too sure I could recognize what is or isn't suspicious, Captain."

"Yes, Doctor, I understand. But we have to work with what we know, don't we?"

"Just be circumspect about what you *don't* know."

Carol knelt down and kept digging at one end of the rectangular metal slab.

"There's a hinge."

"What?"

"A hinge. Actually, hinges. Two." She sat back on her legs so the others could see clearly. "Anything up there that looks like a handle?"

George just stared at her. "Lieutenant, have you not been listening to this conversation about how the whole damn thing might blow up in our faces?" Carol looked back at her superior.

"I have, sir, but the question of whether we should open it is secondary to whether we can figure out how."

"Hansen —"

"Yeah, Carol, there are handles," Barnes said, interrupting the XO.

"That will do. Captain Barnes, Lieutenant Hansen, out!"

"But, sir —"

"Out!"

Carol and Wayne's eyes met, and they silently decided that mutiny probably wasn't the answer. With a small nod to each other, they rose and left the building. They walked a small distance away to talk in private.

"Hinges?"

"Yeah, two heavy ones at that end. What about the handles?"

"Two."

"Well, if they installed handles, makes sense someone should be able to lift it, right?"

"Someone of their species, maybe. Not necessarily one of us weakling humans."

She laughed. "Well, we're not as weak as we were before this trip!"

"No question about that." The young woman Marine that had gone to the ridge with Carol joined them.

"Corporal?"

"Just checking on how the insubordination plan was coming, sir."

"Well, Kendra, we'll keep you posted."

"As you say, Captain. But I think we're all in it with you."

Carol smiled. "That's comforting, Corporal Case. That way, we can all be shot together."

"Have to catch us first, Lieutenant Hansen. And, come on, they can't shoot *you.*"

Carol stifled a laugh, making quotation marks with her fingers as she spoke, "Oh, but she died so heroically fighting the evil alien attack!"

They were interrupted by James George's voice close by.

"OK, you two. You can cancel the mutiny for now."

"Mutiny, sir? Us, sir? Oh, no, sir!"

"Listen, you two —"

"Jokes aside, Commander," Carol said, suddenly serious, "we'd never do that to you."

"Yeah, Hansen, I know. Anyway, you kids got what you wanted. We're going to try to open it. The boss approved it."

They moved back into the building, just Carol, Wayne Barnes, and Corporal Case.

"First, let's clear out the joint between the door and the floor. Try to get that as clean as we can." They pulled combat knives from their packs and began carefully scraping the remaining dirt from the narrow gap between the metal door and the hard-paved floor. "Watch for wires or a trip mechanism, anything that doesn't seem to belong."

In a few minutes, there was a small pile of excavated dirt all around the door. Carol and Wayne pulled out flashlights. Under the bright light, side-by-side they studied the gap at the top of the door. Kendra Case looked over their shoulders.

"Looks like the pavement goes under the door. Figures."

"Figures?"

"Well, you gotta hold the door up somehow, right?"

Wayne ran his hand around the top edge.

"Nothing that looks like a lock."

Carol looked at him. "So, are you ready?"

Wayne nodded. "Flip you for it."

"Heads I win, tails you lose," she answered, delivering one of her dad's old lines.

"What?"

"Get outta here, Barnes. This one's mine."

Barnes stammered a little, trying to explain. "But, Hansen, Carol, I can't just, just —"

"Leave it to a girl?"

"No, that's not —"

"I found it, Wayne, It's mine."

Barnes looked at the XO and Doctor Bowles, who offered him no help.

Finally, he surrendered. "If you get yourself killed, Hansen, I'll never speak to you again."

"I can live with that."

Kendra Case gently shoved her Captain out the entrance, then snuck back around the side to reenter. Carol frowned at first when she reappeared, but Case just shook her head when Carol pointed for her to go back outside. They didn't speak a word, and Carol relented. They took positions on either side of the door, which was less than a meter wide, and each took hold of a handle. Carol counted three-two-one on her fingers, and they pulled as hard as they could.

The group outside jumped at the metallic crash that came from the building. They ran in to find Hansen and Case lying on either side of the door, laughing as a cloud of rusty dust floated down around them.

"What the hell is so goddamned funny?" George demanded.

"Counterweight, sir. I think I could have lifted it with two fingers!"

As the dust settled around them, Barnes was shining a flashlight down the opening. He saw stairs leading to a narrow tunnel.

"Carol, I think you might have got your wish."

"Really?" She stood and brushed the reddish crud off her isolation suit, then walked to the top of the opening. She started to step down the stairs when Wayne touched her on the shoulder.

"Not this time, Lieutenant. This part is mine." He pulled his sidearm, chambered a round, and started down the steps, flashlight in his other hand, pointed down the tunnel.

"Nothing in sight. Tunnel goes for some distance straight ahead."

Carol stood at the top of the opening, trying to align herself with the tunnel. "It leads to the ocean?"

"If you say so."

Carol carefully descended the stairs, following Barnes.

"I don't get it," XO George said flatly.

"Don't get what, sir?"

"How did they ever have time to build an escape tunnel, paved no less, while under attack?"

"Maybe it was already here."

"We need to get Professor Este's input on that," Bowles said.

"Either way, where the hell did they go?"

"Not too far, Captain," George called out, "Make sure you keep the opening in sight."

"Yes, Commander, understood. It looks pretty straight, but I can hear something ahead."

"What?"

"Something wet."

"Wet?"

Barnes decided not to respond to the XO's question, but continued his slow walk into the tunnel, Carol just a few meters behind.

"It's going downhill."

"Yeah, caught that myself."

They walked perhaps thirty meters when light started to reflect off the floor.

"Water."

"Shit."

They had all seen the small sea animals Marcia had reported in the ocean water samples, and no one was about to get exposed to those. The water moved slightly as they watched, sloshing gently back and forth.

"This is open to the ocean, Wayne. If it was closed off, it would be still."

"Weird."

Reluctantly they turned and walked back out to the opening.

"I got video, Doctor Bowles, but it's just a tunnel that gets flooded not that far in. No writing, no markings that I saw."

After Wayne and Carol climbed out, Bowles and James George did their own inspection of the tunnel, taking more video as they walked cautiously to the point where the ocean blocked their path. It was narrow, just wide enough for two people to pass. It was barely taller than Barnes, less than two meters. As Bowles and George climbed out of the tunnel, Barnes was standing outside, looking out to sea.

"Where did they go?" he asked aloud.

"Well," Carol said, "we have to assume they knew what they were doing, right? That heading down that tunnel was a rational, life-saving act."

"OK, so?"

"We don't think they had gills, right?"

"We don't really know, Lieutenant, but probably not," Bowles answered.

Barnes turned back to them. "So, the tunnel must have been dry, but now it's below sea level. Where did it go?"

Bowles crossed his arms, also looking out to sea. "More importantly, Captain, where did *they* go?"

They stood outside the structure for a few moments, still not fully understanding what they had seen. There was something missing from this puzzle, perhaps some small fact, a seemingly minor bit of data, that would complete the picture and unlock the mystery. For now, they had gathered plenty of data but were left with even more questions than when they arrived.

"Time to get back to the ship," George told them.

Reluctant, but weary of the increased gravity, SLUGs, and isolation suits, they walked back to the shuttle and lifted off for the safety of *Antares*.

After a shower and a meal, Carol sat down with her journal.

Dear David —

So today we walked the battlefield. Gruesome is the best word I can think of. Bowles is the real thing, though. Tough, insightful, demanding. I like him a lot.

There were small children killed here, David. I mean, it's like a Nazi death camp or something. Horrible. Such a beautiful place to find such an ugly scene. Ugh.

Tomorrow there will be more to find, more places to search. I'm not sure I should be looking forward to it, but I am.

Wish me luck.

—Carol

Antares
Big Blue
Saturday, October 8, 2078, 0945 UTC

Greg Cordero did not want to let the books out of his sight. They double-bagged six of them on Blue and then washed and irradiated the bags once they were back on *Antares*. Ship's doctor Marcia Soto looked at the "dictionary" as if it were Pandora's Box itself as she placed it in the isolation glove box in the sick bay and secured the door. Greg sat down at the side of the clear plastic box, putting his hands through the gloves, and began carefully cutting off the clear transport bags. His translation processor, a black box a foot square and perhaps four inches thick, sat on the counter nearby. It was wirelessly connected to his tablet and the camera he'd positioned over the isolation unit.

Soto watched him carefully.

"Something on your mind, Doctor Soto?" Greg asked as he worked.

"There's always something to worry about around here. These books are just the latest."

Greg stopped and looked over at her.

"We've done what we know how to do, right? This should be sterile, right?"

Marcia shrugged. "Should is a big word with a giant loophole right in the middle. I don't like 'should.' I prefer something more definite."

"But, *you're* the expert. Is there anything else you think we could have done to make this safe?"

Marcia shook her head. "No, but the thing I'm most skeptical of is my own expertise. I just don't know enough to be sure, and I don't know when or if I ever will."

"I appreciate that Doctor, I think we all do. But we need to know what's in here if we're going to understand this culture."

"Yes, I know," she said with resignation in her voice. She pulled up a stool across from Greg and opened a soda. "Are we going to just sit here and chat or are you going to open the damned thing?"

Cordero smiled as he finished cutting away the plastic. "You have time for this?"

Marcia looked over her shoulder and then looked back at Greg. "I have some cultures to check but not until after lunch. So, yes, I have time."

"Thanks, I can always use another hand."

The book was about eight inches thick. The top was less rectangular than most Terran books, almost square, but slightly taller than wide, and about a foot on each side. The binding appeared similar to the hardcover books he was familiar with, but the material was not cardboard but something harder, almost like wood.

Greg mounted a multi-spectral camera above the chamber so he could photograph the contents without contaminating the camera. He had Marcia snap a photo of the cover before he opened it. On the first page was the writing that they believed was an inscription of some kind.

Greg opened the next page, revealing the two columns of characters. He had Marcia take the picture and then spent a moment just looking at the page, hoping some insight would reveal itself. He'd approached translation problems in this way many times, simply immersing himself in the characters and letting the innate language mechanism in his brain, amplified with experience and long study, work the problem on its own.

Marcia let him think on it a moment, and when he blinked and looked up at her, she asked: "OK, so what do you see?"

"The paper is interesting. It's kinda green, right? And it's not perfectly smooth. The ink, whatever it is, is flat, not raised. So, whatever the pigment is dissolved in must move through the paper pretty easily."

"Weren't there like ferns along the streets? Some kind of small tree? Might this be a papyrus?"

"That's a thought..."

"OK, what else? I can tell you're not done."

Greg smiled. "The paper is stiffer than ours, but it still bends a little. I'd be interested to see what the print shop looks like. This looks like a mass-produced book to me, so, somewhere, there has to be a printing press."

"What else?"

"Not much, yet. We expect a dictionary, if indeed that's what this is, to be in some kind of rational order."

"Well, it has to be ordered somehow, right?"

"Yes, otherwise it would be useless."

"Even I can see that there is just one blob of characters in the right column and much more text in the left."

Greg nodded. "Yes, so let's take a look."

He pulled his hands out of the chamber's gloves and displayed the page image on the large monitor on the wall.

"OK, so there are three basic ways to organize a dictionary. By sound, by concept, or by graphic."

"Graphic?"

"By its appearance, as if it were a pictogram. English dictionaries are like that. You start with the letter A then B then C."

"Isn't that by sound?"

"Well, not really. Not all letters sound the same all the time. The long e-sound can be either an e or an i, depending on the word. So, it's really graphical. The letter E is still e even when phonetically it's *eh* not *ee*."

"OK, I get most of that. So, what do you see in this text?"

Greg pointed at the screen. "Eight characters in a group. If you looked at an English dictionary, it would start with 'a' and then continue building up words from there."

"In other words, our ordering is actually pretty obvious."

"Right, it would not take an intelligent alien very long to break down the order of the 26 letters and assorted symbols and other junk we use in English to understand what they were seeing, even if they couldn't actually read it."

"But this?"

"No clue yet. If you look at the left side, there are characters everywhere. No spaces to make words or periods or paragraph breaks. But it's likely that those ideas are there somehow. We'll just need to fuss the separators out, whatever they turn out to be. I suspect when we get a large enough dataset, we can look at symbol frequency and begin to guess at what they are."

"Guess? I thought this was a science."

Greg smiled. "Well, there's always a little art involved."

They continued the photographing process, Greg turning pages and Marcia triggering the camera. They chatted about their homes — Greg from Phoenix and Marcia from southern California — and their shared taste for southwest Tex-Mex, the hotter, the better.

"How sure are you that this is a dictionary?" she asked after a longish break in the conversation about thirty pages in.

"Fairly sure, but there are other possibilities."

"Such as?"

"Honestly, it could be anything. It's big, and it was in a prominent location on the shelf. That tells me it's an object of some significance. There's a personal inscription, which might imply that the book is important in a cultural sense. Back home, a parent or grandparent might give a Bible or some other book to a grandchild on their baptism or graduation or whatever. This may be a similar kind of thing."

"OK, so..."

"So, I think it's a dictionary based on size and the first few pages. It just kinda looks like one to me. But truthfully, it could be a book of their moral or religious code."

"Or a chemistry text."

That made Greg laugh. "Yes, I suppose it could be a description of the elements. But, then, I think it's kinda long for that."

They worked steadily, quietly, and after fifty pages Greg stood up, stretched his back, and went to his tablet. His translation process was accumulating data, and he asked it for a list of unique characters.

As she looked at the list with him, he asked her, "What do you suppose is the most frequent character in a block of English text?"

"I dunno. T maybe? E?"

Cordero smiled and shook his head. "Nope. It's a space."

"A space is not a character!"

"Uh, yes, Marcia, it is."

"It isn't."

"OK, fine, go over to your workstation and type a sentence but don't touch the space bar."

"I can't, I need a... shit. I need a space after every word."

"Correct. It's punctuation, just like a period or a comma. We don't speak it, but it's a necessary part of the language."

Greg paused a few seconds to study the display.

"So, looking at the list, this slash-looking thing is the most frequent, and it's the most by a lot, it's seventeen percent of the total. So..." He switched screens and told his translation process that the pseudo-slash character might be a word separator. In a few seconds it popped up a list of words, showing him that if slash was right, there were about five thousand unique words in the data so far.

"And the most common word in English is, what?" Marcia asked.

"'The', followed by other boring words like 'to', 'and', 'a', 'of', and the like."

"So, do you guess that the most common word corresponds to 'the'?"

"I could try that, but I would be assuming there is an equivalent concept in their language. Not all human languages do that, so they may have no need of a 'the' — the idea of specification may be by inflection or just context. Or, just left out."

"What about the Inori? What is their language like?"

Greg leaned back, his hands on each side of his head framing the grimace on his face. "Oh, God, it's like Navajo and Inuit had a baby. Long, long words, some cobbled together like in German but far, far more complex. There are no regular verbs and all of it mostly unpronounceable by humans." He paused, shaking his head, then continued more thoughtfully. "The shadings of sounds are so subtle. I saw a presentation once where the linguist had them say five different words, with wildly different meanings, and I could not tell any two apart. It's a nightmare."

"I'm glad this is your job and not mine."

Cordero smiled. "Yeah. Warrant Officer Long said much the same thing as she left to go run a nuclear reactor. It's not really a confidence-building comment, you know?"

"You know her story?" Marcia asked as they continued scanning pages.

"I had a conversation with her at breakfast on the way out, maybe a week ago. I've said hello a couple times since. She seems like a nice person. Something unusual there?"

"She was in Inoria when it was hit. Her guides and two shipmates were killed right beside her."

"My God that's awful."

"Yeah, it was bad. But she recovered well enough and wanted to stay with the rest of that group when Michael got *Antares*, so here she is."

Greg paused to study the current page, then asked, "There are what, sixteen Inor vets on board?"

"Yes. There were just twenty-six survivors to begin with. Some got other assignments, others decided they were done with the Fleet."

"Understandable."

"Absolutely. I don't know how I would react myself, what with people being ripped open all around me."

"I have zero military experience, but I suppose like a lot of things we all handle it as best we can."

"Yeah, maybe. Still, a shocking experience. Word is that there was a young ensign, a friend of Hansen's, that was kinda interested in her."

"And?"

"KIA in Inoria. Ugly."

"KIA?"

"Killed In Action."

"Ugh, that is heartbreaking."

They kept up a quiet conversation, then after a hundred pages, Greg stood up again and checked the translation's progress.

As he was stretching out the kinks in his back, Marcia asked "How long is this thing?"

"Don't know, maybe four hundred pages? I'd guess we're a quarter done. You getting bored?"

"No, just wondering."

It took several hours of tedious work, but by the end of the morning, the entire book had been scanned. All along the translation process was accumulating data, examining the characters, and looking for patterns. Do the same characters appear at the beginning or end of words? Are there variations in words that might indicate families of related words as in Semitic languages? Were there context hints at the end of sentences as in Asian languages like Mandarin? Were there even sentences, or paragraphs, or were those a uniquely human invention?

Greg spent the afternoon scanning the picture book while Marcia worked on small projects for the other team and checked her cultures. He put in more hours that evening, going back over the data and experimenting with different theories about the structure of the language. He had an enormous amount of data to work with, and he knew it was on him to turn that wealth into results. These people seemed so familiar, so, *relatable*, that he felt that he should be able to crack the language. But, on the other hand, they were *alien*, unrelated to him in any way, and their mode of thought might be so disjunct from his own that he would never be able to understand it.

That would be a serious disappointment.

Antares
Big Blue
Sunday, October 9, 2078, 0800 UTC

It was the first daily planning session after a full day on Big Blue. The two-shift concept was working well, but the teams were already tired. They would have to be careful to not let fatigue lead to serious errors. Ron Harris sat at the head of the wardroom table, Kathy Stewart on his left and Terri Michael on his right. There was a lot of chatter as the groups coalesced and took their places.

"Let's begin with the battlefield. Doctor Bowles?"

"Yes, Admiral, as we briefed you yesterday, we do believe that the real point of the defense at the battlefield was not the shelter in the original images, but rather an escape facility located under the trees to the south."

"Do you have any idea where that went?"

"Other than to the sea, no, we don't."

Harris looked across at the battlefield team. "But if you believe that's an escape route, they must have gone somewhere."

"Indeed, sir, they must," Carol answered. "We're considering what we have on board that we could use to explore the submerged portion of the tunnel. We know it's connected to the sea, but we don't know how or how far out, or what else might be in there."

"I don't suppose there's any scuba gear on board?"

"Uh, no, sir. And given what we know is living in the water, we're not inclined to try that."

"Anything else, Doctor Bowles?"

"Not as yet, sir. We brought back some bone samples that Doctor Soto is processing for us." He turned to Wayne Barnes. "Captain Barnes, can you talk about the weapon?"

"Yes. Well, we've all kept Dr. Soto pretty busy, as she also did an x-ray of the rifle we brought back."

"What did you find?"

"The stock is different from ours, but not as much as I originally thought. These people are a little wider than us, and the stock works for them if you hold it more across your body than at the shoulder."

"There didn't seem to be a trigger from what I recall."

"But there is. It's a metal plate under the palm. You basically squeeze the stock to fire the weapon. It's a single-shot, loaded from above. We found plenty of expended ammo casings, but we're not sure yet what they're made of. It looks like gunpowder inside, but until we get it home for a complete analysis, we can't be sure."

"So, what's the plan for today?"

"The weapon has been fully processed and sterilized, so we're going to try to disassemble it. I don't know how that's going to go, sir, as I'm not yet sure how it's held together."

"And what have you learned about the enemy's weapons?"

Carol spoke for the group. "We're looking into that, sir. They're using some kind of hot weapon that doesn't leave a slug behind."

"Plasma? Laser?" Harris asked.

"We think some kind of hot mass, so some kind of plasma is a plausible theory, sir, but we're working on quantifying the power based on the impacts on the structures. It sure looks like it can melt this masonry the aliens used."

"One more thing, sir," Wayne Barnes added, "that Doctor Bowles pointed out. The dead mostly took one kill shot. There's not much evidence of people being wounded and surviving. Whatever their ground force is, we really need to take it seriously."

"OK. Doctor Cordero?"

Greg Cordero called up a sequence of images from the books he had scanned the previous day. There was general agreement that the picture book seemed the most promising lead.

"We scanned what we have been calling a dictionary and the picture book yesterday. I've been running some scenarios in the translation processor."

"Find anything?"

"Yes, quite a bit, actually. There is a word separator, and I believe I have found a sentence marker."

"So, in a day we've isolated the space and the period?" Kathy Steward asked, her tone something between cynical and humorous.

"Well, yes, but it is an *alien* space and period," he responded with mock defensiveness. "So far, there is nothing that looks like a paragraph mark, but that may be an artifact of the source material."

"What about the picture book?"

"That is interesting but difficult to interpret. There is an image, almost a cartoon, of a person with a caption beneath it every few pages. So, is that 'teacher' or 'parent' or 'next lesson' or what? I can't tell yet."

"Any correlation between the entries in the dictionary and the picture book?"

"I will be working on that today, Admiral, along with scanning the other volumes we brought back. It's a good question."

"Good. Doctor Este?"

"Yes, Admiral, I have a few preliminary conclusions. First, this is a more literate society than we would have thought a priori. After we found the library in the portrait house, I had our Marines check a few houses in the area. All had rooms more or less like the one we found. Some had portraits, some not, but all had libraries of comparable size."

"I heard about the common toilet," Kathy said with no small amount of disgust.

"Yes, that was another surprise for me. Again, the Marine team checked a few blocks north and south, and the pattern was the same. A common toilet in the middle of each residential block. So, elimination seems to not have the same social taboos and controls as in human societies." She folded her hands in front of her. "But I am still puzzled by several things, Admiral. There are no beds in any of the houses. I am not sure what to make of that. There is also no kitchen to speak of, no food storage."

"But there's a cooking area in the courtyard?"

"Yes, but I don't know what they cooked and where it came from."

"No beds? What is in the houses, then?"

"The libraries, then other sitting areas."

"Are there blankets or clothing? Closets?"

"Not that we saw."

"Radio, Television?"

"Not that we saw, but I'm planning to go back for a fuller investigation of the house. I'd like to poke around a little more and see what else I can find there."

"That's fine."

Greg leaned back into the conversation. "I would also like to go back, Admiral. I'd like some time to go through the books in the library and see what else might be of interest. I am hoping there are scientific texts where we can match up words or symbols with our own knowledge."

"I think that's a very good idea, Greg."

Capital City
Big Blue
Sunday, October 9, 2078, 2200 UTC

For the second day on Big Blue, Captain Wayne Barnes picked a dozen Marines that had not yet been on the surface and took them into Capital City. Hearing this, Gabrielle jumped at the chance to see the largest city on the planet and invited herself along. Barnes could hardly refuse, but in truth, he was happy to have her along. An expert to give his informal, ad hoc exploration some direction would certainly be helpful.

Jayvon Dean drew the shuttle pilot assignment for this morning, this time a 'drop and return' mission. He would not be remaining on the surface, which relieved him from the necessity of suiting up. He left them at the south end of a large boulevard, lined on both sides with tall buildings. Four stories seemed to be the limit for this city, and construction was similar to what they had seen in the residences: smooth masonry over a framework that they had not yet identified. But, having failed to include an architect in the crew, their exo-architecture study would have to wait for a later visit.

Once off the shuttle, the team moved up both sides of the street, looking into the windows in the front of each structure, then walking around the back. Gabrielle and Barnes kept pace from the middle of the street.

"So strange, Doctor Este."

"Gabe."

"OK, Gabe. Still strange."

"Yes, it looks so much like home in a lot of ways: the streets, the buildings, even the trees are starting to look normal."

"But, there's no one here."

"No one alive, anyhow," she said as they walked around an RFG crater, its bottom slowly filling in with wind-blown sand and dirt. After about two hundred meters, they encountered two skeletons lying on the steps of a building. The bones were cut, typical of the same kind of anti-personnel darts they had seen at Inor.

"Gawd-awful stuff," Gabe commented quietly.

"Yes, terrible."

They continued the walk, avoiding remains and craters as necessary. The buildings gradually got larger as they approached the center of the city, which was actually fairly small by human standards. The Marines tried a few doors as they went along without success.

Two Marines called for Doctor Este from the left side of the boulevard. Through the windows they showed her numerous shelves of books.

"Looks like a library, Captain," the young PFC said with excitement. Gabrielle clicked open her communication line.

"*Antares*, this is Este. I need Cordero."

"Roger that, Doctor Este, stand by."

Greg Cordero was scanning another volume into the translation process. When the Comm Officer called him, he left the sickbay and jogged up to the Intel office, pulling Jack Ballard into the workroom with him.

"OK, Gabe, I'm here." Este enabled the camera on her helmet so Cordero could see what she was seeing.

"Ohhh, nice find you guys. Can you get inside?"

"We haven't had much success with doors today, Greg. Should we break in?"

"No, definitely not. We can't expose the books to the elements." As Gabrielle stood looking at the door, something near the bottom caught her eye.

"Captain Barnes, is that a handhold?" she asked, pointing to six holes in the bottom of the door.

Barnes shrugged, "Maybe. What are you thinking?"

"Up, not over." The PFC that found the library stepped over to the door and pulled up on it using the finger-holes. Given a strong push, it opened.

"Wow, Gabrielle. You're a genius!"

"You just figuring that out, Cordero?" she responded, laughing.

They went inside cautiously, the Marines circling the interior, as always looking for any threat. Gabe carried her virtual Cordero towards the center of the room.

"What are you looking for, Gabe?"

"Librarian's desk. Maybe a computer. We haven't seen much tech here, but we know they have it."

Barnes looked around. "Yeah, I've been wondering about that myself. But, if you think of this as mid-twentieth-century tech, homes and libraries didn't have computers. They had the Encyclopedia Britannica at home and a card catalog in the library."

"So, what you're saying is that I should be looking for a card catalog?"

Cordero laughed. "Well, in a perfect world, yeah. But the Captain is right. If there is such a thing as an inventory system, it's likely going to be physical, not digital."

"OK, understood. We're looking."

"How many floors to this place, Gabe?"

"Three."

"So, how do you get upstairs?"

"No clue."

Barnes heard this question as well and dispatched a couple Marines to see if they could find the access to the upper floors. "Gotta be a way," he told them, "But don't expect it to look like home."

Meantime, Gabrielle explored the stacks, looking for anything that looked familiar. Reference books, picture books, anything that might give them the key to unlock the alien language.

Greg called Joe Bowles into the conversation with Gabe. "Science books, Doctor Este. If we can get a chemistry or physics text, that would be real gold. Or a medical text."

"OK, Joe, we'll keep an eye out for that."

"Gabe, science books will have equations, drawings. I'm not sure how they will express their math, but it should look different than just text."

"Maybe I'll find a periodic table inside a cover."

"Sure, and maybe you'll find some unpublished Shakespeare."

The Marines found the route upstairs. It was a ladder built into an inconspicuous corner of the building. Three went up to check the next floor.

"Not exactly ADA compliant, you know?" Gabe commented.

"Well, they do look a little like a cross between a simian and some kind of big cat. Climbing that ladder may be as normal to them as walking is to us."

Gabrielle thought about this for a few seconds. "Joe, do we know if they walked on two legs or four?"

"Two, I think, based on the shapes of their doors and the height of openings like at the shelters, that kind of thing. The hip bones we saw at the battlefield also support that idea. If they moved predominately on four legs, all those would be much different."

"OK, thanks. Just wondering."

Gabe climbed the ladder to the second floor, which looked much the same as the one below, but here there were large low tables, apparently reading tables, in the center of the room.

"I wish I knew what I was looking at," she said, mostly to herself, as she pulled yet another volume off the shelf. As she flipped through the pages, she suddenly stopped.

"Uh, guys, I might have something here." She knelt down and laid the book out on one of the reading tables, then adjusted her helmet camera so Cordero and Bowles could see it. It was a drawing of the Beta Hydri system, with Big Blue, Little Gray, and the other planets in the system. There were arrows and annotations in the alphabet she was becoming used to seeing.

"Jesus, Gabe, that's amazing," Greg smiled, but Joe Bowles' face remained dead serious.

"Doctor Este, go back to that same shelf and let's see what else we can find."

"OK." She pulled the next book to the right and walked back to the table. She opened it and found the same dense text at the beginning. As she quickly paged through it, she came to another drawing.

"A parabola?" she asked.

"Yes, that's what it is," Bowles answered.

"So, even here, y is looking for its x?"

"Looks that way, yes."

She kept turning pages and found additional drawings and what might have been lists. "Math book?"

"I can't be sure," Bowles answered.

"You want another one?"

"Yes."

Gabrielle paged through the book she had just pulled from the shelf. She was beginning to see how the Beta Hydri culture expressed formulas. "So, Greg, look at this," she said, pointing. "I saw this same kind of pattern under the parabola. Those are numbers, right?"

"Yes, most of them are. But I don't recognize the rest. Might be part of the alphabet we haven't seen yet."

"Or, they could be math operators," Joe offered.

Cordero shrugged. "Could, sure. But I'd love to find an arithmetic book. You know, one plus one is two. Six divided by two is three. Something like that."

Bowles nodded. "Those probably exist, but we have no idea how their education system is structured. The Inori send the young off to school right after birth. We keep ours at home for five years or whatever and then send them for formal education. We don't know what they did here."

"But, Joe," Gabrielle interjected, "we still have simple instruction books at home, right? Our own children's books sound much like what you're talking about."

"So, maybe we should take another look at the library at the portrait house?"

"I think so, yes. What about the picture book?"

"It's scanned, but the inference engine is still grinding on it."

"We'll keep looking for a while, but Captain Barnes wants to move on."

"OK, bring back the three you've shown us, at least. If you find anything else that looks interesting, bring those, too."

"Will do."

Gabrielle dropped the comm link to *Antares* and brought the three volumes down the ladder. They wrapped them in sample bags and left them by the door to pick up on the way back. Meantime, the search party continued north along the street, stepping over the skeletons of the lost residents as they went.

Antares
Big Blue
Tuesday, October 10, 2078, 0230 UTC

Greg Cordero rushed out of the Intel workroom, almost running Kathy Stewart over as he did.

"Where's the fire?"

"Wayne and Gabe found a library. A whole building full of books. I need to get down there."

"Go see the Captain. I'll find Harris."

Greg moved quickly forward and found Terri Michael on the Bridge.

"Captain, the patrol Gabe and Wayne took down have found a library."

"So I've heard."

"I'd like to get down there, Captain. Today. Now, if possible."

Greg's excitement was obvious, and infectious. Terri looked at her ship status, seeing the shuttle was already back. Lieutenant Dean was just returning to the Surveillance station. She got up from her Command position and walked over to him.

"Lieutenant Dean?"

"Yes, ma'am?"

"Are you up for a return trip to the surface? Doctor Cordero would like to get down there as soon as possible."

"Sure, Captain, I can take him."

Ron Harris arrived on the Bridge as they were talking.

"Are you able to get Cordero back down there?"

Terri nodded. "Sure. Ensign Dean will take him."

"I'm going, too."

Harris had not worked out on the SLUGs on the way out, the assumption being that he would not be going to the surface.

"Admiral, need I remind —"

"I know, Commander, I know. I didn't train. But I need to go."

She was the Captain, and it was ultimately Terri's call whether Harris could go or not. She leaned in close to him.

"You're sure about this, sir? You're *sure*?"

"I am."

She waited just a second more, noticing Cordero and Dean watching this very close conversation from a short distance away.

"OK, then. Go. Take Ballard with you to get you suited up."

It was a quick trip down, with Jayvon Dean moving as fast as he dared in order to give Cordero as much surface time as possible. Jake spent that time wrestling Harris, who was tall and muscular, into an isolation suit and SLUG. Before they left, Terri Michael called Barnes and let him know Harris and Cordero were on their way. Once on the ground, Jake slipped into the cockpit and sealed the door before Jayvon opened the hatch to let the passengers out.

Gabe met them at the library.

They stepped carefully into the building. There was just the three of them now; the Marines were already a kilometer north, still looking in windows and snooping around to see what might be found. There were windows in the rear of the library as well as an opening in the floor above. which gave plenty of natural light to the room. They had wondered about basic utilities like electricity or natural gas or whatever, but today that research was secondary to Cordero's work to crack the language.

Greg and Ron walked the stacks, looking at a book here or there on each shelf. It all seemed so comfortable, so much like a library back home. Each of them pulled volumes off the shelves and scanned them for anything familiar. They could recognize numbers now, at least, and obviously the arithmetic book Greg was so desirous of would be full of them. Greg was starting to recognize words, but only that they were words, not what they meant.

Harris looked around and then said, "I'm going upstairs." As he got to the top of the ladder, he called back to them. "Did anyone go up to the third floor?"

"No, Admiral," Gabrielle replied, "at least, I didn't. I think the Marines may have gone up to check it."

"OK, I'm going up." Ron took a moment to catch his breath once he got up the second ladder. He was in pretty good shape for a guy with a star on his collar, but the extra weight he was carrying in Big Blue's stronger gravity was noticeable. He walked around the room, just as he had done on the second floor, looking for something familiar, something he could latch on to and understand. As he moved around, he pulled a few books out and quickly scanned them. Very few had any images, and those that did were drawings that Ron didn't recognize. He added them to the pile to take back to the ship.

Big Blue
The Battlefield
Tuesday, October 11, 2078, 1845 UTC

Joe Bowles wanted to look further outside the main battlefield and to revisit some odd images he hadn't captured well the first day. So, a few minutes after sunrise, *Antares'* shuttle dropped back onto the PCH near the battlefield to deliver him, with Marcia Soto along to assist. The older, sometimes cranky pathologist was finding Soto to be a very useful second set of eyes.

Jack Ballard dropped Bowles and Soto, then took off again to transport Carol and himself to the 'farms' about ten kilometers to the east. As they got out into an intersection of two roads, the sound of their feet crunching on the gravel road reminded Carol of Inoria and its fine-grained stone streets. That prompted another memory of Marty Baker. *Marty deserves to be remembered,* she thought to herself. *Maybe something to put on my prayer list.*

"Carol?" Jack asked, shaking her out of her memory and back to reality.

"Sorry, Jack. Just had a thought of Marty."

"I understand. He was a good guy."

"He was." She took a deep breath, then seemed to perk up. "Shall we?"

"Yes, let's go."

They headed east along the road. On both sides, they found low metal fences that had not rusted. They had some cutters in the shuttle and would come back for a sample, but based on its appearance they agreed it was probably aluminum or an alloy similar to it. Analysis back on Earth might tell them something about the industry and technology of the culture. Shortly they came to an open gate. Looking across the road, the corresponding gate on the other side was also open.

"Jack, the gates are open."

"So?"

"So, well, I don't know what. I guess I just expected them to be closed."

"You're the farm girl, so, why would they leave them open?"

"Maybe to give the livestock a chance? Otherwise, whatever was penned up in here would probably have died."

"I take it you think these are, well, farms for meat, not some kind of crop."

"Yes, these look like pastures to me, not crops." She walked through the open gate and twenty meters into the field, which was covered by grass perhaps a quarter of a meter high. Carol knelt down to look at it, noticing that it was very different from the low, tight, clover-like ground cover they had found on the battlefield. This was much more a grass, with long, thin leaves.

As she stood, she could see a small group of animals in the far corner, several hundred meters away. They were light brown, about the size of a large dog or small goat. From this distance, she couldn't make out much detail as they were head-down, grazing.

"So, some clearly survived! How many would you suppose?"

"We saw several groups in the surveillance pictures. We didn't get a count, but it only takes two, Jack, at least on Earth, plus a little time for nature to do what it does."

"But they're still here? Why didn't they move on?"

Carol shrugged. "The pasture grass is what they were raised on. It's probably good for them. If there's water nearby, there's a good chance to survive here."

The structures Carol had seen in the early overhead images were nearby, and they walked to them, the long grass pulling at their feet.

On the battlefield, Joe Bowles stopped at the skeleton that had caught his eye.

"Look at this, Marcia," he said. "Look how the upper arm is severed. Part of it is missing." They found the lower part of the arm, hand still more or less attached, a meter away.

"That wasn't shot off. It isn't burned. It's cut."

"More like bitten, I think."

"Post-mortem predation?"

"If there were predators around, scavengers, we'd see a lot more of this. It should be all over the field. I've only seen about ten or twelve with these kinds of wounds."

"I see. And, why the arm?"

"Right. Back home, a predator goes for the organs first, then the muscle tissue. They're more nutritious."

"Well, not enough to get me to eat liver!" Soto said, laughing.

"Me, either, Marcia, me either. Somehow crunching down the body's main garbage processing facility and toxic waste dump is strangely unappetizing."

"But not in the wild."

"Right."

"So, did the enemy do this? Could they have eaten them?"

"That would be my guess."

"What the hell are we dealing with, Joe?"

"Someone very alien, Marcia, someone who thinks nothing like we do."

As Carol and Jack came out of the 'barn,' as Carol had labeled it, they were surprised by the feed animals, which had made their way across the pasture and now rubbed their heads against the humans' thighs through the isolation suits. Instinctively, Carol reached down and petted their round heads, and the animals responded with quiet, low rumbling sounds which she interpreted as expressing pleasure.

Their coat was plain brown, without variation. Their ears were small and triangular, set very far back on their heads. They had no nose, but Carol could hear air moving in and out of openings in the sides of their necks. Carol got several close-up images, including one with Jack kneeling next to one for scale.

"They don't have the eyes, Jack."

Ballard looked more carefully at the 'goats' faces and realized they had narrow horizonal pupils in their dark eyes.

"Oh, you're right. Missed that. But look at those pupils!"

Carol looked at the eyes closely. "Hmm. Horizontal. Interesting."

"Why?"

"Well, back home grazing animals like deer and goats have horizontal pupils. My Dad told me once it gives them better vision to avoid predators. Seems nature found that same solution here."

"Ready to go back for Doc Bowles and Marcia?"

"Yeah, I guess."

Carol took a long look around before pulling herself back into the shuttle cockpit. It all looked so familiar: the fences, a little different, but for the same purpose; gates not all that different than what she had seen back home; and a barn that was, well, a barn. Inside there were a few stalls and tools she didn't recognize. Still, she was surprised at how much it felt her own family farm. The pasture needed cutting and the barn could use some maintenance, but she could almost see herself working these fields. It was a strange feeling to have twenty-four light years from Lancaster.

Columbia
Near GL 876
Wednesday, October 12, 2078, 1325 UTC

SLT Mazablaska 'Maz' Dawes stood his shift at the Conn watching the 'blink scan' occultation search display from behind the Surveillance position, just ahead and to the right of the raised command position. A red circle was flashing where three stars had gone dark, remained dark for a time, and then came back on in quick succession. From the display, he knew the stars were just off to his left and slightly below him. Whatever it was, it was not far off *Columbia*'s course.

They had been here a week already, and so far, they'd only seen small debris, stuff maybe a meter or two in size. They'd considered picking some of that up for examination, but Dan decided against it, keeping to the main mission of finding 'the wreck' and, hopefully, remains.

"Chief, let's get the narrowband radar up on that," Maz requested.

"Moving now." It took a few seconds for the massive antenna to slew over to the direction of the blink. Chief Allen started it in long range mode. Nothing appeared on the radar display. He waited a full minute, then switched to short range mode. Still nothing. He was wondering what to tell Dawes when Hughes and Powell came rushing in.

"What is it?" Melinda asked, looking at the blink scan.

"An occultation, Lieutenant," Allen answered, "and a very long one. But, there's nothing on the long-range radar."

"What?"

"I put the narrowband on it, and it's not showing up."

Melinda looked at Powell as she picked up the ship phone. "Captain."

"Planning to go full power?" David asked.

She nodded as she started to speak. "Yes, sir, we have an occultation that looks like it might be far away. And, sir, I think it's pretty big...Nothing on radar but I would like to go full power and see if we can find it... Yes, will do." She hung up and turned to her techs.

"Full power, longest range. Go."

Chief Allen didn't hesitate to adjust his settings and restart the radar. As he did, the phone at the Conn workstation rang. Maz hustled back to answer, and after a short conversation, he instructed the Nav techs to head directly for the contact.

"There it is...very faint, Lieutenant Hughes, but it's there. Four hundred thousand kilometers."

"Four hundred thousand? Can we get a visual?" Allen pointed the long-range telescope at the target the radar was showing. There wasn't much. A smudge, maybe.

"OK, put the visual in accumulation mode. Maybe with time, we'll get something." They watched the visual display freeze, then fill in, pixel by pixel.

"IR is negative, ma'am," her other tech reported.

"Well, it's pretty cold out here, so not surprised at that."

"Yes, Lieutenant."

After a few minutes, Powell leaned in close to the techs. "Did you ever notice how in the movies everything happens fast? *What's taking so long?*" he cried.

The crew laughed a little, releasing some tension.

Hughes leaned towards David and spoke in her best loud whisper, "Did you ever see the one where the little blonde girl kicks the smart ass across the Bridge?"

"Uh, no. That is, not yet. Ma'am." This brought him more snorts and smirks from the crew. After this light exchange, there were a few minutes of quiet, casual conversation.

Then, Chief Allen spoke up. "Visual is starting to fill in, Lieutenant."

They looked at the display to see an image that was not much more than a shadow, but it was clearly cylindrical.

"Is that battle damage?" Powell asked, pointing to some gaps in the image.

"Too soon to tell, but, maybe."

"Chief, do we have the location and course worked out?" Hughes asked.

"Yes, ma'am."

"OK, radar off."

Dan Smith came on to the Bridge as they were talking. "OK, so what do we have?"

"It's a ship, sir, for sure. An enemy ship. About four hundred thousand klicks."

Smith looked at the image. "That thing looks like shit, Powell."

"Thank you, sir."

Dan smiled and turned back to Hughes. "Can you tell the type?"

"No, the orientation stinks right now. Hard to see the dimensions. We'll know before we get there."

"Fine. We'll close in on it slowly. Don't forget that we just shined a searchlight in a dark room. Make sure we're keeping our heads up for any company."

"Yes, sir, will do."

"For the record, if they show up in force, we're bugging out, clear?"

"Yes, Captain," Maz replied.

Dan turned to David. "Do we know yet if the sphere is still there or not?"

"We don't, sir. It would be on the other side of the star by now, and we've made locating the wrecks over here the priority."

"OK, understood. You're not curious?"

"Oh, sure, I am. My guess is that it's gone, but the only way to be sure is to go looking, and we don't have the time for that right now."

Dan nodded. "We'll see how this goes. If there's time, I want to go take a peek, anyway."

Crossing the four hundred thousand kilometers to the wreck would take a full day at the modest speeds Dan was willing to use. Once they got there, they'd decide how to exploit it. They had two shuttles and the six fully maneuverable EVA suits FleetIntel had sent. Tomorrow, Dan would have to decide what to do. Until then, he would hold the decision for when he had all the data he could get.

In David's mind, however, he was already crawling through the holes he'd happily punched in the side of the enormous relic. After his late evening shower and before turning in, he pulled out his journal. It was past time to put something down for Carol.

Carol —

We found one of the ships that hit Sigma — one of the bastards that killed Paula and John and Lisa and Leah and even that jerk Boyd.

So, tomorrow, I think I'll be heading out there to see what I can find. Maybe find a dead one to punch in the face? A useless gesture, I know, but it keeps playing out like that in my mind.

Despite certain questionable violent fantasies (see previous) I'm doing fine. The job is what I've needed and the crew is great. Melinda Hughes is really fun — a great banter partner. Almost as good as you. Almost.

Be safe, my girl, please be safe out there with the dead culture.

Death and death and more death. I really really REALLY hate these bastards.

But I love you. I hope you can feel it from here.

—D

Antares
Big Blue
Thursday, October 12, 2078, 1800 UTC

Every sunset at the Beta Hydri towns, *Antares* would drop from high synchronous orbit into a much lower fifteen-hundred-kilometer orbit to map the rest of the planet and keep up surveillance against any new enemy presence. This had been their practice on the first visit and was resumed when they returned.

Jack Ballard spent several hours reviewing in detail the latest results from these 'mapping' orbits, and at the post-Sol 57 review discussion, he felt his nagging doubts could no longer be ignored.

"I need to address an issue with the mapping orbits."

The room became quiet, and Terri Michael turned to him.

"Go ahead, Jack."

"We're covering these two other continents, but always doing it at about the same time of day."

"So, you're concerned that we could be missing something?" Harris asked.

"Yes, sir. Let's say, just for fun, that there *are* survivors down there. I mean, that tunnel must mean *something*. Or, the enemy. If we're never overhead when they're visible, obviously we'll never see them."

"We have to cover the exploration teams," Terri Michael pointed out.

"Actually, ma'am, I think they'd be fine. A shuttle can find us anywhere in orbit. If something happened that they needed to get back, they could still do that."

"You've had no unusual results so far?" Gabrielle Este asked.

"No, Gabe, none. And we have the best overhead photographic interpretation software that American, British, and Israeli intelligence could give us."

"So, what's the problem?"

"So, if I keep feeding it the same old stuff it's going to keep not finding anything. We need to get imagery that has more variety."

"OK, Jack, what is it you would like me to do?" Terri asked.

"I'd like us to get as low as we possibly can and stay there for a week."

"A *week*? Wow."

"Yes, ma'am. People, and cultures, have patterns. We don't know what behavioral patterns a 47-hour day creates in an advanced species, but it's likely to be *something*. To be able to see the pattern of anything we want to observe, we have to lose our own patterns of behavior. We have to get to where we see something like a random sample."

Terri looked over at Ron Harris. "Admiral?"

"I understand what Jack is saying, and from an Intel point of view, his logic is solid. Surveillance should be at different dates and times if at all possible."

"What about the risk to the surface teams?"

"He's also correct that a shuttle can get back to *Antares* from anywhere on the planet. But, I'm far more concerned about being out of communications with the surface teams."

"If they need us, we'd be out of range much of the time," Carol said.

"You're sure you need a week?"

Jack looked around the table, thinking. "OK, Captain, maybe, instead of a week let's call it three Sols."

"That's really not much less, Jack."

"Yes, ma'am. But if we want to be confident about survivors or enemy presence here, this is what we need to do."

"Captain Barnes, you're most directly responsible for the safety of the exploration teams. What about it?"

Barnes looked at Ballard for a second. "I agree with Lieutenant Ballard, ma'am. We'll need to keep in mind that we're on our own when *Antares* is out of range, but we'll be fine."

Terri took one last look at Ron Harris, decided to sit on her reservations, and nodded.

"OK, after we drop the next AM team, we'll get down low. Alex, what do you think?"

Navigator Alex Williams was ready for the question. "Yes, Captain. We've been using fifteen-hundred kilometers for the mapping orbits, but I think we could go as low as two-hundred-fifty. That would mean an orbit about every ninety-seven minutes."

"OK, then, two-fifty it is."

Alex raised one eyebrow. "OK, Captain. We'll be able to smell the flowers from that altitude."

"If there were flowers…" Carol answered.

Antares
Big Blue
Friday, October 14, 2078, 1800 UTC

The Sol after they found the library, Gabrielle and Greg spent several hours back in the portrait house. That visit turned up several books that appeared to be primers, long on pictures and less dense with text. The new books matched some of the entries in the picture book they had retrieved earlier, and now, the previously implacable facade of the alien language was starting to crack. Greg was beginning to think he could recognize patterns in the language. He was now able to look at a page and see the words, his mind editing out the word separators. As that happened, more, deeper patterns began to come to his attention.

It started with the original picture book. He suggested 'teacher' as the meaning of the word under the cartoon. That didn't work, so he tried 'parent,' taking the suggestion from Joe Bowles, whose grandchildren had simple books that he frequently read to them. Greg fed that hint into the Swadish software and let it keep working on the text.

They couldn't be sure what they were reading, whether a book was technical, historical, or fictional. They just kept collecting the text and feeding the inference engine. Even now, with no real translation, it was telling him about the language. He thought he could see 'root' words with suffixes. There were many five-letter words that had one of a set of eight different suffixes. That looked suspiciously like verb tenses to Greg. But the idea that every verb would be five characters seemed very unlikely. There were some characters that appeared on their own. One was a circle with a dot near the top, one looked like a 7, and another that looked like a backward 7. They didn't appear in every sentence, and sometimes they were at the beginning and sometimes at the end. That smelled like punctuation to Greg, but he could not yet be sure.

It was late Sunday evening as he and Gabrielle sat talking about the language and what they had each seen on the surface.

"There's some serious weirdness in here," Greg said quietly.

"Weirdness?" she asked, shifting in one of the wardroom lounge's comfortable upholstered chairs.

"The five letter words..." Greg let the subject drop, slumping deeper into a recliner with an ottoman.

"The ones you were saying might be verbs?"

"Yes. There are characters that only appear in the second and fourth places. And others that appear in the first, third, and fifth places never appear in two or four." As he talked, he drew the words in the air.

"Do they appear elsewhere?"

"Oh, sure, they turn up in other places, not usually together."

"Does the same one ever show up in both the two and four positions?"

"Not much, but yes, they do."

"How many are there of these two-four characters?"

"Twelve."

"So, you're still thinking these words are verbs?"

"From my very provincial point of view, yes. I think they're regular verbs. But, like, anal retentive regular. All exactly alike."

"You don't ever find that in human languages?"

"Not that I can recall. Farsi has the regular endings but not the fixed length. Beyond that, I can't think of any that do this."

"And the characters, maybe those belong to a class, like vowels or consonants?"

"That's what I believe. I know I'm assuming that their writing is like ours — speech on paper. But I suppose it's possible that writing is just writing and they wouldn't speak it."

"Well, that sounds unlikely." She changed the subject slightly. "Since you named the system 'Swadish,' I read a little about the Swadish list. It's supposed to be for measuring similarities between languages?"

"Right, but it also lists a set of more or less universal ideas that most any language is going to include. I did have to trim it, though."

"How?"

"Well, our body parts for one: nose, tongue, breast, navel, stuff like that. Those might exist for an alien, but I thought they might be more confusing than helpful."

"What else?"

"Earth-specific stuff, like ant, louse, or fish."

"Louse is a universal word?"

Greg smiled, "Yep, a universal word for a universal annoyance."

"You'll get it, Greg. I know you will."

His smile disappeared and Greg was suddenly serious. "Doctor Este, I am grateful for your confidence. I just hope you're right."

Columbia
Enemy Wreck Near GL 876
Saturday, October 14, 2078, 2100 UTC

They arrived after thirty hours; their cautiously slow approach dictated by the expectation of finding more debris near the main part of the wreck. They now had a very close view of it and spent several hours examining the derelict in detail from a few kilometers away. The Bludgeon holes were obvious, but the largest opening was aft, or at least, what they thought of as 'aft.' Both sides of the ship had a hole something like a hundred meters across, with edges bent outward. That, they decided, was likely the massive IR plume that David and his Intel crew had seen from *Sigma*. They couldn't be sure which ship this was, and *Sigma* had scratched three from the enemy's inventory.

The enemy ship was rolling slowly, about once an hour along its long axis. There was no way they were going to stop that, so it would just have to figure into their planning. As his officers gathered in the wardroom, Dan started the discussion.

"OK, folks, this yapping little puppy has finally caught up with the big fancy car. Now what?"

"We're already documenting the wreck externally with hi-res photography," Melinda Hughes began. "We should be done with that in a few hours."

Katch spoke up. "My guess, sir, is that these ships are mostly gas tank and weapons. I think we should start up front and see if there's a way to get inside to whatever passes for a crew compartment."

Dan nodded. "Based on how brittle they are, I agree about the general design. But we should be looking to explore that as well. But, first things first. Our first trip over there is to install the Comm repeaters FleetIntel sent us. That way we can talk even if you're deep within the wreck."

"Clark and I can do that, sir," Katch offered.

Mike Clark suddenly sat up. "When do we leave?"

Dan waved them off. "We'll get to that. Melinda, what does the photography say about the openings in the forward end of the ship?"

Melinda flipped through some images and then settled on one to show on the wall monitor.

"Windows, sir. A couple are blown out, as you can see."

Dan turned to his Weapons officer. "Victor, get both rotaries loaded, a balanced load of half Spartans, half Bludgeons."

"Not fooling around, Captain?"

"No. If we need to shoot, we're gonna shoot fast and hard, and then we're going to run."

"Yes, sir. I'll be ready."

"OK, back to the windows. If there are windows to look out of, there must be someone on the inside to do the looking." He turned back to Melinda. "How large are those openings?"

"You mean, are they large enough to get an EVA suit through?"

"Yes."

"I think so, but we'd have to inspect them, get rid of anything sharp."

"Fair enough. We'll drop a comm relay in one of those on the first sortie, and whoever does that can get the exact dimensions and get us photography of the condition. Clear?"

"Yes, sir," Katch responded.

"Anything to add, Doctor Scranton?"

"We're looking for remains: whole, partial, skin, organs, whatever you can find." She turned to Katch. "But I can also use anything you can tell me about the inside. Chairs, switches, hatches, whatever might tell us something about this species."

Dan looked around the table for a moment. "We all want to get these bastards, I know. But remember we need to live to do that. Stay calm. Stay cautious. If we need to go back later, we'll go back later. We've got plenty of consumables this trip, and all the time we want to take."

"Katch, you and Clark go place the Comm relays. Stef, you can fly them out."

"I'll go, sir," David offered.

"Nope. If Katch goes, you stay, and vice versa. Same goes for all of you. I only have two of you for each division, so I'm going to cut my downside by keeping one aboard at all times."

As the briefing broke up, Dan gathered the small exploration crew together, along with David and Melinda.

"OK, Katch, only low-power VHF comms."

"Right."

Dan turned to Katch and Mike. "Watch out for each other over there. I can see a lot of lovely battle damage that could still bite you in the ass. Am I clear?"

"Yes, sir," Katch answered, "We'll be careful."

"OK, then, get going,"

The small cargo shuttle was pulled from its storage and positioned just inside the hangar from the ShuttleLock. For this trip, seats were placed in the cargo bay for Mike and Katch to get in and out of their EVA suits.

David Powell and Melinda Hughes walked with them to the hangar deck. They talked about the approach, how to set the comm network nodes, but mostly they walked in silence.

Once at the shuttle, Melinda took one more look at her tablet, then looked up at Stef.

"OK, we're abeam the wreck, forward of the BGH."

"BGH?"

"Oh, sorry. Big Giant Hole. Anyway, you have the placements for the relays in your suit displays. Set up all eight and we should be good to go."

"Fine. Thanks for the escort but I think we know the way from here." Katch opened the hatch, and he and Mike Clark followed Stef through, slamming the hatch behind. David and Melinda glanced at each other, sharing a hope that this would all go well, and turned to head back to the bridge.

Katch and Clark moved through the shuttle cockpit and into the cargo bay. The EVA suits were waiting for them. Stef wore a flight pressure suit, and her small frame made it easy for her to slip into the left seat and strap in. Mike and Katch loosely pulled on the EVA suits and strapped themselves into the seats.

Stef clicked the intercom. "You boys ready back there?"

"Yes, mama, are we there yet?" Clark whined.

Stef laughed as she waved to the hangar crew that they were ready. They moved into the ShuttleLock, and in a minute were outside the ship.

"Holy shit," they heard Stef say.

"What?"

"It's, like, huuuuge! It takes up the whole sky up here."

"Just get us over there, Stef, so we can see it for ourselves."

"Workin' on it." She took the shuttle to the first comm relay placement. She turned the docking lights on so that both she and the work crew would have enough light. Katch and Mike had agreed to alternate roles, one would place the relay, the other would hover nearby, to assist if necessary and be the 'safety' guard.

They opened the sliding door on the side of the cargo bay.

"Holy shit!" Clark said.

"What is it?" Stef asked.

"Damn thing takes up the whole sky out here."

"Clark?" Katch asked.

"What?"

"Just place the damned relay and stop trying to be funny."

"But I don't have to try —"

"Clark!" It was Dan Smith's voice.

"Sir?"

"Just get the relays placed and get back here alive, OK? You can do the standup routine Saturday night."

"Yes, Captain. Sorry."

"I like it that you all try to keep a good attitude. I really do. But time to focus, gentlemen. *Focus.*"

"Yes, Captain, understood."

A minute later they heard "Set number one is in place. We're back in the shuttle, so take us to the next stop, Stef."

"OK, on to spot two."

After three placements, they came to the front of the ship. Stef backed off a couple hundred meters so they could see the whole surface, and pick a broken window to exploit. She saw one more or less in the middle and maneuvered the shuttle to it.

Katch moved out of the sliding door, a laser ruler in his gloved hand.

"Captain, I can get through this one easily. Laser says it's one point nine tall and one point two wide." Katch stowed the laser and flipped on the flashlight on the top of his glove. "I'm going to have a look inside."

"Katch, watch yourself on that broken stuff at the top," Clark warned. He was hanging in space just a few meters behind.

"Yeah, I saw that. There's nothing at the bottom so I'll keep low." Katch crawled over the opening, looking around at the interior.

"OK, so?" Stef asked.

"Openings left and right, they look more or less human-sized. No hatch or door. There are some controls under the window."

He pulled out a camera and took several pictures of the interior. He then swapped the camera for the laser ruler and got what dimensions he could, calling them out over the radio since he had nothing to write with.

"See anybody?" Stef asked.

"Nope. Not even part of anybody."

Katch took a last look around and then pulled back from the window. "OK, let's move on."

They worked their way around the wreck, placing the relays so they could see and hear one another whenever they were inside. It was a tedious task, but necessary for their safety later on.

Despite the weightlessness and the easy maneuverability of the EVA suits, both men were tired when they walked out of the shuttle back on board the ship. Mike's Weapons Maintenance crew would clean and reset the suits for the next trip. Meantime, Stef headed forward to her quarters for a shower and some rest.

Katch had much the same in mind but stopped first in the Intel section. David took the camera and loaded the photographs to the ship's central network. After Katch left, he sent Doctor Scranton the pictures taken inside the enemy ship. David could not tell much from them, but maybe she could.

David went back to his quarters before dinner in the wardroom, with Carol on his mind.

Dear Carol —

Katch and Mike Clark did the first EVA to the wreck today. Melinda Hughes and I did the final brief before they launched. Watching the two of them I think Melinda has a thing for Mike but I don't think he gets it yet. Such a good guy but even more clueless than me about this stuff.

Anyway, Melinda and I were walking back from the hangar, just talking, and I turned to say something to you. It felt strange that you weren't there, but that's how it is for me — I feel you next to me all the time, your voice in my ear. I know it sounds weird, but I love that you're there. I hope I'm there for you, too.

—David

Chaffee
Near Enemy Station
Saturday, October 15, 2078, 1045 UTC

FleetIntel Senior Lieutenant Chuck Anderson watched from the Intel workroom as *Chaffee* exited FTL about two million kilometers from the estimated position of Enemy Station. Mark Rhodes thought it best to arrive well short, then see if they could find the facility from a safe distance. Enemy Station had been chatty lately, and while they were enroute, FleetIntel had refined its position to within about five hundred thousand kilometers. At that distance, assuming the facility was as large as they expected, they should be able to find it easily.

As soon as they were out of FTL, Mark maneuvered *Chaffee* to get away from the FTL exit point. If they had made any 'noise' at all coming in, he wanted to be clear of it as soon as he could.

They spent the first twelve hours just gathering data about the surrounding area. There wasn't much to see here in the middle of nowhere. The red dwarf Gliese 687 was the closest star, but it was less than half as bright as the Sun and over ten light years away. Beta Hydri was almost twelve light years, but from there it was just a bright star, giving no real illumination to the area.

Once they finished the initial survey, the Intel and Surveillance teams worked carefully to find Enemy Station.

"So, what are we looking for, Lieutenant Anderson?" one of the Intel techs asked after several hours of watching nothing on his screen.

"I wish I knew."

"So, is it going to be big like Kapteyn? Or small like a satellite or something?"

"Our best guess is that it's going to be big, and I mean, really, really, big."

"With respect, sir, that's not very scientific."

"Agreed. But it's the best guess we have. And, yes, we could well be wrong. I suppose it could be nothing more than a *Sigma* Sphere."

"How are we ever going to see it? There's not much light out here."

"Well, that depends on what you consider light. Activity creates heat, and the enemy so far hasn't tried to hide themselves. So, IR might show them."

"Or?"

"Or, if it's as big as we think it is, occultation might reveal it. We'll just have to see."

146

After sixteen hours, Mark Rhodes called a meeting in the wardroom. Neither of his Intel and Surveillance officers had anything to report.

"Lieutenant Anderson, how good is this location? I mean, you're doing TDOA on a signal traveling almost six thousand times the speed of light."

"FleetIntel is fairly confident of the location, Commander. With the updates we received on our way out, they have about a dozen intercepts to work with. Averaging those locations should put us in the right place."

"But we don't really know what we're looking *for*, right?" asked Sherry Collier, the Surveillance officer.

"True. We think it's a supply depot, which based on the size of their ships would be very large. But we don't *know* that."

Rhodes looked around at his officers, slowly coming to a conclusion.

"OK, here's what we're going to do. Weaps, get me two Sleuths loaded out. I may not need them, but get them prepped and on a rotary."

"Yes, Captain."

"Nav, turn us towards the location FleetIntel has given us. Give me a course to miss that point in space by one hundred thousand kilometers."

"Sir, that's one-fifth the accuracy FleetIntel gave us. We might as well just head for the center!"

Mark looked at his Navigation officer, Australian Cathy McPherson, for a few seconds. She was sharp, but perhaps just a little too direct. She reminded him of Cook. On the other hand, she had a point.

"OK, just go for bullseye then."

He looked around the room.

"Maintain minimum EMR. If they're out there, our job is to slide by like a dead asteroid and get intel. We're not to let them know we're here."

"Yes, Captain, we understand," the Nav officer replied.

"Good. Keep the watch going, but all of you get some sleep. Nav, how long to that position?"

"Uh, your call, sir, but I was thinking two days at forty thousand."

"OK, fine. Proceed."

Mark Rhodes rose and left the wardroom. He'd been up almost thirty hours himself, and it was past time to get some sleep. He took one last tour of the Bridge and slipped into his Duty Cabin.

Chuck Anderson also went to the Bridge, remaining behind the Surveillance position. After two more hours of nothing-to-report, he headed for his cabin, showered, and flopped into bed. *Tomorrow will be another day,* he thought, *and maybe tomorrow will tell the tale.*

The next morning Chuck was standing behind the Surveillance position on the Bridge when the alarm went off.

"IR target, Captain."

Rhodes came down from the command chair to see for himself. It wasn't much — just a couple pixels that weren't as black as the ones around it.

"Where is it?"

"Reads zero-two-five plus twenty. Up and to our right."

"How far?"

"Too early to tell that, sir. Give us a couple hours."

"Get the long-range telescope on it."

They moved the large-aperture visual telescope to point at the IR target and started an occultation search. The visual spectrum didn't show anything, which was no surprise since there were so few photons around to work with. But they would keep the telescope on it, and over time they might collect enough light to reveal something. Sherry Collier took Rhodes and Anderson aside.

"I'd like to get out the high-gain radio antenna, sir. But, as you know, it's not very stealthy."

"Anderson?"

"I have nothing on enemy radio transmissions, sir."

"But is it worth looking?"

"Yes, I think so."

Rhodes turned back to Collier. "OK, go ahead. Let's put it out there for a couple hours. If you don't hear anything, we'll pull it back and try again tomorrow, OK?"

"Yes, Captain."

Less than a minute later, the big dish was up and pointed at the IR return. Almost as soon as it came online, a tech called out.

"Whoa, sig-up 180." The tech pulled up the signal analysis processor to identify it. The result surprised him.

"Lieutenant Collier? Analyzer claims it's a constant wave signal. No modulation at all."

"Let me hear it."

"The only way to hear a constant wave, Lieutenant, is to tune off to one side..."

"Yeah, I know, Scott. Just give me a thousand cycle tone or whatever." She listened for several seconds, then had Scott turn it off.

"Get the antenna down," she said abruptly as she turned to the command chair. "Captain, that signal could be a constant-wave radar. I've stowed the antenna so we don't reflect back."

Anderson looked at her. "So, we've found the station?"

"No question in my mind, Chuck. That IR target is broadcasting a signal, whether it's a homing signal or an intruder detector, I can't be sure."

"OK, understood. Do we have a range to this target yet?"

"Not yet, Captain. Should have it in a couple hours."

Rhodes walked to the Nav position. "Cathy, we need to adjust course to bring us closer to the target. Bring us up ten degrees and move ten right."

"That's going to take some serious gravitons, sir."

"Yeah, I know." He paused to consider his options. There was no evidence that the enemy had an artificial graviton detector. Some experts claimed it couldn't be built, or if it could, it would be too enormous to have any practical application. Given what this enemy had already shown, Mark wasn't all that sure they couldn't build one.

Cathy McPherson waited patiently as her new captain considered his options.

"Do it slowly. Take an hour."

"Yes, Captain."

The Surveillance techs worked to reacquire the radio signal on their less-sensitive but far stealthier hull-mounted antennas. After two hours, they were able to find it and start monitoring. They also began scanning the full radio spectrum for other signals. The IR view had not changed much in that time, just growing by a pixel or two.

The time passed slowly, but finally, Cathy McPherson could make an estimate of the target's location. She pulled Rhodes, Anderson, and Cathy McPherson together in the right corner of the Bridge.

"Range is about one-point-five million klicks, sir. On our current course, the closest approach is about two-hundred-sixty thousand."

"Almost the distance to the Moon," Rhodes said, thinking. Then he turned to his Navigator. "Slow us down, Cathy. Now that we have a real target, there's no hurry to get there. And turn us another five degrees towards them."

"And, slow us down slowly?"

Rhodes smiled. "Yes, exactly. Let's make it twelve thousand."

"Yes, sir will do."

As his officers went back to their tasks, Mark looked around the Bridge of his new ship. *Chaffee* was so far untested in combat, but he liked what he saw. Lots of strong personalities getting along and sharing their strong opinions. He'd been on ships with far less functional Bridge officers. While he knew the captain had much to do with the work environment on his ship, he'd just inherited this crew and could take little credit for what he now saw. He'd have to remember to thank the former captain and XO. They'd clearly left him a very good crew.

As he was considering how he could best maintain the spirit of the ship, the occultation alarm went off.

Antares
Intel Section
Monday, October 16. 2078, 0830 UTC

Antares had been in the low orbit Intel Chief Jack Ballard had requested for more than three days. This morning the automated image analyzer kicked out several images, and he was now trying to understand what might be there. There were hot spots, for sure, that appeared right after local dusk and then faded. They'd never been over this ground at this time of day before, and Jack smiled inwardly that his hunch might turn out to be correct.

The hot spots were arranged in a line behind a beach on the east coast of the continent. This island continent was smaller than the first one they had explored, but it was at about the same latitude, and so maintained a similar climate. Most of it was flat grassland, but towards the east there was a mountain range that terminated suddenly at the shoreline.

"If I needed to hide," Jack said to himself, "This is where I might go."

Carol Hansen heard him and got up from her own review of photography of the third continent in the southern hemisphere.

"Show me."

Jack pointed to the IR scans with no heat during the day, then hot after dusk.

"So, cooking fires?"

"I don't know, Carol, but maybe, yeah. If that's right, there aren't enough for it to be a very large group."

"Not if they were human."

"So, what are you saying?"

"Well, based on the portrait, I did a little research. Back home, large predators don't eat every day. If these people have that kind of physiology, they might not be feeding everyone every day."

"Interesting. I'll keep that in mind. But, Carol, large predators back home don't cook their food."

Carol smiled. "Depends on your definition of predator, Jack."

"Huh. Point taken."

"Now, what are they cooking, and where did they get it?"

"Carol, you know this thing you do where I work all day to get answers and all you have is more questions?"

"Yeah, it's one of my better character traits."

"It's annoying sometimes."

"Yeah, that, too."

She stood up to go back to her work, giving Ballard a quick squeeze on the shoulder as she went. Her continent was completely different. It was further from the equator, nearly halfway to the southern polar cap. People could live there, but it would be like living in Siberia in the late fall, only more so since there would be no summer. It would just be cold all the time.

Aboard the Enemy Wreck
GL 876
Sunday, October 16, 2078, 1000 UTC

David shifted his stance, trying to remain on the deck of the enemy ship as he switched on the small magnets in the soles of his boots.

"There. Better!" He turned around to watch Melinda Hughes slide easily through the window, and gently guided her to a standing position. She flipped the same control and settled quickly to the floor.

"OK, I have the map open." Melinda took the lead as they made their way past the compartments that had already been examined. Katch insisted on a methodical, compartment-by-compartment investigation of the wreck, starting from the window he had first peered into. This was the second day two-person teams had entered through that broken opening and awkwardly made their way further back in the ship.

There were already a few areas where the damage was severe and ragged shards of wreckage were hanging loosely, ready to tear the EVA suit of any careless passer-by. So far, there was no sign of the crew in the dozen or so compartments they had searched. The controls they found were a mystery, too, but didn't appear to be anything more advanced than what might have been found on an early Forstmann ship. The tech seemed to be more analog than the fleet's, with physical dials instead of flat screens. David felt a little like he was exploring an old battleship in a museum. The walls were a plain off-white, covered with some kind of paint or other coating. But for now, understanding the tech was not a priority; finding the enemy was.

Melinda stopped at a new opening to photograph it. "So, David, where do you suppose they went?"

"Beats me. At the time, I thought they had all been incinerated. But these spaces don't really support that."

"The BGH is bent outwards. I suppose it's possible all that heat went out the sides and not up into this space?"

"Seems reasonable." David looked around as he waited for Melinda to finish her pictures. They would be used to add to the map they were creating of the interior of the wrecked enemy ship.

"And then somehow they got off? Got away?"

"Again, seems logical. But we gotta keep —"

His sudden mid-sentence silence caught her attention. "David?"

"Turn around, Lieutenant Hughes." Melinda, struck by the suddenly serious tone of David's voice, slowly turned to look over his shoulder. He was now kneeling, as best he could, and shining his flashlight on the floor.

"What?"

"Does that look like blood to you?"

There was a small, dark, rust-colored smear on the deck. The ship had been spotless up to now, something all the previous teams had commented on.

"Could be, I guess. That's the first thing anybody's seen." She took her camera and photographed the scene.

"Correct me if I'm wrong, but this looks like a hatch to the lower level."

"Maybe, sure." Melinda started her helmet video and looked over David into the compartment.

"It's a blood trail, Powell, look where it goes." She was pointing to another hatch opening, but since she was behind David's bulky EVA suit, he could not see where she was pointing.

"Look where?"

"Oh, sorry. Ahead and to your right a little." David, now stowed the flashlight, turned on his own suit video and turned up the brightness on his helmet-mounted lights.

"Yeah, looks like a blood trail to me. Are we online?"

"No." Melinda switched her communications settings, opening a link to *Columbia* and transmitting their suit video.

"*Columbia*, this is Hughes. We need Doctor Scranton."

Susan Scranton had been haunting the Communications position whenever someone was in the enemy ship. She snatched up a headset.

"Hughes this is Scranton. What do you have?"

"Are you seeing the feed, Commander?"

"Yes. I see something on the floor."

"It's thin and kinda smeared. We think it's a blood trail. It ends at this hatch."

Scranton asked the Surveillance tech to show her both feeds, so she could follow both Melinda and David at once.

"Where does it go, Lieutenant?"

David turned and looked towards the next hatchway. "It goes that way, Doctor. You want us to follow it?"

Katch and the Captain joined Scranton. She turned to them. "Gentlemen?"

"This is your project, Doctor," Dan said. "I think they should see where it goes but it's your call."

Scranton nodded her agreement. "Yes, Powell, follow it but watch your step. Stay out of whatever that stuff is."

"Understood. Because you'd mind, don't walk the line." That earned him a slap on the back of the helmet from Hughes.

They carefully moved through the new compartment to the hatchway.

"It goes straight on through the next compartment. Wait...Melinda...is that a footprint?" They both looked at the odd shape that crossed the blood trail.

"Maybe. If so, it ain't human."

"Lieutenant Hughes, can you get a hi-res photo of that?" Scranton asked.

"Yes, Doctor. Already on that." They got several good images, then continued to the next hatchway. David, now in front, suddenly came to a stop.

"Powell?"

"Well, I'll be damned."

"What?"

"See for yourself." David slid sideways, just enough for Melinda to get a look. "Oh, shit."

Scranton, now out of patience, slammed down her push-to-talk switch. "Please stand still so I can see, and tell me what it is that's so damned shitty."

"Sorry, Doc, but there's a Bludgeon sphere embedded in the bulkhead, and there's what appears to be a forearm lying on the floor."

Scranton was not sure she had heard correctly. "A what?"

"A forearm, I guess. Ends in some really nasty looking claws." By now the entire Bridge was crowded around the Surveillance console.

Scranton stared at the image for several seconds, the recognition freezing her in place.

"Oh my God. Five digits."

"What?" Dan Smith asked.

"Five digits."

"So?"

Scranton recovered quickly, realizing she might have said too much too soon. "Nothing, for now."

"That's a little spooky, Doctor," Alona Melville said quietly.

"Yes, Lieutenant, it's strange. We'll know more when we get it back here." She turned back to the image. "Can you look around and see if there's any more of him?"

"Him?" David asked as he looked around the compartment.

"It, whatever."

"There's a hole on the opposite bulkhead, bent inwards, so that's where the sphere came in. There's some serious blood splatter around where it embedded."

Melinda Hughes had worked her way across the compartment, avoiding the mess on the floor, and now looking back at David. "Sure, looks like the forelimb was taken off by the sphere, Doctor. I'll get some good images."

They heard Dan Smith's voice next. "That was some seriously good shootin' Powell."

"Thank you, sir. We did our best. I confess I would have preferred center mass."

"Where's the rest of him?" Melinda asked.

"My guess," David said as Melinda took photographs, "is that they took him."

"What now?" Melinda asked.

Scranton's response was clear. "Bag it and bring it back."

Melinda pulled a sample bag from her pack and handed it to David.

"What? Why me?"

"Shut up and bag the damn thing."

David carefully picked it up by one of the 'fingers.' It stuck to the deck at the stump and he had to move it back and forth several times before it broke loose. He looked briefly at the individual claws and noticed that they were trimmed at the end, almost like a fingernail would be. The appearance of the flesh reminded him that Scranton had suggested the samples would be freeze-dried. He placed it carefully in the sample bag.

"OK, let's get that back here soon as you can."

"Understood, Doctor."

They scraped up and bagged some of the concretized blood from under the rough end of the forelimb, then started moving back out. It still wasn't much, David thought, but it was a start. He still secretly hoped to find a whole alien body somewhere in the wreck. Given how enormous it was, they'd have to be very lucky to find one.

Still, they'd keep looking as long as they could.

David laid on his bunk for a half hour that night, then abruptly flipped the light on and pulled his journal off the shelf. It took him a minute to find a pen, but he had to get down what he was feeling.

Dear Carol —

I held an enemy arm today. Honest. I'll show you the pictures. It's purple.

Melinda and I found it in the wreck. Looks like we severed it when we hit them with a Bludgeon.

Cool, huh?

I watched Melinda as she sat with Clark at breakfast before we went EVA. She looks at him with those huge blue eyes and he just keeps on talking. I thought about pushing him into a wall or something to knock some sense into him but decided against it. They're both such great people. I hope they can get out of their own way long enough to see what's up.

Miss you desperately. But I heard you in my ear today telling me I'm not as funny as I think.
Pretty sure M would agree.

—D

Antares
Big Blue
Sunday, October 17, 2078, 2030 UTC

It happened much as Greg Cordero thought it might. One moment there were only a few words with possible meanings out of the dozens of books that he had laboriously scanned into the translation engine. The process had identified thousands of words, tracked their associations and disassociations, their placements before or after others frequently nearby, and their position in what he now clearly saw as sentences. Whatever the Beta Hydri culture might call them, to Greg, there were words, sentences, and paragraphs. It made sense, he thought, since knowledge has to be organized logically. Combinations of individual words made complete thoughts. Then combinations of thoughts were added together to create more complex concepts. And on and on it went, each level of comprehension building on the last. Start with one plus one is two, and from there you eventually get to quadratic equations.

The translation engine had the semantic structure of every written human language to use as possible templates, and it would try to match those structures with the words it was given. Even lacking meaning, the process would try to match the words it found in the Beta Hydri language with human syntax patterns.

This evening, messages from Swadish lit Greg's tablet up with three simultaneous notifications from the inference engine. Then, six more a few seconds later. Then twenty, and then they were coming faster than he could understand them. He turned the tablet off and headed for the Intel section. He called Gabrielle on the way, and she met him there, lugging a full mug of coffee from the wardroom.

Greg accessed the translation monitor from the large display in the workroom. Each book was identified by a reference number and whatever title they had located on the book's cover, knowing full well that they were only assuming it was a title.

As Greg watched the monitor, newly translated titles appeared next to the originals. Some were incomplete, and where it could not translate a word, it simply left the original in place. Gabrielle pointed to the top title, which Greg had called 'The Dictionary.'

"Greg, look: 'Path of Knowledge.' I think your grandfather would agree."

Greg nodded. "He would, absolutely he would."

More titles filled in as they watched, and the picture book they found that first day became 'Start of Knowledge.'

"It's a primer, just like we thought."

Gabrielle called in Ron Harris, Carol Hansen, and the rest of the team working on Big Blue. They opened the electronic version of the primer and could now read what it said on the first page. Not every word was confirmed, and the inference engine would sometimes equivocate if it wasn't sure.

Knowledge is start knowledge is end seeking knowledge [journey?]. Today [parent?] start future life [journey?].

Greg opened The Dictionary and looked at the inscription, which he had manually transcribed into the translator.

[NAME?] past [journey?] [good?]. [Wish?] future [consciousness?] long and knowledge grow [time?]. [love?] [parent?] [NAME?].

He turned to the first content page of The Dictionary. He thought he knew what it might say.

Knowledge: Knowledge [root?] life [together?] goal each [person?]. Knowledge past teach meaning future prevent error give [confident?] direction.

He flipped to the second page.

Consciousness: We alive [sentient?] [people?] we [aspire?] think reason apply knowledge in [strict?] application. We past future value preserve consciousness our life our [children?] our [neighbors?]. Attention thought seek new knowledge and [then?] find future [wisdom?] giving future knowledge. This our [path?].

It occurred to Greg reading the translation that while he'd found what amounted to a space and a period, there didn't seem to be a comma yet.

"So, it's not just a dictionary," Ron Harris said. "It's also a book of philosophy, a moral guide?"

"Yes, sir, I think so. Something like that, anyway."

"*Past future?*" Gabrielle asked.

Greg flipped to a detailed display of the translation, a word-by-word breakdown. "Maybe it means something like 'always' or 'forever,' but in the text, it is 'past future.' Perhaps there's an implied 'and' in there for them."

Carol leaned back in her chair, arms crossed as she frequently did when deep in thought.

"Can we try something, Greg?" she asked.

"What did you have in mind."

"Can we do a reverse comparison test? We're translating from their language into ours. It makes me wonder what words in the English language do not have a translation."

Gabrielle agreed. "Hmm. Interesting thought, Carol."

Greg took a few seconds to generate the reverse missing words. Kathy Stewart gasped at the list, prioritized by the 'weight of meaning' in English.

god
worship
supernatural
war

"So, a society that has no concept of the supernatural. Of any kind of 'god'?" she asked.

There was a moment of silence before Greg responded. "I would have expected to see those in the sources we've processed so far, especially The Dictionary, but it is possible that we just haven't found those concepts yet."

"Seems unlikely to me," Harris said. "Based on what else is being taught, wisdom and the search for new knowledge."

"So, sir, you think this is an atheist society?" Carol asked.

"Well, in a way, yes, but I would not say they're 'anti-God' like a human atheist might be. A human atheist has at least heard about the idea of an omnipotent God but rejects it for whatever reason. If this list is right, and I do agree we need to remember our research is not complete, but if it is correct, the concept of a supernatural deity just does not exist for these people."

"Nor does the idea of worship — the emotional reverence for someone or something," Jack Ballard added. "So, a society based solely on rationality, on the preservation of conscious existence, and the accumulation of knowledge?"

"That's what I'm hearing," Carol responded. "And, you know, in a way it's a bit like the Inori. Very different from us, but somehow a people we can still understand and admire."

"Agreed," Ron Harris said, thoughtfully. He turned to Cordero. "So, Doctor Cordero, what shall we call these people? Just calling them the 'Beta Hydri Culture' has gotten pretty awkward."

Greg nodded, looking at Gabrielle. "They're searchers of wisdom, seekers of knowledge. So, the 'Seekers'?"

Gabrielle agreed. "Makes sense to me."

Terri Michael had watched most of this process standing in the doorway, ready to run back to the Bridge if necessary.

"Congratulations, Doctor Cordero. I do believe you've earned your pay today."

Cordero smiled and continued looking through the translations, making notes and fixing ambiguities as best he could. It was all a draft, he knew. The final translations might be different in tone or nuance of meaning, but for now, he was getting real results. His thesis about language and his translation algorithm were correct. That, in itself, was an enormous accomplishment.

Gabrielle was reading his mind as he worked. "So, thinking Nobel?"

Greg snorted a laugh. "Actually, *not* that. I was thinking about how I was going to explain it. It's gonna be a monstrous paper to write."

"So," Carol asked, "this language is, what, *Seekerish*?"

There was laughter all around.

"Yeah, I guess that's as apt as anything," Greg responded. "Seekerish it is."

The Fleet officers left after a short time, off to other duties. Joe Bowles was in the sickbay working with Marcia Soto on cultures and studies on the remains they had brought back from the surface.

"Congratulations, Greg. It's really an amazing accomplishment," Gabrielle said quietly.

He sat back and looked at her, the relief clear on his face and in his voice.

"I wasn't really sure it would work, Gabe, not until this moment. I was terrified I had missed something obvious, and the whole thing was just bullshit."

"That," she said, pointing to the translation display, "is the very opposite of bullshit."

"Thanks, Gabe."

They sat in silence for a long time after that, watching the words fill in, the new pages flowing across the screens.

Antares
Big Blue
Monday, October 17, 2078, 0900 UTC

Jack Ballard presented his results to stunned silence. He and Carol had held the secret until they had enough orbital passes to raise their confidence level to where they felt they could credibly present to the senior officers. But this was Jack's idea, and Jack's show. Carol was happy to support and be his cheerleader, but he was the expert this time. His images were unmistakable, irrefutable. There were several images that appeared to show figures — presumably Seekers — on the beach, apparently fishing. What kind of gear was unclear, but the figures moved into and out of the surf, then back into the low forest just behind the beach. Whether they were using nets or poles or something else, Jack couldn't tell.

"So, to summarize, we think there are some hundreds of Seekers still alive down there. They're living a decent but subsistence lifestyle. The best comparison I can think of to consider them as 20th-century people living with 18th or early 19th-century tech. They're fishing, but I'd be surprised if that was all. There is an interesting area just to the south of where we see these fires. It's several square kilometers of grassland and small trees, cut off on each end by cliffs. It's a natural corral, and we see quite a few small animals living in a natural enclosure, kinda penned in by the sea and the cliffs. They may be consuming those as well."

"Yes," Carol added, "those could well be the same small animals, the 'goats,' we found out in the farm areas in the original settlement."

The next bombshell came from Cordero and Este.

"You want to do WHAT?" Harris asked, incredulous.

"I want to go down and talk to them," Greg repeated.

"Out of the question," the Admiral responded.

"Sir, hear me out..." Cordero and Este reminded the Admiral that one key question had never been resolved: What was the point? The enemy had come here, killed a lot of people, then left. They didn't seem to take anything; they didn't use the planet for any purpose. So, why bother? It was a conquest with no measurable spoils. It didn't seem to make much sense.

"You've been talking to Ballard, haven't you?" Harris finally asked.

"We've discussed it, sir. But even without the intelligence value, we have a chance to sit down with a new alien species."

Harris looked at Carol, then at Terri Michael, who was suppressing a smile.

"Do you think you have enough of the language to even have a conversation?"

"I think so, sir. We'll have to keep it simple, and we'll have to be flexible in how we explain things to one another, but, yes, I think we can."

"I agree with them, sir. They should try it," Kathy Stewart offered.

"Et tu, Stewartii?" Harris asked, surrendering.

"Sorry, sir, but they've got the goods on you this time."

"What are you going to talk about? What *could* you talk about?" Michael asked.

"I don't know," Cordero answered, "I'll say hello and see where it goes."

"I know what we're *not* going to talk about," Gabrielle stated flatly.

"Oh?" Harris' skepticism had not yet completely disappeared.

"We're not going to talk about God, or sleeping, or how they go to the bathroom, or anything else that might trigger some kind of cultural problem."

"Yes, Gabe, I agree. We need to avoid those topics. But, Admiral, if we just stand across from them and *try* to communicate, I think it will be worthwhile. They're smart. They're literate. They'll get it."

"I have to remind you all that our return date is coming up," Terri Michael pointed out. "And I fully plan to meet that deadline. If you're going to the surface to have this, this, *conversation*, it needs to be soon."

"Yes, Captain."

Harris looked over at Cordero. "When would you go?"

"They come out after midday to fish. I'd think we should be there then."

"They're probably armed. How many Marines would you want to take?"

Carol looked at Gabe and Greg and answered for them. "None, sir."

Harris turned to her. "None? You want to go down there and get shot?"

"Greg has a good idea about that, sir. We'll put a message on the side of the shuttle."

"A message?"

"Yes, sir."

"What message could you possibly put on a shuttle?"

Cordero answered. "One word, sir. *Friend*."

Harris looked over at Michael. "Are they all as crazy as I think?"

"Maybe, sir. But we were once young, too, and maybe slightly foolhardy —"

"You were never 'foolhardy,' Commander." He looked around the table once more. "OK, fine. Go."

They were out of the Intel workroom as if there had been an explosive decompression.

Columbia
GL 876
Wednesday, October 18, 2078, 0900 UTC

The samples from the wreck came in properly double-bagged and marked with their source. Susan Scranton and ship's doctor Gerry Knight examined them and agreed that this was probably some kind of forelimb. The limb and the blood were far too hard to process as they were, so she placed them in the sample freezer, which was much warmer than where they had been. Once they came up to normal freezer temperatures, they'd be workable.

The next morning, in full isolation gear, they carefully cut samples from the amputated end of the limb and sectioned them for staining and microscopic examination. Additional samples were taken for DNA analysis, which would take another full day. Once the samples were out of the alcohol-mediated stain and safely under microscope slide coverslips, they could ditch the isolation suits and begin looking at what they had found.

The digitally-enhanced microscope had a high-def video port along with traditional eyepieces, so Gerry could see on the large wall monitor the same field Susan was examining.

Since they arrived at the wreck, Susan had lost some of the edge on whatever chip was on her shoulder. She was now polite to most everyone, and almost cordial to Knight, whom she apparently viewed as some kind of colleague. Or, at least, an intellectual equal. As the sample came into focus, she stared at it for a full minute.

"Gerry, are you seeing this?" she asked quietly.

"Yes, I am. Looks like muscle tissue to me, nothing remarkable."

She looked up from the eyepiece. "But, Gerry, that's the most remarkable thing about it."

"Not following, Susan."

"This is *alien* tissue, Gerry. *Alien*. It doesn't even look like Inori tissue."

"OK, so no surprise that these are different aliens than the Inori, right?"

Susan looked again through the eyepiece. "I'm not sure they're really alien at all."

"What?"

"Mitochondria, Gerry. They have mitochondria."

Gerry walked to the monitor and looked at it for a long moment. "Well, I'll be damned."

"Should we tell the captain?"

"Yes. Smith will want to know right away. Powell, too."

Susan got up from the microscope and called Dan Smith. In a few minutes, he, Alona Melville, and David Powell were in the sick bay, staring at the image on the wall monitor.

"Mitochondria?" David asked, his voice full of the confusion he felt.

"Very good, Powell. Very good."

"But that would mean, would it not, Doctor, that this species is —"

"Terran. Yes, Powell, it would. As best we know, anyway, only organisms from Earth have mitochondria. Inori don't, and neither do the microbes on Enceladus."

"DNA?" Dan Smith asked.

"Tomorrow. If indeed this is a Terran species, it should give us a hint as to the origin."

"But, how on Earth..." Alona said, unable to finish the thought.

"Not on Earth, I think," Dan answered. He stood looking at the cell images, considering what he should do next. "OK, we'll wait for the DNA tomorrow. Meantime, we keep looking for more evidence on the wreck."

"And?" Susan asked.

"Once we see the DNA results, we can decide next steps. If, Doctor Scranton, you feel your mission goals here have been met, I need to know that."

"Meantime, we keep looking?" Alona asked.

"Yeah, we keep at it."

They stood there for what felt like a long time, Dan and Alona leaving after a while to discuss their options privately. David remained for several minutes, eventually heading back to the Intel workroom and his biology texts. He could not be the experts that Scranton and Knight were, but he needed to try to understand how this could possibly be true.

"Who are these aliens?" he wondered to himself aloud. "If they're not really *aliens*?"

With the immediate biological goals met, Dan ordered additional search teams to enter the BGH and explore that space. They found that the aft portion of the ship was indeed six enormous tanks, all shattered by *Sigma's* attack. Near the top of the ship, they discovered a passage which the crew must have used to get to the far aft end. It was ripped open from the bottom, and the damage was such that they could not get very far in either direction. There was just too much sharp and shattered metal for them to pass safely. If they wanted to get to the Drive apparatus, they'd have to find another way in.

The next morning, Susan Scranton called David and the rest of the officers to the sick bay.

"I have the DNA results. They're Terran."

Dan just looked at her. "You're sure the enemy is from *Earth*?"

"I am. There's really no question about it."

"Can you identify the species?" Alona asked.

"They're not a known species, obviously not human or any hominid that we know about. There are some markers that look close to, well, birds."

"Birds?" Dan asked, surprised.

There was a long silence as they considered what this news meant.

David looked at her. "Don't we think of birds as the last living dinosaurs?"

"Yes, that's been proven pretty conclusively."

David held her eye. "What about you, Doctor Scranton. What do *you* think? You're the exobiologist in the room."

"I think this is about the last thing I expected. I thought I might be able to find some markers similar to others, if we could find a body then maybe tell something about their home environment."

"But?"

"But, I never, ever, thought we'd find out the enemy was a species that originally developed on Earth."

"You're sure?" Dan asked again.

"Sorry, Captain, but yes, I'm sure. There are far too many commonalities with other organisms for it to be otherwise."

David had a different thought. "Could they and we share some kind of common ancestor? Could this possibly be telling us something new about where life on Earth came from?"

"Not in my opinion. Life on Earth arose on Earth, period. There is no serious evidence to indicate otherwise, Martian theories notwithstanding."

"You said they're related to birds."

"Yes, Lieutenant Powell, there's little doubt about that. Yesterday, Doctor Knight and I did a close examination of the skin." She put an enlarged picture on the screen. "This is from a macro lens, the kind of thing we use to look at ticks, bed bugs, that kind of thing."

"That looks like a feather," Alona said.

"Indeed, Lieutenant Melville, that's exactly what it is." She switched to a larger scale image. "They're actually kind of a pretty, dark purple, all from very fine feathers that almost look like fur."

"Incredible," Dan said to himself.

David's mind was racing, looking for the next question. "I seem to recall that you can tell how long populations have been apart by looking at the number of DNA differences between them."

"Yes, that's true."

"Do you have enough information here to determine that?"

"Not in any way I'd be willing to stand behind."

Dan, who had been looking down but listening intently, looked up. "Explain, please."

Susan took a deep breath, then sat on the stool next to the microscope. "Let's assume I am correct. If so, whatever this species is split off from all other Earth organisms a very long time ago. It would be as if I was suddenly presented with fresh T-Rex DNA. The DNA separation in both time and speciation is just too great for me to measure."

"Could someone else?"

Scranton thought about that for a few seconds. "Perhaps. It would be a long and tedious research project, but given enough expertise, I think an educated guess could be made."

"Come on, Doctor," Alona Melville pushed, "tell us what you think. Are we talking thousands of years? Hundreds of thousands? Millions?"

Susan looked over at Gerry McKnight, then back to Alona. "We were discussing that this morning before I called you down here. It's nothing more than a hunch, really, but I would say multiple millions of years."

"Wow," Alona whispered.

"Are you saying, Doctor Scranton, are you really saying," David struggled to gather his question, "that there was a technologically advanced society, one with an FTL drive, on Earth *millions* of years ago?"

Scranton was taken aback by the question. "Yes, I guess I am. I had not quite thought of it in just that way, but yes, that's what the evidence I see here tells me."

"Well, wait," Katch said. "We know the enemy is from Earth, but the tech could have come to them from somewhere else."

"What are you saying, Katch?" Dan's incredulity was clear.

"The crew is Terran, sir. I accept Doctor Scranton's expertise on that. But they could have been abducted, or bred, or taken somehow to where they are now."

"So, now, you think it's possible that some *other* aliens picked up some handy dinos while vacationing on our little third rock a couple million years back and bred them into what they are now?"

"It sounded less ridiculous in my head."

"It's *not* that crazy, Katch," Alona said, her hands emphasizing her point. "We now know of three other intelligent species, all not that far from home, none of which we knew anything about just twenty years ago. There must be many, many more out here."

"Could be, I guess," Dan said quietly.

"This changes everything," Alona said.

"With respect, XO, this changes nothing," David said, anger in his voice.

"But when people hear that they are from Earth, won't they want to help them somehow? Understand them?"

David was unmoved. "We've been killing other Earthly species — including uncounted members of our own — for generations. I think they'll get over it."

Dan looked first at David, then Alona. "It will be a shock to everyone, that far I agree with Alona. But David is right, the war goes on regardless."

"One more thing," Doctor Scranton said, regaining their attention.

"Yes, Doctor?"

"I x-rayed the claw this morning."

"Yes?" Dan asked.

"Well, calling it a claw doesn't do it justice. It's far more complex and well-articulated than any current Terran bird. It's a fully functional hand, regardless of what it looks like."

"Interesting."

Another long moment of silence hung in the air.

Finally, David turned to Dan. "So, what now, sir?"

"Damned if I know, David. What would *you* do?"

"It would still be good to find a complete body for Doctor Scranton to dissect."

"True," Alona agreed. "Gross, but true."

"And, we could try to get to some of the other levels in the front of the wreck."

"OK."

"There are controls and dials, sir, but other than that so far there are no manuals, no books, no writing. We need to look harder for that kind of stuff."

"That is strange."

"Really, Captain," Katch added, "this information does not provide any kind of tactical advantage to us. It's interesting —"

"And weird," Alona interrupted.

"—but not terribly useful in a fight."

"So, what are you getting at, Katch?"

"There's no hurry to get this news back to the Fleet. I agree with David. We might do better to exploit the wreck itself for whatever intelligence value it has, instead of spending so much time trying to understand who was riding in it."

Dan nodded. "OK, that's how we'll play it. We keep exploring both up front and in the aft section, in order to understand *the technology*. If we hit on more remains, fine, Doctor Scranton can see what she can learn." He looked around the room. "Agreed?" He received a quiet chorus of "yes, sir" in response.

He looked at Susan Scranton. "Doctor?"

"Yes, Captain, I agree. I have what I came here for. More would be better, to be sure, but I've met my primary mission goals. We know what we're up against."

"OK, good. Let's get back at it."

The group flowed quickly out of the sickbay, scattering to their various areas of expertise. Susan Scranton found herself strangely intrigued, not so much with the aliens, but rather the crew around her. They were surprisingly smart and insightful, and they were far more flexible in their thinking than she expected. Her mission had just become Priority Two, but she agreed with that assessment and looked forward to whatever she might still learn.

As for the enemy, she wondered what their prehistoric reptile lineage meant in terms of behaviors and tendencies. Are they fully *sapient,* like humans and Inori? Or, are they intrinsically more primitive, less able to understand the evil they do? Would a reptile like this even understand something as being evil? Yes, she decided, they would. They've built a complex society with advanced technology. That society would require some level of societal moral compass, some kind of behavioral norms, to support it. *They have to be sapient,* she thought, *but not necessarily in a way that we can accept.*

She allowed herself a few moments to think of her father. He would be proud of her work, she thought. He was large, strong, sometimes a little too loud, but he lavishly loved his only child. His loss left her alone in a world now colder and emptier than it should have been. Once the tears had stopped flowing after his death on Inor, she had set herself the goal to destroy those who had taken him from her. Her pain quickly transmuted into a singular hatred that was intense beyond words. It spilled over into her relations with others, turning her into a tough, sometimes rude, overbearing presence that only furthered her isolation. She didn't care about that. She just wanted them all dead.

David found himself in the wardroom after dinner, thinking about everything that had happened over the last two days. He picked up the worn notebook that was his inner channel to Carol and began to write.

C —

OK, you won't believe this. The alien enemy isn't really alien. They're an Earth species. Yes, really. No kidding. Doctor Hardass dropped that nuke on us this morning. I don't know how I feel about it — betrayed, maybe? Like they're turncoats somehow.

I'll be going back over tomorrow to see what else we can find. I like being in the EVA suit — it's just me and the team, and maybe someone at the Comms station. Sometimes I turn off my mike and just talk to you while I'm working. Sounds a little crazy, yeah, but it makes me feel like we're together.

Which is, you know, something I'm really looking forward to.

—D

Big Blue
Seeker Beach
Wednesday, October 18, 2078, 1000 UTC

Carol Hansen set the shuttle down on the Seekers' beach, just before the time they usually appeared. She and Jack Ballard unstrapped themselves and went back into the cabin to help Gabrielle, Greg Cordero, and Wayne Barnes unload Greg's materials. They had painted Greg's first message, 'FRIEND,' in Seekerish on the side of the shuttle. Harris had again argued that they take a detachment of Marines with them for protection, but Gabrielle and Greg argued just as forcefully that the Seeker culture was not by nature aggressive. If they displayed too much force, Greg pointed out, it would contradict the simple message they were trying to express. They compromised that Carol, Jack, and Wayne would carry sidearms. None of them thought a .45 would be much use in a firefight, but it got Harris to back off, so they agreed. They wore small body-cams on their uniforms which would be sent live to *Antares* through the shuttle, and they all had a small earpiece to allow Harris and Michael to talk to them if necessary.

Doctor Soto had done enough research and cultures by now that the SLUGs and isolation suits could be left behind. They'd have to go through an anti-microbial shower when they returned, but beyond that Soto no longer thought the planet was out to kill them. That was a major breakthrough for everyone.

Greg set up his table about ten meters away from where the forest met the beach. He wanted to be close, but still give the Seekers room to observe him from a distance. He placed his stack of prepared words and phrases on the table. Greg set a stack of blank paper to one side with a black marker. Hopefully, the Seeker, or Seekers, would be willing to write their responses. His tablet now contained all the words they had translated, and if the Seekers wrote something, he could scan it and read the translation.

"OK, what now?" Carol asked, sounding a little nervous.

"We wait, Carol, we just wait. We know they're in there, and I believe they know we're here."

Not a hundred meters from where Greg Cordero stood, inside the cave the adult males were hastily putting away their fishing gear and bringing out what few weapons they had left. The scramble in the main part of the cave as the warriors gathered frightened little Ullnii Dagt, and she grasped Eaagher Fita's soft hand tightly.

"Grandfather, I am afraid. What if they are like the others?"

"I do not believe they are, child. "

"I don't like them. Naaron says they're ugly." The grandfather in Eaagher closed his eyes in joy. She was such a delightful, smart child.

"They are likely not so beautiful as you, Ullnii, but they seem very different from those you fear. They are few, not many. They send a message in our language. They do not attack, they wait."

"Naaron says they have dull eyes, like prey. Where did they come from?" His soft words had not assuaged her fear. The warning of the first to see them, her older cousin Naaron, had alarmed the child perhaps more than necessary.

"You have just learned about the stars, Ullnii, and the planets. They have come from somewhere else. I do not know where."

"Will they let us go Home?"

The question pierced the grandfather's heart. He had asked as much of his own grandfather many years before and received no answer.

"It is not up to them to tell us that, Ullnii. We will go Home when we know it is safe."

"Is it true that there are buildings there taller than you are, Grandfather? Have you seen them? And books? Many books?"

"There are such things, girl. You have seen the pictures of them yourself. And yes, there are still many more books there, I believe."

167

He did not mention what time and inattention might have done to those volumes. Better now for her to have hope.

The warriors arrived at his door, weapons ready.

Tuegar Bindir, their captain, called to Eaagher. "They are here, Leader, they wait on the beach."

"Go forward, then, I will be there shortly."

"You should come now," Tuegar complained.

Eaagher drew himself up to his full height. "Tuegar, I said to go forward. I will be there." The warrior waved his left hand and moved out of the cave.

"I must go see them now, Ullnii. I will tell you all about it when I return."

"I will wait for you at the mouth of the cave, Grandfather. I want to hear." He started to lift his right hand but deferred.

"You must be very quiet, and if I call your name, you must run quickly back into the cave. Do you understand?"

Her small left hand came up, and he raised his in answer.

"Now, let us go see if they are friend, or prey, or predator. We know now that there is no other kind."

On the beach, Greg stood patiently at the table, Gabrielle at his right side, the other three officers standing nervously behind, watching the dense forest with its low brush so thick they could not see more than a few meters past the edge. He went back over his instructions to himself: patience, flexibility, acceptance. He had a good idea about this culture, but the distillation of a few dozen books was nothing next to being face to face with a mature adult. Humility, too, would be required, he reminded himself. *Know that you don't know!*

After a few minutes there was movement and eight Seekers appeared, weapons raised. At the first sound, the humans switched on their cameras. Wayne slowly moved his hand to his .45, but otherwise, they gave no reaction. They'd come here to talk, and Gabrielle had emphasized the need to be unthreatening, even at the risk of being threatened themselves.

Carol scanned the faces across from her, seeing now that two were looking directly at her, weapons ready. She, of course, knew about the multi-colored green-and-sky-blue eyes from the portrait, but they were far more vivid in person. They had a luminous quality that reminded her somehow of Inoria. The two watching her locked their eyes on hers, a lock she could only break with focused intention. They weren't looking around at the other humans, the table, or the shuttle. They looked only into her eyes, blinking occasionally. They stood perhaps six feet tall, some a little shorter, their simian-like faces atop a strong neck. Their fur was mostly white, she realized, with splashes of other colors — browns, blacks, greens. Their coat reminded her of a calico cat. Otherwise, they looked as she expected

168

from the skeletons they had found — muscular, bipedal, very human-like in their form, except for the three fingers and six toes.

After a long minute, a ninth individual came forward and stepped two paces in front of the defenders before stopping. He also stood tall, something over six feet, and he first looked Cordero directly in the eye. After a few seconds, he looked directly at each of them in turn and appeared to take notice of Wayne's hand on his holster. Wayne did not miss that, the Seeker's eyes fixed on him. He took his hand off the handle and let it drop to his side.

The Seeker observed this action, then turned to his escorts. He said something in a gruff-sounding, low voice and they also lowered their guns. He approached the table, looked at the shuttle, and then waved his left hand and touched his forehead. Greg pulled out 'No understanding' and showed it to the Seeker as he waved his left hand and touched his forehead.

The Seeker looked at Cordero, looked at the sign, then again at the shuttle. He waved his left hand again, touched his forehead, and spoke several syllables in the same manner as before. Cordero took the 'No Understanding' sign down and then brought it back up, waving his left hand. The Seeker turned to his compatriots and moved his hand in a circle next to his head. The others responded with the same gesture, at the same time making a sound almost like a growl far back in their throats. They then seemed to relax, their bearing less tense than before.

"I think they're laughing at you, Greg," Gabrielle said quietly.

"I'll take laughter. Laughter is good."

The Seeker looked at Greg for another moment, then at the stack of signs on the table. He approached slowly, then touched the stack and his forehead at the same time. Again, Greg waved the 'No Understanding' sign. The Seeker shuffled through the stack, reading each one as he did. He stopped and put aside the 'No' and 'Yes' pages. He looked back up at Cordero, waved his left hand and pointed to 'Yes' with his right. Then, he waved his right hand and pointed to the 'No' sign with his left.

Greg did the same in return, and when he was done, the Seeker waved his left hand, Greg pointed to 'Yes,' and the Seeker waved it again.

"Well, we now have 'yes' and 'no' defined."

Greg pointed to the shuttle and waved his left hand. The Seeker just looked at him.

"I think he's unconvinced."

"Yeah, I think I would be, too, Wayne."

The Seeker looked at the pad of paper and the marker but didn't touch it.

"I'll show you," Greg said to the Seeker. He opened the marker and wrote 'GREG' in large letters. Then, he pointed to the word, spoke it, and then pointed to himself. The Seeker disclosed no emotion but looked at the characters on the page for several seconds. The Seeker pointed to the word and then moved his hand, indicating all the humans present, then touched his forehead.

"No, pal, Greg is just me." Greg mumbled as he waved his right hand, then pointed to his name and then again to himself, repeating "Greg."

"Did you catch the forehead thing?" Carol asked.

"Yeah, maybe means it's a question?"

"So, at the start, he was giving you 'yes' and 'question,' so maybe he was asking if we're really friends?"

"Maybe. Makes sense." Greg laid a blank page on the table and then pointed to the Seeker and touched his own forehead.

"So, who are you?" he said out loud. The Seeker wrote neatly, eight characters. Greg lifted the tablet to scan the word. The Seeker watched his movement intensely but did not flinch or retreat.

Leader.

The next word he wanted was not written out, so he found it on the tablet and showed it to the Seeker while pointing to himself.

"Learner."

The Seeker looked at him again for several seconds, then wrote another word.

Teacher.

Greg smiled at that, saying, "I think I've just been paid a compliment," as he wrote the English word at the bottom of the page. The Seeker studied his face as he did this and then wrote again and touched his forehead.

Happy.

"He's asking if I am happy."

"You smiled."

Greg waved his left hand. The Seeker took another page, wrote, and touched his head.

Past where you child?

"I think he's asking where we're from. What should I tell him?"

Jack leaned forward. "Well, even if they know the Sun as a star, we don't know what they would call it. How about 'far away'?"

"No, I'm going with 'other star.'"

The Seeker looked at those words and then wrote again, touching his forehead.

Past how learn language.

"He's asking how we learned the language."

"Whaddya mean 'we,' Cordero? You're the linguist!" Gabrielle pointed out.

Greg thought this question might come up. He selected 'past study many books' from the stack and showed it to the Seeker.

The Seeker looked at him again, then wrote several words and touched his forehead.

Where exist not friend not prey past kill.

Greg scowled in frustration and picked up the 'No Knowledge' sign. The Seeker wrote one word and pointed to his forehead.

Sad.

"Damn right I am," Greg mumbled as he waved his left hand. Greg took a blank paper and drew a simple picture of their planetary system, with a circle indicating Big Blue's orbit. He pulled out a prepared sign 'past here how many' and touched his forehead. The Seeker looked at the paper, then wrote several numbers. By now Greg could do the base-six conversion in his head.

"Ten years, so, thirty-six solar years?"

"Yes."

Greg typed his next question on the tablet and displayed it for the Seeker.

"Past how you alive here."

Past many dead protect secret.

"He's not telling."

"Can't say I blame him, Jack. I want him to know they're not the only ones."

Greg wrote out "Past others kill many other planet."

The Seeker read that, then re-found and pointed to the 'sad' word. Greg waved his left hand.

The Seeker asked a different question.

Past time you here?

"Past here little time past future return 14 suns learn to understand."

The Seeker carefully watched the exchange between Greg and Wayne. After reading the translation, he pointed to Wayne and lifted the Leader word, touching his forehead.

Greg pulled out the 'friend' word, pointing to himself and the four others.

The Seeker waved his left hand and wrote another question.

Where leader?

"Orbit."

Talk Leader?

"Future. Learn speak first."

The Seeker waved his left hand, then laughter again. Greg pulled the Happy sign then touched his forehead and waved his hand around like the Seeker had just done.

The Seeker waved his left hand. *Yes.*

He then wrote several words and laid the page on the table for Greg to scan.

Past hard faces not friend not prey kill many.

"Not friend not prey?" Wayne asked, looking over Greg's shoulder.

"Yeah, he used that phrase before. You know, we've not seen a word for 'enemy.' Maybe that's what he's expressing."

Greg typed 'hard faces' and touched his forehead.

The Seeker wrote quickly. *Hard faces past come kill many.*

Greg repeated his question. Maybe on the second try, the Seeker would get it.

Hard faces sharp mouths not like you. Not like us. Want we work we extreme respect we obey.

"Well, that's interesting. Sharp mouth?" Gabrielle wondered.

"'Sharp' in Seekerish only means physically sharp, like a knife. It doesn't mean smart or anything else like it can in English."

The Seeker heard this exchange and pointed to the 'knowledge' sign and touched his forehead.

"No, I don't know who they are," Greg said aloud as he waved his right hand.

Afraid?

Greg waved his left hand. "Yes, we're afraid."

Wise.

Greg reread the last part of the Seeker's response. "Extreme Respect?" He pointed to it and touched his forehead.

Many die we past not understand. Not friend not prey kill.

He continued to write as Greg read the lines.

Not friend not prey leave future past return many. Past future kill.

Carol thought about what that might mean. "Leave future past — they left and then came back to kill them?"

"That's my reading. I wonder if they have a picture of the hard faces." He pointed to an image in his dictionary, then to the 'hard faces' words, and touched his forehead. The Seeker considered this for a moment and wrote.

Picture.

"OK, I guess I missed that one." Greg wrote, "Past picture hard faces."

No.

"No pictures. That would have been helpful." Jack said quietly.

Sad? The Seeker was looking at Jack now. He dutifully waved his left hand.

Hard faces future return?

"There's a hard question to answer. What should I tell him?"

"The truth," Carol said forcefully.

Greg nodded and pointed to the 'no knowledge' sign.

The Seeker went back to a previous question.

Talk Leader?

"He wants to talk to our Leader. Admiral, what would you like me to tell him?"

Harris' voice came through clearly in their ears. "Go ahead and tell him I can see and hear him now."

"How am I supposed to tell him that?" Cordero asked, annoyed.

The Seeker watched him carefully. This was the most emotion he had heard in a human voice.

"OK, let's try this." Greg pointed to the camera on his shirt.

"Leader see and hear with this machine."

The Seeker looked at the camera, then back at the others and the shuttle.

Truth?

Greg waved his left hand, looking the Seeker in the eye the whole time. The Seeker pulled an old page from the stack and touched his forehead.

Afraid?

Greg waved his right hand, then wrote: "Leader send learner to understand first."

Again, the Seeker pulled a page.

Wise.

"He thinks you're wise, Admiral."

"He's an unusually smart person. Tell him we sympathize with his people. Ask him if there is anything we can give him."

Greg flipped through the words, finally crafting, "We know past bad events hurt."

The Seeker waved his left hand in understanding as Greg kept working.

"We offer now help what now need?"

The Seeker shook his right hand and wrote.

Now need nothing. Future desire home future safe.

"They just want to know it's safe to go home, sir." Greg then typed out, "We also future desire you home safe."

You past see home?

"Yes."

Home now exists whole and safe?

Greg pointed to the 'whole' word and shook his left hand for 'yes.' Then, he pointed to 'safe' and touched the 'No Knowledge' sheet again.

Sad.

As this exchange was going on a small Seeker came out from the brush and stood behind the Leader. It was smaller, perhaps half the Leader's height, and delicate in stature. The Leader spoke to it.

"Ullnii, you were to remain at the entrance."

"I hear their voices, Grandfather. They are almost like music. They do not sound like the hard faces."

"No, they do not. I believe they are good, Ullnii, but you should have remained where I told you to stay."

"Sounds a little like Kalmyk...I don't hear any tones..." Greg said to himself as he listened to the quiet exchange between them.

The Leader looked back at Greg and the rest, who were now looking at the small Seeker. He picked up the marker and wrote.

My male child female child.

"That's his granddaughter," Greg said quietly. Carol walked around the table and knelt before what she now understood was a little girl.

"What is it doing, Grandfather?"

"I think this one is a female, Ullnii. She and the shorter one are different than the others. She has a different shape, and the tone of her voice is different."

Carol extended her hand to the little girl, flat and open, as an invitation.

"Greg, tell her that I would like to know her name."

Greg typed "child name" and touched his forehead.

"She wants to know your name. Shall I tell them?"

"Yes, tell them."

"Would you prefer to tell her yourself?"

"No."

"Ullnii," said the grandfather, slowly and carefully so that the humans could hear.

Carol nodded and repeated, "Ullnii." The child raised her left hand and shook it.

Carol pointed to herself and said, "Carol."

The child turned to speak to her grandfather.

"Does it mean itself, or all of them?"

"They have names just as we do, Ullnii. This one," he said, pointing to Greg, *"is called 'Greg.' She is telling you her name."*

"It sounds very strange to my ears. I don't know if I can say it."

"Try. Don't talk about them as if they were prey, Ullnii. They are friends. They are like us."

Carol waited out the conversation. Hearing something that sounded like Greg's name come from the Seeker was strange.

"Callal," the child said finally.

"Pretty close," Carol said, smiling, then she repeated her name more slowly, "Carol."

174

"Callol," the child tried again. Carol nodded without thinking, then raised her left hand. The child stepped forward and took her outstretched hand. The palm was soft, and the dark tan skin was bare of fur. It was not at all like a feline paw, which was what Carol expected. The fur was fine and soft on the back of the child's fingers, then longer and thicker on her extremities. Her grip on Carol's had was firm and warm, but restrained, as if the child knew she could hurt Carol if she squeezed too hard.

"Her hands are warm, Grandfather, like yours."
"Yes, Ullnii."
"I like her, Grandfather. But she still has dull eyes."
"Yes, Ullnii, I think I like her, too. Not everyone can have eyes as beautiful as yours."

Greg picked up the child's name as the Leader spoke. Later, he thought, maybe we can parse out the sounds.
"We have to think about getting back," Wayne said. "The longer we're here, the more chance we have to be observed."
Ullnii moved close to Carol, then sat on the beach next to her. She drew Carol's arm around herself and leaned against her. Carol held the child gently, looking up at the grandfather.
"Tell him, Greg, tell him I am... honored, if there is such a word...that she would come and sit with me this way."
"I don't know, Carol. How about I just tell him you're happy?"
"Close enough."
The Seeker, as careful an observer of behavior as any of the humans present, was not surprised when Greg pointed to Carol, then to the 'happy' sign.
"We still need to get back!" Wayne repeated.
Greg typed, "Must now leave. We short future go home. We future return."
The Seeker waved his left hand, then wrote.
New friends welcome future return.
Then he wrote *New friends future help go home* and touched his forehead.
Greg looked at the words with some sadness. "Admiral, he wants to know if we can help them go back home."
"I can't promise that. Tell him we will try."
Greg found the words "Hope future try help. Now must find hard faces."
The Seeker understood that.
Greg had one last question. He pointed to himself and said, 'Greg,' then pointed to Carol and said, 'Carol.' Then he pointed to the Seeker and touched his forehead.
"Eaagher."

"Eaagher," Greg repeated, and the Seeker raised his left hand.

"They are leaving, Ullnii. They must go home to their own world."
"What about the hard faces?"
"They are looking for the hard faces, I think to fight them."
"As my great-grandfather did?"
"Yes, Ullnii, as he did. But they are strong. Stronger, I think, than the hard faces. It is time to go."

Greg picked up the word signs he had made, but instead of packing them away as he had planned, he handed them over to Eaagher. If someone else came here, those might come in handy.

Eaagher seemed to understand, waved his left hand, and stepped back from the table. Ullnii gently pulled away from Carol to stand with him. They turned and walked back through the brush to the cave entrance. After a moment, the eight guards also filed back down the hidden path and were gone.

The humans stood for a long moment, in awe of what had just happened. Finally, they picked up the rest of their gear and walked to the shuttle.

"I will never see this place the same again," Carol said as she strapped into the co-pilot seat.

Jack, sitting left-seat for the return trip, nodded his agreement.

"None of us will, Carol. This is not just a planet anymore, it's the home of people we know."

Checklist complete, Jack pulled the door closed, and the shuttle rose silently away from the beach, climbing rapidly on its course back to *Antares*. No one spoke until they were back aboard and had cleared the decontamination facility.

Before dinner in the wardroom, Carol took a few minutes in her quarters. She thought about how the day had gone, the sound of Ullnii's voice, how she related to her grandfather, so much like a human relationship. After a moment, she pulled out her journal and picked up a pen.

David —

You would have been proud of me today. We met the Seekers face to face and they were as we'd hoped. Cordero is a confirmed genius, by the way. How he and the Seeker leader held a conversation starting from zero was something incredible to watch. I guess maybe when you really want to have a conversation, you'll figure out how?

There was a child at the meeting — a little girl. The leader's granddaughter, Ullnii. She was strangely strong but still so innocent and vulnerable. Sooo beautiful — I got a good pic off my body cam feed I'll show you when you read this.

I talked to her — best I could — and it was such an emotional experience. How do we connect so easily with a species so different? Something transcendent about it.

Will we have a little girl someday? If we do, I want her to know Ullnii. Something very beautiful about her.

Love always,
Carol

Antares
Big Blue
Wednesday, October 19, 2078, 0930 UTC

The contact team spent an hour reviewing the meeting with the Seekers. They began by replaying Greg's body-cam footage.

Ron Harris had been quiet throughout the conversation. "Is there something we can give them? Is there a...a... gift we could leave with them?"

"What did you have in mind?" Terri Michael asked.

"I don't know...just something to help them out somehow."

"The best thing we could give them," said Jack, "would be a SLIP transmitter. If they could somehow contact us if the 'hard faces' come back, that would be good."

"Yeah, but we don't have a portable SLIP system. Maybe someday," Comm officer Lori Rodgers said sadly.

Carol drummed her fingers on the table. "You know, it's a long shot, but if we could give them a hand-held radio, then put a Sentinel in orbit with the right alert criteria. That would do the same thing..."

"Ohh, not bad, Hansen, not bad at all," Kathy Stewart commented.

"But that presumes we can get a Sentinel here."

"Not a problem," Harris said easily. "But it'll take time."

"We'd need a hand-held that would be easy for them to use. Plus, we would not be able to understand them."

"Well, we might be able to manage that."

"How, Greg, would we do that?" Terri asked.

"Let's get Eaagher to read us some words. Something like 'need help' or 'hard faces' or whatever."

"Hmmm..." Harris sounded skeptical.

"Or give him a list of numbered messages, and all he has to do is say the numbers."

Kathy's initial enthusiasm was fading. "I think this *could* work, but it's an awfully complicated solution. How is he going to keep the handheld powered? When will the Sentinel be in a position to hear him? There's a lot of questions we can't answer right now."

Carol rejoined the conversation. "I agree with Kathy that this is all a little premature. It makes no sense to give them a handheld unless there's a Sentinel in orbit to listen for it." She paused for a second. "I still think another visit to tell them we're leaving would be good. And we can tell them that others might be coming, and later we'll give them a way to call us."

"What about giving him a book?" Gabrielle asked.

"A book?" Terri responded, skeptical.

"Sure. We learned all about them from their books. Is there something in the ship's library that we could print out — a real, physical copy — and leave with him?"

"Well," James George offered, "we have the whole digitized Library of Congress aboard. We should be able to find something."

"What would you want to show them?" Harris asked.

"Nothing political, nothing historical, just us, our planet maybe, the animals on our world, that kind of thing."

"Hmmm. I like it," Carol said. "But there's something else."

"Yes?" Terri asked, inviting her subordinate to continue.

"I think we should go back, and maybe some of us from the first trip should go, so they recognize us."

"Oh," Terri asked, curious, "and who else would you take?"

"Except for Greg, the rest of us who went are all the same, Commander - white kids. I didn't think about it until just now when Gabe brought up the picture book. If we go back, I'd like to also take XO George and someone like my tech Fujimoto Yui."

"A racially diverse group?" Harris asked.

"Yes, sir. We need to show them that there is a wide variation in our appearance. If Commander George were to appear on that beach unannounced, I can't be sure they'd understand he's one of us!"

XO George shifted in his seat. "An interesting thought, Lieutenant. I never wanted to be the token but, in this case, I think what you say makes sense. If they are as homogeneous as they seem, the concept of a wide variety in physical appearance within a species would not be part of their experience."

"I agree, it's a demonstration we should probably make," Harris said.

"OK, so," Terri spoke in her best 'time to wrap this up' tone, "Tomorrow at the expected time we'll visit the Seekers again, as Carol has described. Gabe, I will leave it to you and the rest of the surface team to find an appropriate book to take to them. I would think some kind of children's book would work. Greg, you may want to add some annotations in their language to help them along."

"Yes, Captain, good idea."

"Very well. We're adjourned."

Central Council Chamber
The Preeminent Home World
Earth Equivalent Date: October 24, 2078

The Revered First stood at the narrow end of the long Council table. The reports from the monitoring station on the moon in the scholars' System 849 lay on the table. His eyes moved from side to side, moving around the table, reflecting his irritation with the current situation.

"The Vermin have found System 849."

"Yes, Revered First," Jaf Seen Toft, the Respected Second, said quietly.

"And yet we have not found where these despicables come from?"

"We have not, Revered First."

"Are we not the Preeminent?"

"We are, Revered First," they all said in unison.

"The monitor reports that they landed and walked the ground where those clueless scholars lived."

"Yes, Revered First."

They waited in fear as the Revered First looked around the table at his counselors. His eye finally came to rest on one near the far end of the table, one who seemed to be leaning back, almost to conceal himself from The First's view behind the others.

"Ashil Kiker, it was you who found such fault with Hess Tse Sim. Take a quarter cohort and go see what these disgusting creatures have found."

"Yes, Revered First. We will see what they saw, and we will prevail."

"We are the Preeminent," the First repeated.

"We are the Preeminent," they echoed.

Kiker was one who rose from obscurity through careful political maneuvering, not through conquest. Nevertheless, he was confident that he could easily crush any feeble opposition from this new invasive species in their small, dark ships. They had a sting, that much he knew, but they were only small insects to be eradicated. An inconvenience, no more.

System 849 was nearby; they would be there in twenty rotations.

Antares
Big Blue
Tuesday, October 25, 2078, 0830 UTC

Once again, Carol set the shuttle down on the wide beach. After a few moments finishing the post-landing checklist, she got out and followed Admiral Harris, Greg, Gabe, and James George to the point where Eaagher had talked to them. Weapons Technician Yui followed her, feeling some uncertainty, as meeting with aliens was not part of her usual job description.

"CALLOL!" she heard a small voice call, followed quickly by its owner bursting out of the brush. She stopped when she saw the others with Carol. She looked at Greg, and spoke a decent version of 'Greg,' but she was surprised at the others.

She finally came to Carol and reached out her hand. Carol took it, and Ullnii led her along the beach. Carol went along, uncertain of what Ullnii had in mind since they could not hold a conversation about anything beyond their names.

Eaagher appeared shortly after Ullnii, carrying the word signs.

"Greg," he managed.

"Eaagher," Greg responded.

Eaagher looked at the others with Greg and touched his forehead.

Greg pulled the 'friends' sign and showed it to Eaagher. He didn't say yes, or no, but looked at Yui and XO George. Finally, he wrote: *Different.*

"He gets it, sir. He understands." Greg waved his hand at all of them, then again held up 'Friends.'

Eaagher waved his left hand. Ron Harris came to stand next to Greg.

"Eaagher," he said, then pointed to himself and said, "Ron."

"Ron."

Greg picked the 'Leader' word and showed it to Eaagher, who waved his left hand and touched his forehead.

"What was that?" Ron asked.

"I take it like we would say 'really?' or 'is that so?' — that kind of thing."

Ron waved his left hand. "Yes, really."

Eaagher wrote *Wise leader past send good teacher first. Respect welcome friend leader.*

"I want to say 'thank you' but is that a concept they understand?"

"Not really, sir, that I can see. Just respond with a 'yes.'"

Ron waved his left hand, which Eaagher returned. Eaagher looked at James George, said 'Eaagher' and touched his forehead.

'James," he said.

"Yamz," Eaagher replied.

180

"James," XO George said again, more slowly.

"Yames," Eaagher tried again, then wrote, *Friend names hard speak.*

Then he wrote again, *Friends look different all same?*

Greg waved his left hand, then wrote: "Friends home world many more numbers. Much difference in appearance still all Friends."

Eaagher read that, then wrote again, *What Friends name selves?*

"What do you think, sir? Human? Terran? People? Earthlings?"

Fujimoto Yui laughed at the question. Eaagher looked at her, circled his hand next to his head and then touched his forehead.

"What was that? What did I do?" she asked, suddenly a little alarmed.

"You laughed. When we were here before, we thought that hand movement was laughter. Tell him yes."

"Yes?"

"Yeah, lift your left hand and wave it a little."

Harris leaned in to speak quietly to Cordero. "Go with human, Greg."

"Human," Greg said, looking at Eaagher.

"Oomahn," Eaagher said.

"Close enough."

As they finished, Carol and Ullnii came walking back to the group.

"So, Greg, you should spend more time with Ullnii. Her name means 'sky', by the way." Hansen had that sly smile on that told everyone she'd found something interesting.

"Oh, and what else?" Harris asked.

"Sand is 'deez.' The beach is 'lideez.' Water is 'kel.'"

"And so ocean is...'likel'?"

"Yup."

"That follows what I see in the written language — pretty regular suffixes and prefixes, but I couldn't know what they sound like."

Eaagher followed much of this exchange, then spoke to Ullnii.

"I hear her speaking our language, Ullnii. Did Callol tell you their words for these things?"

"Yes, Grandfather."

"Show me!"

The girl pointed to the sky and said 'sky' so clear that the humans' heads snapped around as one. She picked up a handful of sand and said, 'Sandh.' She pointed to the beach and said, 'beachk.' Finally, she looked at the ocean and said, 'uceeanh.'

"Amazing," Greg said quietly, then started typing out a new message for Eaagher.

181

"We must go home short future. We bring a gift."

Eaagher waited as Harris drew the book from his backpack and handed it to Eaagher.

"Simple book to help learn Friends world," Greg typed.

Eaagher opened the book, looking first at the paper, thinner and whiter than he was used to. It was a children's picture book, a first dictionary of sorts, with many different people, places, and animals. Where he could find correlations, Greg had added the Seekerish word to the page. He also added simple explanations where he could work them out.

Eaagher knelt down and looked at the first few pages with Ullnii. He rose and wrote, *Will study Friends book.*

Greg typed out "Simple child book to start. Future learn more together."

Yes.

Greg kept typing. "Future bring device to call Friends."

Long future?

"Yes. thirty suns possibly more."

Sad.

"Time to go, Greg," Carol said.

He turned to her abruptly. "I'm getting really tired of hearing that sentence, Carol."

"I know, Greg, I know. Me, too."

Greg looked at her for another second, then turned back to Eaagher, who was writing. *Friends future come when?*

"I don't know, Eaagher." He said out loud as he typed "No knowledge," then "Hope short future but more than thirty suns."

Eaagher waved his left hand, then turned and walked with Ullnii back to the cave.

It was a somber Bridge as Terri Michael gave the command to turn the ship towards home. They were at the limit of their supplies, and for only a three-week visit, they'd made incredible progress. Greg's translation engine kept digging at the language, picking out a few new meanings every day. Joe Bowles was mapping the battlefield in precise detail, his attention more focused, more immediate, knowing now that there were survivors to defend. Gabe looked at her results, the complex, rich culture they had before the enemy appeared. They could rebuild it, she knew. Everything was there for them, they just needed to know it was safe.

ISC Fleet HQ Intel Section
Ft. Eustis, VA
Thursday, October 26, 2078, 0830 EDT (1230 UTC)

Don Curtis had the TDOA review task this morning, Frances Wilson taking a rare day off with her husband. Kristin Hayes sat nearby, looking through the computer analysis of the message patterns of the last few days. The alarm turned both their heads to the display.

"Beta Hydri?" Don said quietly. He dug into the details of the intercept, looking at the signal quality and the stations that had reported it. It was a solid report, no question about what or where.

"When?" Kristin asked.

"1433 on the twenty-second."

"But *Antares* would have still been there."

"Yes. But they should have left yesterday."

Roger Cox came into the office. "Did you see the Beta Hydri hit?"

"Yes, just talking about it." Kristin answered.

"Well, it's strange we haven't heard from *Antares*. If they'd seen anything, we should have heard from them by now."

Don nodded. "So, perhaps they didn't see anything?"

Roger scowled, "Or they're all dead."

"Now, Roger," Kristin said quietly. "Let's not get ahead of ourselves."

"We need to push this up the chain. This might mean *Antares* was observed. Whatever, I don't like it."

They went to Elias Peña, who took them to Chief of Operations Patty Cook, who then pulled in CINC Admiral Connor Davenport.

Their conversation was short and pointed.

"*Antares* should have left," Cook declared, "but we don't know that she did, and she won't be calling in for at least a week. I want you to tell them, just in case."

"They may not respond," Elias pointed out.

"Maybe not. Send it anyway."

```
FLASH 207810261400UTC
TO: ANTARES
FROM: FLEETINTEL

HIGH CONFIDENCE SLIP INTERCEPT ORIGINATING 207810221423UTC INDICATES
ENEMY PRESENCE BETA HYDRI.

PENA

END
```

The message sent, Elias got up from his desk and walked to Kristin and Don's small space, leaning against the door jamb.

"Done?" Kristin asked, looking up.

"Yes. I'm not sure what good it will do them. If the enemy's already active there, the message may be moot, or, at least, anti-climactic."

"I take it *Antares* doesn't have a SLIP scanner?"

Elias shook his head. "No. They're putting one in *Intrepid* while she's here, so that's hopeful."

"*Canberra* got one before she left for Inor?"

"Yes."

"Well, that's something..."

Elias was unsatisfied. "Something, sure, but I am not sure it's enough. The SLIP delays, the time to travel, it's like fighting a war in neck-deep molasses. I know right now that *Antares* might be in serious danger, but I can't get the word to them fast enough to be of any help."

As always, they had done everything they could. And, as always, they had a nagging feeling it somehow wasn't enough.

Antares
Enroute Earth
Tuesday, October 27, 2078, 1600 UTC

Antares left Beta Hydri on schedule, 1200 UTC on October 25. That was the mandate they'd been given, and Harris and Michael had agreed to stick to it despite their remarkable discoveries. The message from FleetIntel that there was an enemy presence at Big Blue came as a shock to them all.

"We need to go back."

"No, Jack," Terri Michael insisted. "We're low on consumables, and we're already two days away."

"I'm not sure going back would be a good idea, Jack," Ron Harris said. "If the enemy is watching somehow, coming back might just draw more attention."

"Fleet doesn't know about the Seekers," Carol pointed out. "We need to tell them so we can get someone out there to cover the planet. If the enemy finds the survivors..." Her thought drew nods around the table.

Greg Cordero shook his head sadly. "God help us if we led those bastards back to these people."

"Yes, Greg, I agree. Our worst nightmare," Carol responded, her face reflecting her pain.

"I guess we better tell them," Jack said quietly.

"We'll be breaking our EMR routine, but I agree we need to let Fleet know what's at stake."

Terri Michael nodded her agreement with Ron. "OK, I'll get it sent right away."

```
FLASH 207810271610UTC
TO: FLEETINTEL, FLEETOPS, CINCFLEET
FROM: ANTARES

ANTARES INITIATED RTB EARTH 207810251200UTC AS PLANNED.
FULL EXPLANATION TO FOLLOW BUT MUST INFORM YOU SOONEST THAT
THERE ARE AT LEAST HUNDREDS OF SURVIVORS OF THE BH CULTURE - WHICH
WE NOW CALL 'SEEKERS' - ON THE EAST COAST OF THE SECOND CONTINENT
IN THE NORTHERN HEMISPHERE.
STRONGLY RECOMMEND YOU DISPATCH WARSHIP TO COVER THE PLANET IN
CASE ENEMY RETURNS.
DEEP FEAR HERE THAT OUR EXPLORATIONS MAY HAVE PUT SEEKERS AT NEW RISK.
RECOMMEND DEPLOY SENTINEL IN ORBIT THEN PROVIDE RADIO SO
SEEKERS CAN CALL IF ATTACKED.

MICHAEL/HARRIS

END
```

ISC Fleet HQ Operations Section
Ft. Eustis, VA
Monday, October 28, 2078, 0915 EDT

Chief of Operations Admiral Patricia Cook read the message from *Antares* four times, making sure she was really seeing what she was seeing. CINCFLEET Connor Davenport sat across from her, with Fiona Collins of Plans and Elias Peña alongside.

"I can hardly believe it," she said quietly.

"How does she know what to call them?" Fiona asked.

"We sent an expert on lost languages. Seems like maybe he found enough to understand them," Elias commented.

"What are we going to do?" Davenport asked.

Patty looked at her fleet status. "*Intrepid* is here, they'll be back from leave in three or four days."

"But Patty, do we really want to send them back out on another long trip?" As CINC, Davenport had always placed a high priority on crew rest and avoided any order he felt placed an undue or repetitive burden on a ship.

Cook knew what he was thinking. "Sir, they're what we have on hand. Besides, Joanne and her crew are who I'd pick anyway."

Elias sat up as he spoke. "They'll need ground troops, too. We sent Terri Michael with three squads. I think we need to give *Intrepid* more firepower."

Cook nodded. "Agreed, I'll find her a rifle platoon. She can't carry much more than that."

"We have a Sentinel we can send?" Fiona asked Elias.

"Yes. There's several in the supply depot waiting for delivery. I'll get Ann on the programming."

"What's this radio thing?" Davenport asked.

"Oh, I get that, sir," Elias answered. "If we give them a handheld transceiver, and set the Sentinel to alarm if it sees a signal on whatever frequency we pick, all the Seekers would have to do is click the transmit button."

"Assuming the Sentinel is in view," Cook pointed out.

"Yes, Admiral, very true. I'll get Ann and her team on how to solve that."

"I want them underway in three days. Get the Marine racks and other materials they need up there and get an engineering crew on it."

"Yes, Admiral, I'll get that moving."

"Get a Sentinel back from the Depot and get Ann Cooper and whoever she needs up to *Intrepid* to program it."

"Yes, sir, I'll get with her right away," Elias responded.

Davenport stood up and turned back to his Chief of Operations, who was taking rapid notes on her tablet. "Call Henderson. Let her know what's up and get her back here."

"Yes, sir, I will."

CINCFLEET turned and walked out of the room as Admiral Cook picked up her phone to arrange for a shuttle to fetch Joanne Henderson. She didn't even notice Elias and Fiona as they left the room.

Elias Peña went back to the main Intel workroom.

"Ann!"

"Sir?"

"Get Scott and Kelly and find a small room." He turned without waiting for an answer and went to Rich Evans' office. He just put the tablet with the message on his desk.

"Good Christ, man, what the hell is Harris thinking?"

"He's suddenly got people to defend, Rich. This is him."

"So...what now?"

"Let's go put Ann and her crew on it."

They went to the same small workroom where Ann and her team had invented the Sentinel. The three young officers looked at their superiors with a mixture of dread, anticipation, and excitement.

Elias made it hard and quick. "*Antares* has found survivors on Beta Hydri. Meantime, there's been a TDOA hit from there." He handed the tablet around, Ann taking the last look.

"OK, sir, so you need us to figure out how to do this last little bit?"

"Yes." Only Ann Cooper could describe the deployment of a Sentinel and all the associated work as a 'bit.'

"Give us an hour, sir."

"You can have until lunch."

"We won't need it." She turned to her team, "Scott, get the Big Blue system up on the display. Kelly, take a look at the UHF handheld transceiver specs. I'll go back over the Sentinel navigation system." The three began digging through the data they needed to absorb, and much like Ops, they failed to notice when their two Lieutenant Commanders slipped out of the room.

Within a few minutes, the digital dry-erase board was showing images of the Beta Hydri system, with numbers, circles, and arrows here and there. An hour later, the board was cleared and replaced with a neater table of numbers and ideas. Ann, seated on the front table sipping her usual diet cola, started to close up the discussion.

"OK, first, we'll use the UHF emergency frequency, 243 MHZ. That's a preset so all the Seeker would need to know is to push the right preset, then use the push-to-talk button to communicate."

"And, turn it on."

"Duh, yeah, let's not miss that in the procedure, OK?"

Scott nodded. "Right, nice and simple. And, it doesn't matter what they say, they just need to talk."

Kelly looked up from her tablet. "We put the Sentinel in synchronous orbit over the second continent?"

"No," Ann responded, "Too obvious."

"We can't put it over the old town — it would not be above the horizon where the survivors are."

Ann smiled. "No, but we could split the difference a little, right? If the Sentinel is even fifteen degrees above the horizon, it'll have no problems hearing the signal."

Scott nodded. "Cool. What about navigation?"

"Should be no problem. We designed it to lock onto three guide stars and orbit another. This is a little different, but the nav logic can handle it."

Ann looked at her team for a few seconds. "OK, Let's go see Peña."

"You better call Stan first," Scott told her as they stood up to leave the room. "Stan? Why?"

"'Cause I think you're going to Beta Hydri in, like, three days."

"Huh. I hadn't thought of that."

"Go call — Peña can wait fifteen minutes."

"Fifteen? Wishful thinking."

"Nah, won't take you even ten."

Ann smiled as she retreated to her office to make the call.

It took only five.

November 2078

ISC Fleet HQ Intel Section
Ft. Eustis, VA
Tuesday, November 1, 2078, 0730 EST (1130 UTC)

Lieutenant Commander Elias Peña read the dispatch with satisfaction. It was the news he'd been waiting for ever since *Chaffee* left.

```
PRIORITY 207810301200UTC
TO: FLEETINTEL
CC: CINCFLEET FLEETOPS
FROM: CHAFFEE


CHAFFEE UNDETECTED THROUGHOUT.
ENEMY STATION IDENTIFIED NEAR EXPECTED POSITION AS FACILITY
SIX KM LONG.
IMAGES SHOW LARGE (500M) SPHERICAL STRUCTURES ASSESSED
AS H2 AND O2 TANKS.
FOUR TYPE I TWO TYPE III ENEMY SHIPS OBSERVED DOCKED.
ONE TYPE I OBSERVED TO ARRIVE THEN LEAVE EIGHTEEN HOURS LATER.
RADIO SIGNAL CONTINUOUS WAVE 180 MHZ DETECTED WHICH INTEL
BELIEVES IS PROBABLE RADAR/INTRUSION DETECTOR.

END
```

Six kilometers? Was there anything these creeps couldn't build? Harris would be back in a week. Peña forwarded the message to *Antares* so Harris would have it in advance of his return. Peña had previously sent Harris notice of *Chaffee*'s mission, but with *Antares* running silent, Harris could neither agree nor object. But Elias was confident the boss would support his decision. Certainly, Plans and Ops thought it was a worthwhile project.

The outcome seemed to confirm that opinion.

Intrepid
Earth Orbit
Friday, November 1, 2078, 1230 UTC

The wide beach on the south shore of Fiji seemed a long way away to Joanne. Just seventy-two hours ago she'd been waking to the sound of breaking surf, soaking up the sun, sipping fruity cocktails she'd never order anywhere else, and enjoying her home planet in complete solitude and anonymity. No uniform, no NetLink, no weight of command, no war; just the rumble of the ocean and the quiet of her own thoughts.

189

Then came the call from Cook and the scramble that followed to pack and be ready for pickup in ninety minutes. The Fleet shuttle landing on the beach made quite a show, and the other guests were left wondering who that woman in Hut Six had been, after all. *She seemed so normal, like a regular person,* they said to each other.

Now, here she stood on the second-lowest level of *Intrepid* watching the closing scenes of the construction of a bunk area for nearly fifty Marines. Joanne's ship would be carrying more than twice the additional load that had been put on *Antares*, which meant that much more work for the engineers. There was plenty of space, really, but Joanne was still concerned about getting the job done and getting underway on schedule.

She'd just come from the very cold and somewhat dark communications equipment room, a place not far forward of the reactor, where the Fleet Engineers were completing the installation of a SLIP Scanner. They would now be able to know if the enemy was transmitting, and might possibly contribute to a TDOA solution if they happened to be in the right place at the right time. That seemed unlikely to Joanne, but she'd gladly accept the additional capabilities. Who knows, it might save their collective hides someday.

Weapons Maintenance Officer Natalie Hayden disrupted her worried face as she appeared in the former storage area.

"Load complete?" Joanne asked her.

"Yes, ma'am, all done. Forty-eight Bludgeons, twenty-four Lances, seventy-two Spartans."

"Good. What about the Marines?"

"Due in a few hours. The ammo and weapons lockers are complete downstairs. My guys will build the rifle range on the way."

"OK, works for me. Ben?"

"Came aboard with me. He's head-down in the reports from *Antares*."

"Is the Sentinel aboard?"

"Yes, about an hour ago. Lieutenant Cooper is here as well. She'll be doing the programming on the way."

"She's really great, Natalie. The Sentinel was her idea. You should get to know her while you have a chance."

"Yes, I'll try to make her welcome."

"Good. She knows Price pretty well, so that's an 'in' for you."

"Yes, Captain."

Joanne expected Natalie to excuse herself, but she hesitated, looking a little uncomfortable to Joanne's eye.

"Something else?" Joanne asked with a wry smile.

"About Price and me, ma'am..."

"Yes?"

"We're here to do our jobs, Captain. We know that comes first."

"I expected no less from either of you, *Lieutenant* Hayden."

"Yes, ma'am."

"And don't *worry* about it, Natalie," Joanne said more closely, taking Natalie's arm and giving it a gentle shake. "You're not the only pair on the ship. You know the rules, you'll be fine. Just don't forget I have my job to do as well."

"Yes, ma'am."

"OK, good. Carry on."

Natalie took her dismissal with good humor and headed back to her magazine. They'd taken on a full weapons load, every spot in every rack filled with lethal potential. She wished she could stuff a few more in the empty spaces below, but that wasn't the Fleet way. If they did run into any trouble, she was confident it would be the trouble that would be sorry.

As Natalie was climbing out, Navigator Larry Covington and FPI Engineer Pope were waiting to come down the access ladder.

"You sent for us, Captain?"

"Yes, Lieutenant Covington, I did. Ms. Pope, I need all the speed I can get all the way to Beta Hydri. Can we squeeze anything more out of the Drive?'

"We do 1.05 routinely, Captain, as you know. I can give you 1.1 for a while, but I will have to keep an eye on the Drive internals. I might have to take some of that back."

Joanne thought for a second and decided to push the FPI Rep as far as she could. She needed the speed.

"Any chance we could go any faster? We don't know what's going on and we need to get there as soon as we possibly can."

Pope looked at her for a moment. "Not with this version of the Drive, Captain. I'm stretching it as it is."

"Fair enough." She turned to Covington, "Larry, we'll be leaving as soon as we get the Marines on board. Be ready."

"Yes, ma'am, the navigation is already programmed. We can go at any time."

"Very well, and thanks. I appreciate it."

Covington and Pope were about halfway up the ladder when Joanne took a call from her Logistics Officer, reporting that the additional food and other consumables were on board. They were ready for a hundred days, Ensign Cantrell told her. *A hundred days!* she thought. *He said it like it was normal!* She took a final look around, spoke briefly with the construction chief, and climbed up two levels to the main deck.

Ben Price was reading the *Antares* reports for the third time, trying to get his head around what was in front of him. The first alarming message from *Antares* had been followed up the next day with a lengthy report of where and how they had found the Seekers. Cordero also reported that he'd left the word signs he'd created with the Seekers, just in case someone else had to talk to them. He'd also left the tablet with the translation software. According to Cordero, all you had to do was land on the right beach and call Eaagher's name. Ben was skeptical how well he could pull that off, but if they were going to get the radio to Eaagher, he'd have to manage somehow.

He looked up in surprise as Joanne came in, closed his office door, and dropped into the chair across from him. She looked a little thinner, her hair was shorter and combed back, and she'd clearly picked up some color on her face and hands.

"You got some sun," he observed.

"Yeah, two weeks in Fiji will do that for you."

"Nice. Got a haircut, too."

"You approve?"

"Not my place to approve, but you'd be insulted if I didn't notice."

"Sometimes I forget you were married."

"Yes, dear."

She looked at him for a few seconds, waiting for his eyes to meet hers. "How are you, Ben? How are you, really?"

Ben leaned back from the *Antares* reports and looked back at her, a wide smile on his face.

"I'm better now, right this moment, Joanne, then I have ever been since you've known me."

She nodded and gave up a small smile. "Good, very good." The smile quickly faded. "It might get dangerous out here this time, Ben. We won't be sneaking around."

"You say that like it's a bad thing." He pointed to the reports on his desk. "If this culture is one-tenth what Jack Ballard says it is, we *have* to stand up for them."

"I'm more worried about *our* species, Ben, and more specifically, *this ship.*"

"I understand that, Joanne. But this is a good mission. If those bastards come out on the surface, with this many Marines, we could have some serious fun."

Joanne wasn't so sure it would be 'fun,' but she understood the feeling. They had been chasing the mystery too long, the enemy frustrating all attempts to get at them, and it was time to get some answers. Their last mission, zipping silently around a significant portion of the local universe dropping spy-bots, was necessary but frustrating to the crew's appetite for more direct action.

She decided to change the subject.

"So, it goes well with Natalie?"

Ben looked away for a moment, then nodded. "I have you to thank for that, Joanne. If you hadn't asked me to come along, I'd never have met her."

Joanne shook her head. "No, you have only *yourself* to thank. I put you here, but you put yourself in that relationship."

"We've spent a lot of time together these last three weeks, that's for sure. But she also went home to Bozeman for several days to see her folks, and I had some time to get up into the mountains by myself. It was good."

"Did you get back to *your* mountain?"

"Sugarloaf? Oh, yeah. Natalie and I hiked it a few times—trails there are really fun. I got up into the Blue Ridge for a couple days while she was away. Nice and cool up there in the morning."

"I'll take the warm, you can have the cold."

"Thus, Fiji?"

"Exactly!"

"So, any company for you in the south seas?"

Joanne looked away, then back, shaking her head. "That time is for me, alone. And, in truth, there's no one, Ben, that I would *want* to take along."

"I see." Ben waited to see if she would take that any further, but Joanne switched topics, heading off that thread.

"OK, back to business. What do you think of the SLIP scanner?"

Ben shrugged. "It might be useful if we're kinda looking around and they happen to transmit and accidentally tell us they're present, but other than that I'm not sure how much good it will do."

"You're setting up a workstation?"

"Yes, we can access the display from the Intel workroom. We'll put it up on one of our regular monitor screens. There's an alarm if it sees anything."

She started to stand, then stopped and sat back down.

Ben looked up in surprise. "Is that all, Joanne? Or was there something else?"

"You know how I feel about you."

"I do. And, so do you. We've talked about this before." Ben was not sure where she was going with this line of conversation.

"I am the captain of this vessel, Ben. If whatever happens out there turns to shit, I have to do what's necessary."

"Of course, you do. What are you thinking about, Joanne?"

"You're the one with the data on the Seekers. If we need to talk to them, you're the one who's going to the surface."

"So, I'm the one who could be left behind?"

"This isn't a movie, Ben. But, yes."

Ben reached over, taking her suntanned hands in his and holding tight.

"Joanne, let's be clear, OK? Let's say this once and be done, OK?"

She nodded.

"I trust you with my life, just like everyone else on this ship. I will willingly follow you into combat under whatever circumstances we face. If something bad happens, I expect you to do the right thing, regardless of what that means for me, for Natalie, or any other single person." He hesitated a second. "Does that clear it up for you?"

"Yes, it does."

"OK, so, you go do your Captain thing, and I'll do my Intel thing, and we'll just see how this all works out. OK?"

"OK."

Joanne, feeling strangely encouraged, left the Intel section to check out the Bridge.

Ben, feeling less brave than he had sounded to Joanne, went back to his reports, and pushed the anxiety that Joanne's comments had seeded back in his mind. *Do your job, let her do hers, and we all might just live*, he thought to himself.

Maybe.

They wouldn't be to Beta Hydri until at least November 12th. If anything bad was going to happen to the Seekers, it might well be long over before they got there. Ben allowed a small prayer that this trip would all be for nothing.

But he knew it might go very, very differently.

Preeminent Ship 254
Beta Hydri (d)
Earth Equivalent Date: November 8, 2078

Ashil Kiker stood at the viewing port on the main deck of the ship. Exploration and the natural conquests which flow from it were not his skills; he was an individual of more subtle action. But, after all, he was a Preeminent, and therefore he would be able to vanquish any opposition and bring whatever culture he found to obsequia, or death.

The planet below him was attractive, but for the Preeminent's purposes, it was far too much water for too little land. It also had no value to them since the population could not be brought to heel and serve. It was a suboptimal outcome, Kiker thought, as the Scholars, as ignorant and hard-headed as they might be, were productive farmers and the animals they grew were reported to be succulent to the palate. But, without the bent-kneed workers to farm them, it meant little.

Scad Nee Wok, the ship's commander, came to him to report.

"There is nothing new here, sir Kiker. Yes, the Vermin may have been here, but we have found nothing left behind."

"And the Scholars? The ignorant ones?"

"They also have not returned to their former place."

"They are all dead, are they not?"

"Such was the report, yes, sir Kiker."

It had all started with the Deists, he knew. This new species, such trouble that they called them the Vermin, had first appeared at the Deist's System 352. What if they were from beyond 352? That was an area not scheduled for exploration for another lifetime, perhaps more.

"How far, Scad Nee Wok, can this vessel explore?"

"Where is it you wish to go, sir Kiker?"

"Past 352. I want to find the source of these Vermin."

"I have the resources, yes. But I will require the permission of the Council to go so far."

"You doubt my authority?"

"I do not doubt my own, sir Kiker, and it does not extend to such an exploration. It is unheard of for a ship to go so far without the direction of the Council."

Kiker turned to look again out the port. Wok, annoying as he was, was correct in his response.

"Send a message to the council. Tell them I wish to see what is beyond 352."

"As you say, sir Kiker."

Hatred welled up inside Kiker, the hatred of that which presumed to threaten not only his life but his place in the universe, indeed, his entire culture's place. He would not accept that they could have any equal anywhere. They were the Preeminent, and they were meant to be worshiped and served. So far, they had overcome every world they found, crushing resistance, and placing the surrendered remnants under their rule. Six species had already come to obsequia and were living far better lives, in Kiker's expert opinion, than they had heretofore.

They were the Preeminent. This was the will of the Universe.

The direction of the Council was that he should proceed not beyond 352, but to a stable, yellow-white dwarf star in System 201, which was actually closer than 352. Kiker relayed the order to Scad Nee Wok, and they departed.

What the Council concealed from Kiker was that exploration to find the Vermin was already underway, a decision taken after Kiker had been dispatched to Beta Hydri. They also hid from him the consensus among the scientists that 201 was exactly the kind of star that could harbor the Vermin.

Columbia
Earth Orbit
Saturday, November 12, 2078, 0930 UTC

The message had come in a few days before they returned home.

```
ROUTINE 207811081200UTC
TO: COLUMBIA, CHAFFEE, ANTARES
FROM: FLEETINTEL

1. ANTARES (ON ORBIT 20781109) REPORTS SURVIVORS OF THE BETA HYDRI
   CULTURE THEY CALL 'SEEKERS.'
2. CHAFFEE (ETA 20781115) HAS LOCATED LARGE ENEMY FACILITY
   APX 25 LY SOUTH.
3. COLUMBIA (ETA 20781112) HAS SPECIFIC INTEL ON ENEMY SPECIES
   AND SHIP DESIGN.
4. FLEETINTEL TDOA RESULTS CONTINUE TO REVEAL USEFUL PATTERNS IN
   ENEMY COMMAND STRUCTURE.
5. CINCFLEET HAS TASKED FLEETINTEL TO MANAGE CONSOLIDATION AND
   CROSS-EVALUATION OF ALL INTEL STARTING 207811221300UTC.
6. ALL TEAMS SHALL PREPARE ABSTRACTS OF PERTINENT RESULTS FOR
   DISTRIBUTION IMMEDIATELY ON RETURN.
7. DETAILED REPORTS WITH SUPPORTING DATA TO BE FILED WITH
   FLEETINTEL NLT 2078111701300UTC

PENA

END
```

David and Katch set to work on the abstract, with Susan Scranton providing the details on the alien remains. They never did find a full body. The several partial remains they did locate testified to the violence of the Bludgeon attacks, but gave only a few hints at enemy anatomy.

But overall, the wreck had been a confounding and mostly disappointing endeavor. Most of it was tank; three pairs of enormous spheres. The piping led to the aft engineering spaces where they apparently ran a hydrogen/oxygen fuel cell to produce electricity. The drive system was not sealed like a Forstmann drive, but neither could they make any kind of conclusion about how it worked. They coerced red-headed FPI Lieutenant Tom Herring to take an EVA trip over to the enemy ship, but he had very little to say about what he saw. He promised to write a complete analysis and send it to Forstmann, but he could not, he said, tell them anything about how the enemy drive compared to Forstmann. This made sense, of course, since the operation of the Forstmann Drive was perhaps the most closely guarded secret on (or off) Earth.

"You know what?" David asked Katch after Herring left the Intel office following their last discussion.

"What?"

"I don't think Tom knows jack shit about how the Drive works. They monitor dials, check levels, assert commands, but I don't think any of them have the slightest clue what's actually back there."

"So, what was he doing on the wreck?"

"Pictures for Forstmann. *He* might understand."

"Yeah, maybe. We'll have to see what happens."

They convinced Mike Clark to take some of his small supply of C4 and blow the hatch that the blood trail that Powell and Hughes had found seemed to pass into. It made a mess of the room, but other than some writing on the wall, nothing interesting was found in the next level down.

With careful, patient work, they had managed to explore the aft end beyond the broken passageway, and there they found more controls, and more writings, which they bagged, sterilized, and brought back with them. There were a couple of close calls with nicked EVA suits, but everyone got back whole and safe.

They carefully documented the outside of the wreck with photographs, hoping that they might find something more. David, keenly aware how the enemy used SLIP to their advantage, wanted to find the SLIP apparatus. It should be on the outside of the ship, he was sure, but he was equally sure he had no idea what it might look like. When they got back, Katch shipped the whole package to Fleet-Intel, who forwarded a copy to Lloyd at FPI. Perhaps he could find something interesting. The written materials – both the internal pictures and what looked like technical manuals – would be delivered to Greg Cordero at FleetIntel.

Antares had beaten *Columbia* back to Earth, but Carol had not been waiting for him as he got off the shuttle late Sunday evening. She was still working aboard *Antares* and would be down the next day. They'd both managed to wrangle a few days off. The real intelligence discussions would begin Friday, after *Chaffee*'s return, so their commanders could afford to let the crew have some free time.

So, this time, it was David who waited for Carol to step off the *Antares* shuttle the next morning, well-bundled against the cold November wind. They held each other for a long time before they spoke, relieved to be together again. They slipped into the autonomous vehicle David had brought and headed out of town for the day.

ISC Fleet HQ Intel Section
Ft. Eustis, VA
Wednesday, November 14, 2078, 0845 EST

Kristin Hayes walked into Frances's small office and sat down, all without looking up from the printout in her hand.

"Good morning?" Frances asked.

Kristin glanced up only briefly. "Oh, yes, good morning."

Frances let a full thirty seconds go by. "Something on your mind?"

Kristin blinked and looked up. "I think I found something in these Beta Hydri messages."

"Oh?"

"The first one is at the lower end of the SLIP channels, 70. The second is much higher, 652."

"So, what are you thinking?"

"I think those are separate sources. Same place, but not the same transmitter."

"Interesting."

"Yes, but there a message from further south, somewhere around Alpha Mensae, on channel 76 which looks to me like a response to the 652 message."

Frances pulled up the history of SLIP intercepts on her workstation, looking more closely at the channel numbers. "Yes. All 76's locate to Alpha Mensae. The Enemy Station source is only on 248."

Kristin shifted in her chair. "Don was telling me last week that he thought there might be a pattern in the channels. That's what got me going in this direction."

"Looks like he was right."

"So, any other hits on 652 or 70?"

"No. But we've only been at this for a few months. They could have both been involved with Inor or *Otbara* or even *Sigma,* and we might not know."

"Yes, it took a while to get this all working correctly."

"But if we could match channels to transmitters, even imperfectly —"

"We could track individual enemy ships. That would really be something."

"I'll bring it up at the staff meeting today. Maybe some of the others will have more ideas."

"Right, good idea."

There was spirited discussion of the meaning of the channels around The Table later that morning, with a conclusion that they were likely on to something very significant.

Roger Cox started the discussion. "OK, try this...the enemy has an eye on Big Blue, somehow...and it sees *Antares* poking around, and it calls home, just like a Sentinel would. Then, home sends a ship to go see what's going on."

"Makes sense so far. It's what we would do," Frances responded.

"Maybe that's why it makes sense!" Kelly Peterson responded, a sly smile on her face.

"Kelly, you're such a buzz killer."

"That's one of my best qualities!"

Roger continued. "OK, so, then, the ship shows up and there are no humans hanging around, and nothing changed in Capital City."

"So, he's there, but nothing's changed, so he sends a 'what the hell?' back to H-Q and they tell him something."

"Or, where-to-next?" Adrienne McLean asked.

"Sure, could be. In any case, that's a logical scenario."

Peña looked around the table. "*Intrepid* won't be there for four or five more days. Is this something we should tell them?"

Rich Evans spoke up. "If we think there's a decent chance that some surveillance station exists, then yes, we should clue them in to look for it."

"Ann will understand, sir."

Peña nodded. "Roger, draft the message, and I'll get it off to Henderson."

"Yes, Commander."

```
PRIORITY 207811141515UTC
TO: INTREPID
FROM: FLEETINTEL

FURTHER STUDY OF ENEMY MESSAGES FROM BETA HYDRI LEADS US TO BELIEVE
THERE IS AN ENEMY SURVEILLANCE FACILITY IN THE VICINITY.
THE TWO MESSAGES FROM BH WERE ON SEPARATE SLIP CHANNELS
WHICH WE BELIEVE IMPLIES SEPARATE TRANSMITTERS.

END
```

ISC Fleet HQ Intel Section
Ft. Eustis, VA
Friday, November 18, 2078, 1400 EST

Ron Harris had not been away from his family for so long in several years. Their reunion was sweet, but overladen with the frustration and fear of having a loved one at risk so far away for weeks. It took a few days to adjust back to a normal life, and Ron did his best to be home and present as much as possible, given how much work there was to be done at FleetIntel.

Today, he was back in familiar settings at The Table, going over the results of *Columbia*'s photographs of the enemy Drive with Dan Smith, David Powell, and Randy Forstmann. Forstmann had studied Tom Herring's pictures and come to the conclusion that the enemy Drive was inferior to what the Fleet was using.

"It's less efficient and less powerful. I'd expect they'd only be able to do point-eight-five light year per day at the most."

"How can you tell?" David asked.

Forstmann just looked at him. "I can tell, Lieutenant Powell. Leave it at that."

"But, Mr. Forstmann, we saw —"

"Leave it at that, Lieutenant." Forstmann, someone known for good manners and patience, had cut him off mid-sentence. David looked at Dan, who just shrugged, and gave up.

"I must ask, Lieutenant Powell, do I have all the images? Have all the others been destroyed?"

Dan answered for him. "Yes, Mr. Forstmann, Herring was emphatic about that. We've erased and bit-washed everything we had."

"I am sorry to be so prickly about this, Commander Smith, but this is a secret that must be protected. The entire Fleet, the entire new economy, is largely based on the Drive."

"That close, eh?" David asked, his inner smart-ass leaking out.

"That's enough —" Harris started.

"It's alright, Ron." Forstmann interrupted. "I understand a young man's frustration at not being allowed to understand something he's seen with his own eyes. It's OK."

Powell and Smith were dismissed, heading back to the BOQ for the night. After walking them out, Ron returned to the conference room.

"Randy, how about dinner with us tonight?"

"That would be very nice, of course, but you should clear it with your wife," Forstmann responded, cautiously.

"Oh, I will, Randy."

"Make sure she's willing, Ron. My presence can create a real circus."

"I know, I know, but we live on the base, so I think we're well enough insulated from the cameras. But, yes, I'll talk to her."

"Good."

Ron returned to his office and dialed his wife on his personal phone.

"Can we do a dinner for a guest tonight?" he asked.

"I guess, yeah. Who?"

"Well, Fiona —"

"Fiona's not a guest."

"Yeah, I know. It's Fiona and someone else."

"Who else?"

"Can it be a surprise?"

"I guess. Depends on the surprise."

"It's a good surprise."

"OK, fine, be that way, Admiral Mysterious, but is this a lasagna surprise? If so, I have one in the freezer. If this is a burgers surprise, I have those, too."

"OK —"

"But if this is like a beef tenderloin surprise, I need to order it, get the asparagus, get some fresh horserad—"

"Yes, this is definitely a beef tenderloin kinda guest."

"Hmm. VIP, huh? Let me guess —"

"Please don't."

"HA! Gotcha old man."

Ron never tired of Meredith's laughter. Every time he heard it, he felt twenty-two again. He hung up smiling and walked back to the conference room.

"We're set."

"Wonderful. Did you tell her who was coming?"

"No. I just requested the menu."

"You're a brave man, Admiral Harris."

Just after six, the kitchen door opened and Fiona came in, followed by a small, older man in jeans. As Meredith turned from the stove to greet her guests, she froze as she saw him.

"Mr. Forstmann!"

"Good evening, Mrs. Harris, thank you for inviting me tonight."

Meredith looked at Ron, then back at Forstmann, and smiling with one hand on her hip, and pointing to Ron with the carving knife in her other hand, she replied, "Actually, sir, this guy invited you."

"Something smells wonderful," he answered.

"I sure hope so! Do come in Mr. Forstmann."

"Randy, please."

"Meredith." She shook his hand, then turned back to the grill on the stove.

"Fiona?" she called without looking away.

"Yes?"

"Why is there not a glass of wine in my hand?"

Fiona gave her a gentle hug as she passed by and headed for the wine rack. "One Norton, coming up. Randy?"

"Oh, when in Rome..."

"Three Nortons it is, then."

After dinner, they sat around the table, talking about the war, and about family. Meredith put down her glass and looked down the table at Ron.

"I've had Ron gone for months before, but this time was so different. There were always dangers, but I never had that feeling that someone might actually hurt him."

"And this time you did?" Randy asked.

"Yes. It was much harder to keep a normal life going. The girls picked up on it and they tried their best to help me."

"I can see how that would be."

"Any children in the Fleet, Randy?" Fiona asked.

"No. But there are several cousins, nieces, nephews, that kind of thing. I only have the one son, and he's a little old even by Fleet standards."

"But you worry about them?"

"Yes, Meredith, I do. But really, I worry about all of them. It's my invention, my dream of practical space travel, that's at the root of this conflict, and that concerns me very much."

"So, are we going to win?"

"Meredith!"

"No, Ron, it's fine." Forstmann took another sip of his after-dinner coffee. "I am not a military man, certainly no strategist. But I believe our victory is almost certain. We have several tactical and technological advantages. From what I have read, we understand combat better than they do."

"But?" Fiona asked.

"But this won't be some bloodless walkover. They *are* powerful. And, ruthless. So far, they're also unpredictable, which makes them even more dangerous. But Ron's people are working very hard on that."

Meredith shook her head gently. "I think you are too hard on yourself, Randy." Forstmann set down his cup and looked back down the table at her. "How so?"

"Without your invention, seems to me very likely they would have shown up here someday just like they did at Inor and we would have had no answer for it. But for you, we might have lost it all on the first day."

Forstmann nodded slowly to himself. "I think that's overly generous. We have other kinds of defensive weapons that we would have used had that happened. But, thank you for that, Meredith. I appreciate the thought."

Fiona and Ron cleared the table as Meredith and Randy talked children and family. Randy had grown up not far from Meredith's home town, and they shared memories of a few places: restaurants, parks, and theaters. She was surprised that he was aware of her education, her two master's degrees, her work with the families of young fleet officers.

"But, even with all that, Meredith, I think I'd really like to send my chef here for a week."

"Say what?"

"Yes, I think you could give him some lessons."

"You have *got* to be kidding. "

"Not really. This meal was beautiful, and I know it was expensive because I pay the bills for ours, but it still felt like a home cooked meal, and I miss that part."

"Well, Randy, there's a small trick to that."

"Oh?"

"Yeah, don't try to be too perfect. If it's not exactly medium rare, if the potatoes are in for ten minutes too long, nobody really cares. The food is only part of the meal."

"The rest is good company?"

Meredith smiled. "Yes. And, good wine!"

For dessert, there was a classic, simple New York cheesecake, made from a several-generations-old family recipe. It was excellent by any standard, and Randy went back to his penthouse apartment with a new appreciation for the Harrises. He made a note to send Forstmann Foundation Scholarships along when their three daughters headed for college in a few years.

It had been a good day, and he slept more soundly than he had in some weeks.

Intrepid
Approaching Beta Hydri
Saturday, November 19, 2078, 2110 UTC

Ben found Natalie Hayden head-down in her office. She'd spent the last six hours back-checking weapons inspections. It was boring but necessary work for the Weapons Maintenance Officer. Ben slipped in as quietly as he could, but Natalie looked up before he got to her.

"Stalking me, Price?" she said, laughing as she sat up straight.

"Naw, just looking," he said, smiling, and nodding as he continued, "for you."

She regarded him carefully for a moment. This late-evening visit wasn't a business call, that much was obvious.

"So, what's up?"

He leaned against the steel frame of her office door. He paused a moment before speaking. His voice was quiet, intense.

"We're going to be there in two days, Nat."

"Yes, I know," she responded quietly. Something else was going on here, she thought, but she decided to let Ben come to it at his own pace.

He looked away as he asked her, "What do you want, Nat? I mean, what do you really *want?*"

She sat back in her chair and stretched her arms above her head, leaning back to let out some of the stiffness she felt after hours in the stacks and then pouring over the reports. After a moment, she pulled herself back down and leaned her elbows on the desk. She was stalling for time to think, but the stretch felt good, too.

"You mean today? Later? What?"

He turned to look at her directly. "I mean forever."

She thought about it for a second and then looked steadily back at him. "I want to do good work, hard work, work that I love, and at the end of the day I want to fall into bed with someone who wants nothing more in the world than for me to do just that."

Ben looked up at her. "Then, I am your man."

Natalie looked at Ben for a few seconds, her head inclined a little.

"So is that —" she began to ask, but he leaned over quickly and kissed her.

Straightening up, he repeated quietly, "I am your man, Nat, and yes, that's a question. Think it over."

A step after he turned to leave, she said, "*Mister* Price?"

He turned back to her. She was smiling slightly as she looked off into the distance.

"Yes, *Lieutenant?*"

"OK."

He smiled. "Is that an answer?"

"It is."

"You're sure this isn't too soon? You're sure you're ready?"

"I've been ready since we launched the second Sentinel."

He smiled, recalling the time they spent head-to-head inside the second surveillance drone, troubleshooting a problem with the RTG. He had enjoyed that interplay, too, but clearly it had made an even deeper impression on her,

"Cool. Should I, like, ask the captain for your hand?"

Natalie laughed. "I kinda thought I'd have to ask her for yours!"

"OK, well, then maybe we should ask her together?"

"Sure. But Ben, we're not waiting around, OK? Let's get this done right away."

"You're sure about that? I mean, I don't have a ring or anything—"

"Buy me a ring after this is all over if you want to. For now, just give me your word. That's all I really need."

"Well, you know you have that already."

"OK, then."

"So, I'll get us an audience with Henderson, and we'll see what she says, OK?"

Ben and Natalie appeared in Joanne Henderson's office the next day. Ben had asked the captain for an appointment but left out any mention of Natalie or the subject. None of that was unusual, as Price would meet with the captain routinely to cover Intel or administrative topics.

So, Joanne was surprised when they arrived together and closed the door behind them. She suppressed a smile, but there could be no doubt, in her mind, what this little gathering was about.

"We've decided to get married," Ben reported.

"Well, there's the least shocking thing I've heard today. Congratulations."

"Least shocking?" Natalie asked.

"Yes. Least shocking, most obvious, whatever. But, contrary to popular belief, I can't help you. Fleet Captains can't marry people."

"No, we just thought you should know. And we had to tell *somebody*."

"Well, thanks for that. And I appreciate the notice, I do. When we get back, you'll have to file the relationship declaration with FleetPers. For now, your status doesn't change."

"Yes, Captain, we understand."

Joanne smiled now, her laugh barely suppressed. "But I am very glad for both of you. You'll be great."

They rose and left the captain's office happy, and as the door closed behind them, Joanne Henderson was left unsure whether to laugh with joy or cry that her best friend in the world — in the universe, she corrected herself — was yet another step away from her. She missed him brutally already, their deep and free-wheeling conversations now past, but the rules and realities of command required a distance between Captain and crewmember. Their friendship was a rare thing. She had once called it *lightning in a bottle* talking with Fiona, and would likely never be repeated.

But life goes on, she reminded herself. We live, we find people to enrich our lives, and we enjoy them while they are present. The patterns of life change, the lights dim or brighten, and everything looks different. She shook off those thoughts, picking up Ben's synopsis of what Fleet knew of the Seekers, what Sol it would be when they arrived, and what FleetIntel thought they might find. She could hear his voice in her head, reading each word to her, laying out for her the nuance of what was important, and what probably wasn't.

She finished the Intel summary and returned to considering what had just happened in her office. She wasn't jealous, that much she was sure of, because she never wanted the kind of relationship with Ben that Natalie now enjoyed. But she missed what she once had, and how it had made her life more tolerable. *Perhaps,* she thought, *the time has come to think differently*, to allow for new options, new choices. For now, she had her ship to attend to, but she let herself consider, however briefly, that when they got back home, she might be making some changes.

ISC Fleet HQ Main Briefing Theater
Ft. Eustis, VA
Tuesday, November 22, 2078, 0900 EST (1400 UTC)

The four briefings, summaries though they were, took all morning. The sudden wealth of information now rolling around in CINC's mind, and that of his staff, was almost overwhelming. The enemy was ultimately Terran. They had a giant supply facility of some kind in the middle of nowhere twenty-five light years to the south. The Beta Hydri culture — the 'Seekers' — were alive and in hiding. The enemy had returned to Beta Hydri. And, finally, FleetIntel's message intercepts now had a revealing new source: Alpha Mensae. Some of this knowledge would confirm decisions he'd already made, and some would cause him to pursue new and more promising modes of action.

As they left the long morning meeting, David and Carol came across Susan Scranton.

"Good morning, Doctor Scranton."

"Hello, Lieutenant Powell."

David turned back to Carol. "Oh, Carol, this is our exobiologist, Doctor Scranton. She led the investigation of the wreck and did the DNA analysis." He turned back to Scranton. "Doctor Scranton, Carol—"

"Hansen," Scranton said firmly, clearly recognizing her.

Carol found herself looking carefully at the tall, thin physician. "Scranton..." Carol looked away, then back at Scranton. "Susan Scranton?" she asked gently.

"Yes, Lieutenant."

"Chief Vaughn Scranton's daughter?"

Tears grew around the edges of the doctor's eyes. David found himself completely lost.

Susan reluctantly nodded and said, "Yes."

David's question was plain on his face.

Carol leaned over to speak quietly in his ear. "Chief Scranton was the senior enlisted man on *Liberty*. He used to talk all the time about his daughter the doctor, but I didn't make the connection to your Doctor Scranton until now."

They moved to the side of the lobby where they could sit down. Scranton's hardened armor guard was clearly gone, her emotions coming fully to the surface. Susan turned to Carol, seated next to her on a small bench.

"I've wanted to talk to you for so long, Lieutenant Hansen, *so* long."

"Oh?"

"You found him. I read your report."

"I did."

"Tell me about it. Tell me everything."

Carol looked down, wondering how to answer her pain-filled question. "He was a brave man, Doctor Scranton, brave beyond whatever words I have to express it."

"That's not much of an answer, Lieutenant Hansen."

"It's the best answer I can give you. The rest is irrelevant."

Susan looked at David, the mask that once occupied her face now gone. "So, now you know why I was so single-minded. I had to get them, Powell, I had to find them and somehow make them pay."

David just nodded in response.

"Everyone told me I was nuts. Told me to calm down and stick with my research. Stay where I belonged."

"Of course."

She looked back at Carol. "For you, he was an admired shipmate. But he was *my Dad*, he was all I had, and they took him away."

"So, you joined FleetIntel."

"They'd take me. Nobody else would. Besides, I could make a good case for a geneticist if we could find something to examine."

"Turns out you were right," David said softly.

"Yes, I suppose so."

David looked at Carol, sharing an understanding, then back at Scranton. "From what I see, Doctor, you belong just fine right here. I can't see Harris letting go of you now."

"I hope that's right, Powell. But I've never counted on people doing the right thing."

"You can here, Doctor, and that's a promise," Carol responded.

"I wish, Doctor Scranton, that you had told us who you were back on *Columbia*. We never understood what was behind the demands, the stress."

"I've never really been able to trust people other than my Dad."

"Well, then, start with us." Carol reached around and gave her a gentle hug. Scranton nodded and relaxed a little.

David stood up from the kneeling position he'd been in, rubbing his sore left kneecap.

"I think you should talk to Harris, tell him why you're here. He'd respect that." She looked up at him.

"Yes, I'll do that. I suspect he already knows."

"Well, that's possible. He is the head spy after all. If you don't mind, I'll let Commander Smith know?"

"Yes, that would be fine."

207

Carol looked up at David, who returned her look with a slight nod.

"So, how about some lunch?" she asked.

Scranton let go a small laugh, wiped her eyes, and stood.

"Sure, that would be lovely."

David smiled as he responded, "Doctor Scranton, that is a word I never thought I'd ever hear from you."

"Oh?"

"Yes, but I like the sound of it. Shall we go?"

They headed off for the HQ commissary.

After lunch, Connor Davenport sat with his senior staff and the most experienced ship captains available: Kieran Barker, Terri Michael, Mark Rhodes, Anna Nonna, Nobuyuki Kawaguchi, and Dan Smith.

Smith felt like an intruder in this company, the rest being much more senior officers, but CINC had called him in, so he went. He tried his best to be listening far more than talking.

For Rhodes, it was familiar territory but a very unfamiliar role. He was accustomed to sitting off to the side, taking notes and passing questions to Cook. Now, he was at the table between Barker and Michael and expected to help figure out what to do with what they now knew.

CINC opened the discussion. "What do we think, folks, about this idea that the enemy is an ancient Terran species?"

"Let me say, sir, if I may, what my Intel folks said," Dan Smith started, contradicting his own initial thoughts about keeping quiet. "The fact that the enemy is originally Terran is interesting, but it gives us no useful tactical advantage."

Nippon's Captain Kawaguchi turned to him. "So, Lieutenant Commander Smith, you discount that finding?"

Did Kawaguchi really just emphasize the *Lieutenant* part, or was that just Dan's imagination?

"No, Captain, I just don't see how it helps us defeat them." There were nods around the table, so he continued. "Now, sir, on the other hand, knowledge of their drive system, which we brought back photographs of, could well give us an advantage."

"Forstmann has reported on that. He believes the enemy is capable of only about point-eight-five light years per day."

Barker looked surprised. "That's gives us a significant advantage, sir."

"Yes, it does." CINC looked around the table, changing the subject. "So, let's move on to the Seekers."

"Well, sir, that question has been answered by the enemy. *Intrepid* will be there soon," Operations Chief Patricia Cook stated. "Whatever happens with

Henderson's mission, we should keep a ship there as a sentry until we have determined that they are safe."

"Yes, there's really very little choice, now. We're going to guard Big Blue." CINC's tone closed off any argument. He turned to Cook. "Get a rotation going, using the frigates as much as possible. Fill in with whatever else you need. I think six weeks on station would work, which makes for about a ninety-day trip overall."

"Yes, sir."

CINC picked up his tablet, slipped his glasses back on, and continued the discussion. "Based on more recent SLIP locations, FleetIntel's working theory is that the enemy homeworld is at Alpha Mensae. That's about thirty-three light years to the south. They also have this depot or supply facility, Enemy Station, at twenty-five light years."

He set down his tablet and laid his glasses on top of it.

"I want a recon of Alpha Mensae to see if it really is the enemy's home, or, at least, their main base."

"A recon?" Terri asked.

"Yes, much as Commander Rhodes did with *Chaffee*, a fly-by just to see what's there. Admiral Harris?"

"Yes, sir. Over the last few months, Rich Evans' primary task has been the conversion of a frigate hull under construction into a surveillance ship. This one started out as a Memorial Class, and I want to say that the original name for this vessel will be assigned to the next one in line. We just kinda cut in and took one."

"It's OK, Admiral," Anna Nonna said with a smile, "Cosmonaut Volkov would understand."

Ron continued, "Thanks, Anna. We now have a platform designed specifically for this kind of trip. That ship, *Cobra*, will be ready shortly and will be making the trip to Alpha Mensae."

"Who will be in command?" Terri asked.

"Evans. The crew, I am sorry to say, will sound very familiar to most of you as I am planning to raid your Intel staffs pretty heavily."

This revelation was met with groans of widespread sadness and somber head shaking. Ship commanders love their Intel chiefs, who will from time to time either make their careers, or save their asses, or both at once.

CINC picked returned to his notes. "I am concerned that Enemy Station is only fourteen light years from Kapteyn. That's an asset too valuable to lose, so I want at least one combat-ready warship there at all times."

No problem there, Dan thought. *Being on guard duty at Kapteyn would be the equivalent of guarding the best hotel in town.*

"These next two items will be in reverse order for reasons that will become clear."

CINC paused for a sip of water. Or, was it just for dramatic effect?

"I am directing Operations, Plans, and Intel to prepare an offensive for early next year, the objective being the destruction of all known enemy assets."

CINC looked around the conference table. No objections were raised, but there was unmistakable surprise on the faces of the ship commanders.

"In support of that, I want every star that we examined in our first randomized search revisited in the next 45 days. We can skip the dozen or so that have Sentinels in orbit."

"About the offensive, Admiral," Captain Kawaguchi asked, "Are we not then telling the enemy which facilities we know about and which, assuming they exist, we do not? Are we not telling them something we should keep to ourselves?"

"There is that possibility, but I believe the strategic initiative would then be ours."

"That is an ambitious agenda, sir," Terri Michael responded.

"It is. But there's actually more. I have decided to establish a forward command deep in the south so that we can keep our ships in action more and in transit less, and have better command awareness of what's going on."

There was a long silence after CINC finished. Barker spoke first, breaking the tension in the air. "Sir, that would make an enormous and very juicy target for the enemy."

"If they could find it, yes. So, let's not get found."

Anna Nonna, quiet up to now, had a different concern. "You would be taking crews away from home for much longer, sir. Much longer."

"In earlier wars right here on planet Earth, soldiers and sailors were gone for years, Commander, *years*. Yes, we will be asking more of our people than we have before, but I believe they are up to it if we are."

"What would this command station look like, sir?" Dan asked.

"And who would be there?" Fiona asked, somewhat anxious about what the answer might be.

"As to who, I will be appointing a new commander for the southern theater of operations, designated CSTO, whose first task will be this offensive."

The silence in the room grew to an unsustainable level.

"Responsibility for Inor, Earth, and anything else north of ten light years south of the Sun will remain here." Davenport pointed to Admiral Yakovlev, seated next to him, "Stan will remain my deputy, but will add operational command of the northern area to his portfolio — as if keeping me out of trouble isn't a full-time occupation. Stan and I will remain here at HQ."

"As to what form it will take, I will let the CSTO decide that. My expectation is that they will select a flagship and remain mobile. That makes the most sense for operational security." CINC looked around the table and saw only agreement.

"ISC is also giving us an older, small mining ship as a supply vessel: the *Ceres*. It should be ready sometime in January. That ship will be positioned with the flagship to provide support to the deployed warships."

Again, he laid down his glasses and leaned his elbows on the table.

"I know you're all wondering who I will appoint to command the southern theater. I will finalize that today and you'll all be notified tomorrow, Thanks, everyone, for your input."

The ship commanders excused, CINC and his senior staff continued the deliberations. There were some radical names proposed for CSTO, like Terri Michael, but despite her obvious talents, she was junior to many more experienced commanders. Joanne Henderson was discussed, as was Mark Rhodes, but he, too, while smart and resourceful, was probably too junior for the job. He needed more time in command.

Yorktown's commander, the Virginian Captain Harry Hess, was a good candidate. He was just slightly junior to the late Dean Carpenter, having also started out with Forstmann in the early days. He wasn't already an Admiral only because he said 'shove it' every time the Fleet tried to promote him. Kieran Barker had already handled a small task force from *Dunkirk*. His performance was solid. Captain Kawaguchi from *Nippon* came up as well.

In the end, CINC selected Barker, whom he saw as the most appropriate officer for this command. When called, Kieran accepted his orders with good humor, and spent the night outlining who he would want to join him, and how he would stage the offensive. He was still outlining when the sun interrupted him as it spilled a yellow glow into his BOQ room.

ISC Fleet HQ, ISC Board Conference Room
Ft. Eustis, VA
Wednesday, November 23, 2078, 0900 EST

The next morning, CINC Connor Davenport met again with his available ship commanders, this time without his staff assistants. They ate breakfast from an extensive buffet in the ISC's large, formal conference room, a venue equal to the board room of any major corporation. Forstmann's money was well spent here in large windows and fine black walnut paneling.

After a leisurely period of friendly talk, and a couple good war stories from the commanders, CINC was ready to get down to business.

"We need to talk about some new assignments."

Davenport turned to Dan Smith.

"Is Melville ready?"

"Ready, sir?"

"For her own ship."

"Oh, yes, sir. I've already submitted my recommendation to that effect."

"Think she can handle a new frigate?"

"Yes."

"Good. She gets *Jarvis*."

"Oh, I see. I think she will do a fine job, sir."

"Find another XO and let me know."

"Maz Dawes," Dan responded immediately. "Stef Tsukuda can handle Nav, so send me an Ensign to back-fill her position."

Davenport made a note on his tablet. "Very well."

"Thank you, sir."

Terri Michael shifted in her chair as CINC's eyes landed on her. "I'm hitting you hard, Commander Michael. You seem to bring out the best in these young-sters."

"Thank you, sir, I guess, but who did you have in mind?"

"Jim George is getting *Yankee*."

"Yes, sir, excellent choice."

"I thought to send Hansen with him, but you can keep her if you like."

"Yes, I'd prefer that."

"Do you want a new XO from the crew or should I send you someone?"

"I have three good young officers who are ready, plus Hansen."

"You think she's ready to be an XO?"

Dan heard himself talking out of turn again. "Admiral, in my opinion, she's as qualified to command, if not more so, than I am."

Davenport smiled. "The loyalty of friends is a good thing, Dan, but she's not you. Not quite yet."

He turned back to Terri. "I'm moving Ballard, too. "

"Really, sir?" she asked in mock annoyance.

"Really."

"He would have been a strong candidate for XO."

"Let me know what you want to do."

"Ryan Lewis, sir. Send me a good Surveillance officer to be Jayvon Dean's new assistant."

"As you wish."

"If I may, sir, where is Ballard going?"

"*Cobra*."

Terri smiled and looked around the table. "Oh, now I see what Harris was talk-ing about."

CINC turned back to Dan Smith. "Dan, what about Powell?"

"Sir?"

"I'm inclined to put him on *Cobra* as well, with Ballard and Evans."

Dan thought for a second before responding. He'd expected something similar since Harris' announcement the day before.

"I guess I have a couple things to say, sir. First, Lieutenant Khachaturian is senior. I would think he might be a more appropriate candidate. Second, David is great at Intel, there's no denying that. But his ambition has always been to command, and I would not want to sideline him into an Intel track that would not take him where he really wants to go."

"Needs of the Fleet come first, Dan, as you well know."

Dan nodded his agreement. "I do, sir, and if you order David Powell somewhere, he'll go, and he'll do a hell of a job for you."

"Good." He turned to Barker. "*Dunkirk* isn't getting away unscathed, Captain Barker."

"I did have hopes you'd just pick off all the decent Yanks and Kiwis and leave us the hell alone."

That got him a laugh.

"Sorry. I need Myra Rodgers for *Cobra*. They need a first-class Surveillance officer."

"She is that, sir, to be sure. I will miss her."

CINC looked at Barker with some anticipation. "Well, *someone* will miss her, anyway."

"Yes, sir, time to let that stupid cat out, I suppose." Barker looked around the room. "I've accepted the assignment to command the southern theater. I know many of you were considered, and I have enormous respect for all of you—"

"Just as we do for you, Kieran," Anna said quietly.

"Thanks. I will be assembling a staff, so some of you may be hearing from me soon."

"Well, congratulations, Kieran," Terri offered.

"Thank you all very much."

"Captain Barker will be picking up a star to go with this little task."

"Yes, Admiral, thank you."

"So, *Admiral* Barker takes command December 1st," CINC declared. "He will execute the reexamination of the southern sky and the offensive against the enemy. I know you will all support his efforts."

CINC looked around the table one last time. *Such good people,* he thought, *so many I can count on.* "That's all."

The meeting broke up with the typical handshakes, bad promotion jokes, and sincere well-wishes. Kieran Barker had a massive task in front of him now, and from a standing start he had just seven days to recruit a staff, consult with Plans and Intel to develop an operational strategy, and start another quick round-robin search.

Finally, they were going to make a major strike. There was plenty of searching to be done yet in order to really pin down the enemy, but at least they were planning to draw serious blood. Barker had been on Inor. He'd seen the streets, the shattered buildings, and smelled the stench of death and decay. He and Len Davis had helped move human remains to be buried at sea. Now Len was gone, too, and enough others to make Barker's stomach grind in anger. Payback, sure, that was part of his mindset, but more so was *never again*. This species had to be put back in their place and kept there. If that meant killing them all, Barker figured that was their choice. He hoped it would turn out otherwise.

Terri Michael, in the meantime, had to hustle back to the main Fleet conference room for a very different kind of discussion. Ron Harris was about to tell the world about Beta Hydri.

ISC Fleet HQ Main Conference Room
Fort Eustis, VA
Wednesday, November 23, 2078, 1100 EST (1500 UTC)

Donna Wright began with a degree in Political Science from Iowa State, then a Master's in Communications from Michigan. Her career started slowly with a year of finding no jobs that really made sense to her; those she did find were so tepid about facts and shallow about meaning she was embarrassed to put them on her resume. She happened to see a media ad promoting ISC Fleet's one-year officer training class. Curious if the ad matched the reality, she called the number on the screen and found herself talking for an hour to the screening officer, one Captain Connor Davenport. He understood her reservations about a military career, how command influence worked, and how someone with her skills might find a place with the kind of rigorous integrity she wasn't finding elsewhere. After a few months of conversations with Connor and others at Fleet, up to and including the then-CINC, she decided to make the move to Ohio and take the course. She negotiated a clause that if after the year she didn't want to stay, she could buy out her commitment and leave. If she remained, she would be commissioned a Senior Lieutenant and assigned to the Public Information Section at HQ.

Fast forward a few years, and Donna found herself a full Commander, the Fleet's Chief Public Information Officer, and Connor Davenport now CINC. Since the war began, she'd made herself a household name with her daily press briefings, fighting against the ill-advised and uninformed opinion makers in the news media. But even now, months into the conflict, too often they ignored her words of caution and the facts were lost in the shouting between talking heads.

For the public reveal of the Beta Hydri culture, Donna went to CINC and laid out her case for a detailed presentation for the media by an authoritative voice. She proposed Ron Harris or Terri Michael, and they settled on Harris. After all, Donna said, Ron had actually been there. He'd seen the Seekers personally.

Donna contacted each of the recognized national and international news networks, as defined by the United Nations and the US Government, and informed them of a detailed briefing on a major development in the war. The condition, she told them, was that there could be no announcement of this briefing until after it was held. Any news outlet revealing the planned briefing would be barred from attending. It was the best cudgel she had to keep them honest. Several were angered or resentful of the constraints she put on them, but all eventually relented, if only for competitive reasons. After all, the on-air 'experts' who had heard what the Fleet had to say would be far more credible than those who did not, and it was, in the end, really all about the ratings.

On the day of the event, Ron put his youngest, most attractive foot forward to greet the reporters, producers, and analysts. Ann Cooper was at Beta Hydri with *Intrepid*, so Kelly Peterson and Kathy Stewart greeted the attendees as they arrived. Young, smiling, and engaging, they checked ID's against the roster, wrote out name tags, took all electronic devices, and thoroughly searched every person. Scott Morgan ran interference when necessary, always pleasant, understanding their problems while ensuring they were properly checked. Tim Jackson did a final electronic scan at the door to the theater-like Main Conference Room. Several people were sent away when he found that they had tried to bring in concealed recording devices. After Security escorted the third offender to the front door, more devices seemed to appear in the storage bins provided, and no one else had to be removed.

The news people generated quite a racket in the conference room, which grew with each new entry. Who knew these presumably serious news people could talk such nasty trash? Ron was actually worried that a fistfight might break out as rivals called each other names across the room, lobbing insults and hyperbole about who had the larger or better audience. But, as it turned out, the only shots landed were verbal. Ron found himself strangely disappointed. A real altercation amongst this carefully groomed and made-up group might have been entertaining.

The front of the room held a few chairs, a lectern with microphone, and a large video monitor behind and above the stage showing a boilerplate 'Welcome to ISC Fleet HQ' slide. After the last person had entered, the Intel personnel came in and sat, ready to assist as necessary. Ron then picked up his phone and made a call. In a moment, the back doors opened, and Admiral Davenport came down the aisle to the front, accompanied by Donna Wright's familiar face.

Terri Michael, Cordero, Este, Bowles, Hansen, and the rest of the *Antares* exploration team leads snuck in after Davenport and took seats in the darkened rear of the auditorium, in case they were needed. David Powell slipped in right after, taking a seat behind Carol. He really didn't want to miss this.

CINC and PIO Wright stood at the lectern, and the room rapidly became quiet.

"Good morning. As you all should know by now, I am Commander Donna Wright, Chief Public Information Officer. Thank you all for coming. To get us started here is the Fleet Commander, Admiral Connor Davenport." She moved aside and slightly behind the Admiral as he stepped to the center and the microphone.

"Good morning. I want to welcome you all to Fleet HQ. I know this is the first time for many of you, I hope this will be a useful experience. We have some very significant finds to report. I want to emphasize your duty to give the public a clear picture of what we tell you today. It is important to our mission that the news that reaches the general public is accurate and complete. Commander Wright?" CINC took a seat on the aisle in the first row and Donna retook the lectern.

"Your presenter today is the Chief of FleetIntel, Rear Admiral Ron Harris. You have all received the embargo rules and don't think we aren't monitoring your channels."

"Embargo? What could we do? You took all our devices!" a voice called from somewhere in the back.

"Yes, yes, we did. But if something leaks out, you'll be out on your ass."

"Is that on the record?"

"Oh, yeah, it is, every word up to and including 'your ass.'"

That got her some nervous laughs.

"Admiral Harris will give an initial presentation and will then take questions. One more rule — and to be clear, this was in the packet I sent your organizations — FleetIntel may refuse to answer a question. In that case, you may *not* report the question or that it was not answered. I will tell you right now that there are sensitive facts that we are not going to share with you today, facts which may place lives at risk."

She looked around the crowd, seeing plenty of smirks and scowls but no objections.

"Very well. Admiral?" Donna stepped back and sat in one of the chairs behind the lectern, ready to intervene if necessary

"Good morning, all. I am Admiral Ron Harris, Chief of FleetIntel —"

"We can't be subject to this kind of control, this kind of censorship!" interrupted a familiar voice, belonging to one of the larger talking heads. Ron looked directly at him and pointed to the back of the theater.

"There's the door."

After a moment, he added, "No one is keeping you here. Donna's warning aside, no one is telling you what to think or what to report regarding anything you learn in this briefing or after you leave."

Ron paused another three-count. "So, are you staying or going?"

"Staying, for now," came the arrogant response.

"Well, well, that's a relief. I guess now we can go on." Ron's sarcasm made his crew laugh.

"So, let's get to it. On May 31st of this year, *Antares*, under Commander Teresa Michael, discovered an Earth-like planet in the Beta Hydri system." On cue, Scott Morgan put up the initial 'beauty shot' of Big Blue.

"Although very similar to the Earth, 'Big Blue,' as it was named by the *Antares* crew, is about ninety percent ocean. It's also just under ten percent larger than the Earth."

Ron paused to look around, and when no questions came, he continued.

"As part of their normal examination of this new planet, *Antares* discovered this —" The first image with a definite street grid appeared on the monitor. He let the sounds of surprise die down. "Yes, those are roads. Yes, there is, or was, as you will see, an intelligent species living there."

"Was, Admiral?" came a familiar voice from the crowd, one of the daily main-line news anchors. Harris looked up.

"More on that later, OK?"

He waited for the second buzz of surprise to subside.

"After some initial observations from orbit, *Antares* dispatched a fleet exploration drone to obtain high-resolution images of the area."

A picture of the main avenue in Capital City appeared on the screen, complete with skeletons and craters.

"Again, yes, those are skeletons, and yes, those are craters. The pattern of attack and other details developed subsequently leave us with no question that the same alien species that struck Inor attacked this planet."

The slide of the battlefield followed, and there was a gasp of surprise from even this most cynical, hard-bitten audience.

"There are thousands of dead here. This culture, which based on later information we now call the 'Seekers,' fought a desperate, to-the-last battle against our enemy. Their bravery was remarkable."

He gave them a few seconds to examine the photograph.

"Pictures obtained as part of the exploration revealed writing on the buildings. Along with that evidence, and other information they developed, we believe this was a culture with approximately a 1970's level of technology. They had chemical rockets, geosynchronous satellites, and radio communication. There remain many aspects of their technology and society that we do not yet understand."

On cue, Roger put up the portrait.

"Then, there was this." Ron turned to look at the image himself and was instantly reminded of Eaagher and Ullnii. If only he could show *their* pictures, tell *their* story. But for now, he knew that was unwise. He turned back to the microphone.

"It's an image of someone now long dead, someone who sat for a portrait, much like any of us might do. The eyes are the most remarkable I have ever seen, with vivid blue and green heterochromic irises. The human-like quality of the eyes is also, well, captivating."

"After a review of their initial results here at HQ, *Antares* was sent back to Big Blue, her crew augmented with an archeologist, a linguist, and a battlefield pathologist. And, your humble presenter. We returned from three weeks at the planet on November 7th, and the crew and those of us in FleetIntel are still processing the results. Next slide, Roger?"

The slide of the picture book appeared.

"This seems to be a child's early education text. Through hard work and the examination of the library, which was in the same room as that portrait, our linguist has been able to break out much of the meaning of the Seeker language. We also now know from *Antares*' groundwork that they were destroyed something like thirty-five years ago."

The buzz that small number generated took a full minute to die out. Ron let them talk a little before taking back control.

"So, we can say with certainty that our opponents have been on the move for some time. We don't know what brought them to Big Blue, or why the population was exterminated. We are still working on the evidence we have, and we may go back for more, so, at some point, we may understand better what happened."

Ron took a breath, a sip of water, and looked around the room.

"So, to summarize, we've located a new habitable planet, a new intelligent species, and managed to learn quite a bit about their society and fate. We'll deliver a package of images, including all of these, to your organizations immediately after this briefing. That's all I had for now. I'll take your questions."

"How far is Beta Hydri?"

"Twenty-four light years."

"Who were the academics that went with you?" the big talking head asked.

"The list is in the data package, but the archeologist was Gabrielle Este from Ohio State; our linguist was Gregory Cordero from Arizona State, and the battlefield pathologist was retired US Army Colonel Joseph Bowles. All three are well-respected, published experts in their fields."

"Will they be available for interviews?" came a female voice. He vaguely recognized it from a popular discussion program, but he couldn't quite recall the name.

"It is my understanding that they will be. It's their choice who they talk to, not Fleet's, but for simple convenience Commander Wright is handling their scheduling. Again, it is their choice whether or not to do whatever interview is requested."

"What about Michael and Hansen and the rest? Will they be available? They refused to talk to me after Inor."

Ron recognized that voice. The woman speaking had a nightly interview show that was one of Meredith Harris's favorites. She did her homework and treated her guests well. Ron managed a quick glance at the back of the room, where Terri and Carol sat impassively.

"Well, let's remember that the entire *Liberty* crew agreed that they would do no interviews. So, really, those officers were honor-bound by that agreement."

"And now?"

"My information is that they are not interested. They have duties to attend to and prefer not to be in the spotlight."

"Can we ask them ourselves?"

At this question, Donna Wright came to the lectern. "No, you can't. We're telling you how they feel —"

"Donna!" came Terri Michael's voice from the back of the room. They all turned to see Terri Michael and Carol Hansen standing at their seats, the rest of the exploration team around them.

"Yes, Commander Michael?" Half the room stood and turned around to see Terri, and Carol in the back of the auditorium.

Terri looked at Carol, who nodded, and Terri said simply. "We're not interested."

Donna looked at the interviewer. "I guess you have your answer, eh?"

Ron stepped back to the microphone as the attendees sat back down, a murmur of disbelief and frustration moving through the seats.

"OK, now, more questions?"

"How many remains did you find?" A different voice, one of the former-Fleet analysts he had seen. Ron could tell from his commentary that there was a perfectly good reason he was a 'former' Fleet officer.

"We don't have a specific number — that was not really a priority. Doctor Bowles puts it on the order of ten thousand, including both the battlefield and what we found in the cities."

"Why so vague?"

"Well, we didn't actually *count* them, right? Also, there are areas of the settlement that we have not examined in detail."

"Are there any of these, these, *Seekers* still alive?"

The pause in Ron's answer after this question caused another stir among the news people.

In the back of the auditorium, Jack leaned over to Carol. "What's he going to say?" he whispered.

"Dunno," she responded just as quietly. "He doesn't want to lie to them. But he can't let that out."

"He's screwed," David said, his head behind and between Carol and Jack, "It's obvious from his reaction that there are."

"Yeah, maybe," Jack responded.

After a few seconds, Ron answered carefully. "We found none alive in the cities and towns we explored."

David leaned forward between Jack and Carol again. "Nice move. A lie wrapped in the truth."

Jack leaned back towards him, "Yeah, if they buy it."

One of the better analysts spoke next. "You understand, Admiral, that if there are survivors, and you've seen them, that's the real story here?"

"I do understand that, but I stand by my answer. Next question?"

"Is the enemy aware you've been to Beta Hydri and seen this, uh, genocide?"

"I can't answer that on the record directly, but we would make this announcement either way. It's important that the public hears this news."

"I still feel like there's something you're not telling us."

Ron's shrug was the only answer she was going to get.

The interviewer spoke again. "I still struggle, Admiral, with how we know what we're hearing is the whole story, and how we talk about this discovery and just skip over what might be the most important part of it."

"Ma'am, that is always a problem between the news media and the military, so let's explore it. People want to know what's going on, and we have a duty to tell them as much as we can about what is happening to their loved ones. We really do want people to know as much as we can safely tell them. We have that responsibility. You all obviously have a profit motive to tell those stories, since they gain you audience, which then sells ads."

"We don't do it for profits!" came yet another familiar voice.

"Bull-shit you don't, asshole. Everybody knows about your contract," came the voice of an avid competitor.

"Yeah, and you're welcome, blowhard."

The room laughed at that. They didn't just compete for ratings.

"Nothing wrong with making money," Harris said quickly, regaining control. "It pays the bills. Back to the actual question on the table, we're having this side discussion specifically because we've decided that as an organization, we're going to do our very best to tell the truth. But we have a fleet to protect, so we do sometimes have to refuse questions, or leave out what you might consider relevant facts."

"The enemy committed a genocide against this race, a modern, apparently well-ordered society. What can you tell the world to reassure it that the enemy is not going to attack here?" It was the competitor again, fishing for a snappy quote for his program that night.

"Nothing."

"You won't tell the people they're safe here?"

"No, because I don't know that." Ron frustration was plain on his face. He had to make them understand, somehow, why he said what he said. "OK, here we are. Yes, we have ships overhead to guard the planet, as we do at Inor, but that may or may not protect everyone in the event of an actual attack."

"People are frightened, Admiral. You have nothing to offer them?"

"No, I don't. Look, this is an Intel briefing, not Operations. I don't want to get too far off topic. But in FleetIntel we take pessimism as axiomatic. We have to be coldly realistic about what we know, versus what we believe, versus what we have no damned idea about."

He thought for another few seconds.

"But you mustn't be alarmist about this. Just because I can't say we're safe here doesn't mean we aren't. It just means I can't prove it. Just like I can't say that there *won't* be an epic battle with the enemy between here and the Moon tomorrow. But that doesn't mean I think there *will* be. Please try to understand what I am saying, and don't make inferences that aren't intended."

"You mean, as in, that there might be survivors of this Beta Hydri race?"

"Exactly."

PIO Wright got on her feet, closing up the meeting and sending the media people on their way.

After they were gone, she dropped into Harris' office and flopped into the chair across from his desk.

"Ron, you were really good today. I hope they hold the line on the survivor issue."

"Any complaints?"

She shook her head. "Nothing serious, just whining about stuff they had already agreed to. They like you, though. They like the young staff, too."

"They're young, for sure, but they're here because they're smart. I hope we got that part across."

"I think they did. The media people were happy with their treatment, and that says a lot."

"Good. Anything else?"

"Nope."

"Well, hopefully, it will have some effect. I'll have to watch the news tonight and see."

Donna got up to leave. "Hopefully, yes, but somehow I think there's still going to be a lot of chaff amongst the wheat for a while yet."

And, indeed, when Donna watched the evening news programs, she could see the chaff was clearly winning.

Intrepid
Big Blue
Thursday, November 24, 2078, 0950 UTC

Intrepid came out of FTL at Beta Hydri ready to shoot but found no targets. They made two wide swings around Big Blue, looking for any sign of the enemy. Joanne drove the ship hard, moving quickly around to try to get a look at the planet from every angle. This was no Newtonian orbit — she was pushing the Drive to get them around as fast as practical.

After three and a half hours, Surveillance Officer Marco Gonzales left his Bridge workstation to report his results.

"Nothing new in orbit, Captain. No evidence of the enemy in the cities, either."

"This is all pretty strange, Marco, don't you think?"

"Yes, ma'am. Sure is."

Joanne called Ben up from Intel. Ann Cooper came along, intrigued by the November 6th alert from her colleagues back at FleetIntel about messages from Beta Hydri.

"OK, so, *Antares* says they didn't see anything in orbit when there were here, either."

"Right," Ben answered.

Joanne pointed to her tablet. "But, according to this update from FleetIntel, there was a message from here while *Antares* was still present, then another about eighteen days later."

"Again, correct."

"So, where is it?"

"Well, the FleetIntel advisory is pretty clear," Ann said. "If they have a spy installation here, it could be anywhere. On one of the moons, maybe even in orbit so far out *Antares* didn't see it."

Ann studied the layout of the Big Blue system on the display above the Surveillance station, then turned to Marco Gonzales.

"So, Lieutenant Gonzales, we've looked for Sigma Spheres, right? Checked the old satellites in orbit?"

"Yes, Lieutenant Cooper, that's standard procedure on arrival in any system these days."

"Would you say that includes anything in high orbit?"

"We would have seen a *Sigma* Sphere out to about three times the orbit of Little Gray, so, say, a million and a half klicks."

Ben nodded as he kept looking at the map of Big Blue and her eight moons.

"What could be transmitting that *Antares* would not have noticed?" he said, thinking out loud.

Joanne, Ann, and Marco followed his eye to the system map as Ben continued. "I mean, Lewis and Jayvon Dean are smart officers, and Ballard is maybe the best ship Intel guy in the Fleet. They would have seen a sphere if it was here."

"What are you thinking, Mr. Price?" Ann asked.

There was a long silence before Ben spoke again. "The moons, Lieutenant, the moons."

"No! Surely *Antares* would have mapped them?" Joanne's voice showed a combination of surprise and concern.

Marco went back to his station and retrieved the detailed surveillance images on the moons from *Antares'* first visit. There wasn't much. The moons had all been mapped but at a relatively low resolution. It just hadn't been a priority.

Ann's surprise was clear in her voice. "Oh my God."

"I could not agree more, Lieutenant," Ben said quietly.

"What now?" Joanne asked.

Ben turned to Marco. "OK, so they're almost all tidally locked, right? Same face always towards Big Blue, just like at home."

"Yes, so?"

"So, would that not be a perfect platform for an observation post? Sort of, a *Sigma* Sphere on the ground?"

"I suppose, but really, even a moon that rotates would probably do."

Ben shook his head, still looking at the data. "No, if I were planting one, I would not want blind spots that could be exploited."

"OK, so, big moon, or small?" Joanne asked.

"Big. Easier to conceal something that size on a large surface," Ann responded after a moment. "A *Sigma* Sphere on the surface would stick out on some of these smaller bodies. On Little Gray or one of the other larger ones, they might be able to hide it somehow."

"So, start with Little Gray?" Marco asked.

"Yes. And hope to God they haven't seen *us* already."

"But, let's not tip our hand," Joanne said. "We'll go into a high orbit, say, halfway up, same plane as the moons but counter-direction? "

"Makes sense to me, Captain," Ben answered.

They made one last pass over Big Blue, checking that the evening cooking fires were where they belonged. Reassured by their presence, *Intrepid* moved into a high orbit and began studying the moons in detail.

Intrepid
Big Blue
Saturday, November 26, 2078, 1935 UTC

"What the *hell* is that?" Ben heard one of the Surveillance techs say. He walked over as the tech put the image on the display.

"Spectrum matches," said the other tech on duty.

"So, it's enemy?"

"By the book, Mr. Price, yes, it is."

Tucked near the tall outside wall of a crater, nearly dead-center in the face of Little Gray, there was a dome. There were dark spots on top, presumably windows or viewing ports.

"There ain't no natural domes like that. Craters can be really, really, round, like to a few percent, but domes? Domes just ain't natural."

"Especially domes with windows?"

"Gotta admit, it looks pretty suspicious."

Joanne joined them.

"OK, gentlemen, what now?" she asked.

"We keep looking," Gonzales said firmly. "Yes, we found this one. That doesn't mean there aren't others."

Ben nodded. "Yes, I agree. We should finish examining Little Gray and then all the others."

"And then?"

"Well, Captain, I'd love to just smoke the bastards, but we really should ask FleetIntel what they think."

"They'll tell you to leave it in place," Ann said, having arrived about halfway through the conversation. "Basic counter-intelligence: leave the enemy's asset in place until we can either exploit it or we really have to kill it."

"Yes, I agree," Ben commented.

Ann went on. "If we kill it now, we both tell them we know it's there and we give them a chance to replace it with something better that we won't find."

Joanne nodded her agreement. "OK, let's wait until we've completed the survey, then we'll send a quick message home. Do we think the enemy is copying our SLIP messages like we are theirs?"

Ben answered, "Not enough data to say either way. They know we have SLIP, for sure, but beyond that, no proof. Harris has always insisted that we assume they are, but, in truth, we don't know."

"OK, that's how we'll play it."

"We still need to finish mapping Little Gray, then do the others."

"Yes, Marco, I agree. We check everywhere. When we're done, I'll signal Fleet-Intel and see what they say."

Ben had been on duty for twenty hours, so he headed for his cabin for some rest, but not before a short stop in the Weapons Maintenance office.

Joanne returned to the command position and spent a couple hours watching the Surveillance team work their process on the little moon. She briefed XO Bass when he came on for the midnight Conn shift, then retired to her duty cabin. It had been a long and eventful day.

Intrepid
Big Blue
Sunday, November 27, 2078, 0630 UTC

After they completed the survey of Little Gray, Joanne decided that they would proceed with the deployment of the Sentinel. She wanted it in place and working as soon as possible. Once that was set, they would finish surveying the other moons and then visit the Seekers to let them know how to contact their new friends.

Putting the Sentinel out was like a day at an amusement park for Ann. She'd read the final procedure that Ben and Natalie had devised, of course, but to watch it in person was a treat for her. She buried her head in the Sentinel to connect the RTG as Ben talked her through the procedure, with Natalie looking on from the other side. This was what Ann had wanted to do all along. She rode out with Natalie in the shuttle to deploy it, and had a chance to watch it orient itself and begin its lonely, monotonous, invaluable work.

As they got out of the shuttle back in the hangar, Ann gave Natalie a massive hug.

"That was GREAT!" she exclaimed.

Natalie smiled and returned Ann's embrace. "Well, it was your idea, after all!"

After the half-day excursion to install the Sentinel, they returned to mapping, and it took them another day to survey the rest of the moons in detail. They now knew that there were no other facilities on Little Gray or any of the other small bodies that orbited Big Blue. Joanne sent a message to FleetIntel, asking what to do with the dome they had seen.

"I also requested instructions on where they want us to go from here," she reported to the wardroom. "But, with a full rifle platoon aboard, I have to think they'll order us back home. I can't keep them cooped up forever."

December 2078

ISC Fleet HQ Office of the Commander in Chief
Ft. Eustis, VA
Thursday, December 1, 2078, 0930 EST

New Admiral Kieran Barker met with Fiona Collins in Plans and together they created a new search plan to satisfy CINC's requirements. This plan used a less randomized and much more efficient routing. It deliberately included stops at Kapteyn, Inor, and Tranquility II to give the crews relief from the monotony of transits. The training and education plan that Joanne Henderson had started months before was useful, but one could only study and exercise so much before boredom naturally began to creep in.

Ron Harris's staff provided the locations of all known enemy observation posts, the so-called 'Sigma Spheres,' and they would be paying special attention to those. They needed a more precise definition of their orbits so they could be easily found later.

By late November *Aurora* had already deployed four more Sentinels, and Fleet-Intel expected all eight to be released by mid-January. Harris argued strongly that any offensive should be delayed until all of the new Sentinels were operational, and *Cobra* had completed its mission to Alpha Mensae. Both had the potential to change their understanding of the enemy, their location and behaviors, and their weaknesses. But *Cobra* would likely not return until late February or early March. CINC wanted an attack before that, and further discussions had not moved him from that opinion. If Barker really wanted to wait, he'd have to push CINC much harder than he had so far.

Barker made his initial report to CINC on December 1st as ordered. His staff was now complete. Harry Hess had agreed to join him as his Chief of Staff, Operations Officer, and de facto deputy. As long as they didn't ask Harry to put on a star, he'd go. Not happily, as he loved *Yorktown* like a mistress, but he'd go.

The same could not be said for several ship commanders Barker tried to recruit. Terri Michael, in particular, expressed her support for him but would not come unless ordered by CINC. Mark Rhodes said something similar, something about prying *Chaffee* from his 'cold dead hands.' They all wanted to stay with their ships, and Kieran, who *had* been ordered by CINC to take the southern theater post, respected that.

On the other hand, Elias Peña agreed to come over from FleetIntel, which, along with Evans' new assignment commanding *Cobra*, seriously depleted Ron Harris' senior staff. He didn't care, he said; he had great people, and they'd manage

227

just fine. CINC could find him some new blood whenever he had the time, according to Ron. Elias was glad to get off Earth, away from his personal distractions. He'd have arm-wrestled any other candidate for a chance to get on the front lines.

Fleet Logistics sent Commander Ed Mendez, the Chief of Staff, to handle supply for Barker. They expected to have significant requirements, and Mendez would know how to make it happen. The ship that ISC had promised was undergoing the needed modifications and would be ready after the first of the year. Mendez and Barker talked at length about how best to use that asset, and how to integrate it with Barker's flagship. They decided to put Mendez in command of *Ceres,* and keep Barker's flagship and it together.

"What I want to do, sir," he told CINC, "along with the flag vessel, is to keep one or two frigates in convoy with *Ceres.* They can hang out with us for a few days, a week, whatever, and then back to search or attack."

"So, you're both protecting *Ceres* and giving them a small break?"

"Exactly, sir."

"Good, I like it. What are your thoughts on a flagship? You really need to decide, Kieran, so we can get them in place."

"Well, *Yorktown* and *Dunkirk* are out right off, sir; too deep a connection with Harry and me."

"OK, then, cruiser, destroyer, or frigate?"

"Destroyer, I think. It can handle the additional staff I'll be bringing. Four additional Intel, then Hess and his three staff, my three assistants."

"Right, that would get seriously tight on a frigate. So, who?"

"Well, sir, might I ask your opinion? What's available?"

"This is a major priority for the Fleet, Kieran. You can have whatever you want. But if you're asking what's immediate and not inconvenient..." Davenport continued while he pulled up his status display. "*Antares* and *Intrepid* have both been modified to carry more Marines. Let's skip those." The display populated with the current position and condition of every ship in the Fleet. "OK, so, *Yankee* is here, she's brand new and getting a new Captain, Jim George. *Aquarius* happens to be in orbit, but she's expected to leave, uh, tomorrow for the search."

He paused as he read the display.

"*Mir* is due back day after tomorrow, then a quick turnaround — three days then back out."

"*Ceres* won't be ready until January, and the search is going already forward..." CINC set down his glasses and looked across his desk. "What are you thinking, Kieran?"

"Smith is a young shit, you know, all smart-ass and guts."

CINC nodded and smiled, crossing his arms. "Remind you of yourself?"

Barker grinned slightly and looked out the window at the blowing snow. "He can be a real pain the ass, just like his friend Powell. But, he's not one to quit, and he ran that intel op on the wreck about as well as it could be run. Dicey thing, that, and they got what we needed."

CINC leaned forward on his desk. "Well, Powell is going on the first trip on *Cobra*. I need to get them back before she leaves."

"Well, then, sir, I'd like *Columbia*, if I can."

"*Columbia* it is, then. When do you want them back here?"

Barker smiled as the snow outside the window gave him an idea. "Oh, let's get them back for Christmas. It will be a small gift before they get the really bad news about being the flagship."

CINC sent the message to *Columbia* but did not hold back the 'bad' part. Dan Smith should know what was up, and be able to prepare his crew for what was now ahead of them.

Intrepid
Big Blue
Thursday, December 1, 2078, 1800 UTC

The message back showed that Fleet clearly agreed with Joanne.

```
PRIORITY 207811282200UTC
TO: INTREPID
FROM: CINCFLEET

FLEETINTEL INSTRUCTIONS ARE TO LEAVE LITTLE GRAY FACILITY IN PLACE.
IT WILL BE DESTROYED WHEN TACTICALLY NECESSARY OR DESIRABLE.
LEAVE RADIO WITH EAAGHER THEN RTB EARTH YOUR EARLIEST
CONVENIENCE TO DISEMBARK MARINES.

END
```

Joanne read the message to her officers before dinner on Friday.

"What's the time on the surface right now?" Joanne asked.

"Sunrise on Sol 93 where the survivors are was three hours ago, ma'am," Marco Gonzales said.

"If you want to go today, we need to get on it," Ben said.

"Where is Little Gray with respect to the Seekers' position?"

"Uh...one second, ma'am," Gonzales checked his tablet. "Little Gray set about three hours ago."

"So, we have, say, twenty-one hours before it rises again?"

"Yes, ma'am."

"OK, Lieutenant Covington, get us in a position over the Seekers. Ben, you'll lead the discussion with Eaagher. Natalie, you'll fly this mission."

Joanne turned to her left. "Ann, are you interested in going to the surface?"

Her excitement at this invitation was obvious in her voice. "Yes, ma'am. I can help explain the radio procedure to Eaagher."

"The Sentinel is up?"

"Yes, ma'am."

"OK, the three of you get down there and get back. I get all creepy knowing the enemy might be watching."

Big Blue
Seeker Beach
Friday, December 2, 2078, 0100 UTC

The arrival of the *Intrepid* shuttle, well ahead of the normal fishing time, was a surprise. The few Seekers on the beach moved away as it landed. As the three humans walked to the place *Antares* had described, body-cams running, the child they knew had to be Ullnii came out.

She called "Callol! Yames! Grag!" as she looked from face to face. Finally, she stopped, her disappointment at seeing no familiar faces obvious.

Ben, remembering his instructions, waved his right hand 'No,' said "Eaagher," and touched his forehead. It all seemed very awkward and overly complex, but the little girl waved her left hand and went back into the brush at the edge of the low forest.

"Oh my God, the eyes!" Ann said quietly after Ullnii left.

Natalie agreed. "Yes, amazing."

Eaagher returned a few minutes later with two of his guards, carrying the word signs Greg Cordero had left with him. Greg had also left a Fleet tablet with the translation application. Eaagher handed it over to Ben.

"Eaagher," the Seeker said and touched his forehead.

"Ben."

Eaagher lifted his left hand. "Benh."

Ben typed on the tablet, then pointed to the handheld radio in Ann's hand.

"You may contact Friends this device."

Eaagher pulled the 'happy' sign and pointed to it. Ben smiled and lifted his left hand.

Ann came forward and said, "Ann," as she touched her forehead.

Seekers didn't smile the way humans do, but Eaagher was pleased with the respect this female had shown him, introducing herself properly. Their oohmann friends were learning, and this seemed to confirm his hope that they were 'good.' He tilted his head to the left and responded, "Eaagher."

Ann was able to show Eaagher how to use the radio with the liberal use of the 'Yes' and 'No' signs, along with 'On' and 'Off.' Eaagher understood quickly what was being asked of him. The Seekers once had radio, Ann knew, so this was not an idea that was foreign to them. Natalie watched all this from a small distance, her earpiece on the ship's tactical frequency. Ann had Eaagher speak into the radio, and Communications Officer Jesse Woodward confirmed that it worked by answering Eaagher's message with his name. Again, he inclined his head and made the laughing gesture, accompanied by a mid-range rumble in his throat.

"Is he laughing?" Natalie asked.

"I think so," Ben answered, "But Cordero didn't mention a sound, just the gesture." Ben touched the 'happy' sign and touched his forehead.

Yes.

Ben typed, "Friends home far. Message to Friends must travel one and one-half sun."

Eaagher wrote his response and touched his forehead.

Suns Friends future come?

Ben turned to Ann. "I think he's asking how long for us to come if he sends us a message."

"Well, it's twenty-two-plus days, so, twelve Sols?"

"OK." Ben typed "twelve suns" and put it in front of Eaagher.

Hard faces kill many 14 suns.

Ben looked at the message and then showed it to Ann and Natalie.

"That's the hard truth, Ben," Ann answered.

Joanne and her Bridge crew were casually watching the body-cam feed from the surface, listening as Ben did his best Greg Cordero impression, when the Surveillance console lit up with alarms. Marco Gonzales jumped in response and ran back to his position.

"Captain, we have multiple IR transients. I read them as four enemy ships arriving."

"Four?" Joanne exclaimed. "Jesse, get Ben on the line and tell him to wrap it up."

Ben waved his left hand in response to Eaagher's comment, then turned suddenly, holding his ear.

To Eaagher's eyes, all three humans turned suddenly away as if stricken in pain. He saw how they held their ears, and he knew from the first visit that they had devices that let them hear their leader. Whatever had just happened must be bad, and might be dangerous. He called Ullnii to his side. There was a rapid conversation between them, and they frequently looked back at Ullnii and him.

Joanne put on her headset. "Ben! We have company. Four Type I's just arrived."
"We best get the hell out of here, Captain. We can't let them see a shuttle here."
"Agreed."
"We can't just come back — we'd be leading them right to you."
"OK, Mr. Price, what do you suggest?"
Ben looked around to the west. "Lots of mountains west of here, Captain. We'll just have to go hide."
Ann and Natalie nodded their agreement. Ann took the tablet from Ben and walked back to Eaagher, typing as she went.
"Hard faces return. Friends must leave now to keep your secret."
Eaagher waved his left hand, then wrote.
Where hard faces?
"Orbit"
Many?
Ann waved her left hand. Yes, many.
Eaagher typed *Friends leave* and touched his forehead.
Ann waved her right hand then repeated, "These Friends must go now to keep secret."
Eaagher waited for her to continue.
"Friends in orbit not leave. Fight hard faces."
Eaagher waved his left hand.
"Ann, finish up with Eaagher, and then we gotta go."
"OK, just one more." She typed as quickly as she could. "We three now go hide ship to protect you. These Friends hope to see you again short future."
Eaagher looked at the sky. To Ann, he looked nervous, but she knew that was just projection on her part. She had no idea what 'nervous' looked like on a Seeker. She shut down the tablet and handed it to Natalie, who flipped it over and replaced the battery in a few quick motions, then returned it to Eaagher.
Ben was getting increasingly worried. "Gotta go, gotta go!"
They ran to the shuttle, Natalie in the left seat, Ben on the right, and Ann stuffing herself in the jump-seat just behind and between the pilots. Natalie pulled the shuttle off the sand and moved quickly north just a few meters off the water.
"We need to get as far away as fast as we can," she said quietly.
"Right," Ann answered. Ben just nodded as he pulled up the imagery of the continent.

"Where are they, Marco?"

"They're still moving around, Captain. I can't tell for sure, but I think they're setting up over Capital City."

"Yeah, too much snooping around down there by us humans."

"May be, ma'am, may well be."

"Weapons are ready, Captain," Jim Kirkland reported. He'd loaded their two rotary launchers with Bludgeons. Joanne had no plans to hang around if fired on, so she'd ordered no Spartans. The rotaries remained inboard, maintaining the stealth of the ship.

Joanne stood at her command station, wondering what she should do next. *Intrepid* was now as buttoned-up as she could be: a silent, nearly invisible ghost in space. The shuttle crew would have to fend for themselves for now. There was nothing more she could do for them, so she tried to put that worry off for the moment.

Intrepid Shuttle
Big Blue
Friday, December 2, 2078, 0225 UTC

As Natalie hurried the shuttle north, flying just above the swells a couple kilometers off the beach, Ben and Ann were studying the landscape.

"There's a pretty deep valley right here," Ben said, pointing. "With a decent sized river. We could use that to get inland."

"And then what?" The stress was starting to show in Natalie's voice.

"And then we'll figure something out," Ben replied evenly.

Ann looked from one of her companions to the other. She knew they had a relationship, and that could be a problem in this scenario, but so far, they seemed to be handling themselves well. Still, it would be something she'd need to observe. She outranked both of them, and if necessary, she'd pull that trump card, but for now, Natalie was the best available pilot and Ben the resident expert on the planet. Her best option was to listen, advise, and let the *Intrepid* people take the lead.

They turned up the valley, which was enormous — several kilometers wide and at least a kilometer deep. Natalie cruised westward at two hundred kilometers per hour, not more than a dozen meters over the river, the tops of the trees at eye level, Ann watching quietly, but nervously, from behind as the world zipped by a few meters away.

"OK," Ben said, "there's a fork in the road about fifty klicks ahead."

When he didn't say any more, Natalie couldn't resist. "So, what? Take it?"

"You can't have your fork and take it too, Nat. Go right."

"Why right?"

Ben shrugged. "Honestly, there's no good reason other than it moves us further away from the Seekers."

"That works."

A few minutes later they saw the mountain that split the valley in half rising out of the horizon. Once it grew to dominate their view, Natalie moved the shuttle right, up a long and rising area of whitewater, then settled down near the surface again as they followed the smaller tributary northwest. The valley was rising gently, the water flowing swiftly in the opposite direction. The walls were gradually closing, and Natalie could see that they would come to the end before long. After all, the mountain range that ended in the sea was not that wide, perhaps a hundred kilometers.

"How far should we go?" Natalie asked.

"West of here is the plains. I think we should maybe double back south a little and find a notch somewhere to hide in."

"I don't get it," Ann said.

Ben leaned back, showing her the images on his tablet. "Look at how the mountains come up out of the plains. There are some pretty rough areas right on the edge, here and here," he said, pointing. "If we tuck in there somewhere, hopefully we'll get lost in the rocks."

"OK, fine. We'll be out of cover here shortly."

Natalie flew up and out of the remnant of the valley they had been following, then turned hard left and dropped back down to skim just above the low foliage of the foothills. She kept her eyes ahead, sneaking only a few glances at the sharp mountains just off to her left.

Ben and Ann agreed on a promising site to put the shuttle down.

"OK, Nat, just a little ahead there should be a big stone outcrop, slide around that to the left and then set us down somewhere soft."

"Soft?"

"Yeah, soft. As in, not hard enough to break the belly."

"Smartass."

Natalie found the massive stone prominence easily, slowing the shuttle as she gently moved around it and laid the shuttle down as close to the rocks as possible. There were boulders strewn all about, and it took her a few tries to find a suitable spot. She shut down the Drive, and some of the tension that had her shoulders, her whole body, feeling like a coiled spring started to release. "Now what?" she asked, shaking the stress out of her legs and shoulders.

Ann shrugged. "Now we wait, I guess. Is there anything to eat?"

"Sure," Natalie answered, "there's food and water in the back. Hungry?"

"Yes. Being scared out of my wits does that to me."

Ben looked at her with surprise. "You hide it well."

"I'm married and I've delivered a child, Ben. It's required."

Intrepid
Big Blue
Friday, December 2, 2078, 0830 UTC

Captain Joanne Henderson paced the Bridge, impatient for something to happen while at the same time dreading that something actually would. They had tracked the shuttle up the coast, but once Hayden ducked into the river valley, they had lost it. Marco Gonzales guessed that they would follow the valley west, and he was able to pick them back up when they came out but lost them again not long after that.

"I think, Captain, that they've holed up in one of these little canyons along the western edge of the mountains." He pointed at a picture of the landscape they had taken only a few days earlier. "Plenty of cover there, and the black shuttle will blend in as well there as anywhere else."

"OK, where are the Type I's?"

"As we expected, they're in synchronous orbit over the old settlement."

"OK, so, they're about 120 degrees off our position, but at about the same altitude..."

"Yes, Captain, that's correct."

"...but from here I can't just go get the shuttle. We'll need to figure out how to get them back."

"Yes, and assuming they're in one of those canyons, our line of sight from here sucks."

"Put up a tactical display, Marco, let me see it in 3D." In a few seconds the main display screen revealed the four enemy ships close together over the old city, with *Intrepid* around to the east of the enemy, more or less over the Seekers' hideout. The Sentinel appeared about half-way between Joanne and the enemy ships.

"We can't stay here for long. If they see us, it'll compromise the Seekers."

Her line of thought was interrupted by the arrival of the lead Intel tech, husky Texan Colin Garrett. He was nominally in charge now, what with both Ben Price and Ann Cooper not available.

"Captain? Ma'am, the Sentinel just phoned home. It sent an automatic alarm back to Fleet."

"What? Explain."

"Well, ma'am, it's programmed to call in a significant IR event. I'd say the arrival of four Type I's would qualify."

"How long ago?"

"About five minutes. I came as soon as I saw it on the SLIP scanner."

"Fine, Garrett, thanks."

He made no move to leave the Bridge.

"Something else?"

"Yes, ma'am. We should be watching the enemy ships for a reaction. If they're hearing our SLIP transmissions, they might move to find and take out the Sentinel."

Jim Kirkland had been listening to the conversation. "He's right, Captain. But the Sentinel just did us a gigantic favor. We don't have to tell Fleet that the enemy is here."

"Yeah. Except, it can't tell anyone else."

Garrett turned back to Joanne. "Did you want a Fleet report, ma'am?"

Joanne looked at the young tech, just months out of Advanced Intel certification school, with new eyes. He was no slouch, this one. "Yes, Garrett, go ahead."

"The best we have is *Eagle* at GL 66, that's ten light years."

"And, almost ten days."

Garrett nodded sadly. "True, ma'am. Regrettable. The next is *Friendship*. She's at GL 293, about twelve light-years. Then —"

"Never mind, Garrett."

"Ma'am?"

"None of them are close enough to be any help. I can't call them myself without exposing us, and any order from Fleet is three days away. So, we're on our own."

"Yes, Captain."

Joanne looked at the young, disappointed face of the tech. Disappointed, she noticed, but not afraid.

"Thanks, Garrett. Keep an eye on the SLIP. If the enemy starts talking, we may have to act."

"Yes, ma'am. We'll be watching."

Garrett left the Bridge and headed back to the Intel section. He'd given the captain what they had. If it wasn't enough or wasn't what the captain needed to hear, that wasn't Garrett's problem. Price had taught them over and over that the truth was the truth, and their job as Intel techs was to deliver it as completely and objectively as they could. Commanders would do whatever they could with it, but once the information was delivered, he had done his job.

Intrepid Shuttle
Big Blue
Friday, December 2, 2078, 1030 UTC

After a forgettable lunch of pre-packaged *what-the-hell-was-that*, Natalie opened the side entry stairs of the shuttle, and they took some time to relax outside.

Ben walked back the way they had come in, and finding nothing interesting after a hundred meters, returned to the shuttle.

"Not much out there, really, just some scrub and rocks."

"Yeah, I felt a little like Neil Armstrong coming in here. Too many boulders."

"But you weren't running low on fuel."

"Don't pop my balloon, Price."

"Or fighting a 1201 alarm—"

"Price!"

"Yes, you're right, Nat, it was exactly like Neil and Buzz."

Ann laughed at the exchange, encouraged at their sense of humor. They were all stressed, but the danger was not immediate. They were down, safe, with food, heat, and whatever else they might need for at least a week, probably longer.

Ann sat on the entry stairs, sipping coffee as she studied the landscape around them. Natalie had set the shuttle down in line with the east-west orientation of the small canyon they were in, although 'canyon' might be too generous a term for it. *It's more of a gorge,* she thought, *but no stream.* The sides were not more than fifty meters apart, and the walls rose steeply for about twice that distance. The stone was gray and flecked, like granite, and small foliage grew on ledges in the walls. Except for the wind in her ears, it was silent. There were few insects and no birds on Big Blue, so the planet at rest was unusually quiet to human ears.

"Are we worried about being seen out here?" Ann asked.

Ben leaned back, stretching. "I don't think so. *Antares* reported some larger wildlife, not a lot, but there are human-scale animals here. If they see us on IR, they might not notice."

"Might," Natalie said from just inside the shuttle.

"There are no guarantees, Nat. If they spot us, it'll be trouble, yeah."

"We should stay inside at night."

"Yes, that would be smart. We'll be a more obvious target when it's cooler outside."

Natalie stepped out of the shuttle, handing Ben and Ann holsters with sidearms.

"You think this is necessary?" Ann asked.

"We don't know the wildlife. Where there are animals our size, there are likely predators who eat animals our size."

"Fair enough." Ann slipped the leather over her shoulder and cinched it up around her waist. "And if they enemy shows up, at least we can take a few hunks out of them."

The sun had come around now and was fully illuminating the gorge. The three humans retreated to the back of the shuttle, finding some shade and a few cool rocks to sit on.

"We should talk about that," Natalie began.

"About what?" Ben asked.

"If the enemy shows up."

"What do we have besides three .45's?"

"There's three 2K7X's and about a hundred rounds each in magazines. There's also a couple hundred .45 rounds."

"Well, that's better than nothing," Ann responded.

"Maybe," Ben said. "Two things you both need to remember. We can't be taken, and we can't let the Shuttle be taken."

"Ben, you're not leaving us much of a choice."

"Ann, you know this as well, maybe better, than I do. They show no indication of understanding atomic energy. We can't hand them a working reactor, no matter how small it is."

"And we can't let them have us, either," Natalie said, a distance in her voice.

"And we can't lead them to *Intrepid*."

"Let's just hope they don't find us."

Ben nodded his agreement. "Yes, Ann, I hope that, too. But if they do, I'll try to hold them back, you and Natalie get in the shuttle and get out of here."

Ann shook her head. "This is no time for chivalry, Ben."

Ben looked at her, frustration clear on his face. "It's not that, Lieutenant Cooper."

Ben stood, walked to the corner of the shuttle, and looked out into the sunshine. "It's really pretty simple. I'm single. You have a family. Nat is the best pilot. If you think about it rationally, I stay and shoot as long as I can while you two bug out."

"And you get to save me in the bargain?" Natalie asked.

"Well," Ben said, smiling, "there's that, too."

Ann leaned back against the rock wall. "Before we get all emotional about who might live and who'll probably die, how about we let this process play itself out?" Natalie and Ben nodded their agreement.

"Don't forget who's senior here — that would be me — and if it comes to the worst case, I'll be making the decisions."

They looked at Ann in surprise. Neither Ben nor Natalie expected her to pull rank. She was an HQ Intel wonk, after all. But, she was indeed senior.

Ben looked at Natalie and then replied for both of them. "Yes, ma'am. We understand."

"Good. I don't suppose there's a deck of cards on this tub?"

Intrepid
Big Blue
Friday, December 2, 2078, 1430 UTC

Twelve hours was a long time to sit around and watch your enemy organize themselves. Joanne watched the tactical display as the enemy dispatched a shuttle to the surface. So far, they were concentrating on the old city, and she was happy to let them have it. She called her staff together on the Bridge to decide what to do next.

"They don't seem to know we're here," she began, "So, let's keep it that way. Any suggestions for what we should do about the shuttle?"

Marco Gonzales answered, "I've been thinking about that. We need to pick them up somehow, and we need to keep an eye on the Seekers. If the enemy should discover them —"

Marine Captain Andy Martin spoke up. "Then I'll have to go down there and help them un-discover them."

"Yes, Captain, indeed you might," Marco agreed. "But I was thinking if we set up a high-inclination elliptical orbit —"

Joanne looked at him in surprise. "A Molniya orbit? I haven't thought of that in years."

"Molniya?" Martin asked, puzzled.

Marco Gonzales explained. "Early Soviet spacecraft could not easily reach synchronous Earth orbit – their launch sites were just too far north, A practical alternative was a high-inclination, highly-elliptical orbit with its apogee over the northern hemisphere. The satellite would linger for a long time over the service area. Once several were in place, you could have continuous communications – or intelligence - coverage."

"Wow. Inventive."

"Yes, they were always good at overcoming problems with simple, reliable solutions."

Martin was starting to understand. "So, with this orbit, we could hang out for a long time over the Seekers."

"Yes."

"How does this help with the shuttle?"

"Well, the perigee of a Molly orbit is deep in the southern hemisphere. If they could work their way around the other side of the planet to that third continent, they could meet up with us as we go by."

Communications Officer Jesse Woodward agreed. "And a high inclination would give us a line of sight to where we think they're holed up. We could talk to them with the laser, let them know what we're thinking."

Joanne nodded her understanding. "And we could do all of this out of sight of the enemy on the other side of the planet?"

"Yes, Captain, I think we can."

She looked over at Larry Covington, her Navigator, who'd said nothing throughout the discussion.

"Lieutenant Covington?"

"Yes, Captain?"

"Your opinion?"

"Oh, well, yes, we've been talking back and forth about this for a couple hours. I agree with what Marco and Jesse are saying."

"What about the shuttle?"

"I looked at the geography, and if they can leave from the far western edge of the southern continent as we come around the planet, it should be no problem for them to catch us before we are in the line-of-sight from the enemy ships."

Joanne was skeptical. "No problem?"

"Not for Hayden, ma'am, no. But we will need to set up our orbit to pass right over that point as we come up from perigee. That will minimize the lateral distance and save some time."

"The Sentinel is in synchronous orbit on the equator, about sixty degrees west of our current position."

"Yes, Captain, that's correct."

"We picked that position so it could see both the old cities and the Seekers' hideout. I think our apogee should be over that same longitude."

"That makes sense, ma'am."

"Lieutenant Gonzales, what would that do for our line-of-sight to the shuttle?"

"If the inclination is high enough, say, seventy degrees, we should see them, assuming a good apogee. Since I don't know exactly where they are, it's hard to say for sure."

"Do I dare risk a maneuver to put us right over them, tell them what we're doing, and then another to get into the right orbit?"

"Cooper, Price, and Hayden are all pretty cool customers, Captain. If they're down and secure, they'll stay put for at least a Sol or two."

"I hope so. They don't teach this scenario at the U."

"They will next year!"

Joanne thought hard about what she should do, finally deciding to make one long maneuver to get them into the elliptical Molniya orbit. Once they got high enough, Marco could try to raise the shuttle. But that would be at least 12 hours away, maybe more.

Intrepid Shuttle
Big Blue
Friday, December 2, 2078, 1500 UTC

Sunset came slowly on Big Blue. With a rotation speed roughly half that of Earth, the star took its time crawling behind the horizon. But despite the warm weather, on a planet with almost no tilt there was little gradual twilight as in North American summers. Once the star set, pretty soon it was dark. Ben took another walk out to the mouth of the gorge, just to check, and returned.

"Nothing?" Ann asked.

"Nope. Nada. It's as quiet as a cathedral on a Monday out there."

"OK, good."

The evening was clear, the night air cooled quickly, and soon the stars were out. Big Blue's atmosphere was very clean, and there were no city lights to haze the skies. They enjoyed the beauty for a while, but soon they moved inside the shuttle and closed up for the night. They weren't aware of exactly how long they'd been awake, just that it had been a very long time, they were dead tired, and now it was dark outside. Probably a good time to sleep, they decided.

They folded down a few seats and pulled blankets from the emergency supplies. Natalie did an inventory and found they had almost two weeks' worth of food and water, a small reward for being only three individuals. The toilet would hold out that long as well, a relief for everyone. The only amenity they lacked was a shower, but they'd at least all get ripe together.

Ann found herself a spot in the back of the passenger area. Ben and Natalie took a spot in the front, nearest the cockpit and the communications gear. They finally gave up on the seats — this was not a Fleet shuttle designed for long trips — and managed to nest together on the floor, a few layers beneath them to cushion their hips and shoulders. Ben drifted off quickly. Despite her fatigue, Natalie laid there for a couple hours listening to the rhythm of his breathing, watching his chest gently rise and fall in the dim glow from the red and green LED status displays and illuminated switches. She was unable to sleep, reliving the dash up the coast and then between the trees just over the water. It didn't scare her at the time, but now, as she thought back on it, she was a little frightened at what she had done. She hoped if she had to do that again, she'd be as cool as she was today.

Ben stirred and looked at her, and seeing she was still awake, he hugged her gently. She smiled in response. As he readjusted his position a little and went back to sleep, she refolded the blanket that served as her pillow and closed her eyes, wrapping one arm around Ben's waist. Before long, she was snoring quietly.

Intrepid
Big Blue
Saturday, December 3, 2078, 0330 UTC

Jesse Woodward pointed the long laser communications boom at the general area where Marco seemed to think the shuttle would be and put it into acquisition mode. It would transmit a few millisecond-long bursts of light, then wait a few seconds for a response, then try again. The communications dome on top of the shuttle would detect the call and respond.

On the surface, local midnight was almost an hour away, but the three fugitives had already scored a full night's sleep. Ben walked out again to have a look around. There was nothing new to be seen, no sign of any enemy activity, no wildlife. It was still very, very quiet. Little Gray was over the mountains in the east, and Ben greeted it with a single, well-chosen digit.

As he returned the comm system sounded a connection tone. Natalie pulled on the headset.

"*Intrepid,* this is Hayden."

Jesse responded with a smile. "Good evening Lieutenant Hayden! Enjoying your shore leave?"

"Oh, yeah, it's a real paradise down here. Good to hear your voice, Jesse."

"Same here. Get Price and Cooper on the line and stand by for the captain."

Joanne put her headset on and brought the shuttle crew up to speed on what they had done in the last twenty-four hours. *Intrepid* was now in a twelve-hour elliptical orbit, its forty-five-thousand-kilometer apogee placing them in a position to monitor both the old cities and the Seekers' new settlement. Larry Covington data-linked the orbital details to them and then explained how they could get back aboard with a sprint from the southern continent. The enemy was concentrating all four ships over Capital City, so it would be possible for them to sneak around the other side of the planet to get themselves in position.

"How long to get over there?" Ann asked.

"It's halfway around the planet," Natalie responded. "Once we're out of sight of the enemy, we can go up out of the atmosphere. I'd say, maybe three hours?"

Ben looked at the orbit Larry had sent down on the cockpit display. "Right now, they're just a few minutes past apogee. So, it's six hours, or eighteen. What do we think?"

Natalie pulled up a visual of Big Blue, showing where it was day or night. "In three hours, it will still be dark on that continent. In five, it'll be light. So, I vote we wait three hours, then go. We meet *Intrepid* in eighteen hours."

Ben looked at Ann. "Any other thoughts?"

Ann shook her head. "No. Natalie's the pilot here, so I'll go with her decision. But I do agree that it would be better to arrive there in daylight, especially in the morning where the shadows will be exaggerated."

Natalie clicked the transmit switch. "*Intrepid*, this is Hayden."

"Yes, Lieutenant."

"OK, our consensus is that we meet you in eighteen hours. We want to get over to the other side in daylight."

On *Intrepid*'s bridge, Larry agreed. "I expected that, Captain. It's the safest course for them."

"OK, fine. Jesse, tell them that's approved. We'll close up comms for now and see them at the start of rev three."

Joanne looked at the chronometer over the Nav station for the time. It had been twenty-seven hours since the Sentinel had sent its alert. The message should be at Earth in nine more hours. Then, another thirty-six hours for HQ to sound the alarm and then ten days for anyone to get to them. So, she was on her own for at least fourteen or fifteen days. *Two weeks!* she thought to herself. *A lot can happen in two weeks, and all I have is one ship and a rifle platoon against four enormous enemy ships with God-only-knows how many troops.* She could strike them and probably win, but that would reveal two very important facts: first, that *Intrepid* was here; and second, that there was something still on this planet worth killing for. She would avoid revealing either of these facts until the danger to the second outweighed the risk to the first. So far, they were OK. Intel was doing well watching the enemy move up and down, exploring the destroyed cities, but likely finding nothing. *Antares* had done a good job of cleaning up after themselves.

So, for now, it was status quo. Orbit quietly, pick up the shuttle, keep watching and be ready to act if necessary. She sat at her command position, oblivious to the nervous tapping of her right foot.

ISC Fleet HQ Intel Section
Ft. Eustis, VA
Saturday, December 3, 2078, 0920 EST (1420 UTC)

Rich Evans was in his office, reviewing the status of change orders for the new spy ship, *Cobra,* when all hell broke loose in the hallway. The shouts of alarm echoed around the Intel section like a ricochet. Soon the entire Intel crew was crashing into the large workroom, Evans trotting along behind.

Roger Cox put the data up on the large wall display.

"The Sentinel at Big Blue called in with four, yes *four,* enemy ship arrivals. The data is solid, there's no question about it."

"*Intrepid?*" Scott Morgan asked.

"They're still there, far as we know." The immediate cross-discussion among the technical experts rose to a crescendo which broke as Chief of Operations Patricia Cook entered the room, followed by FleetIntel Chief Ron Harris.

"OK, Intel, talk to me."

Roger looked over at Harris, who indicated that he should brief Cook.

"Yes, ma'am, we got the report maybe 15 minutes ago. The Sentinel at Big Blue has reported four enemy ships arriving. It's a really high confidence report, ma'am. The enemy must have been very close."

"We've heard nothing from *Intrepid?*"

"No, but Henderson would have seen this arrival the same time the Sentinel did, so it's no surprise we haven't heard from her."

Cook looked at her tablet. "We have *Eagle* at GL 66, and *Friendship* at GL 293. Everything else is too far away." She turned to her new assistant, a dark-haired, bearded new Lieutenant named Eaton. "Send a flash to *Eagle* and *Friendship*, copy *Intrepid*. Order them to Beta Hydri immediately, minimum EMR. I don't want them to acknowledge the order. Henderson should take command as they arrive. Clear?"

"Yes, Admiral, right away."

Eaton was out of the room in a rush, headed back to his desk to send the order.

"Four ships. What do you make of that?" Cook asked the room.

"They only sent six to take Inor," Roger pointed out.

"Can we tell the type?"

"Yes, Admiral, four Type I's."

"So, perhaps not an invasion force? Did we not propose that the Type II's were the troop carriers based on size?"

"Yes, ma'am, that's what we *think.*"

Evans spoke up from the back of the room. "*Columbia*'s wreck was a Type I, and from their reports, I think it could easily carry several hundred ground troops."

"So, we're looking at the possibility of something like eight hundred enemy troops?" Cook asked.

"From what they reported about that wreck, I think that's conservative, Admiral."

"Damn."

"Yes, ma'am," Evans answered, "Double damn if you ask me."

ISC Fleet HQ Operations Section
Ft. Eustis, VA
Saturday, December 3, 2078, 1530 EST

Six hours later, Ron was across from Chief of Operations Cook in her office, along with Rich Evans, Elias Peña, and CINC Connor Davenport.

"Nothing from *Intrepid* yet. How do we interpret that?" CINC asked.

"It's exactly what I would expect," Peña stated. "The Sentinel did Henderson a huge favor. She doesn't have to call in — the Sentinel did it for them. So now they can clam up and see what happens."

"If Joanne were under attack, she'd tell us before it was too late," Cook said, trying to reassure everyone, including herself.

"I have to wonder, sir, if the Little Gray facility saw *Intrepid* and called home."

"It's possible, Rich, but we saw them check in at Big Blue, then nothing more. I wonder if this could be a follow-up to that previous activity."

"There's no SLIP activity to support Little Gray transmitting," Ron said with some authority. "So, this feels like they're sending more resources to see what those annoying little humans were doing there."

"So," Cook asked, "More of a recon-in-force than an invasion?"

Ron nodded. "Right. There's no one there to invade, far as they know. They think the Seekers are all dead."

"Well," CINC said, leaning back in his chair, "That's what *we* think they think, at least."

Elias Peña responded, "Based on their behavior at Big Blue, sir, I can't see that they would have just let some of them get away."

"Not if they could help it, I agree," Rich added.

CINC shook his head slowly as a scowl grew across his face. "As usual, there's little we can do to help them." His voice rose in both volume and tone as he continued. "We're too far from the action, with control levers that are far too long and assets too far away from where they're needed."

He slammed his cup on Cook's desk, spilling some of its contents, then rose and left with a full-throated obscenity echoing down the hall.

Intrepid
Big Blue
Saturday, December 3, 2078, 2200 UTC

As the shuttle came out of the ShuttleLock, Joanne, XO Alonzo Bass, and several other officers were waiting. Natalie opened the cockpit door and slipped out, Ann and then Ben just behind her.

"Well, well," Joanne said, smiling, "I'm glad to see you three!"

"Thanks, Captain. We're glad to be back," Ann responded.

"And you, Mr. Price?" Joanne asked.

He pointed to Ann. "Don't ever play cards with that woman."

"What?"

"Just don't, Captain. We played Hearts for a buck a point, now I owe her half my next paycheck!"

"Really, Price, you're talking about a superior officer!" Joanne scolded.

"What I'm talking about, my dear Captain, is a superior card shark! What kind of a game is it where the high score *loses*? What the hell is that?"

They laughed at his feigned ignorance. Ann snuck up behind Ben as they walked out of the hangar to give him a hug and whispered, "Sore loser?" in his ear.

Ben smiled and answered, "Well, yeah, sure, sore in the wallet, anyway."

He turned to Henderson. "Seriously, Captain, what's going on?"

"Well, the Sentinel did us all a favor and called in the enemy arrival. Other than that, we're watching them moving personnel, I guess, up and down into Capital City. We can see some of what they're doing but not that much."

"But nothing around the Seekers?"

"Nothing."

"OK, good."

"What did you think of them?" Joanne asked Ann.

"Amazing, Captain, truly amazing. Eaagher is a very smart man. I can see why he's the Leader."

"Interesting. I hope to meet him in person."

Joanne stopped outside the Intel section, holding Ben, Ann, and Natalie with her as the rest of the shuttle greeting committee returned to their duties.

"OK, back to your quarters, all three of you. Get a shower, a few hours rest, then we'll all get back together and see what we need to do next."

"I'll second the shower," Alonzo Bass said as he walked past, headed for the Bridge.

Intrepid
Big Blue
Sunday, December 4, 2078 0500 UTC

After his mandated hot shower and a short rest, Ben returned to the Intel work-room, taking a seat across the table from Colin Garrett.

"OK, so, tell me what's happening."

"They're all over Capital City. I don't know what they're doing, but they're walking all over the place. They take shuttles down and up, which are, you know, a hundred meters long, at irregular intervals."

"No pattern? Not like they're relieving on a day/night cycle or anything?"

"Nope. Once in a while, one goes down, or one comes up."

"What about our friends?"

"They have not been out fishing since this started, and no cooking fires on IR."

"So, they're hunkered down."

"That would be my conclusion. So, what now sir?"

Ben looked at the data feeds, then back at Garrett. "Maintain our surveillance. Not much else we *can* do until the enemy shows their hand."

Intrepid
Big Blue
Sunday, December 4, 2078, 0830 UTC

The wardroom filled slowly as Henderson's officers gathered to discuss their situation and work out their next steps. Joanne sat at the head of the table, and Ben Price dropped into his usual place on her immediate left. XO Bass sat on her right, and the rest filled in more or less randomly as they arrived.

"OK, let's get started. Mr. Price, what is the current state of the enemy?"

"As of now, there are three large shuttles on the surface, all near Capital City. We can't quite count the number of individuals from this range, but there are several hundred, at least. Technician Garrett made an estimate of one hundred fifty per shuttle from the images we have, but really, it's just an estimate."

"And the ships?"

"The four Type I's remain in equatorial synchronous orbit near Capital City. They moved into positions about seventy-five kilometers apart just after they arrived and they've been in those positions ever since."

"Any indication that they are aware of us?"

"No. There have been no RF transmissions, nothing on SLIP, they haven't moved, nothing that would make me think they know we're here. And, no indication that they're aware of the Seekers on the second continent."

"What do we know about them?"

"They're hiding — no fishing and no cooking fires since the enemy arrived."

Joanne turned to face the table. "Nothing back from Fleet, yet, but I don't expect anything for at least another eight or nine hours. When we see it, I am quite sure they'll be ordering *Friendship* and *Eagle* to reinforce us. But they are at least ten days away." She looked down the table to her left. "Ensign Cantrell, how are our consumables?"

"We're on schedule, Captain, with about seventy days left, plus the usual reserve."

"Good. I am open to discussion, but here is how I see our situation. Our first priority is the defense of the Seekers. The best way to do that is to keep the enemy ignorant of their presence; but, failing that, we'll act decisively to protect them." She looked around the table and saw no disagreement. "Then our second priority is our own safety and, of course, the safety of the ship. Again, if the enemy moves against us somehow, we'll act."

"So, Captain, if neither of those come to pass, what do we do?"

"That, Lieutenant Kirkland, is what we're here to discuss."

Several officers were skeptical of Henderson's 'wait and see' approach. They favored more direct and immediate action to eliminate the enemy presence. Others supported her stealthy patience but proposed other activities, such as running a Sleuth past the enemy ships or dropping into a lower orbit to better see what was happening on the ground. Big Blue was near its perihelion, and the weather was marginally warmer and drier, meaning clear skies for overhead observation.

In the end, Joanne decided against either. She hated doing nothing as much as anyone else, but in this case, inaction *was* action; they would remain observant and unobserved, and wait for *Eagle* and *Friendship*. Larry Covington reported that the current orbit was holding well, and would be stable for as much as a month without any further maneuvers.

They had time, they had plenty of supplies. They would keep their eye on the enemy. Tactical patience, hard as it was to maintain, was clearly the best option. If the enemy moved in the 'wrong' direction, they would counter.

Meantime, they'd wait.

ISC Destroyer *Faith*
Earth, Outer Picket Position
Monday, December 5, 2078, 1400 UTC

It was *Faith*'s turn in the boring 'picket' work of guarding her home planet. She was orbiting the sun about three lunar distances, about nine hundred thousand kilometers outside the Earth's orbit, always remaining in opposition, so to speak, with the Earth between the ship and the Sun. Frigate *Grissom* had the trailing position, behind the Earth as it orbited the sun, with *Komarov* currently in the lead on the other side of the planet. The three ships maintained a laser link for instant, secure communications. Each also had a direct line to the Operations Center at ISC Fleet HQ.

It was a quiet, boring day shift until the Surveillance alarm sounded, making the young tech's head snap back from the casual conversation she was having with the Comm tech just a foot or two away.

"IR transient, 125 minus 15." She called out as she worked the identification process. When the answer appeared, all she could do was mumble "Holy God..." Collecting herself, she then announced in a clear voice "Assess IR target as enemy ship entry." She turned to the young Ensign manning the conn. He looked back at her in shock for a long second, then reanimated himself.

"Set Alert Status One! Comms — inform *Grissom* and *Komarov*." The bridge came suddenly alive with action as they prepared the ship for battle. The captain arrived to take control, and the Ensign left the Conn and ran aft to his place in the Life Support section.

In a few minutes, they had a firm track. The Surveillance officer came to his Captain.

"Bastard came up from the south, Captain, pretty as can be. We have him for now."

The Captain called across the Bridge, "Weaps! Can I shoot at this thing yet?"

"If they can track it, we can hit it, sir. But closer would be better."

"Very well."

His command phone rang. "*Faith* actual," he answered. He was not at all surprised at the voice on the phone.

"This is CINC." Davenport was clearly aware of the transmission delay, about four seconds at this distance. "I want all three of you to hold your positions for the moment."

There was a ragged chorus of 'Yes, sir' responses.

"It could be a single, or they could be trying to pull us off the planet and come in behind. So, stand pat for now."

The captain hung up and turned to his Surveillance station. "Keep on it, but we're holding our position for now."

The Fleet had never detected an enemy ship in Earth's home system. That it would happen midday on a Monday was almost too lucky. Everyone was at work; every analytical resource was available.

Standing in the Fleet HQ Operations Center, Davenport turned to his new COMNORTH. "What do we have?"

"The pickets, then a few ships either just returned or about to leave."

"No, who do we have that is combat capable *right now*?"

"*Dobrovolski* is leaving tomorrow, but her Captain is here on the surface."

"Get her going, Stan. Now."

Yakovlev picked up the phone. "*Dobrovolski*."

The Comms officer on *Dobrovolski*, Dan and Carol's old friend Senior Lieutenant Joe Scheck, happened to have the Conn.

"*Dobrovolski*, Lieutenant Scheck."

Yakovlev didn't hesitate.

"This is Yakovlev. Get yourselves underway and put yourself in a position to attack the enemy contact."

"Yes, sir. But, sir, the captain —"

"We're not waiting for your captain, Lieutenant. Whoever's senior on board right now is in command. Now get moving!"

"Yes, Admiral, right away."

Shortly after this, Captain Sultanov appeared in the Operations Center.

"Admiral, I have a shuttle here. I can get back to my ship!"

Davenport shook his head. "No. I can't risk that. Who's in charge up there?"

"Comms officer, Senior Lieutenant Scheck."

"Weapons?"

"She's here with me. Weapons Maintenance Officer is there. He should be fine."

"Let's hope so. Listen, Jora, I don't think this is a major attack. Let's just see what happens."

Back on *Dobrovolski*'s Bridge, Joe Scheck was on the move.

"Where is it?" he asked the Surveillance techs.

"It's about twenty degrees to the right of opposition, RA twelve hours ten minutes, declination five...looks like about one AU out. According to *Faith*, he's doing something like twenty klicks per second."

"Holy crap — that's outside the orbit of Mars. If he was coming here, what is he doing way the hell over there?" Joe rubbed his beard absentmindedly as he wondered where the enemy ship was headed, and why.

"Yeah, no clue here, Lieutenant. Mars is about 90 degrees behind us right now, so he ain't going there, either."

The second Navigation Officer, an Ensign, joined them.

"OK, what's it going to be Lieutenant Scheck?"

"Put me on his ass."

"Fast or slow?"

"Not FTL, but quick as you can."

"On it."

Joe went back to the command position. "Listen up, everybody." As they turned to face him, he could see their anxiety. The Captain, XO, and Weapons officer were on the surface, so this wasn't the best time to head into battle. He took a deep breath. "We've all done bandit intercept exercises before, both at the U and aboard this ship. You all know your jobs, so just execute like you've done it fifty times before and we'll smoke this guy if that's what COMNORTH wants, OK?"

They all nodded in response.

"OK. Cool and competent, take your time, get it right."

He sat down, wondering if that little speech had done any good, but at least it made him feel like he'd done *something* to set the tone.

As *Dobrovolski* accelerated towards the enemy contact, Ron Harris and Fiona Collins answered CINC's call to the Operations Center.

"I don't get it, sir," Ron said. "They're just passing through?"

"Yes, it makes little sense except as a diversion," Jora Sultanov agreed.

Fiona leaned against a console. "Unless..."

"Yes?" Yakovlev asked.

"They were just checking out the system like we have at any number of stars?"

"They just dropped by?" Sultanov asked, incredulous.

"I understand the rule about coincidences, Captain, but it is possible they didn't know we were here."

Yakovlev smiled. "Well, Captain Collins, if so, they're about to get educated."

On the Preeminent ship's Bridge, Third Counselor Ashil Kiker stood stolidly at the view window as the chaos roared around him. They had arrived at System 201, but it was unlike anything Kiker or Scad Nee Wok had ever seen or heard of. The blue third planet was alive with radio transmitters. They detected numerous small and large artificial objects in orbit around it. It was beautiful to Kiker's eye as he examined it through the telescope. There was a red one, too, not very far from the blue. Then, a white one off to one side, but closer to the star.

A white, a blue, a red, rocks, a giant, then rings.

The *Ultimate Origin* legend, something he had always dismissed as a ridiculous myth, came to Kiker's mind. But it could not be so. This was just another species to be put to the knee.

"Wok, what have you learned?" Kiker asked impatiently.

"Thousands of radio transmitters, sir. Whatever this race is, they have tech as advanced as our own, and they make no attempt to conceal themselves."

"Good. They are naive, then."

"Perhaps, sir. We are continuing to detect objects in orbit at many places. The red planet has large ships nearby as well."

"And the blue?"

"I cannot tell you how many yet, but many. The ones that worry me —"

"You are Preeminent, Wok, you need not worry."

"We are indeed, sir Kiker, but we are one and they are numerous. As I said, there are objects as large as this vessel not far from us. If they are warships —"

"If they are warships, we will defeat them."

"I must remind sir Kiker that if these are the Vermin, no ship has yet come away undamaged from their sting."

Kiker's face displayed his disgust. "Their *sting*, Scad Nee Wok? Perhaps we should sting *them*!"

"I must remind you, sir Kiker, that the Council sent us to explore, not to attack. The knowledge we now have matters far more than the few vessels we might destroy. And we would do that at the risk of being destroyed ourselves."

Kiker, always the politician, the maneuverer, initially resisted Wok's advice but finally accepted it. There would be more credit in the knowledge gained than in a conflict that could very likely kill him. Death was never his goal, for in death one never rose further, one could never become The Revered First.

CINC turned impatiently to his ad hoc brain trust.

"So, what do we want Scheck to do?"

"Eliminate it," Captain Sultanov answered immediately.

Ron Harris shook his head in disagreement. "I don't know, maybe, or, we could have him put a Lance up its ass and knock out the Drive."

"What then?"

"He's only doing twenty kilometers per second. At that distance, he's below the Sun's escape velocity. Take out his Drive, and he's ballistic."

"So, he'd be stuck here?"

"Exactly. Then we can do what we want with him." Ron's enthusiasm was growing.

"He'll deorbit," Fiona reminded them.

"If he can, sure, he might. With no Drive, I don't know how he'd do that."

"They can still talk," came a stiff female voice from behind them. Frances Wilson had just run over to Operations from FleetIntel.

"Talk?"

"Yes. I just heard from Lloyd at Forstmann Propulsion. They already know about this intruder."

"How did *they* find out?" Ron asked, alarmed.

"I don't know, boss, but they did. Anyhow, he says he's identified the SLIP apparatus on *Columbia*'s wreck."

"OK..." Harris wasn't sure where she was going with this line of thought.

"OK, so hit that, and they can't communicate. I heard a little of this conversation, and if you're thinking about disabling it, you need to silence it, too." She handed the photographs over to Harris.

"It will take Scheck a couple hours to get into position. When he calls in, we'll send him the image."

Sultanov looked at the photographs, making note of the long elliptical dome near the front of the ship. "That's a pretty obvious structure. A Lance should do it."

Scad Nee Wok kept his own counsel on the wisdom, or lack thereof, of remaining in this bizarre system. They knew of the pulsed radio-locating technology that had been seen at System 248 when Hess Tae Sim was defeated. Some of the radio transmissions they were hearing from the blue planet were pulsed in the same way. But nothing was close by, so there was no reason to believe they had been detected.

To Wok, those transmissions meant that this must certainly be the Vermin's home. Never before had they encountered a species so extravagantly advanced. There were ships everywhere, it seemed, and radio transmissions on a multitude of frequencies with a bewildering variety of signal types. It felt dangerous, threatening, even as a part of Wok's mind reminded him that *they* were the Preeminent. Still, Wok's tail stump quivered slightly, reflecting his nervous unease.

Wok considered sending a message to the Council telling them of this discovery, but Kiker refused, wanting to wait until more information was available. Waiting, Wok knew, meant more data to take home, which was good. It also left more opportunity for misfortune or miscalculation, something he, as a Preeminent, tried to dismiss. Still, the rational part of his brain told him over and over that this could end badly for him and his crew.

Pacing *Dobrovolsky's* bridge, Joe Scheck thought the two hours would never pass. Finally, his Nav came to him.

"We're almost in position, Lieutenant Scheck. We're about a thousand klicks off his butt."

"Good. Comms, get me a laser link to COMNORTH."

"Delay will be about ten minutes, Lieutenant, and at this distance, we're better off with the X-band channel."

"Whatever you think best, just get us connected and request instructions."

It was a full twenty-five minutes before the Communications tech called Joe back over.

"They sent a couple of photographs and a text order."

```
FLASH 207812051725UTC
TO: DOBROVOLSKI/SCHECK
FROM: COMNORTH

CINCFLEET ORDERS ARE TO DISABLE REPEAT DISABLE INTRUDER TO
PERMIT CAPTURE AND FURTHER STUDY.

PHOTOGRAPHS PROVIDED INDICATE SLIP APPARATUS ON ENEMY SHIP.
FIRST PRIORITY IS TO DESTROY THIS APPARATUS.
SECOND PRIORITY IS TO DISABLE ENEMY DRIVE.

CPT SULTANOV EXPRESSES HIS CONFIDENCE IN YOUR ABILITIES.
ALSO STRONGLY ADVISES YOU NOT DENT HIS GODDAMN SHIP.

YAKOVLEV

END
```

"Oh, don't dent his ship, huh? Very funny."

Joe Scheck laughed. "Sounds like Sultanov."

They put the photographs up on the large monitors above the Surveillance station. One was a wide shot showing the position of the SLIP apparatus on the enemy ship. It was far forward, under the 'chin' of the vessel as seen from the front. The second photograph was a detailed image of the apparatus itself.

Joe called his Weapons Maintenance officer, Ensign Adrian Lucas, over, along with the Surveillance tech. Adrian would stand-in for the Weapons Officer on this attack. He was a tall Oklahoman, dark of hair and his skin deeply tanned from years spent chasing steers on his family ranch. He was new to the ship, smart and insightful. The product, Joe thought, of working all those seasons on horseback.

"By the book, we should be able to hit this small a target, right?"

"Sure, by the book. The dimensions are on the image, so I could, I guess, tell it to find the front and then offset the target that far aft. Yeah, we can do it."

The Surveillance tech, the most senior member of his division aboard, was skeptical. "OK, but if they see it coming, they'll bug out. Or, shoot back. Both are, you know, problems."

"Lances are not stealthy, Joe," Adrian commented.

Joe thought about that for a few seconds.

"No, they aren't. But Sleuths are."

"What are you thinking, sir?" the Surveillance tech asked.

"I want to slap a Sleuth sock on a Lance, cut out whatever we have to in order to make it work, and then bring the weapons in real slow, maybe final at something like ten meters per second. If we use only passive sensors, they'll never know until the warheads go off."

"Sneaky, Joe, very sneaky."

"Can we do it, Adrian?"

254

"Yeah, we can do it. I think. We're close enough to the sun that visual and IR should work. We don't need the radar. But, there's a thousand klicks to cover, Joe. At ten meters per second, I'm not sure the math works."

"We'll manage. Get it done."

Joe walked back to the Comm station to let the brass know his plan.

"Well, it's imaginative, I'll give him that," Admiral Yakovlev commented after reading the message from *Dobrovolski*.

"He's going to sneak up behind it and launch at point blank range?" Ron said, surprised.

"That about covers it, yes. He'll pull within ten klicks and then launch. When the SLIP attack goes off, he'll fire the second Lance at the Drive system at normal speed and pull back."

Captain Sultanov let out a low whistle. "Scheck. I should have known. Sneaky little SOB, that one."

Harris smiled. "He's part of that Hansen, Powell, and Smith group. Trouble, all four of them."

"Good trouble for us, sir, but bad trouble for the enemy!"

"Let's hope so."

Yakovlev smiled as he told the Comm officer, "Tell Scheck to proceed."

"Sir Kiker, we have seen a very strong radio message from something orbiting the blue planet. It is too intense not to be aimed at us, or at something close to us."

"What of it?"

"I believe it may be a communication."

"They're communicating with us?"

"Doubtful, sir Kiker. If this is the Vermin planet, as my crew believes it is, they may be communicating with a ship close to us."

"And you have not detected any such ship?"

"As you well know sir Kiker, their ships are small, dark, and hard to locate."

"We are the Preeminent. Locate it."

Joe Scheck ran back to the Magazine when Adrian Lucas reported that the Sleuth/Lance mashup was ready.

"It's a ragged job, Joe, but's it's on."

'Ragged' was a generous word for it. The head of a Lance was not much like the spy-head on a Sleuth. There were a number of knife cuts and strips of black utility tape wrapped around the weapon, but in Joe's eye, they'd done what he asked.

He was smiling broadly as he told them, "Get it on a rotary, and deploy the rotary as soon as it's ready."

As he turned to head back forward, his phone rang. It was the Surveillance tech. "The one-eighty megahertz signal just came up, sir. FleetIntel thinks that might be an intruder detector and we're awful damned close. "

"Fine, on my way." He saw the questioning look on Adrian's face.

"They may be on to us. The one-eighty is up. Get that thing out!"

Joe turned and ran the hundred twenty meters back to the Bridge, thinking all the way that it would nice if their ships were, well, smaller somehow.

He went directly to the Weapons station. "As soon as the rotary is out, fire at the SLIP antenna!"

"But it's already out!"

The sound of alarms and frightened voices suddenly filled Wok's ears.

"There it is! Something just appeared close behind us, sir Kiker. We're leaving!"

Before Kiker could object, Scad Nee Wok was commanding his crew to engage the engines and depart.

He turned to Kiker angrily, "We could have left long ago. You may have killed us all."

When he saw the enemy ship shift slightly, Joe didn't hesitate.

"Switch to direct path, max velocity, and shoot!"

It took the tech perhaps five seconds to make the changes and release the Lance.

"Weapon's away. Ten seconds."

There was a call from the Surveillance station. "Something's happening!"

Joe looked at the display, the enemy ship seeming to waver, to shimmer.

"Shit. They're bugging out. Nav! Pull us back!"

"How far —"

"JUST BACK! I don't want to get caught up in their graviton flow." It would take a few seconds. Maybe he had time.

"Weaps! Fire at their drive!" The second Lance was quickly away.

"We've been fired on!" Wok reported. The only answer now, he knew, was to finish engaging the engines and get away as soon as possible. Just before the ship started to accelerate, there was a loud explosion below him. Wok had never been under attack. Few ship commanders that had been ever returned to tell the tale. The ship began to move more quickly and soon slipped into FTL.

They would be safe for the moment. The course was incorrect, but that could be fixed soon enough.

The important thing now was to escape, and that they had.
Barely.

"Dammit. They got away!" the Weapons tech whined after the second Lance exploded harmlessly in the flood of anti-gravitons generated by the enemy ship's rapid departure.

Joe returned to the Surveillance position.

"Show me the hit on the SLIP apparatus." The Surveillance tech ran it in slow motion, backward and forward. Joe saw the enemy ship begin to move, then a bright flash near the front. Then, pieces flying off.

"Are those hunks of the Lance or parts of the ship?" he asked.

"Hard to say, Lieutenant, but hold on." He ran the video forward a few frames. Just before the enemy ship departed, there was a single frame that showed the SLIP apparatus. Or, more accurately, the lack of one.

"There's just a hole. You did it, Lieutenant Scheck. They can run, but they can't talk."

Joe smiled. "I'll take it." He turned to the Bridge crew. "And I didn't do this. *We* did this."

Now safely in FTL, Scad Nee Wok seethed with anger.

"They are evil, these Vermin," he said through his sharp clenched teeth.

"We are the Preeminent. We will prevail."

Wok turned to Kiker. "They struck the communications device, Sir Kiker. They did not want us to be able to reveal their location."

"We are the Preeminent. We will prevail."

"They knew where the communication device was! How could they know that?"

"You should have detected them sooner, Wok. This is your doing."

"And had you not insisted on waiting so long, we would have been gone long ago!"

Kiker opened his maw to strike at Wok's neck but found himself restrained by the crew. Wok looked at his guards with satisfaction. He'd expected Kiker to strike at him, but he could not know when. But he was a Preeminent. He was prepared.

"Lock Sir Ashil Kiker in his compartment, and keep him there until I tell you otherwise."

"You'll suffer for this, Wok!" Kiker screamed.

"Feed me to the Council, Sir Kiker, if you can convince them that it is I, and not *you,* who is not Preeminent. But at least now we will all live to have that conversation."

Kiker, shocked that Wok would know of the Council's secret practices, struggled vainly to attack his keepers.

"Take him!" Scad Nee Wok was less positive than he sounded about his ultimate fate. And it would be a very long trip home.

Kiker gone, Wok's second-in-command, Tesn Lei Dott, came to stand with him.

"The crew has heard, Sir Wok. They all whisper of *Ultimate Origin*."

"Myths and legends, Dott, can have a root in some remote truth. I don't understand it myself, but I doubt there is any real meaning to it."

"But the crew, sir Wok, many in the crew believe."

"Let us not discuss it further, and instruct the section commanders likewise." Dott signaled his obedience, but his tail stump betrayed his inner conflict. *He believes*, Wok thought to himself, *I would not have thought that possible.*

These Vermin were different than any race they had previously encountered, and while they were Preeminent, these Vermin were well advanced in ways that the Preeminent were not. He was not supposed to 'worry,' as Kiker had said, but to blindly deny facts was the path to death, and that was a path Scad Nee Wok had no intention to tread.

Dobrovolski's battle report included the use of the Sleuth-Lance and the one image of the enemy's destroyed SLIP apparatus. Scheck also lauded his crew from the Weapons Maintenance Officer to the Surveillance techs.

Ron Harris frowned. "I really wanted the whole ship."

Yakovlev shrugged. "As did I. But now, they can't call it in. They'll have to get to another facility or another ship to phone home."

Fiona was rereading the report. "The intrusion detector came up right before they left. That makes me think they had an idea someone was there."

Ron was unconvinced. "But *Dobrovolski* would have been invisible to it. They weren't moving, and I don't think we're visible in that frequency anyway."

Jora Sultanov smiled grimly. "Until they deployed the rotary, that is."

"Oh, shit. The launcher!" Ron groaned.

Fiona nodded her agreement. "The downside of getting so close, I guess. I'd still want to know what tipped them off."

"Yes, we'll have to see what Scheck's thoughts on that are."

"So, Ron," CINC asked, "What should we be expecting next?"

"Their drive is slower than ours. Forstmann told us they might be able to do point-eight-five, no more. If he's going back to Enemy Station, it will take him, oh, maybe thirty days. If he's going back to Alpha Mensae, then, uh, more like forty."

Fiona looked from Ron to CINC. "I'd go to the Station. He can probably get repairs and call home from there. I doubt he'd spend the extra time to go all the way back."

Davenport nodded. "Yes, I think that makes sense."

"We can be at Enemy Station a week earlier. He's incommunicado for now. He can't call for help or hear messages from his commanders."

"So, wherever he's decided to go, that's what's going to happen no matter what we do?"

"Right. If we smoke Enemy Station, he'll still show up if that's where he's headed."

"A nice thought, Fiona," CINC said with regret, "but we're not going to do that now. Let's get to work on the assumption that he's going to get the message back home in thirty days."

Intrepid
Big Blue
Monday, December 5, 2078, 0315 UTC

Joanne Henderson awoke to the alarm from her phone announcing a FLASH message. She sat up on the hard bunk in her duty cabin and struggled to focus on the small print. *I'm not old yet,* she thought to herself, *but these eyes are not what they once were.*

```
FLASH 207811211500UTC
TO: EAGLE, FRIENDSHIP, INTREPID
FROM: FLEETOPS

1)  BETA HYDRI SENTINEL HAS REPORTED ARRIVAL OF FOUR
    REPEAT FOUR ENEMY TYPE I VESSELS.
2)  INTREPID HAS NOT REPORTED INDEPENDENTLY BUT IS ASSUMED
    TO BE SILENT FOR OPERATIONAL SECURITY.
3)  EAGLE AND FRIENDSHIP SHALL PROCEED IMMEDIATELY BETA HYDRI
    MINIMUM EMR
4)  ON ARRIVAL EAGLE AND FRIENDSHIP MAKE BEST EFFORTS TO COVERTLY
    ESTABLISH COMMUNICATIONS WITH INTREPID.
5)  ALL SHIPS SHALL NOT ACKNOWLEDGE THESE ORDERS.
6)  HENDERSON TO COMMAND THE TASK GROUP ON ARRIVAL.

COOK

END
```

She dressed and headed up to the Bridge, where XO Bass was keeping watch. She sat next to him at the command workstation and showed him the message.

"So, how exactly do we 'covertly' establish comms?"

Joanne shrugged. "I don't know, Alonzo. We can ask Woodward in the morning." She looked around the Bridge, which seemed very quiet.

"It's just past sunset in the cities," he offered.

"What are they doing?"

"They pulled out maybe an hour before, no one left on the surface, best we can tell."

"They don't like the dark?"

"Yeah, maybe not."

"Interesting."

ISC Fleet HQ Office of the Commander in Chief
Ft. Eustis, VA
Tuesday, December 6, 2078, 0800 EST

Ron Harris looked up from the data on his tablet. "So, far as we know, there aren't any enemy locations closer than the sphere at GL 674."

"So, that's what, fifteen light years?" CINC asked.

"Well, about that, so, at point-eight-five, almost seventeen and a half days."

"Minimum."

"Correct."

"And from there to Alpha Mensae?"

"Twenty-eight. So, a SLIP could get there in about another forty hours. So, in round numbers, the word can't get to Alpha Mensae before nineteen days."

Fiona leaned back in her chair. "So, we have almost three weeks to decide what to do."

Kieran Barker shook his head at the irony. "Right. We have until Christmas day."

CINC nodded his understanding, then looked at Ron. "What is your assessment of yesterday's event?"

"My people have looked at that really hard, and we went late into the evening yesterday trying to digest exactly what happened."

"And?"

"We think they came to check out this system, much as we do other systems, but did not specifically come here for us. We believe they did not know we were here."

Barker was clearly uncomfortable with this. "What makes you think that?"

"First, their entry angle and course. They came in well outside the orbit of Mars, and nowhere near any planet. To me, that's not the kind of entry to make if you're planning an attack."

"What else?"

260

"If we think about Inor, and now this new appearance at Beta Hydri, when they mean business, they come in force. Six ships at Inor, four at Big Blue. One ship, to me, is a recon, not an attack."

Barker was starting to be convinced. "Hmm. That does make sense."

"If they knew we were here and wanted a look, they would have come in much closer to Earth."

"Does any of this really matter?" CINC asked.

"Sir?"

"Does it matter if they knew we were here or just blundered across us?"

"It does to me!" Ron answered, agitated. "If I thought they already knew where we are, I'd be telling you to pull back everything we can and prepare for an invasion."

"Yes, I see."

"But they know now. And we need to be thinking about what that means."

"What do you suggest?"

"That's more a question for Admiral Cook, sir, but since you asked..."

"Go ahead, Ron."

"We've not been careful about resupplying ships when they return. We put the crews on leave, then take a week or more to get them reloaded with supplies, update their weapons, all the small tasks required to get them ready to go back out."

"You're suggesting we do that more quickly?"

"Yes. When a ship returns, we need to get it turned around immediately. The crew still needs some time off, so we might have to put in a temporary crew, just enough to run the ship and put it into a fight if necessary."

"OK, I'll talk to Admiral Cook about that."

Fiona agreed with Ron. "All that, sir, and we might want to beef up the pickets. Three might not be enough."

"Yes, a stronger defensive posture at our three important points makes sense. I'd already planned to do that."

"From a Plans point of view, sir, I think we should rethink the schedule for the offensive."

"Oh?"

"Yes, sir. If we commit forces forward against them, when they're actually coming here, seems to us that we'd be needlessly vulnerable."

"I understand your position, but for now the offensive is on."

"But, sir —"

"I understand your position, Captain Collins, and I will consider making some adjustments to accommodate it. I've given Admiral Barker his directions, and I expect him to move as I have ordered." CINC looked hard at Fiona, his body stiff, tense.

Fiona had made her point, there was only one thing left to say. "Please note my exception to that decision, sir."

"So noted."

Ron watched the old friends argue, wondering if Davenport would relent to Fiona's caution. If he were CINC, he would have. But Davenport was dead set on making a statement to the enemy. They walked out of CINCs office together.

"He's overplaying, Ron, he's being Len Davis." Ron nodded his agreement, recalling how *Sigma's* Captain had held on to a bad tactical idea too long and gotten himself and much of his crew killed.

"Let's see how much he modifies the forces. If he leaves us with enough to cover the three planets, maybe we can still support the offensive after all."

"Maybe. I don't know. I don't want him to throw me some minor concession that won't get the job done. This isn't about saving face."

"I know, Fiona, I know." He looked at her sympathetically. "Hard to tell the old man he's wrong."

"Yeah, very hard. I owe him a lot, but I owe him the truth even more."

Kieran Barker came out of CINC's office as Fiona was finishing. She and Ron looked at him, wondering at his silence during Fiona's discussion with CINC.

"For my part, I agree with both of you, but CINC is adamant. Let's talk tomorrow and see if we can pare back the offensive without weakening it too much."

"It's a zero-sum game, Admiral," Fiona pointed out, "Whatever we keep here, we take away from you."

Barker nodded his understanding. "Let's talk tomorrow."

They left for their own offices, promising to get back together and see what it would take to defend their planets against an enemy attack. The answer, unfortunately, turned on what assumptions they made about the numbers and types of enemy ships that would appear. Would it be like Inor? Twice Inor? Ten times Inor? If they found out too late that they were short-handed, there would be no time to get help back from Inor or Beta Hydri. Or, to get help *to* Inor or Beta Hydri.

They'd have to fight it out with whatever was on hand, wherever the fight appeared. Fiona liked that thought not one bit.

Intrepid
Big Blue
Wednesday, December 7, 2078, 1145 UTC

"Mr. Price!" Colin Garrett called from the workroom. Ben hustled out from his office, Ann Cooper right behind him.

"Yes, Colin, what's up?"

He pointed to a live video feed from one of *Intrepid*'s long range telescopes. "This shuttle, it's not going where it's supposed to. It's heading towards the Seekers."

Ben picked up the ship phone. "Gonzales...Price here, Lieutenant. Are you seeing this shuttle heading east?" Ben hung up.

"Gonzales and the Captain are coming. Stay on it."

"Where the hell are they going?" Garrett asked himself as Henderson, Gonzales and Marine Captain Martin rushed into the Intel work area.

"Oh, no, oh, *shit*!"

"What is it, Garrett?" Joanne asked.

"The herd."

"What?"

"The herd, ma'am. I should have thought of this."

Ben looked at him. "Keep talking, Colin, and eventually we'll understand what you're talking about."

"Yes, Mr. Price, sorry. There's this area, a pasture, really, of about four square kilometers just south of where the Seekers live."

"OK, so?"

"They raise the little animals they eat in there, remember? The cliffs and the sea make for natural fences. They can't get out."

"Again, OK, so?" Henderson asked.

"So, that's not a natural situation, ma'am. They would not just be there on their own. They would have to have been introduced artificially."

"Shit. It's a tell," Joanne said, surprised she hadn't thought if it herself.

"Yes, Captain, I think it is. And I think the enemy might have figured that out."

Joanne picked up the ship phone without looking away from the display. "Kirkland...James, do we have firing solutions on the enemy ships? Good. Designate two Bludgeons each. Get with Marco when he gets back up there and target the shuttles on the surface near Capital City....Yes, I want a clean sweep if we can."

She hung up the phone as Marco Gonzales took the hint and headed back to the Bridge. She turned to Martin. "Get your Marines up and ready to deploy. If they actually land, which I'm pretty sure they will, we'll need to move quickly."

Martin acknowledged the order and moved aft quickly to get to his people.

Ben caught Joanne's eye. "I should go with the Marines. I can talk to Eaagher if necessary."

"No."

Ben didn't want to have this discussion right here in the Intel section, out in the open, but here is where he decided it had to happen. "Captain, I should go. I didn't sign on as a Warrant Officer ten years ago to sit on the sidelines. I am your Intel Chief. It is my job to see what this enemy is in person. I should go."

Joanne looked at him for a few seconds, looking for a good reason to turn him down, then decided she couldn't. He was right after all. "Bring me back a souvenir, OK?"

"Sure, I promise. The Leader's head on a platter?"

Joanne smiled. "That would do nicely Assuming, of course, that they have a leader and you can find and kill him."

"Assuming all that, sure."

Decision made, Joanne turned and headed back to the Bridge.

Ben turned to Ann Cooper, who was looking at him with dread in her eyes.

"Take over for me, till I get back?"

"Yes, of course, Mr. Price..." She started say something more, but Ben headed her off.

"Thanks, Ann. I'll see you after High Noon in The Pasture!"

Ben was suddenly gone, trotting to his quarters to change into field colors. Garrett looked at the door, then back at Ann.

"Good work, Garrett," Ann said, resting her hands on his shoulders, trying to reassure the young tech.

"Yes, Lieutenant, thank you." Garrett swallowed hard. "He is coming back, right?"

"He better. He owes me money."

"Yes, ma'am."

Natalie Hayden was darting around her hangar deck, loudly directing traffic as two shuttles were pulled out of storage and placed in line for the ShuttleLock. They would launch them in quick succession, the second perhaps a minute after the first. The hangar deck was large enough, just barely, but dispatching two shuttles like this was not a typical procedure, and the geometry was tight. Natalie pushed, pulled, pointed, and yelled her way through it until the two small spacecraft were in position and ready to go. She'd also changed into field colors to match the Marines, a .45 in a shoulder holster on her left side. When Ben arrived, he stopped a meter away and looked at her.

She met his eye with determination. "I'm driving. Don't argue."

The words that Ben wanted to say couldn't be said at that place and in that moment, so he nodded his acceptance of her decision. He could hardly argue with her for going on a mission for which he'd just volunteered.

Fleet Marine Second Lieutenant Liwanu Harry had been sent up by Captain Martin to see how things were progressing in the hangar. The tall, angular young man from Montana asked a few questions of Natalie, got the answers he needed, then followed Ben below.

As Ben arrived in the Marines' barracks area, Captain Andrew Martin, late of the New Zealand Special Air Service, was standing before his Marines. They were good men and women, Martin knew; careful, well-prepared, and, he hoped, brave. But suddenly the time had come to set the rules of engagement, and these were nothing like he had ever seen before.

"OK, the enemy is down there, and we're probably going to meet them on the field. Hopefully, we're going to get them into a fight they're not ready for." He paused to look around the room and found every eye was on him. "We've come from all over, I know. Aussies, Brits, Canadians, Arab League, United States, Europe, and the Central African forces. But now we are all Fleet Marines. Some of us have seen combat, but most of you have not. But from what I just saw in Intel, you will today."

He paced, thinking how best to say what he had been instructed to say.

"There is one thing I need to make very clear, and this comes from the top, understand? The enemy is not a signatory of the Geneva Convention. The usual rules of war are out the window."

The Marines now looked at each other, wondering where exactly this was going.

"That said, we're warriors, not butchers. You must each be true to your own personal code of honor. But no one, and I do mean *no one,* will second guess your actions on the field today. At home, we would never finish off a wounded or defenseless enemy soldier. Here, it's your call whether they pose any risk to you. Protect yourselves and each other. Don't forget what this enemy did at Inor, and what they've already done here." He paused to look around the room. "The gloves are off, people. Am I clear?"

He was. He turned to Ben.

"Mr. Price?"

"Yes, Captain. I just want to say that best we know, the enemy uses some kind of plasma rifle. None of us understand how it works, but it shoots fast, and according to what I read from *Antares*, it's pretty lethal."

"Your point?"

"Don't underestimate them. They've killed tens of thousands, and they don't seem to care."

"Anything else?"

"This is likely to be a gold mine for Intel, so keep your eyes out for anything useful about their appearance, communications, weapons, even their behavior."

"You want any prisoners, Mr. Price?" a Marine asked. She had very short hair that accentuated an angular but pleasant face and an engaging smile.

"If you think you can capture one, sure. I am not at all sure what I would do with it, honestly. Lock it up and feed it, I suppose, until we get home?"

That made them laugh.

"Hey, Joanie," one called to the woman who had asked the question, "Don't you bring home a pet unless you're ready to feed and house train it!" That really got them going as they headed up the ladder and into the hangar. Ben followed them up, with Martin right behind him.

Martin went directly to Natalie as he came up the ladder. "Do you have a briefing board?"

They went into the Weapons Maintenance workroom, where there was a large planning board on the wall.

"This will do. Can you get the relevant officers in here in, say, ten minutes?" As Natalie left, Andy Martin started drawing quickly on the board. The required officers crowded into the workroom: Henderson, Gonzales, Kirkland, Ben Price, and XO Alonzo Bass, who would be piloting the second shuttle. Ann Cooper joined them late with the news that the enemy shuttle had landed about two hundred meters off the apex of the pasture triangle. Too close to ignore, but the Seekers were not in any immediate danger. Martin marked the enemy position on the map.

"OK, here we are. As you all know the area is roughly a triangle, with these cliffs on two sides and the ocean as the base." He looked around and saw that they understood. "Fine, good, so these cliffs are not actually all that high, something like five or eight meters. Also, there is a small bluff over the beach here," he pointed to a spot about a third of the way down from the north corner of the triangle. "That bluff really is small, but it will suffice for the plan. The first shuttle will cross over the enemy's position at low altitude, maybe twenty meters —"

"Twenty?" Natalie interrupted, "They can smoke us with those hot rounds that low."

"Not at high speed. The first shuttle will pass over them, then scoot over the cliff, spin around, and set down about fifty meters behind it. There's a spot here," he circled an area on his hand drawn map, "where there is room. The second shuttle, with Lieutenant Harry in command, will set down on the beach behind this little bluff thirty seconds after the first one passes over."

"So, you're expecting them to be looking the other way?" Ben asked.

"Yes." He turned back to the map. "There is abundant scrub along the verge of the cliff, so my team will establish themselves along that line. Lieutenant Harry will bring his force up from behind and establish a diagonal blocking position two hundred meters northeast of the enemy's location. If they head towards the Seekers, the L-T's squads will eliminate them." He turned to the tall, muscular man with the angular features. "Is that clear enough?"

"Yes, Captain, I understand."

"I believe they will come towards the cliff to investigate the first shuttle. On my signal, my team will open up on them. If they retreat towards the sea, or the Seekers, again, the L-Ts squads will reduce them." He stopped and looked around.

"Questions?" There were a few about timing and exact positions, but Martin had devised a reasonable plan in almost no time. Keeping it simple also kept the questions and options to a minimum.

"Here is what *Intrepid* is going to do," Henderson announced. "There are still three shuttles around Capital City. We are going to strike three of the four Type I's all at once at time zero, which is the time the shuttle passes over the enemy. We're hoping that once this all starts, the enemy on the surface will run to their shuttles to get off the planet. If they do, we'll wait for them to gather and then we'll hit the last ship and the shuttles with Bludgeons simultaneously. If they don't return within a decent time, we'll hit them anyway and then clean up the survivors later."

"What about the station on Little Gray?" Second Lieutenant Liwanu Harry asked.

"We'll hit that just before we hit the three ships."

As the gathering broke up, Henderson, Kirkland, Hayden, and Bass went over the timing and set a specific time zero. Everything else would work backward and forward from that time.

Intrepid Shuttle
Big Blue
Wednesday, December 7, 2078, 1415 UTC

Natalie tried desperately not to recall her post-escape fear as she again flew the shuttle ten meters off the water, the beach rapidly growing larger ahead of her. She lifted up just enough to get over the shore and, in a flash, they were over the top of the enemy shuttle. She had a fleeting impression of purple heads turning, but she was pretty sure that was her imagination. She slammed on the 'brakes' in the Drive and spun around to land where Martin had indicated. No scratching around for a spot this time, the area was as smooth and clear of obstructions as Martin had said. She was barely down before the last Marine was out the door. She reset the shuttle for rapid return, with the flight director programmed to take them back to *Intrepid*. That done, she pulled a 2K7X out of its locked storage and headed towards the cliff.

Martin's two squads arranged themselves just behind the cliff, peering through the scrub between them and the enemy. Fleet Marine helmets had an integrated communications system, with earpieces that both protected their hearing and provided communications. The whole company was on a single circuit, allowing them to pass information, or orders, instantly.

As they looked carefully through the scrub, they could see a large group of enemy coming towards them. Martin had been right—they were coming to check out the shuttle.

"I ain't never seen no giant-assed purple turkey carrying a gun before, Captain," one whispered.

"That turkey can shoot back, asshole, so mind your manners," his corporal responded quietly.

"Still, ain't never seen that."

"Looks more like a weird mutated ostrich to me," came a female voice.

"Yeah, I ate ostrick once," the first voice responded, "Shitty meal."

The Seekers had fought this enemy and lost, but today would be different. Today, the enemy would encounter something it had not seen before: experienced, professional warriors who were prepared, well-trained, and disciplined. This was no rabble, no ad-hoc collection of hunters fighting desperately shot-by-shot for their lives.

Martin smiled at Natalie as he stifled a laugh and motioned for her to stay down. He was still smiling as he clicked open his mike. "Sights up. Disambiguate."

The Marines clicked on their laser sights, searching through the low foliage for targets. They looked down at the enemy as they approached the cliffs, drawn by the passage of the shuttle overhead, just as Martin had hoped.

The sights on the 2K7X were individually coded, and as each Marine put the scope on an enemy soldier, they could see if someone else was already on that target. In a few seconds, each Marine had his own personal alien to eliminate. They approached haphazardly, something that surprised Martin. He expected more structure, but he did notice a single figure in the rear, looking back and forth and up at the cliff face.

"Do ya suppose they taste like chicken?" someone asked.

"We could have a helluva bar-bee-que tonight!" said another.

Finally satisfied, Martin lined up who he thought was the commander with his own weapon, then said quietly over the comm, "Fate whispered to the warrior, you cannot withstand the storm!"

Twenty-four voices whispered back, "No, sir, we are the storm!"

The first volley dropped twenty-five enemy, most with headshots. The presumed commander was down, and the rest of the foot soldiers looked confused for a few seconds, but then they knelt and raised their rifles as more shots from the Marines cut down another twenty. The rest kept firing at the cliff until the Marines eliminated them.

Big Blue
The Pasture
Wednesday, December 7, 2078, 1500 UTC

Ben Price lay in the high, coarse grass just up from the beach, a meter to the right of Marine Lieutenant Liwanu Harry. They had heard the firing from the cliff face; one massive blast of rifle fire followed by more random shots, and a few muted pops that Ben thought must be the enemy weapon. He could also hear something else, something like a flock of geese or some other large bird squawking with alarm.

He heard Ann Cooper's steady voice say in his ear, "There's more coming out of the shuttle."

Lieutenant Harry, hearing the same on the secondary circuit, looked at him with the obvious question in his eyes.

"Which way are they going, Ann?" Ben asked.

"They're moving northeast. There's a lot of them, Ben, more than fifty, I'd say."

As Ben rose slightly to look for the enemy, he could see the polished top of their hundred-meter-long shuttle reflecting the sunshine. Beyond that, he could also see three bright lights low in the sky to the west, the enemy ships burning to death under *Intrepid's* Bludgeons.

"Sights up!" Lieutenant Harry called. Ben switched on his weapon but remained low as he had been instructed. He was to keep down and sort through the remains, not get his head shot off, to quote Captain Henderson's last unequivocal order, given pointedly as he boarded the shuttle. She also sent him down with Bass, which he suspected was intended to keep him and Natalie apart. No distractions or confused priorities for either of them. As usual, Joanne was right even when you really didn't want her to be.

The Marines around Ben opened up on the enemy from fifty meters. The enemy responded by firing ahead of themselves, not really aiming but firing low into the brush where their tormentors must be. Two Marines were hit and fell in the first few seconds of this offensive. Ben looked to his left where XO Alonzo Bass was firing methodically. Aim. Shoot. Reacquire. Focus. Aim. Shoot. He heard a sizzle and a thud to his right and saw a Marine was down. Another loud, hot sound and a Marine five meters to his left was down, writhing in pain, then deathly still. PFC Joanie would not be bringing back any prisoners today.

The plasma bolts were coming in fast, one after the other, landing close in front of him, some passing over his head to strike the ground behind. Ben felt a rising sense of alarm, and he could see the same in the Marines around him. As he kept down, holding the weapon tightly to his chest, another Marine was hit off to his right.

"That's three. Sorry, Joanne," he said aloud to himself. "There's only so much I can watch." The Marine on his right was dead, so Ben pulled him back from his position and crouched down to peek between the spikey fronds of the thick, fernish shrub he had been hiding behind. He could see the enemy still moving forward, swaying side to side in their strange gait, like oversized birds. He leveled the weapon, aimed quickly, and fired. He was shocked at the damage he did, splitting open the enemy's head. There was still a dangerous volume of incoming rounds, and some small fires had been started in the brush. Ben could smell the smoke, and it reminded him of what the *Liberty* crew had told of the acrid, terrible smoke on Inor. This stuff just smelled like normal smoke. He'd have to remember to share that with Evans someday.

Ben looked to his left, found another target, and fired. Another hit. He saw motion in front of him and fired hastily. He missed. As he repositioned to fire again, he felt his chest on fire as he was thrown back, the weapon flopping to the ground next to him.

When he opened his eyes, a young Marine Lieutenant was kneeling over him. Ben thought he looked awfully worried. *Wait,* he thought as confusion invaded his consciousness, *I know him, what was his name? It was weird, like a first name for a last name.* His chest felt heavy, and he thought it strange that the Marine would be standing on him. He wanted to tell him to get off.

"Mr. Price! Mr. Price is down!" the officer called on the communication link.

His head clearing from the initial shock, Ben now fully understood what was happening, and suddenly there was too much to say and no air to say it with. Ben tried to breathe, but his chest refused to move. Desperate, he looked the Marine hard in the eye as he reached for his uniform shirt and pulled him down.

"Nat... *Nat...*" Ben squeezed out.

"Yes, Mr. Price, yes. I understand you. I will tell her, Mr. Price. I swear I will." Ben nodded slightly, then he pulled again on the shirt, weaker this time.

"Joanne..."

"Yes, what about the captain?"

"Thanks..."

"Yes, I will tell her. You have my word."

Price nodded again weakly as he let go, then settled back flat on the ground, let out one long last breath, and was gone.

"Captain Martin, Price is dead."

As Lieutenant Harry said this, a tipping point seemed to flex, and the enemy fire started to diminish. He got his Marines up, and they began firing continuously into the enemy. Bewildered and nearly surrounded, the enemy stood their ground and died where they stood. Never did one take a step backward once engaged.

Once the firing stopped, Harry returned as quickly as he could to where Price lay, smoke rising from the massive wound on the right side of his chest. Natalie Hayden, who had heard everything on the comm link, had beaten him there, and he found her kneeling over Price, holding his hand as the tears ran off her face and dripped onto his shirt. Liwanu stood guard over them, giving Natalie this moment as best he could. As he looked high and to the west, there was now a fourth fire in the sky.

A clean sweep, he thought, *just as Henderson had hoped.*

A few minutes later, without warning, the enemy shuttle lifted off. Clearly not every enemy soldier had been out on the surface, and the remnant was making a run for the relative safety of space. Captain Martin had to yell at his people to not shoot it as it departed. The last thing they needed was for that thing to explode in their faces. It was greeted with a Lance as it exited the atmosphere.

They had lost five, including Ben Price. The enemy had lost over a hundred. Captain Martin picked three of the least damaged alien bodies to bag and return to *Intrepid.* One was the 'leader' he had dropped with his first round. Those bodies would be a gold mine for FleetIntel.

PFC Joanie McCarthy, who had laughed about bringing back an enemy pet, was laid next to Ben. The Marines put them carefully in body bags, after first gently moving Natalie aside.

On the other side of Ben was Gunther Hartwig, a tall dark-haired man originally from the German Army. Gunther had been a teacher but decided he'd rather see history made than just talk about it. Harry had known Gunther well and enjoyed their long discussions on historical subjects, especially where they saw the same events from opposite points of view.

But they had taken the field from the enemy and protected the Seekers.

Harry heard the crackle of someone walking the brush behind him and turned quickly, reflexively raising his weapon. He saw three Seekers not ten yards away. *How the hell did they get that close?* he wondered to himself. There were others further back, walking towards the now silent battlefield. His eyes met those of the taller Seeker in the middle, who pointed to his forehead and said, "Eaagher." Harry lowered his weapon, his eyes still riveted on the Seeker's.

Hearing Eaagher's voice, Natalie turned to face him. She pulled herself up and walked to Eaagher, reaching for his hand.

"*Nathelee,*" Eaagher said, recognizing her. He took her offered hand and let her lead him to Ben. Eaagher knelt beside him and crossed his arms around his abdomen.

271

"*Benh*," he said quietly, then placed his right hand on Ben's head. Natalie knelt on the other side, watching, her tears still wet. He looked at her and said something she did not understand. She shook her head, then remembered to raise her right hand. Eaagher raised his left, which Natalie took to mean that he understood that she didn't understand. She wished she could just hear what Eaagher had to say. Ben would have appreciated it, she was sure.

Eaagher rose and walked to the next body on the ground. He looked at Liwanu Harry, then pointed to his head and said, "Eaagher."

Natalie's voice came from behind him. "He's asking who that is, Harry. Just tell him the name."

"Gunther."

"*Gunther.*"

"Yes."

Eaagher looked directly at him and asked his name in the same way.

"Liwanu"

"*Lahkwhyooh.*"

Again, Eaagher knelt next to the fallen warrior and spoke Gunther's name as he touched his head. After a moment, he rose and went to the next in line. Eaagher continued this pattern until all five casualties had been visited. The Marines watched this process in wonder, as this tall and somber looking alien offered a gesture of respect, a benediction of sorts, to those who had fallen. That emotion was something they understood and respected in turn.

As he finished, another Seeker arrived with Cordero's tablet, paper, and marker. Eaagher handed the tablet to Natalie and wrote on the paper. Natalie scanned the writing.

I immediate past say extreme regret conscious end of friend Ben and much sadness in you.

As Natalie read it, Eaagher touched her arm and said, *'Benh.'* She lifted her left hand.

Sad five conscious lifes end today. Future always remember sacrifice names.

He wrote more and handed it over to Natalie.

Future always grateful Friends loyal brave fierce.

Natalie just nodded and handed the tablet to Alonzo Bass, who had come to see Ben and try to help Natalie. Nearby, the medics were getting the wounded on their feet and helping them towards the shuttle on the beach. There were six, all with burns from near-misses, none critical. The three enemy bodies were already bagged and on the shuttle.

It was time to go. She knelt down once more and kissed Ben on the forehead, then stood, picked up her weapon and started walking back to the shuttle she'd flown down. She would not dishonor herself, or Ben, by failing to complete her duty.

Second Lieutenant Liwanu Harry watched Hayden leave, then helped close up the bags. He picked up Ben's weapon and followed the body bags back to the shuttle, a grim sadness walking with him.

Intrepid
Big Blue
Wednesday, December 7, 2078, 1800 UTC

Natalie Hayden returned to her quarters, a double she shared with FPI Engineer Pope. She angrily ripped off her dirty, blood-stained field colors and stood for a long time under a hot shower, begging it to wash away the pain and tension gripping her body.

It didn't help much.

The knot in her stomach had not lessened even a bit as she redressed and headed for the magazine, and neither had the dull pain in her chest, or the faint headache behind her eyes. Ben or no Ben, she had work to do, duties to perform, the first of which was to write a detailed post-engagement report for Henderson. She walked silently to her small office next to the magazine and closed the door behind her.

Her crew let her be. They saw her arrive, moving almost in slow motion, and knowing what she had lost that day, they kept at their own tasks as quietly as possible so as not to disturb her. They knew what she had to do.

She hung her head in her hands for a few minutes, willing the emotions to subside and the grief to abate. Giving up, she pulled a note pad from a drawer and started writing down, in long-hand, whatever she could recall, in whatever order it happened to come to her. She would organize it later, then dictate or type it into the ship's record. For now, she just needed to get everything in her memory on the page as quickly and accurately as possible.

Struck by her own grief, after the shuttles were back aboard Joanne Henderson spent an hour alone in her cabin, thinking about her friendship with Ben Price, what they had meant to each other, and how it had all ended so suddenly. The Fleet was still new to war, and most commanders did not yet know the feelings that naturally flow from ordering good people to their deaths. Ben had volunteered, no, she reminded herself, he'd *demanded* to go on this mission. He was prepared for the consequences. The enemy is fighting for their lives, too, and an unlucky break can cost you your life. Today, from what the Marines told her, Ben had done well, but it just hadn't worked out for him.

But it had been her order, her decision, that put him on the surface.

She got moving again and headed for the Intel work area. Ann Cooper looked up at her as she entered, then finally remembered to stand up. Colin Garrett remained seated and looked sullenly in the other direction.

"Yes, Captain?" she asked, the regret clear in her voice.

"Sit down, Ann, please." Garrett turned at the sound of Henderson's quiet voice. "Tell me how you're all doing."

Ann sat up straight, a habit she knew she had when she was about to tell someone something difficult.

"It's hard, Captain, very hard for the techs, especially. They identified with Mr. Price, and they seem to have gotten very close in the time he's been here."

Joanne nodded sadly. "He has that effect on people." She relaxed a little and leaned back in her chair. "Back in Plans, he called me an idiot to my face the day after Inoria. I almost slugged him." The techs looked at her in surprise. "Ben could really stick it to you when you had it coming."

"Did you?"

"Probably. Anyhow, night after that he wanders into *The Drive* looking all lost and lonely and the next thing I know we're debating the proper way to drink Scotch." She paused for a moment, remembering their evenings in the old bar. "I don't think I ever laughed so hard as I did with Ben and Fiona."

"I'm sorry, Captain, that he's gone," Garrett said.

Joanne turned suddenly serious. "No, Garrett, no pity for the Captain. I put him there. In the end, I'm why he's dead."

Ann let the silence go for a few seconds, then moved the conversation elsewhere.

"Was there something you needed, Captain?"

"Yes. Did they transmit at all before we hit them?"

"They did," Garrett replied. "Once right after the first three were hit, a long message. Then another short message just before we hit the last one."

"Same channel?"

"Yes, ma'am. We assess that as the undamaged ship reporting the first strike and then reporting that they were under attack."

"Did they finish the message?"

"Yes, ma'am. But only by a few seconds."

"Very well." She looked around at the four Intel techs, their shoulders sagging as they sat at their positions. "Thank you, all of you. I know you all admired Ben Price. I did, too. We'll all miss him." She looked around at them again, meeting each eye. "Lieutenant Cooper will be in charge for now, at least until we get back home."

Ann followed Joanne out into the passageway, closing the workroom door behind her.

"Yes?" Henderson asked.

"Natalie?"

"I talked to her briefly when she got back, but not since. I'll catch up with her later tonight, maybe. They were going to get married."

"Oh, no!"

"Came to me about a day out of Beta Hydri." Joanne shook her head. "I made a joke about how I couldn't marry them."

"And you? How are *you* doing?"

Joanne smiled grimly. "I meant what I said, Ann. No pity for the captain. I'm fine."

"But, Captain —"

"Really, Ann, I know you mean well, I do, but this is a warship in a combat area, not Fleet HQ. People can die here, and for every one that does there's some-one aboard who wishes it hadn't happened."

"Yes, I see."

"I need to go." She pointed to the Intel door. "Let them work through it tonight, but tomorrow they need to be back on their 'A' game. If you need to push or kick a little to make that happen, I understand."

"Well, I'm more of the mothering type, but we'll be ready."

"Good."

Joanne walked the few dozen meters quickly to the Bridge. Alonzo Bass looked at her as she stood outside the Command position where he sat.

"Well?"

"They got off two messages."

Alonzo nodded grimly in response. "You know what that means, Captain, right?"

"Yes. They'll probably be back. In force. And soon."

Joanne climbed the three steps and sat in her command chair, silently staring out at the cold light of the stars, wondering which one spawned this curse, which one sheltered those she so completely despised. The stars weren't telling, and their willful silence angered her for a moment; a feeling that passed as she recognized the irrationality of it. *There will be more Bens*, she thought to herself. *Maybe many more. If not here, then somewhere.*

Damn it.

After two hours, Natalie was almost done with her first 'brain dump' draft when there was a knock at the office door. She thought about telling whoever it was to get lost, but instead decided to accept the interruption. She set down her pen and turned the pad over.

"Come in."

The door opened slowly to reveal the young Marine Lieutenant who had been standing over Ben when she found him.

"Lieutenant Hayden?" he asked, tentatively.

"Yes. Liwanu, right?"

"Yes, ma'am. I need to tell you, Lieutenant, about, well, about Mr. Price, ma'am."

Natalie felt suddenly vulnerable, suddenly even more alone. What could this young Marine possibly know about Ben? She swallowed hard before responding.

"OK. Care to sit down?"

"Yes, thank you, ma'am."

Liwanu stepped forward nervously and sat in the hard steel seat across from Natalie. It was the same seat where Ben had said 'I am your man!' just a few days before. And, indeed, he was. Could it possibly be only that long ago? It already felt like a lifetime. In a way, it was. There was her life before Ben, her time with him, and now she was in the first day of her life without him.

There was a long pause, as if he was unsure how to say what he needed to say.

"What did you need to tell me, Liwanu?"

"Mr. Price, ma'am. After he was hit, he only had a few seconds, and I think he knew that, but he wanted me to tell you how much he loved you."

Natalie looked down at her desk, then back up, the image of him on the ground raging back to the front of her mind, the smell of his burnt flesh, the quiet sounds of Marines trying to not be where they were, trying very hard not be in the middle of the worst moment of her life. She hadn't missed that, and someday she'd be able to tell them she noticed, and appreciated, what they were trying to do. But, no, not today.

Liwanu saw the renewed pain on Natalie's face.

"I'm sorry, ma'am if this is hurtful for you right now, but I swore to him I'd deliver his message and I couldn't live with myself if I didn't."

"I see. Thank you."

For Liwanu, there wasn't much more to say. He was ready to move on and leave Hayden with her pain.

"I'll just go now, ma'am."

"Thanks, Liwanu, for keeping your promise. Mr. Price would appreciate that."

"Yes, ma'am."

"Anything else?"

"No, ma'am, just that I'm very sorry for your loss, Lieutenant. He was brave, ma'am, and I think what he did today mattered."

Liwanu rose and left the office, closing the door softly behind himself. He walked to the bridge, directly to the command position.

"Captain Henderson, ma'am, might I have a word with you?"

276

Henderson looked at him, saw the seriousness of his expression, and walked down off her position.

"Sure, come with me." They walked a few meters aft to the captain's duty cabin. Inside, Joanne offered him a seat, which he accepted with relief.

"So, marine, what's on your mind?"

"Mr. Price, ma'am."

"Oh?"

"Yes, Captain, before he died, he gave me two messages to deliver."

"OK."

"The first was to Lieutenant Hayden. You can guess what that was."

"Yes, I suppose I can."

"I think he loved her very much. But to you, ma'am, he wanted me to say 'thanks.' He didn't say exactly what for —"

"I know what for," Joanne responded, cutting him off, then instantly regretting having done that.

"Sorry, Lieutenant Harry, I should not have interrupted you. Price and I had a conversation before we left on this mission. He talked about it then. I know what he meant."

"OK, well, that's good, Captain, I guess. That's all I had, ma'am."

Liwanu was ready to be dismissed, but Henderson had more questions.

"What was the fight like?"

"Hard, ma'am, hard, and fast, I mean, we had them dead-on, but they just kept coming and shooting that hot shit at us. Price put himself on the line after Joanie and Gunther went down. I was surprised that he'd do that, ma'am, he was just an Intel guy, you know?"

"Yes, I know. I specifically told him not to get shot."

"It was pretty fluid, Captain, they were pushing us pretty hard, and I think Mr. Price thought he needed to pitch in or we'd be in real trouble."

"That sounds like him."

"Yes, ma'am. Just for me, Captain? I heard you were friends with Mr. Price, and it's none of my business, really, but I just wanted to say I'm sorry for your loss, ma'am."

"Thanks, Harry. And thanks for telling me how it played out. You can go."

"Yes, ma'am."

He slipped out of the captain's duty cabin, worked his way aft then down the ladder to the Marines' barracks area. The Marines were listening to music as they talked and cleaned their weapons. Normally the music would be loud and occasionally drowned out by shouted banter or laughter. Tonight, the music was quiet and the talk subdued as they restocked their packs and made sure if another call came, they were ready. Harry took a short walk around the room, talking to most and encouraging a couple that seemed more sullen than the rest.

He left and headed back to the cabin he shared with Captain Martin.

"So, how did it go?"

"OK, I guess, sir. I've never had to deliver messages like those, you know?"

"I do. But you did it, Liwanu, you did what someone in a desperate, really hopeless, condition asked you to do. Good work, if you ask me."

"Yes, sir, thanks."

After they switched off the light, Liwanu replayed his first day of combat command. He hadn't frozen, he hadn't even hesitated. He felt on the verge of a well-earned tear or two afterward, what with both Gunther and Joanie lost, but he hadn't cried or vomited as some did. He'd killed several times that day, but after seeing the Seeker leader and his people, his conscience was clear. He thought about Price, what he had said, and what that said about the kind of man he was. If there was a regret to take away from this day, he decided, it was that he had not known this man better before he was gone.

Intrepid
Big Blue
Wednesday, December 7, 2078, 2030 UTC

Joanne spent two hours preparing her report to Fleet. SLIP's limited bandwidth meant she had to keep the text to a minimum. But there was an awful lot to say, so if she was going to send a message, she'd thought she'd best make it count.

```
FLASH 207811242030UTC
TO: CINCFLEET, FLEETOPS, FLEETINTEL
CC: EAGLE, FRIENDSHIP
FROM: INTREPID

REPORT OF 207811240915 ENEMY ENGAGEMENT

1) ENEMY MOVEMENTS EARLY AM THIS DATE INDICATED PROBABLE
KNOWLEDGE OF SEEKERS.
2) AT 0915 UTC INTREPID STRUCK LITTLE GRAY AND THREE OF
FOUR ENEMY SHIPS.
3) CONCURRENT WITH THIS STRIKE INTREPID LANDED MARINES TO
COUNTER ENEMY FORCES IN PASTURE NEAR SEEKERS.
4) ENSUING GROUND ENGAGEMENT REMOVED IMMEDIATE THREAT.
5) AT 1020 UTC INTREPID STRUCK THREE ENEMY SHUTTLES IN THE
PROCESS OF LOADING GROUND TEAMS IN CAPITAL CITY AND
SIMULTANEOUSLY THE FOURTH SHIP.
6) SLIP SCANNER REPORTS ENEMY TRANSMITTED MESSAGES AT
TIME OF INITIAL STRIKE AND JUST BEFORE FINAL ATTACK.
7) INTREPID WAS NOT ENGAGED BY ENEMY.
8) ALL ENEMY AT GROUND ENGAGEMENT KIA. THERE ARE BELIEVED
```

```
TO BE SOME DOZENS OF ENEMY SURVIVORS IN CAPITAL CITY.
9) REGRETFULLY SUFFERED 4 MARINE KIA PLUS WO4 BENJAMIN PRICE.
6 WIA NONE SERIOUSLY.
10) FROM ENEMY SLIP ACTIVITY WE EXPECT ENEMY RESPONSE IN
FORCE IN THE NEAR FUTURE.
11) INTREPID WILL REMAIN ON STATION UNTIL DIRECTED OTHERWISE.
12) EAGLE AND FRIENDSHIP PING 121.5 ON ARRIVAL IF NO
ENEMY PRESENT.

HENDERSON

END
```

"That is going to shake some souls at HQ," her XO said after reading the report.

"Maybe. They're too far away, Alonzo, to be of any real good to us. *Eagle* and *Friendship* are coming, but we won't see them for at least a week."

"So, for now, we're all there is."

"Yup. If the enemy sends enough ships, we'll have a damnable time holding them off."

Bass pulled up the ship's Weapons Status on his workstation. "Still, thirty-five Bludgeons, twenty-two Lances is a long way from nothing. We should be able to hold them off for a while."

"As long as we can keep from being detected, yes. As soon as they find us..."

"It could get ugly, like, *Sigma* ugly."

"Yes."

Alonzo changed the subject. "What are we going to do about the bodies in the pasture? We can't just leave them there to rot."

"No. After dawn tomorrow I'll go see Eaagher and see what he wants us to do."

"Tomorrow? There's still at least fifteen hours of daylight left down there."

She shook her head. "Not today, Alonzo. I can't send another shuttle down there right now."

Alonzo let that go. He'd have gone back immediately, but Henderson was the captain, so they'd wait. "So, again, what will we do with them?"

"I don't know what the Seekers' practices are, but they might have a sugges-tion."

"What about the enemy's practices?"

"I don't care. No, that's wrong. I do care, and if I knew what they wanted, I'd make sure that was the one thing we *didn't* do."

"Ugh, you do ruthless very well, Captain."

Joanne smiled grimly and shrugged. "It's a gift."

As Alonzo smiled in response, she got back up and returned to her cabin for a few hours' sleep.

There was nothing more to be done tonight. Sunrise at the Seekers' location was forty hours away. She needed the time, and she suspected most of her crew did, too.

Columbia
Kapteyn Station
Thursday, December 8, 2078, 1730 UTC

The Fleet's newest and most popular starbase was in the southern constellation Pictor, near the red sub-dwarf Kapteyn's Star, almost thirteen light-years southeast (in Right Ascension terms) of Earth and about ten light-years south of Inor. Kapteyn's Star is too faint to be seen from Earth with the naked eye, so it didn't get a name from the Greeks or Romans or even a designation as part of Pictor. First identified in the late nineteenth century, Kapteyn is about one quarter the mass of the Sun, with an even smaller fraction of its luminosity, just over 1%.

Kapteyn Station was much bigger than Tranquility II, intended to provide ample space for rest and relaxation for visiting crews. Off-ship hotel space was available, and a small-town 'Main Street' of restaurants, pubs, and shops gave it a feeling of being back home. The 'sky' above Main Street was occupied not by a familiar yellow-white sun but by the red dwarf, a strange yellow-orange color to human eyes.

The better rooms in the hotel looked out at Kapteyn, and the view was spectacular, with the small 'sun' in the foreground and the diamond-like stars behind. The rooms were comfortable and reminiscent of those in any of the better hotels on Earth. But the view, beautiful as it was, reminded them that this was not home but a strange and dangerous place very far away. One of the station's best attractions was a long, wide walkway, the 'Promenade,' which ran on the outside of the station behind Main Street's shops.

As Barker's plans for offensive operations were being developed, the Fleet was out reexamining the stars in the south that had been part of the original randomized search. This time, the routes were less random and more efficient, and they frequently included a visit to Kapteyn. *Columbia* stopped there after checking two typical systems, neither of which had any enemy presence.

Late in the afternoon, Mike Clark, Ramon Flores, Melinda Hughes, and a few other officers from *Columbia* spilled out of the airlock, a high-volume mass of cascading gregarious noise. David Powell had passed on this outing in order to complete some Intel reports he had promised Katch he'd finish. He'd watched them rumble down the central passageway, catching Melinda Hughes' eye as they made the turn for the airlock. She leaned back with a sly smile before disappearing around the corner.

They squeezed themselves into a booth in Main Street's best (and only) Italian place, Uncle Vito's. They had a great time recalling the search for body parts, at least, those events that could be repeated in public, over generous plates of lasagna, chicken parmesan, and pizza, and numerous bottles of the house red. The wine was pretty good, if a little weak by home standards. Still, it went well with the food, and they enjoyed the meal and their company together. Clark found himself between Melinda and Ramon, people whose company could be counted on for plenty of laughter. Tonight was no different.

Somewhere after the salad and before the main course, about two glasses of wine into the evening, he felt Melinda wrap his right little finger with her left. Her touch was gentle but firm. He waited a moment for her to pull her hand away, but it didn't seem to be going anywhere. He glanced at her, but she was looking at Lieutenant Abbas, across the table and to her right, intently sharing a story about Katch. He returned her gentle pressure and shortly they had two fingers together.

Confirmation received.

Mike now had a real problem. A good problem, really, but a problem nonetheless. He was as right-handed as could be, and he now had to eat his dinner left-handed, single-handed, all without drawing attention to himself or Melinda. He was suddenly glad he had ordered the lasagna, which he could eat with only a fork. He made it through the rest of the meal as he and Melinda worked their way through their remaining two fingers to be fully intertwined. His head was spinning a little, and not from the wine. Mike knew Melinda very well, liked her, and respected her abilities. They had spent quite a lot of time working together recently, including several lunches and dinners, but this overture took him by surprise. Their hands held fast until the time came to pay the check and leave. He disengaged as gently as he could, saying nothing, and they moved on out of the restaurant.

Flores, no fool, had caught on to the whole thing about halfway through dinner. He grabbed the rest of the officers and insisted they head back to a pub he had heard of to finish off the evening. He managed to get everyone away from Mike and Melinda without anyone noticing. Or, without them admitting to having noticed. Slick. Once they were a few steps down the walkway, he threw Mike a smiling 'you owe me pal' look over his shoulder, then returned to moving the group away.

They stood for a moment, neither sure what to say.

"Let's walk," Mike said, "there is an entrance to the Promenade at the end of the street." Melinda nodded, recaptured his hand, and they moved slowly down the walkway, away from the fading noise of their shipmates. The street held a variety of small businesses, from bakery to ice cream to souvenirs to jewelry. They were quiet until she stopped at a Christmas shop full of Russian nesting dolls, small lit trees, tiny replicas of 19th-century English buildings, and a great many Santa's. For a moment she just looked in the window.

"Melinda —"

"My Dad always did the tree," she interrupted, her voice quiet and somber. "It was fake, of course, but we loved it. He dragged it out of the basement every year and spent most of the day piecing it together. The world always seemed to change that day. It's funny, every year, that tree went up and suddenly we were happier."

He looked at her, then down at their hands. "I think I know what you mean."

She laughed a little, smiled, then went back to the wistful look she had had when they saw the shop.

After a moment, Mike went on. "We had a line of blue spruces that we pulled from each year. Then the next spring we'd replant where we took the last one. It was fun when I was a kid, but later, I thought it was just another shitty chore that got black stains on my hands." He paused. "What an idiot I was."

Melinda didn't seem to hear him, still looking in the store. "He's gone, you know? Just like that, one day he wasn't there anymore." Her grip became stronger on his hand.

"We need to talk, Melinda. I need to understand —"

"Oh, we'll talk, Michael Clark, we're gonna talk a *lot*!" her voice reflected her smile, the melancholy quickly fading. "But for now, let's just walk, OK?"

They moved on down the street, which was maybe a hundred meters long, and at the end crossed over to the hotel's Promenade. It was built of a double layer of glass that stretched three meters from ceiling to floor. The Promenade faced away from Kapteyn, and with no star to diminish them, the stars were bright and vivid. The glass wall was set out from the station, with a clear floor and ceiling a meter wide. The walkway was dimly lit to enhance the view, and if you stood close, it gave the illusion of being in space, not looking out on it. Some found the illusion a little too real and became nauseous, nervous, or even agoraphobic when they first saw it. But for most, it was a wondrous place to see.

Mike loved it, and so did Melinda. They walked a fair distance and then found themselves a seat on one of the benches that were installed every ten meters or so.

They sat quietly for a few moments, then Mike began.

"Melinda we've been on *Columbia* for a while now. We've worked together a lot, had a few meals lately. You're wonderful to be around, that much I know, and most people you meet love you. But I had no idea —"

"Oh, Mike, Mike, Mike..." she said quietly, gently cutting him off. "They like me, some respect me, and some, I am sure, want something far less high minded from me. But love? I don't think so. Love..."

"Is a choice," he continued for her, "a commitment, something conscious, not completely emotional."

"Exactly."

"So, why tonight? What's changed?"

She shrugged. "I have had these feelings since before this last mission. I just decided I wanted you to know it, now, and not wait until some supposed 'right time.' You're kind, you're thoughtful, you don't look at me as an object instead of a person. I just have had this solid feeling around you, Mike. You can be counted on, even when it's hard. I've seen it."

"As can you, I think."

"I'd like to think so, but I've watched you work, and I see how you are with your crew, how you are with the rest of us. It's great, Mike, really."

"Melinda, I am just another junior officer doing his job." He was going to say more but decided not to. He was going to say he was flattered that she felt this way, or maybe honored, but neither of those words or anything else he could think of really expressed the feeling he had.

She spoke intently as she continued to look out at the stars.

"Mike Clark, you were never and will never be just another officer. You, and Powell, something about you is just a cut above the rest of us. You'll see."

"I have never considered myself any —"

"Of course not," she interrupted him again, waving her hand dismissively. "If you did, it would ruin it."

He let the matter drop, doubtful that her assessment was entirely objective. He'd worked hard to be good at all the things she mentioned, but he never considered that it was anything other than the way it should be done.

She sat back a little and looked at him.

"So why take *my* hand tonight? Why not push it away? It would have been easy to do."

"Well, you did catch me off guard. But by now you must know that I like you as well. Everything you say about me — and David — many of us would say about you. Yes, there's no getting around that you are an attractive woman, as you say, but no one I know thinks of you first in that way. It's part of who you are, just like being too tall and too skinny is part of me; but what I see when I look at you is not a pretty girl but a smart officer working very hard to get stuff done. The outside stuff, for me and for most others, I think, is way less important."

They became quiet as a few small groups of people and couples passed their bench. They shared a few quiet 'Good Evening' greetings with others taking in the view.

"I like the skinny."

"I like the blue eyes."

After a moment looking out at the stars, Mike spoke. "So where do we go from here? I don't have a class ring to give you."

"Very funny. Let's just spend some time together, OK? Maybe some movies, listen to some music? Let's see who we are when it's just us."

"Sure. I would like that. So, what do we say to the others?"

"Nothing for now. There's nothing to tell, yet."

"Works for me. I have the watch in the morning. Are you ready to head back?"

"I could sit here a very long time," she said.

"The stars will be here tomorrow," he said brightly.

She gripped his hand tightly again. "I wasn't talking about the stars."

As they stood, she reached up, her hand on the back of his neck, and on tiptoe she kissed him lightly. They had a brief embrace, then headed along the Promenade towards the ship. As they reached the entrance and headed back out on to Main Street, by some silent agreement they dropped their hands.

After they separated, Mike felt suddenly cold and disconnected, and the feeling surprised him. He began to think as they walked off Main Street and down the passages to the ship's airlock that the evening had shown him more than he realized at first. He was no loner, but neither was he one to rush into a relationship like he just had. She said she felt 'solid' around him. Her presence had had that same kind of effect on him, too, making him feel somehow secure, that he was somehow in the right place in his life. She had opened a door to a future he had not even known was possible. This would be an evening that he would always remember, even if nothing ultimately came of it. Someone he admired, admired him as well, was willing to take a risk to tell him, and wanted to see what else there might be found between them. Not many people get that, he thought, and he was happy that Melinda Hughes would give him this gift. She had her own reasons, he was sure, and he had no illusions about that, but it was still a gift, and he knew it.

His alarm waking him at 0515 for his 0600 watch disturbed dreams he would never have dreamt just a day earlier. It was a new day in a new universe, and he was glad to see what was next.

Columbia
Kapteyn Station
Friday, December 9, 2078, 0700 UTC

Dan called his staff together early in the morning. They were anticipating a trip to yet another red dwarf.

"We have orders."

"Orders, sir?" Melinda asked.

"Yeah. Orders. First, we're going directly home from here. Today."

"Home?" David asked hopefully, visions of Carol suddenly dancing in his head.

"Yeah. Merry Christmas."

Maz Dawes studied his Captain's face carefully. "If this was good news, you'd be smiling."

"Yeah, Maz, that's true. We've been assigned to be Barker's flagship."

"Us?"

"Yeah. I guess I pissed him off more than I thought."

"Or, he likes what you've done."

"Katch, I'm not looking for compliments. Barker is a fine officer, don't misunderstand, and he would have been my choice for the southern theater. But we're going to be taking on a pile of staff weenies and our freedom of action will be nil. Our main job as the flagship will be to keep Barker breathing."

"Not what you came out here for, sir?" Weapons Officer Victor Shoemaker asked.

"No. Not even close." Dan sighed, then continued with resignation in his tone. "OK, tell your people. I want to be underway by 0900."

"How long have you known?" Melinda asked, holding Smith back from leaving the wardroom.

"About a week. I didn't see any need to tell you until we were ready to go home, and I didn't want it leaked on the station."

Dan started again to leave, then turned around. "Oh, one more thing."

"Yes?" Maz asked, clearly worried.

Dan looked at his old friend. "David, you're going with Evans on *Cobra*."

"What, sir?"

"Evans asked for you and CINC agreed."

"Yes, sir. Thank you, sir. May I have some more, sir?" he responded with a mixture of sadness and sarcasm.

"David, *Cobra* is a huge opportunity for you. Don't discount that part. I'd rather you stayed here, too, but CINC has other ideas."

"Yes, sir, I understand."

"They're pulling Myra Rodgers off *Dunkirk* to handle Surveillance and taking Jack Ballard away from Terri Michael, too."

"And Carol," David said quietly, "She adores Jack. They've made a pretty good team."

"Well, there's a good recommendation. So, David, go be the good spook we all have always known you really are."

Dismissed, they went out to prepare the ship to undock from Kapteyn, and to prepare the crew for a very different mission.

Dan stopped by the Intel section a few minutes later.

"Lieutenant Powell, may I have a moment?"

David left his discussion with Katch and stepped out into the passageway with his Captain.

"Sir?"

"Listen, David, there's going to be an offensive."

"I thought so. Fleet has to get something positive going."

"Yeah, but that's not exactly why we're here."

David looked at Dan with some skepticism. "OK, so why *are* we here?"

"Linda and I have moved up the ceremony."

"Oh?"

"We're getting married December 27th at the new Fleet place in the Keys."

"Nice."

"You're going to be there. So is Carol. *Antares* is still at Earth."

"OK."

"Buddy, for someone who talks way too much you're not saying much."

David smiled. "Sorry, Dan, just thinking. Who else is available?"

"Joe and Larry will both be there. Some others from the U."

"Kinda short notice."

"It is, but I checked with Evans, and *Cobra* can't go before New Year's. It won't be ready. So, that pushes the whole offensive planning back a month or two as well."

David nodded his agreement. "Makes sense. But once it starts, it's gonna get hairy."

"That's why we made the change."

"That, and..."

"Let's not think about what might or might not happen, David. But, if it does, she'll be taken care of."

"Understood. Anything else?"

"No. I just wanted you to have the scoop. I already sent Carol a SLIP."

David stepped back into the Intel workroom and finished his conversation with Katch, but he was suddenly disconnected from the moment. It seemed incongruous to him that within three weeks, he'd be feeling real sunshine and smelling salt breezes with the other half of himself at his side. It was too soft a picture to feel real, too much removed from his current steel-and-glass existence to believe. But now there was much more to look forward to than a few presents and an eggnog by the fire.

Big Blue
The Pasture
Friday, December 9, 2078, 1205 UTC

Beta Hydri was just rising over the horizon when *Intrepid's* shuttle set down in the pasture, near where Ben Price was killed. At his own request, Weapons Officer James Kirkland did the piloting. He'd severely misjudged both Price and Henderson when they first came aboard, and now he regretted that reaction. Price had excelled at his job, and Henderson was as good a Captain as there was in the Fleet. Flying this trip was just the start of his personal penance.

Joanne brought Colin Garrett along so that he would be familiar with how to work with the Seekers. As they disembarked, Joanne was surprised to find no enemy remains. They could see signs of the battle, blood and drag marks on the sandy soil, but no bodies.

Garrett followed the grooves in the soft ground for fifty meters, then turned back to Henderson and Kirkland.

"Looks like they were dragged to the sea, Captain. From the end of that little rise you can see the trail goes right on down to the beach."

"So, the Seekers did this?" Kirkland asked.

"I guess," Henderson replied.

They walked the three hundred meters to the north edge of the pasture, working their way through a herd of the Seekers' food animals, climbed the easy cliff to get out, and then down a gentle slope back to the beach.

Seeker lookouts had seen them land, and Eaagher and Ullnii were waiting. Once the usual introductions were made, Joanne typed a question on the translation tablet.

"Where are the hard faces killed yesterday?"

Eaagher waved his left hand and wrote.

Put in sea then sea animals eat.

"Wow," Kirkland said, "that's cold."

Garrett was surprised. "But, Captain, I've seen the pictures. They walk into the surf when they're fishing."

She typed another question for Eaagher.

"Sea animals not eat you?"

Eaagher waved his right hand, then wrote.

Tiny sea animals eat dead not eat living.

Garrett looked up after reading the translation. "Tiny sea animals — wait — didn't *Antares'* doctor report some kind of nasty-looking near-microscopic sea creature? Told everybody not to go swimming?"

"Yes, that's right."

"So, there are tiny seagoing maggot piranha that only eat dead flesh?" Kirkland suggested.

"Gross," Garrett said with disgust.

"Gross, sure, but convenient," Joanne responded. She turned back to Eaagher.

"Hard faces gone for now but we think they will return. We will stay until new Friends come."

Grateful Friends here.

"You can't see us, but we are there, and we are watching over you."

Eaagher just raised his left hand in acknowledgment.

Joanne kept typing. "We will visit again with new friends within five suns."

Friends future welcome.

The group started to leave when Eaagher got Joanne attention again.

Ullnii has questions for Friends.

Joanne looked at the child, who she now realized was holding a book. Joanne waved her left hand, and Ullnii came forward. Joanne knelt on the beach to get down to her eye level. Ullnii opened the book *Antares* had left her to a picture of a zebra. Joanne smiled. She'd always loved zebras as a kid.

"Zebra."

Ullnii looked at her carefully, watching her mouth.

"*leeba.*"

Joanne said it again very slowly. "Zeeebra."

"*Zebra.*"

Joanne waved her left hand, then realized Eaagher had written a question for her.

Is this a real creature?

Joanne waved her left hand to say yes, this is real. Ullnii looked at her for a moment, in what must have been an expression of surprise. She opened the book to a picture of a blue whale with a human figure next to it for size and pointed to it. Joanne lifted her left hand again.

Ullnii lifted her right and shook it rapidly.

Joanne took the tablet and wrote, "What does her gesture mean?"

Eaagher wrote back, *She not believe. She thinks impossible.*

"Are there not large animals in your ocean?" she typed.

No.

"That is surprising. So much ocean," she typed back.

Know ocean well. Nothing so large.

She looked back at Ullnii and raised her left hand again. Ullnii closed the book and walked back towards the cave.

Joanne stood up and wrote on the tablet. "My home a very different place. Your home a very different place."

Eaagher waved his left hand and wrote *Hope short future see Friends again.*
Joanne waved her left hand and headed back to the shuttle. She wasn't sure her short kindergarten teaching career had gone all that well.
Next time, she thought, *I'll send Ann.*

Eagle arrived December 14th, and after *Friendship* arrived on the 16th, Joanne began making plans to take *Intrepid* home. Two squads of Marines volunteered to stay, so she transferred one each to the newcomers. Captain Martin and Lieutenant Harry would go home on *Intrepid* to make their reports to Fleet in person. She made one last trip to the surface with the new captains to introduce them to Eaagher, then set course for home. She welcomed the safety of FTL travel, but quietly grieved the lives lost, their remains now carried home in the deep freeze behind the hangar deck.

Next to the five they'd lost in battle lay the three enemy bodies recovered from the pasture. Their eventual disposition would be something altogether different.

Columbia
Earth Orbit
Wednesday, December 21, 2078, 1400 UTC

Shortly after *Columbia* was settled into its parking orbit, a fleet shuttle arrived carrying Kieran Barker, Harry Hess, and Elias Peña. They met in the Intel conference room with Dan, Katch, and Dan's new XO, Maz Dawes. Alona Melville was already gone, headed to the ship factory in the asteroid belt to take over *Jarvis*, which was almost ready for delivery. Barker and his most senior staff had come to *Columbia* to set the tone for his flagship.

Barker wasted no time, beginning to speak almost before they were all seated.
"OK, Commander Smith, I just wanted to talk this out a bit."
"Talk what out, Admiral?"
"Right off, I want to reassure you that this is still your ship. I know to have me and my retinue aboard is going to be a distraction. But you are still in command, and I will respect that."
"Well, thanks, Admiral, but we both know *Columbia's* primary task now is not to fight, not to find the enemy, but to keep you breathing."
Barker smiled. "Your reputation for being direct is intact, Commander." He paused a second. "That is typical, yes, but it will not be the case here. On the other hand, Commander, keeping me breathing means keeping yourselves breathing!"
"Yes, sir, true enough."
"There's more, and I think this will help our situation. A FleetShips crew will be here later today. Based on what's previously been done to *Antares* and *Intrepid*

to carry Marines, we're going to take those same two lower levels here for my people. We'll have our own operations area, some quarters, and a communications center. We'll be adding a second SLIP system as well."

"That will certainly help. I had Lieutenant Murphy looking at how we were going to allocate quarters with your people aboard, and it wasn't going well."

"You may still need to give me a few bunks, Commander Smith, but we're not going to totally take over."

"That will be a relief to our crew, sir."

"Good. But we will be around, on the Bridge, in the Wardroom. My instructions to everyone are to remember we are your guests, and to respect that in every way possible."

"Thank you, sir. If your choices in staff are any clue, I can see that this will work well."

Elias Peña leaned forward on his elbows. "Lieutenant Khachaturian, I will need your help with the Intel process between ship and staff. This is part of why we pulled Powell for *Cobra* and kept you here."

Katch smiled. "Well, Commander, truthfully, I'd have ducked that assignment even if you'd asked me. I'd much rather stay operational here on *Columbia* than go snooping around in the dark with Evans."

Dan turned to Barker. "You felt strongly about keeping the HQ mobile. Are you planning to orbit somewhere? Stay out of any system?"

"We'll have *Ceres* along with us, nearby, anyhow. I'm going to go to Beta Hydri first. Our presence will bring additional firepower there, and it puts me closer to where the offensive is going to end."

"Alpha Mensae?"

"Correct. My hope is to push through to the home planet shortly after this first set of strikes."

"After *Cobra* visits?"

"Oh, yes, definitely. We need to see what's there before we can think about staging any action."

"I agree, that's wise. When are you planning to leave, sir? I need to let the crew know."

Harry Hess spoke for the first time. "We're not waiting for *Ceres*. It can come along later. So, plan two weeks here, and then we'll depart."

"Assuming our space is complete," Peña added.

"Right," Barker agreed, "assuming that, we'll head to Beta Hydri January 5th."

"*Columbia* will be ready, Admiral."

"Very good." Barker looked around the room. "Gentlemen, I'd like a word with Captain Smith if I may?"

Dan could not keep the surprise off his face as the four other officers filed out, Maz Dawes closing the door behind him.

"Sir?"

"Listen, Dan, you're a very junior Lieutenant Commander. If you think you got that because it was expedient for FleetPers, you're right. I've been around this Fleet for a long time, maybe fifteen years."

"Your point, Admiral?"

"None of that means shit now. This *is* your ship."

Dan was still very unsure where this conversation was going.

"Thanks, I guess."

"As the captain of my flagship, I expect your honest input on decisions that affect her. Like it or not, your part of my staff now, Dan, and I want you to feel free to speak your mind."

"Never been a problem for me, sir."

"I know. It's part of why I picked you."

Dan finally broke a grin, one somehow sheepish and cocky at the same time.

"I think we'll do fine, Admiral."

"Good. So do I."

The new Admiral and his aides headed back for their shuttle, their goals for the visit accomplished. Barker did see a lot of himself in Dan Smith, and he wanted to sit face-to-face with him and establish a working relationship. Smith was direct, as he'd said. He was also smart and resourceful. If Barker wanted to live to finish off this offensive, *Columbia* gave him the best chance to do that.

South Fleet Resort
Florida Keys
Monday, December 26, 2078

Everyone knew Randy Forstmann was rich beyond anyone's dreams of avarice, but no one ever said that he was ungrateful or ungenerous. Once he realized that his invention had required the creation of the Fleet, he knew there had to be a place for crews have a respite, to have some fun and time away from the stress of their duties.

So, along with a half a mile of Lake Erie shoreline near his boyhood home between Vermilion and Huron, a little east of the Cedar Point amusement park, he made a similar investment in a winter resort in the Florida Keys. Behind the beach, he built a series of low buildings with small apartments where Fleet people could stay for a nominal fee, just enough to cover the costs of services and maintenance. The beach and walkway behind were open to the public, but the facilities were only available to Fleet personnel.

This was the place Carol, David, and the others came for Dan Smith's wedding. Once Dan knew that they would be the flagship in a new offensive, he and Linda decided to move their marriage up six months. They could not know what might happen, and they wanted to 'get this done' as soon as possible. CINC called Forstmann and Forstmann called the resort, and it was done.

The timing was perfect for David and Carol. He was now relieved of duty on *Columbia*, but not due on *Cobra* until after the New Year. Carol asked Terri Michael for a week's leave, as there was at least that much time before they would be headed back out, and it had been easily granted. They would have a few days together away from the war and the death and the fear; a few days to spend feeling the warmth of their own sun, their own wind, and the sand of their own planet between their toes.

Dinner on Monday was a luxurious mixture of good wine, great food, and fine company. They told tales from the University, from missions 'out there,' about friends present and also those now gone, reveling in the inside jokes and puns that only SFU grads would get.

By seven-thirty or so it was breaking up since Dan and Linda and the rest of the official wedding party had a rehearsal to get to. As they left, Carol strolled back over to David.

"So, sailor, can a girl buy you a drink?" she asked, one eyebrow up and the smile clear in her voice.

"Well, let me think..." he responded with mock skepticism. Carol took David's arm with some authority, steering him back to her room. She walked him to the balcony overlooking the beach, then headed back for the small bar.

"Glenlivet or Balvenie 16?" she called.

"Glenlivet, one cube." She poured his drink, then served herself a Southern Comfort, neat. She walked out to the balcony, the stars shining brightly in the clear sky. The evening was cooling quickly, a contrast from the warm sunny day. She stood there for a moment, sipping gently, and feeling the evening beginning to fall around them. She slipped an arm around him, resting her head on his shoulder.

"That was the best thing I ever did in my whole life."

"Oh? What?"

"When I promised that next time I would stay for the sunset," she said quietly. He set down his drink and looked away from the water, into her eyes.

"But tonight, we missed it."

She poked him in the ribs, just hard enough.

"Well, anyway, here I am, still standing here."

They were quiet for a while, sharing the beauty of the moment and the feeling of being together. They stood close at the rail for a long time, sipping their drinks and talking only a little. Carol finally stepped back into the apartment for another pour, and with the sound of the waves David didn't hear her return. In his mind, he was reliving the day, seeing their time together over and over again. Her hair was short now, done in a way that showcased her features very well — David had long thought she looked her best with that style. He could see just a little more of the freshman girl he had fallen for the first day of university, still living there somewhere deep inside the fully mature, experienced Fleet officer.

"David..." she said softly, very close to him.

As he turned, she took his face in her hands, thumbs resting gently on his lips. Her sudden touch felt electric, as chills ran down his back all the way to his toes, a quick knot appeared in his stomach. Her face was mere inches from his.

"I've missed you *so much.*"

David, struck dumb for the moment, could only nod and let her talk.

"I want to tell you, just once, just this once, that I think I always have loved you, ever since that stupid first day."

David, struggling to speak, managed only "Doesn't seem so stupid now, does it?"

"I just couldn't see it somehow. I don't know how I could have been so blind. I mean, there you were, *right there*, all along..."

He pulled her close and finally, found his voice. "I said it before, and now, just this once, I'll say it again. I'll never regret whatever it took for us to be here. Right here, right now."

She nodded her agreement with her face pressed against his chest. She could feel his heartbeat.

He gently pulled her back to him.

"It's time," she said.

He looked at her, puzzled. "Time?"

"Time to read the journals!"

They sat cross-legged on the floor of her room, leaning against the small sofa. They went back and forth, in chronological order, each reading the other's words aloud. There were tears and laughter, questions and answers, the occasional tease and the more frequent hand holding.

By the end, they were exhausted by the experience.

"I think next time we do this a little at a time," Carol suggested.

"Yes, definitely."

As they stood and stretched, loosening muscles made tight by sitting a little too long, she took his hand and gently pulled him close.

The next afternoon, after the wedding midday, David and Carol were back on her balcony. The reception would be later, drinks and dinner and dancing at seven. They both looked forward to a fine evening with people they loved. There was a breeze coming off the ocean, and the air was moist but starting to warm with the sunshine.

David turned to Carol. "So, I guess we should really talk."

She nodded. "You have orders..."

"That's not what I wanted to talk about, at least not yet."

Puzzled, she looked at him with a question in her eyes. "So?"

He got up and retrieved his personal case. Most officers had a small case to carry their personal tablet, phone, and a few miscellaneous small items. As he returned, she could see he was holding a small bag, satin, with a drawstring.

"Oh my God..." she whispered. He stopped mid-stride and looked at her, her eyes wide, her hand over her mouth. He slowly sat down next to her. With a little difficulty he untied the string and dropped the object it contained into his hand and turned to her.

"Carol —"

"Yes."

He smiled as he lifted the ring in his fingers. It was an old style and not large, but it was a beautiful stone in a fine, graceful setting. They both fixed their eyes on the ring as he spoke.

"This was my grandmother's. After everything with my parents was done, there wasn't much left, but she gave me this. She said it had brought her a happy life and she hoped I could inherit some of that joy with it." He paused. "Crazy old lady, I know."

"I remember her visiting you. She was kind and funny and so proud of you."

"And short." David reminded her, and she laughed again.

"Yes, very short."

The breeze felt good against their faces. The day was warming, and it looked like it would be clear and pleasant.

"OK, Carol, if I can finish this time?"

"OK."

He took a breath to get himself together.

"I don't have much beyond this ring, but everything I do have, everything I am, is yours if you will have me."

She took the ring from his hand and closed it in her right palm for a moment, her eyes shut as if in prayer, then she opened her hand, gave it back to him and held out her left hand.

"I want nothing in this world beyond this ring, and everything I am, is yours."

He slipped in on her offered finger, where it looked as if it had always belonged.

South Fleet Resort
Florida Keys
Wednesday, December 28, 2078, 1030 EST

The reception had been everything they had hoped, with plenty of good music and the warmth of the company of comrades-in-arms. Far from feeling up-staged, Dan and Linda made David and Carol's engagement a welcome counter-melody for the reception, something that only added to the joy of the day.

After breakfast the next morning, Carol and David headed out for a walk. This would be their last day at the Resort, so they wanted to make the most of the short time they had there. They circled the apartments, seeing several friends along the way. They were out of uniform in bare feet, shorts, and t-shirts, but the NetLinks on their wrists gave them away as Fleet personnel.

As they walked another lap down the wide path behind the beach, hand in hand, they came upon a family trying vainly to take a picture of themselves in front of a passing ship. Carol, happily incognito out of uniform and with short, colored hair and large sunglasses, went over and offered to take one of all of them together. They gratefully agreed, and shortly they were walking away happy, the parents telling the children about how wonderfully nice the Fleet lady was. As Carol came back to David, he was looking at her strangely.

"What?"

"My grandmother used to do that."

"What?"

"Take pictures like that for people."

She shook it off. "What's so important about that? It's just a kind thing to do."

"Yeah, I know, I guess, but, well, you don't see that much anymore."

They walked in silence for a while.

"I never met your mother," she said offhandedly.

Goddamn right, he thought to himself. Outwardly he just shrugged.

"She was my mother. I was her son."

Carol took his arm in her hand and spun him to face her.

"That tells me nothing," she said, sounding much more than just mildly annoyed. "Don't just make words, David, *talk* to me." He looked surprised as she went on. "It matters to both of us but I think even more to you than me."

"I *am* talking," he began, hesitantly. "That's how it was. She played her role, and I played mine." David looked around as if searching for the right words. "There was never any question that she cared for my welfare, but I can't say that she loved me."

"But you loved her."

He gave her that same hopeless shrug. "She was my mother."

Watching his face, Carol realized that she was perhaps not his first unrequited love, and she shuddered at the pain that must have surrounded his young heart. She put her arms around him and pulled herself close to him.

"*I* love you...I *love* you...I love *you*."

"I know, Carol, I know."

"Do you? Do you really?"

He looked down, still firmly locked in her arms, and nodded.

"This is no role for me, David, this is me — this is all of me — like I said, this is everything I am."

He leaned down slightly and kissed her, fighting the tears forming in his eyes.

"I do know, Carol, I do. And this is all of me, too. "

It took a moment before he could say what he was thinking. "I always dreamed of a Fleet life, but those were a little boy's dreams of spaceships and adventure. Now, together, you and I, we go so far beyond those childish visions, to *real* devotion, the truth of the two of us together, to the beauty of this...this...connection."

He stopped to catch his breath, realizing suddenly that she was still right there in his arms.

"If we survive this war, and you know as well as I do, we're both very lucky to still be alive right now, there is a future waiting that I never imagined. I hardly know how to tell you what it means to me."

She reached up and touched his cheek, smiling. "Three times, fella, I said it three times."

"Yeah, got that."

"Good." She took his hand in hers, and they moved on down the warm, sandy walk.

"So, when do we see Grandma?"

"Tomorrow. When do we see your folks?"

"Right after."

The Home of Virginia Graves
Kendallville, Indiana
Thursday, December 29, 2078, 1000 EDT (1400 UTC)

She was indeed tiny, not quite five feet. Her silver hair was full, and she was trim for a woman in her middle eighties. Her accountant's mind could still drive her bright green eyes to look right through you if necessary. David could clearly see his mother in her eyes and the shape of her face.

She stood as they came in, reaching up to touch Carol's cheek, gently pulling Carol's face down to her own. She held her there a few seconds speaking quietly into her ear, so quiet that David could not make it out. He could see Carol's eyes fill, then as they separated, she kissed the old woman on the cheek and said, "I will...I promise I will." The old woman nodded, smiling, and sat back down.

"I see you've found a good home for my ring!" she said, with a strong dose of humor in her tone.

"Yes, Grandma, as I recall you made me promise to do that when you gave it to me."

She smiled. "Yes, indeed, I did."

They talked about the weather, about Grandma's home and her quiet life with just the one cat and a small rose garden. Just enough, she said, to lighten her day and give her a reason to get out of bed in the morning. Marie had been her only child, and David was Marie's only child, so Grandma Virginia had but one grandchild, and she loved him dearly. After a while, she got moving and served them tea and homemade cookies. As she sat down after pouring the tea, she folded her hands in front of her and looked intently at David.

"David, my dear, there are some things I need to say to you. I need you to listen to all of it with an open heart. Can you do that?"

Unsure of what was to come, but willing to hear it, David nodded.

"David, please try not to judge your father too harshly."

David immediately realized that whatever was coming, it was not anything he expected.

"As you know, David, my family and your father's were friends since I was a little girl."

"Yes, ma'am, I remember. That's a very long time."

"It is. From the day your father Raymond was born, they told him how smart he was, how he could do anything, how wonderful he was. Your grandfather Richard doted on him. I saw it even before he and your mother knew each other. But as he grew, he made his own choices, which usually disappointed Richard, and he made sure Raymond knew just how much. Richard played basketball in college, pretty well, in fact, so Raymond played baseball, but not quite as well. Richard wanted him to be a doctor like himself, so Raymond became a lawyer. Richard was famous for his skills and wealthy, but Raymond never caught on with a big firm and finally settled into some obscure area of the law. He was good at it, and he made a good living, as you know, but as time went on, he questioned his choices. He became disillusioned with himself. Then, he became disappointed with himself for being disillusioned."

She paused, shaking her head slowly, the sadness plain on her face.

"Sometimes, he thought he had done pretty well; other times, he mourned the life he never chose to have. He was a Christian, but he condemned himself for his sins, then condemned his self-condemnation as evidence that he was not, in fact, a true Christian. This was a spiral from which he could not escape, David. He hated himself, and he hated himself for it."

"And Mother?"

Grandma looked away for a few seconds, feeling again the pain of losing a child, even a full-grown daughter as Marie was when she died of a heart attack nine months after Raymond's suicide. When Grandma spoke again, it was quieter, full of sympathy and grief for both her daughter and her son-in-law.

"She saw the pain he felt, she would talk to me about it sometimes. She just never was able to break into his fortress."

She paused a moment again, her hands shaking just a little. She took a sip of tea.

"He held onto the pain, the distance, more fiercely than she could overcome. There is a conceit in that, David, a dangerous one. It's a feeling that no matter what, he knew better than anyone how horrible he was inside. But of course, he wasn't horrible at all, just a flawed human soul like the rest of us, the same strange mixture of beauty and beast. Your mother knew this, she saw the need in him, the beauty he was hiding, and she tried to help it escape, but he was never able to unclench his heart long enough for her to break in. That's what broke her heart, David, the knowledge that with all her love, and all her talents, she could not get her husband to love himself enough to save his life."

"I never thought of it that way."

Carol sat quietly through all this, seeing even more clearly now the pain that David had been surrounded by as he grew up, wondering how he had emerged from that environment as the man he was.

"No, you wouldn't. It's so hard to be in the middle of something like that and see it objectively."

"I always thought I was just an accessory, you know, something they had to have as part of their lifestyle."

"That's unfair, David. But I do understand why you would feel that way. Marie was always preoccupied with Raymond. You probably didn't always get the attention a child needs."

He nodded his understanding, and as he did, Carol reached over and took his hand. Grandma Virginia looked on this approvingly, a small smile on her face.

"I think my dear David, that will not be a problem from here on."

He looked at her, then at Carol. "No, Grandma, I think you're right about that."

They talked about the wedding a little, how fine a match Linda was for Dan, how much they both had enjoyed their few days in the warm sun. Grandma extracted a promise that they would set a date not too far in the future.

"After all, David, I'm eighty-six. I can't wait forever."

"Soon, Grandma, soon as we can work it out. We still need to see the Hansens."

Grandma turned to Carol. "So, do you think he'll pass muster with his future in-laws?"

"Oh, I think I can get him through," she answered, laughing.

"Very good. Very, very good."

They rose and each embraced Grandma Graves, then went back out into the street where their ASV was waiting. The trip to Lancaster would take two hours.

Word was, Laura Hansen was planning quite the feast.

January 2079

ISC Fleet Shuttle Pad
Ft. Eustis, VA
Tuesday, January 3, 2079, 0020 EST (0420 UTC)

David and Carol had their farewell dinner at their favorite, most dependable Chinese restaurant the night before he left. The New Year had brought him an unexpected promotion to Senior Lieutenant, and Carol the news that she would be promoted to Lieutenant Commander within six months, pending an open position. The war had completely scrambled the promotion system, and at this point, the Fleet needed more senior officers than it had. This situation had driven Dan Smith's early advancement, and things had not gotten any better since then. Nor, FleetPers knew, would it improve any time soon.

Carol heard from Terri Michael that she had picked up her silver eagles at the same time, promoted to Captain. Terri appreciated CINC's confidence in her, she told Carol, but she dreaded that it also meant *Antares* might be getting a new commander soon.

That would break her heart, Carol knew.

It was a little after midnight in Virginia, as Carol and David played out the same excruciating goodbye scene at the Fleet Shuttle pad. Except on this night, it was freezing cold, and there would be no crickets or bullfrogs to accompany their farewells. The bright lights that illuminated the waiting shuttle gave it a strange appearance against the surrounding darkness, making it look more like a movie prop or a toy, not a vessel easily capable of space flight.

They held each other for a long time, each trying to memorize what it was like to be together. When they finally separated, David reached up to touch her cheek as they were eye-to-eye for a moment.

"I love you," he finally said.

She gripped his arms. "Make sure you come back, OK?"

He smiled. "I could ask the same of you."

She nodded, then looked down and rested her head on his chest.

"I know," she said, "I'll do my best. I promise."

"Good. We have stuff to do, you and I."

She pulled back from him, again meeting his eye. "Stuff?"

"Yeah, you have a wedding to plan."

She laughed. "Yeah, a wedding."

"And a then a whole life to figure out."

She was smiling. "Oh, that. Right."

"Meanwhile..." he began.

"Meanwhile, we fight," she finished.

They shared one more brief embrace before David turned and headed for the shuttle. Every time they did this dance, he hated it more, but duty was duty, and he could not avoid his responsibilities.

Carol felt this no less than he did. They were as immersed in the war and the Fleet as they were in each other, and they were each required to share the other with it. Painful as it was at times, it was necessary. Had either of them quit, they would not have been the person the other fell in love with. It was a strange, emotional paradox that they lived in; a continually bittersweet existence.

The image of Carol's face as he walked away from her, again, still haunted David as he hoisted his bag from the webbed storage at the back of the Fleet Shuttle and headed out through the airlock to *Cobra*. As he emerged on the other side, he looked up to see three familiar faces smiling back at him.

The short one with the dark hair called out "You're still a royal pain in the ass, *Senior Lieutenant!*"

David laughed. "Hello, Margie! Hello Gregg, Steve!" It was good to see three of his classmates from the Advanced Intel School. As he shook their hands, he flashed back to the day their instructor Ray Salazar caught him in the bar and gave him a figurative kick in the ass.

He'd always be grateful to Salazar for that intervention.

"Oh, we're not alone!" Gregg Browning said with a wide smile.

"Who?"

"Salazar."

David rolled his eyes. "Oh, God, no!" he said in a faux panic. They laughed at him and then headed down the passageway.

"Anyone else?"

"No, just us. Salazar kept us as instructors for a while but come September we were sent out to FleetIntel for temporary duty. Then Evans came around looking for talent and found us!"

"Well, if Evans wants you here, that's pretty high praise."

David heard a distinctive New Zealand accent echoing from behind him. "Yes, Powell, and that goes for you, too!"

He turned to face his new commander, extending his hand, which Evans seemed determined to fracture.

"Good to see you again, sir."

"Welcome aboard, Powell. I see you found your classmates."

"Good group. sir. Nice work."

"Sure, they'll do. Listen, Powell, officer's briefing in the wardroom at 1800, OK?"

"Yes, sir. "

"Get yourself settled, and we'll see you then."

Cobra
Earth Orbit
Tuesday, January 3, 2079, 1800 UTC

The briefing was long, and despite David's previous study of her overall design and specifications, he picked up some interesting new details in Evans' presentation.

Cobra had started out as Memorial Class Frigate #9, the *Volkov*, recognizing the sacrifice of Cosmonaut Vladislav Nikolayevich Volkov, killed during reentry from Salyut 11 in 1971. Shortly after she was started, FleetIntel prioritized the need for a fast deep-space intelligence gathering platform and pulled Hull MCF-9 out of the regular production line for extensive customization.

She had the latest refinement of the Forstmann Drive, and a reactor capable of 25% more power output than the standard model. With those improvements, *Cobra* could regularly run at 1.2 light-years-per day with sprints to 1.4 or 1.5. In general layout, she was still a frigate, two hundred forty meters long, twenty-one high and twenty-four wide. She had seven decks, where a destroyer like *Antares* or *Columbia* had ten. Thinness mattered under Forstmann Drive, just as it had with ships and aircraft on Earth, so Fleet ships generally followed a 1:10 width-to-length ratio. Some scored higher, some a little less, but that was the target for efficient and safe Drive operation.

Seven decks meant only one empty 'insulation' deck at the top and bottom of the ship, and her narrower beam meant only one empty three-meter segment along her sides as well. That should be enough, they said, and with *Cobra*'s extra external stealth treatment, Evans seemed to agree.

The last interior spaces of every fleet ship were unused, filled with a spun-stone foam that provided both insulation from the cold of space and an extra measure of protection from attack. The meter-deep black foam stealth coating on the outside of the ship completed that shield, and when completely closed up in 'Minimum EMR' mode, Fleet ships moved about almost undetectable by infra-red or any other electromagnetic radiation.

Cobra had other surprising new features.

A large fifty-meter dish antenna was mounted on her starboard side, covered in a thick but flexible fabric which effectively concealed it but didn't interfere with its operation. With that antenna, they'd be able to hear radio transmissions over a wide range of frequencies from a long distance. But, only from the right. David didn't see that as much of an obstacle. If you wanted to look left, all you had to do was flip the ship on its long axis, just as he had done with *Sigma.*

There was a twenty-meter-square, flat, phased-array radar on top of the ship, similar but more powerful than that on regular frigates. David doubted that would ever be deployed. Turning on the radar was generally the wrong thing for a stealthy spy ship to do. But, it might be useful in limited circumstances.

There were three enhanced visual spectrum telescopes where the rotary launchers and magazine would otherwise be. These were the latest available: large, sensitive, and on gimbals that allowed fast repositioning and smooth tracking of targets.

Evans laughed as he pointed out the lack of armaments. "Just remember, everyone, we can't so much as throw a stone at the bastards, so be ready to run like hell if necessary."

She'd also received more sensitive IR detectors, six in all, providing complete coverage all around the ship.

Cobra had the latest iteration of the SLIP scanner, able to copy all enemy and Fleet traffic, including Sentinels. Her SLIP communications system employed the latest channel-hopping technology, meant to make Fleet SLIP transmissions harder to detect.

Cobra would run with the least crew possible. To do that, several officer roles were combined. LCDR Elaine DeLeon would double as XO and Communications, with SLT Myra Rodgers the backup. The Navigator, SLT Lena Rice, would handle Administration, too. There would be long shifts for the Intel types, with two officers, four warrants, and eight techs. But, with no weapons division, they were still well under the normal complement for an ISC Fleet frigate. A smaller crew meant she could support much longer missions, a fact not lost on her officers. *Cobra* could easily go six months without a port call.

David did not consider that a positive feature of the assignment.

"This ship is the best surveillance platform we know how to build," Evans said as he finished his description of the new ship's features. Setting down his tablet, he looked around the table at his new collection of officers.

"I asked for this ship, this command, and I asked for each of you, individually. We are not the tip of the spear. We are the eyes that will tell the spear where to strike. Thanks for coming along."

Evans smiled as he turned to his Navigator, Lena Rice. "Enemy Station, Lieutenant Rice, and let's stretch our legs a bit, shall we?"

"Stretching is good, sir, will do."

Within an hour, the black ghost accelerated away from its home, racing away to the south at 1.3 light-years per day.

Intrepid
Earth Orbit
Saturday, January 7, 2079, 0830 UTC

For Natalie Hayden, the end of this trip could not come soon enough. She'd been on the Conn when *Intrepid* slipped out of FTL a few million kilometers from Earth. The little blue ball grew rapidly over the next day as they made their final orbital adjustments. By the time they were set in their assigned geostationary orbit, the planet was bright and beautiful below them, nearly filling a Bridge window from where she sat, by chance once again at the Conn.

When not on duty, Natalie had spent much of the trip in her quarters, or in the gym, grappling with the changes that had come her way since she had last seen her home planet. A man she had unexpectedly fallen in love with had proposed to her. She'd accepted. She'd visited an alien planet and spoke to the race that lived there. She had run like a scared bunny from the enemy, then engaged them in an old-fashioned firefight at the side of the Marines. They had won the day, but her love had died on the field. And now, she was again alone.

She was not weak-willed, that much she was sure of about herself. She met her responsibilities all the way home. She could not disappoint Ben by avoiding her duties. She still loved him, loved the memory of who he was: his humor, his work ethic, his essential goodness, were all still with her.

A Fleet shuttle arrived two hours after they were established in orbit. It carried CINC Connor Davenport, Fiona Collins, Joe Bowles, and a few Intel techs. It also carried five caskets, so those who had given their lives could leave *Intrepid* with some level of dignity. The body bags would be an awful sight. And, they'd gather frost, since the remains had been frozen since their return to the ship. That grotesque sight, at least, was spared those who cared about them.

Joe and his two techs moved quickly to the aft frozen storage area. They made a momentary inspection of the three enemy bodies, shared a grim congratulations with each other, moved the bags into insulated containers and then quickly into the cargo hold of the shuttle. All this was done from the rear of the shuttle, out of the view of the crew except those detailed to help.

As Natalie entered the hangar bay, Joanne Henderson was already there, locked in a long embrace with Collins. They had all been together for years in Plans, Natalie knew, and their pain could not be much less than her own. CINC stood by, looking sad. He approached Natalie, extending his hand.

"Lieutenant Hayden, I am very sorry for your loss." She took his hand, which was surprisingly warm and soft — not at all what she expected. He took her hand in both of his and held it gently.

"Yes, sir, thank you, sir. I'm still not sure what to think of it all."

"I can understand that. If there is anything I as CINC can do for you, or for Ben, do please call on me."

"Yes, sir, thank you, sir." She repeated herself without humor or notice.

There was the sound of a funereal cadence, at which CINC let go of her hand, turned, and came to attention. Six Marines appeared from the aft passageway, carrying a casket draped in the Stars and Crosses of Australia. Behind that came two more caskets under the Stars and Stripes of the United States, then the German tricolor of black, red, and gold. Finally, two more under the Stars and Stripes. Ben, most senior, came last.

The Marines moved in their impossibly slow, respectful cadence to place the caskets on the platforms already set up in the shuttle. Captain Andrew Martin was last into the bay. After the remains had been placed and properly secured, he came out and embraced Natalie. She held on very tight for several seconds, then released him and looked to Joanne.

"Time to go," Joanne said quietly.

They climbed the short steps and took their seats for the trip down to the HQ Shuttle pad. Marine Lieutenant Liwanu Harry, accompanying his comrades to the surface, sat forward. Joanne left the seat next to Ben empty for Natalie, who sat with her hand on his casket the whole trip down, silent in her grief.

As they stepped off the shuttle at Ft. Eustis, the morning was cold and gripped in a misty rain, a gray curtain hanging low over their return. It fit their mood.

A different set of Marines repeated the sad ceremony as they carried each of the fallen to a waiting transport vehicle. Gunther and Joanie were taken to another shuttle to go back to their home countries.

Liwanu, Joanne, Natalie, and Fiona headed for Price's parents' home up in Frederick, Maryland. They traveled by autonomous surface vehicle, a ride of ninety minutes. The car sloshed noisily through the rain and came to a stop in front of a well-kept row house on a narrow street off North Market.

Natalie had been here twice for dinner; generous home-cooked meals on fine china with real sterling silver flatware. The Prices were elegant in their own self-deprecating way, and she felt comfortable and welcome in their home.

The officers carefully climbed the three wrought-iron steps to the small front porch. As Joanne reached for the door knocker, the door opened to a small, older woman, eyes bright blue but rimmed with tears. Behind her stood a taller man with thinning gray hair, combed back from his forehead, dark brown eyes looking out beneath fading eyebrows.

"Hello, Captain," the small voice invited her, "please do come in. I am Mila, and this is Ben's father, Logan."

"Thank you, Mrs. Price."

There was a dark maple hall tree just inside the door which easily absorbed their raincoats. The diminutive Mila embraced Natalie for a long time, slowly rocking side to side. "My dear, my dear..." Mila said quietly. As they stepped inside the house proper, the others introduced themselves. Mila pulled back, eyes now full, and moved to the little sitting area just off the entrance, facing the front window. She sat between Natalie and Joanne, holding their hands tightly. Logan moved sadly to a seat across from his wife, his grief plain on his face.

Joanne began to speak, "Mr. Price, Mrs. Price, I —"

"No, Captain, please," Logan interrupted her. "Mila and I, we have something to say first."

"Yes," his wife agreed, "we do."

They looked at each other for a moment, like old married couples sometimes do, and then Mila spoke.

"Thank you all for coming to see us. I know Ben would be honored that you would do this for him. But, more than that, thank you for caring about our son."

"You all," Logan Price said, "each in your unique way, you all were family to him." He looked directly at Fiona. "Captain Collins, he admired you so much. He would talk about you, your easy leadership, the way you cared for your people, every time we saw him."

Fiona managed to nod as she pulled a tissue from her pocket.

Mila took her turn again, "And you, Captain Henderson, he so loved his best pal Joanne. He would go on about your times together. He loved you, and he knew you loved him, too. For Ben, it was like he'd found a sister he never knew he had."

Joanne smiled. "Yes, that's a good way to describe it. I never had a brother until Ben."

Mila moved to hold Natalie's hand with both of hers.

"And my dear, dear Natalie. I don't think I ever saw him so gob-struck smitten as he was about you."

Natalie laughed a little through her tears.

"Well, it was mutual, ma'am."

The old man turned his intense brown eyes to Liwanu Harry. "And you, Lieutenant Harry, I am told you were with my son at the end?"

"Yes, sir, I was."

"And it was to you then, that he entrusted his last words, his last messages to those he loved?"

"Yes, sir."

Logan reached out, touching the young officer on the shoulder.

"Thank you, son, for listening to him and delivering his words. I expect you had plenty of other things on your mind."

Liwanu smiled shyly. "Yes, sir, it was a, uh, busy moment in all our lives."

Joanne shifted in her chair, stress plain on her face. "I was his commanding officer. I gave the orders. I just want to say how sorry I am —"

"There's no need here for apologies, Joanne," Mila said quickly. "Ben knew what he was doing. This enemy, whoever or whatever they are, are to blame. Not you."

"Thank you, ma'am."

Mila gripped Joanne's hand. "Please, Joanne, do not give that another thought. We all know what he meant to you, to all of you."

Ben's younger brother Isaac came in from the kitchen in the back of the house, carrying cookies, tea, and coffee. He sat with them as they talked about Ben's youth, his education at the University of Maryland, and his eventual choice to join the Fleet. His first marriage was dismissed in a few sentences punctuated with words like 'superficial' and 'distant.' None of the officers had met Olivia Price, so they took the family at their word. They seemed more disappointed than angry, sadder for Ben than vindictive towards his ex-wife. Still, they were clearly glad the marriage ended.

They talked for more than an hour, Isaac and Logan bringing out pictures of young Ben in soccer clothes, on the baseball field, in his cap and gown at Maryland. Natalie gave them a picture of Ben with her that Ann Cooper had taken on Big Blue after their escape. They were sitting with his arm casually around her shoulders, both of them smiling into the sunshine. Mila hugged it tightly to her chest.

Someday, Natalie thought, *I can give her a picture of Ben with Eaagher, but that will have to wait until this is all over.*

"I have something for you, too, Natalie." She climbed the stairs, nimbly for a woman of her age, and returned shortly with a small box. "I was going to give you this necklace on your wedding day."

Natalie looked at her with surprise. "But, Mrs. Price, he didn't ask me until we were almost to Beta Hydri!"

Mila smiled and touched Natalie's arm. "Oh, dear, I knew he was going to ask you before you all left. He had that look in his eye. So, I was ready."

The gold chain held a fine golden cross, a beautifully simple design.

"This is yours now. Think of him when you wear it."

Natalie took the small box from the old woman carefully, knowing what it meant for her to give it.

"I will."

"But, Natalie, I want to tell you something. I know you loved Ben and you're hurting right now. But you have so much life yet to live for, and Ben would never want your life to stop because his did. Remember him, honor him, but you must go on. We want what Ben would want, and that's for you to be happy."

"Yes, ma'am."

There was more talk of Ben, and finally, of the Price's plans for his remains. They would return in three days for the funeral service and internment. More family would be there, more people anxious to meet them.

They left the warm and welcoming 250-year-old row house with its beautiful hardwood floors, classic wainscoting, and delicate plaster crown moldings, and stepped back into the modern world, where it was still cold and raining. It felt like a nasty slap in the face as they descended the iron steps and dropped into the ASV for the trip back to Fleet HQ.

Marine Second Lieutenant Liwanu Harry, just twenty-two and a former summa cum laude economics major from Heart Butte, Montana, sat in uncomfortable silence as three senior officers grappled with their feelings about a lost friend. They shared a few stories about Ben and commented on the grace and kindness of his family. Harry had little to offer that conversation, but he studied their reactions, their tone, their feelings of responsibility for what had happened on Big Blue. He felt he was watching a Master Class in leadership and emotional control, unknowingly presented for his education. He'd remember how this all went down, and he would use what he observed to inform his own decisions, his own reactions to painful events.

He would not be at the funeral in three days. He'd be in Australia seeing to the final rest of Joanie McCarthy in a national cemetery.

Sugarloaf Mountain
Dickerson, MD
Monday, January 9, 2078, 1415 EDT

The ASV parked itself neatly in the second row, having groaned noticeably in the climb up the little mountain to the parking lot. Natalie Hayden got out of the car, pulled her coat tightly around herself, and walked to the trail. She stopped at the stone steps, remembering her first ascent here with Ben, so many months ago. This was a place so very important to him, even from his school days, and they had hiked several of the trails during their October leave. This was the place he first told her he loved her, as they sat on boulders looking out towards the Potomac River on a warm and breezy fall afternoon. They teased each other that they were too old to act like teenagers at a drive-in, but the truth was, they really didn't give a damn.

Today there was snow lying about, here and there, and the wind was definitively cold. She had just left Ben's wake, a well-catered and pleasant event that followed his burial in the Price family plot, in a cemetery on a gentle, tree-scattered knoll. In spring, she knew, it would be a green and beautiful place, and if she lived

308

that long, she'd be back to see it for herself. At the wake she'd met more of his family, more people she would have come to know well as part of her own family had he lived. Now, they would forever be strangers to her, and she just a footnote in the family history.

She stood there for a full minute, replaying their times here and in the restaurant just down the road. It was a quaint, beautiful, expensive little place to get a club sandwich and a salad. But Ben loved it, and really, so did she. They had so much time on board ship, spending almost nothing, that small luxuries like the occasional pricey lunch on their home planet were completely worth the money.

Finally, she forced herself to put one foot before the other and slowly climbed the easy trail. She was surprised to find a few others there at the overlook, mostly solitary, either seated on rocks or standing, looking out at the spectacular view. The snow was as spotty in the fields below as it was on the mountain, and she was reminded of an old painting of a Guernsey cow. Splotchy was perhaps a better word for what she saw. She walked forward and found that the rock where they had confessed to each other was vacant, so she carefully climbed up, wary of ice and slick snow, and sat, again pulling her coat in tight and adjusting her knit cap and tugging her gloves. She thought only of Ben, wondering what they might have been together, how their lives could have evolved side-by-side. She cried just once, as she recalled him lying still in the coarse grass on Big Blue.

She would never forget the smoke, or the smell.

The snap of a branch startled her, but before she could turn, she heard Jim Kirkland's quiet voice.

"Henderson told me you'd be here."

Natalie didn't answer at first.

"I thought maybe you shouldn't be alone."

Natalie looked hard at Kirkland as she pulled her knees up into her chest, wrapping her arms around them for warmth.

"Don't worry. I'm not jumping."

"Not what I was worried about."

Kirkland stood next to the rock, close, but not invading that space where he knew, in Natalie's mind, the memory of Ben still sat. There was a long silence between them, filled only with the random rising and falling white noise of the wind in the leafless trees all around them.

"You hated him."

Kirkland nodded sadly. "I did, at first, I am ashamed to admit. I resented him for taking Craig's place. But I was wrong, Natalie."

"So, now?"

"So, now, like everyone else I'm sorry he's gone. I'm sorry for him, for you of course, and for the ship."

"Really?"

Kirkland looked away in frustration. "Yes, Natalie, really."

Natalie nodded slowly, still looking out toward the Potomac.

"Well, it's OK, I guess. Maybe because you had no part in losing him."

"No, I didn't." There was another long silence. "We've known each other a long time, Natalie. I came here to be your friend. I know I can't undo what I said back before I knew what I was talking about."

She looked at him again and managed a small smile. "So, did you prepare that one or did it just come to you now?"

Kirkland took his eye off the scenery for the first time and met her eye. "I plead the fifth."

"Yeah, I thought so."

"I want to help, Natalie, I do, but I don't know how. I don't know what you might want or need —"

She snapped around to look at him.

"There's only one thing I need, Jimmy, and that is for Ben Price to be alive again and right here next to me where he belongs."

Kirkland just nodded. There wasn't much that he could say to that.

"Yes, I understand," he finally managed.

They waited silently as a small group, which seemed to be two couples, walked past chattering among themselves about the view and the cold.

"How did Henderson know I'd be here?"

"Not sure. I guess Ben told her about the place. She knew it was important to him. A touchstone for him."

"That's a good word for it. Touchstone."

"If you'd rather be alone, I'll go. I don't want to be an intrusion. Like I said, I just thought you shouldn't be alone."

"Well, mister Senior Lieutenant Kirkland, I'm going to be alone now for quite some time. Might as well get used to it." She said this looking out at the country-side, not at him, her tone resigned and sad.

"OK, then, I will see you back on the ship tonight?"

"No. Tomorrow, maybe. I can't say for sure."

"I'm sorry, Natalie. For what happened to Ben and for what I once thought. But I wish you'd let me stay."

"It really is OK, Jimmy, really. I understand how you felt. But I need time, and I need it with myself."

"As you wish."

"And, Jim, thanks for thinking of me. Thanks for making the climb. Tell Henderson she should see it for herself."

"Yes, maybe she should. She has her own loss to process."

"*Process,*" she spat, "What a damnable shitty word to apply to the loss of someone you love."

"Yes, I see what you mean. Goodbye, Nat."

"Don't worry, Jim. I'll be fine."

She remained there another two hours, silently categorizing her days with Ben, trying to squeeze out every moment, every detail so that she would remember it clearly. She also wrestled with her alternate futures; what choices she had and which she thought would bring her some measure of satisfaction, some kind of fulfillment. Even with Ben gone, as Mila had told her, she still had a life to manage, and before long she would have to be making choices about what that life would be. She could try to just go back to her life before Ben, and be that hard-working all-business no-bullshit officer she'd once happily been. Problem was, Ben Price had effortlessly pried open a part of her that could not be re-closed, and that former person just wasn't her anymore.

But, for the moment, she had a job and there was a war and that was pretty much that. *Later,* she thought to herself, *when I have more time, later will be more difficult.*

It was late afternoon when she pulled herself off the ledge and walked down the trail to the ASV. The car requested a destination, and as Natalie sat trying to decide, she realized she was fingering her small, delicate cross, the gift of Mila Price. At that moment she decided to accept a tear-rimmed invitation she had earlier declined. She gave the car the address, and within 30 minutes she was again standing on the little wrought iron porch as the door quickly swung wide and open arms reached out for her.

Columbia
Earth Orbit
Monday, January 15, 2079, 1030 UTC

Admiral Kieran Barker, a man still unaccustomed to answering to that rank, came aboard his flagship for the first time, officially. LCDR Dan Smith and his new XO SLT Maz Dawes greeted him at the airlock. He was followed aboard by his deputy, Harry Hess, Intel chief Elias Peña, and then a succession of techs and officers who comprised his staff. They headed down to their newly installed quarters on the lower level while Barker, Hess, Peña, and the Columbia officers headed for the wardroom.

Once seated, Barker took the lead. "Good morning, all, again. We'll be leaving for Beta Hydri as soon as you're ready, Commander Smith. *Ceres* will come in about two weeks, but I want to get down there right away."

311

"I expected as much, Admiral. We can leave as soon as the Fleet Shuttle is off, sir. Columbia is ready to depart right now."

"Good, Commander, very good."

"*Eagle* and *Friendship* have been watching Big Blue since *Intrepid* left, and they'll be released when we get there. There will be others arriving to take their place."

"Who will that be, sir?"

"Well, Henderson is just back, really, so I'm tapping Terri Michael and her crew for their third trip."

"I take it she didn't argue?"

"No, not at all. I think they've started to think of Big Blue as a second home! Besides, they can carry more Marines than anyone except *Intrepid*, and I want a ground force available."

"I see."

"I'm working with Cook to get a couple frigates scheduled in, but they're still working on the search, so it may be a few days before they decide who we can have. We'll see if Yakovlev needs Henderson – I would not mind at all having both those ships at Beta Hydri."

"It would sure give us a solid option for a ground engagement."

Elias spoke up. "We know there are still something like fifty enemy alive on Big Blue, left behind when Intrepid smoked their ships. We figure they're foraging the countryside to stay alive, hoping for a rescue. We may want to see if we can get one."

"Alive? Really?"

Elias shrugged. "It's worth a try."

"OK, sir."

"You're skeptical?" Barker asked.

"Oh, yes, sir. I sure am."

"Good. Keep being skeptical. But we'll see if we can pull it off."

"OK, sir. We'll see."

In less than an hour, *Columbia* was on her way to Beta Hydri, a trip of almost twenty-two days. Dan smiled at the prospect of seeing Carol again so soon, but his thoughts were mainly of his new wife, Linda, and their plans for their future. He was also thinking about David, already headed for deep space on *Cobra*. It was a dangerous mission, going all the way to what they thought was the enemy home-world, but he could think of no better ship and no better crew to carry it out.

Meantime, he thought, *I got my own problems to deal with.*

Brass.

Silver Search

Central Council Chambers
The Preeminent Home World
Earth Equivalent Date: January 17, 2079

Ashil Kiker felt an emotion he had never experienced before. He was nervous. Scad Nee Wok had submitted to the Council a complete report on their encounter with the Vermin at System 201. During the long trip to Home, Wok had directed an analysis of everything they had seen, with a complete timeline: events, discussions, and disagreements.

Kiker believed it was designed to cast him as the incompetent, and as the Council heard from Wok, Kiker angrily challenged each conclusion.

"These are disturbing developments," the Respected Second intoned. "We have now lost far too many ships and Preeminent lives to these Vermin. The time for proactive steps has come."

"And what of Wok's indictment of me?" Kiker demanded.

"You, Ashil Kiker, should be grateful that Ship Commander Wok was well reasoned and made a precise argument for his position. Had he been less rigorous, you would be in a difficult position."

Kiker was humbled, but he might live. "Yes, Respected Second," he answered quietly.

"As it is, we shall thank Scad Nee Wok for his efforts and move on."

Wok bowed slightly, threw a side-glance at Kiker, and ambled out of the Council Chamber. He'd made his point to the Council but had deliberately avoided getting Kiker killed. He might need to cash in that favor someday.

Before each Council member was a recitation of their encounters with the Vermin. It began with Hess Tae Sim and the Deists in System 352. Two cohorts of Combatants and three ships lost to a single Vermin vessel.

Then, the loss of one vessel in an encounter with several Vermin at System 572.

Their one clear victory had come at System 155. They had tracked a Vermin ship to its destination and then crushed it with a massive attack.

In the final test of the tracking system, they'd destroyed another Vermin ship at System 253, but lost three more ships in the process. Then, soon after this victory, the tracking system failed. The Vermin had apparently discovered their technique. They were despicably smart.

All these and the loss of three observation stations disturbed the council. The rate of attrition was not unsupportable, but it was unprecedented.

Most recently, they had dispatched four ships to investigate what the Vermin were doing at system 849. After several rotations of exploration, all four ships and the monitoring station were lost. The transmission from the last ship to be struck reported no enemy contact, but believed there to be many present, as the attacks

313

on the other three appeared to come from different directions. There may yet be Combatants on the surface, but without communications, they could not be sure.

After this painful recapitulation, the Revered First entered the Council Chamber and took his place at the head of the table.

"The time has come to deal with the Vermin decisively. Scad Nee Wok and Kiker have given us their location. We will attack. We will prevail. We are the Preeminent. We will strike the Deists, too, for we know the Vermin defend them. There is something on the stubborn Scholars planet that the Vermin do not want us to find. There is no other reason they should remain there and oppose our presence as violently as they do. We shall learn what that is."

The Council licked their pitted, dark-stained teeth in agreement, peeling back the skin at the sides of their mouths to reveal their incisors for emphasis.

"The forces will be assembled, then we will strike them everywhere at once. Their ships are faster than ours, but that will become an irrelevance in a single moment. We will suddenly be in all the places they protect at once. They cannot withstand such an attack. They will be defeated."

The Respected Second stood to ask his question. "There are billions of them, Revered First. How shall we bring such a population to obsequia?"

"We will not," The Revered First said dismissively, "give them such an opportunity. I care not for their filthy masses. I care only that they are neutralized."

"But we are the Preeminent. It is our right—"

"It is our right to choose what we do, Respected Second. And we choose to leave them to their worthless cesspool and find more useful species elsewhere. They will learn to leave us alone. That is enough."

Had Ashil Kiker been even slightly self-conscious, had only a hint of objectivity, or been capable of even minimal critical self-examination, he would have recognized this statement as the transparent rationalization it was. But Kiker was a Preeminent, and if they chose not to do something, then that choice was correct.

"The recall has already gone out. We will gather ourselves here first, then we will proceed to these three systems and put an end to this annoyance."

ISC Fleet HQ Intel Section
Ft. Eustis, VA
Friday, January 20, 2079, 0900 EST

Frances, Don, and Kristin looked at the intercept location report carefully. Several Sentinels had seen the signal, as had all four regular monitoring stations. It was long — thirty seconds — and clearly originated at Alpha Mensae. It was SLIP channel 76, which they had tentatively identified as a headquarters source based on its pattern of activity. Based on when and where it was detected, they could tell it had been sent the morning of January 17th.

Roger Cox joined them, standing in the doorway of Frances' small office as he held the same report.

"So, what do we think this means?" Frances asked.

"We've never seen anything this long," Roger observed.

"We've never seen anything one-tenth this long!" Don agreed.

"No responses, either," Kristin Hayes observed.

"Yeah. Here are your orders. Just go do them and keep quiet about it."

"Seems logical, Roger, but it doesn't tell us *what* they're doing."

Frances looked up at Roger. "Our estimate is that the ship that was here on December 5th could have made it back to Alpha Mensae when?"

"If they went direct, something like January 12 or 13." Roger flipped to a different screen on his tablet. "Hard to be sure, but it could not be before the 12th."

"Right, OK, so if they went straight home, no stopping, and got there on January 12th or 13th, a major order on the 17th is no surprise."

Don looked up from the report. "I agree, except, I don't think this reaction took four days to formulate."

At their regular 10 AM Table meeting, the enemy signals team presented the results of the intercept and their initial opinions. The staff had been reduced by a few — Elias Peña, Rich Evans, and Tim Jackson were gone — but also enhanced with the presence of Susan Scranton and Joe Bowles. Scranton, now fully understanding the resources around her, had become a forceful and constructive member of the group. She allowed her formerly hidden sense of humor to emerge, much to the surprise of her colleagues. Once Joe Bowles found himself on the inside of the Intel establishment, he had no desire to leave and Ron Harris found a place for him with Scranton in Exo-Biology. Joe's one condition was his frequent days off for grandchild duty. Ron gladly obliged, knowing how much it meant to Joe.

Bowles's experience as an Army pathologist had returned huge dividends as he and Susan dissected the three enemy bodies *Intrepid* had brought back from Big Blue. They were Terran for sure, likely a lost offshoot of some relation of velociraptor or other dromaeosaurid. They could not tell how long ago they split from the main evolutionary line, but it was easily tens of millions of years. Why and how they got to Alpha Mensae, no one could say. They were meat eaters, for sure, their last meal being some other kind of Terran animal, likely a prey species that they had taken with them. That species' DNA didn't map to anything either, which left Susan and Joe with no further to go. Whatever it was, there were no living relatives to compare it to.

The most important conclusion they delivered was that they were not any kind of super-aliens. They breathed the same air, ate food, and could be killed just as easily as any Terran species. They were intelligent, yes, but nothing in their brains made them seem any smarter than humans.

The Weapons division was also dissecting the enemy weapons, trying to understand how they worked and how they might be defended against. So far, they had been unable to get inside without a small explosion, nor could they make them fire on demand. Whatever the key was, they still hadn't found it.

The conversation over The Big Message went on for some time. There could be no deciphering it, so any conclusions had to be made based on traffic analysis, timing, and context. All of which added up to nothing conclusive.

"Still," Ron said as he looked around the room, "we should notify *Cobra*. They may see something that gives some meaning to this."

Ann Cooper nodded. "Yes, sir, and we should get with Ops and Plans and see what we can do to beef up our defenses."

"I agree with you that this is a fleet-wide message. And it's interesting that there are no responses."

"That, sir," Don said, "tells me that headquarters doesn't need to know their position and status. They either already know or it doesn't matter."

Ron shifted in his chair. "I will talk to CINC and bring him up to speed. Something is definitely up, and we need to be prepared."

Ron sent The Big Message analysis to CINC and Ops and Kieran Barker. He suggested that they meet later that same day to discuss what actions CINC might want to take.

"There's nothing definitive in this, Ron." Davenport stroked his chin as he stood looking out the large windows in his office, his back to Ron, Frances, and Ann.

"That's true, sir, but it's the best conclusion we can make."

"It's pretty thin."

Frances gave Ron a frustrated look, then looked hard at CINC. "It's not as thin as you may think, sir. We've been watching their communications for more than six months. They send messages, they get responses. Normal command behavior."

"Always?" CINC asked as he turned back to face them.

"No, sir, not always. But, usually. We've never seen anything this long, Admiral. That alone makes it unique, and in our business, unique means dangerous."

"I just don't see —"

"Don't be a damn fool, Connor," Frances said sharply. Ron and Ann both looked at her with surprise.

"Listen to us, Connor, for Christ's sake, just listen to us."

"Mrs. Wilson, I will thank you —"

"Oh, Connor, shut up. I've been at this since you were a skinny ensign on loan to NSA for training."

CINC looked at her for several seconds, his expression going slowly from offense to acceptance. He came back to the desk and sat, and when he spoke, his tone carried his full surrender.

"OK, Frances, what would you have me do?"

"There is no question here that something major is up. No, we don't know what, but *something is happening.*"

"And?"

"And, you need to accept that as a fact, or, at least, a very high probability, and *act like you believe it!*"

"Fine. You all think this is a prelude to some kind of all-out attack?"

"Well, sir," Ron said, ignoring the previous exchange, "that would perhaps be the worst case. But we believe that defenses should be strengthened at all three planets and both starbases."

"And what about the offensive?"

Ann looked up from her tablet. "The purpose of the offensive, sir, is to reduce the enemy's fleet, their supplies, their ability to resist, is it not?"

"Yes, of course."

"Is that goal not achieved just as well by letting them come to us? Let them come into a trap of their own making?"

"What if they don't show? Or don't arrive when we think they will?"

"Then there will still be time for us to move forward and strike."

"Actually, Admiral," Ron said, "we could still hit all the Sigma Spheres, the Enemy Station, on a particular date. That would only take a handful of ships."

"To what end?"

"If nothing else, it will put them on notice that we know about these assets. If we're lucky, it will make them pull back."

Ann again consulted her tablet. "*Cobra* is due at Enemy Station in a few days. Another week and they'll be at Alpha Mensae."

"Your point?"

"Let's hold off on any commitments until we hear from them."

"You're talking three weeks, Lieutenant. If what you say is true, we might not have that kind of time."

Ron leaned back in his chair. "Let's get a message to Barker, see what he thinks. My own feeling is that we immediately reinforce ourselves at the five points I mentioned, then see what *Cobra* can tell us."

"And then strike the enemy facilities when we want?"

"Yes, and I would say the sooner, the better."

"Very well. Send a message to Barker describing this intercept and what you make of it. I'll get with Cook and work out the reinforcements and then let Barker decide when and how to strike."

As they returned to the Intel section, Ron turned to his most senior civilian. "Frances, what the hell was that? Getting yourself fired doesn't help!"

She smiled shyly. "Connor wouldn't dare."

She walked confidently to her office, closing the door behind her.

Ann Cooper shared a perplexed look with Ron, then went on with her duties. Whatever Frances had on Connor Davenport was pretty strong leverage. Ron had never seen her use that tone with anyone before, let along the Fleet Commander.

Whatever it was, Ron was pretty sure it was a one-time-only thing.

Cobra
Enroute Enemy Station
Saturday, January 24, 2079, 0600 UTC

As *Cobra* approached its appointment with Enemy Station, David and Jack Ballard spent time looking over the new Operations Center, buried deep within the ship, fifty meters aft of the bridge. The rectangular room was nine meters wide and eighteen long. The lateral walls were lined with workstations, six on each side, which could access whatever sensor its operator required, be it IR, UV, RF, radar, or visual. In the center of the room was a large U-shaped raised island, Center Console, in which sat the shift boss. The technical analyst at Center was essentially the Officer in Tactical Command of *Cobra* and could monitor incoming data, direct operations, and assign resources as necessary to collect whatever data they were after. Forward of Center Console was another small raised platform, with seats meant for the Captain, XO, or another observer to monitor the operation. Aft of Center was a large work table, where references could be accessed and charts displayed.

The room was just large enough for the dozen operators and backup analysts it required. The sound-deadening walls and ceiling made it feel subdued, which helped each analyst focus on the task at hand. The aft wall contained the visual observation complex, with several oversized monitors and controls for the large telescopes mounted back in what would otherwise be the magazine.

In a pause in the discussion of the workstation assignments for the Enemy Station encounter, David looked over at his new supervisor.

"Listen, Jack, I just...well...while I have a chance...I know what your support meant to Carol while *Sigma* was missing."

"Yeah, she was pretty busted up there for a while. It was hard to watch."

"Like I said, your support meant a lot to her, and I just wanted to say thanks for being there."

Jack folded his arms across himself and leaned back against the Center Console. "She's a great person, David, and a fine, fine officer. I was glad to be able to be a friend when she needed one." When David didn't respond, Jack continued. "Everyone on board loved that girl, David, and they were all praying you'd somehow turn up alive."

David smiled. "Thanks, Jack, I owe you."

"I don't think so, not really. We do the right things, David, because they *are* the right things. She would have been there for me if the roles had been switched. I'm pretty sure you would, too. So, no, you don't owe me a thing."

They went back to the minutia of assignments, looking to put the right people on the right source data feeds.

Later that day, David pulled out his journal.

Dear Carol,

I had a talk with Jack Ballard today. I thanked him for being there for you — it seems like that's just natural for him.

They think the world of you over there, but I guess you probably know that. I do, too, and I'm real sure you know that.

This is going to be another long trip. More chapters for the journal, more memories of you that keep me awake when I really should be sleeping. Thanks!

—David

Cobra
Enemy Station
Sunday, January 25, 2079, 0600 UTC

Cobra fell out of FTL well away from Enemy Station. *Chaffee* had given them a good location, well within a few thousand kilometers. As they cruised towards it, at first nothing appeared on any of their surveillance displays.

Ray Salazar was sitting the Center position, with David and Jack Ballard observing.

"D'ya suppose they moved it?" David asked quietly.

"I wonder if maybe they did. After Henderson creamed them at Beta Hydri, maybe they decided to pull back?"

"Sure, but Cooper made the point in her report from the Marines' observations that the enemy never stepped back once engaged, not even to regroup. They stood where they were, even if that meant they all died."

"Fatally stubborn?"

"Well, I think more like unable to cope with opposition."

An hour later, Marge Nixon, watching the radio frequency scanners as she listened intently to her earphones, called out to Salazar. The 180 MHz constant wave signal was up. The 'Dinner Plate,' as the fifty-meter dish had been nicknamed, had proven its worth. The facility was there, and they were on the right course.

There was a long silence as they waited impatiently for the IR and other sensor displays to register.

Finally, David saw something. "Hey, Jack, take a look at that!"

Jack followed David's eye to the IR display, where a large series of spherical shadows were beginning to reveal themselves.

"Hot damn, there it is!"

Jack looked at the ship's status monitor for their exact location.

"Right where it's supposed to be after all."

They moved silently past the enemy facility, at a distance of a thousand kilometers, much closer than *Chaffee* had dared. They could easily see the three enemy ships docked there.

Nothing moved in or out in the thirty-six hours they were gliding by. But, looking back at *Chaffee*'s images, there had been a complete turnover in docked ships. They could clearly see six ships of various types in the *Chaffee* pictures. Some of the ships *Chaffee* saw may have been those smoked by *Intrepid* a few weeks later, but there were no markings that would allow them to uniquely identify individual ships.

Once well past Enemy Station, *Cobra* pulled away and headed for Alpha Mensae, the suspected enemy homeworld. What they would find there, no one had any idea. At a speed of 1.3 light years per day, they'd be there in six days and twenty hours.

It was good to be the fastest ship in the fleet.

February 2079

Cobra
Alpha Mensae
Thursday, February 2, 2079, 0600 UTC

As they approached Alpha Mensae, the Intel crew made preparations for the Fleet's most important, and riskiest, intelligence operation yet. They arrived at six AU from the star. Astrophysicists had calculated the habitable zone to be slightly closer to the star than that around the Sun, but Evans wanted to be a safe distance out so they could assess the system and find the enemy homeworld from a safe distance. That is, if it was actually here.

Jack Ballard assigned himself to Center Console for the initial contact, placing David on the main visual observation post with a young tech to assist. Ray Salazar took the RF task, side-by-side with Gregg Browning. Margie Nixon was assigned the IR data station. On *Cobra*, the Surveillance Officer could access all the same data, but Myra Rodgers' job was to assist the Navigator and look for threats to the ship itself, not collect the intelligence they were there to find.

Ray Salazar deployed his full selection of antennas in the direction of the star, looking for the radio waves that would be evidence of modern civilization. Each frequency band displayed on its own 'waterfall' display on Salazar's workstation. The darkened room was quiet, each analyst focused on their individual task. Except for the whirr of cooling fans and the low whisper of the ventilation, the only sound was the rustle of uniforms as they shifted in their seats.

Rich Evans strolled around the room, making small jokes, and encouraging the analysts as they struggled to detect the enemy. He stopped at David's visual station and pulled up a chair.

"So, Powell, what do we have?"

"Well, sir, survey telescope already sees three gas giants, but small for giants, kinda Neptune-ish, all outside four AU. There's no close-in giant like we've seen elsewhere. We're still looking for an Earth-analog in the HZ but nothing yet. There's a pretty big asteroid belt somewhere around three AU. We'll need more time to pin all that down."

"Understood. Keep it up."

David nodded in response and went back to looking at the time-trail displays they were accumulating. If there was a rocky planet down there somewhere, it should be showing up as a small streak on the display.

David turned to look at Salazar, intently watching the RF displays.

"They've never done much to hide themselves, sir. I thought they'd be obvious once we got here."

Evans followed David's eye.

"Unless, of course, they're beyond radio as a primary communications method."

"Sure, for terrestrial comms, sure, they might have moved on to fiber or laser or something else. But out here, except for SLIP, radio is the most reliable long-range method."

David's head snapped back around as a tone sounded from the survey telescope. His fingers worked the keyboard, calling up the data the computer had found so interesting.

"OK, sir, here we are. Enemy tech signature." He switched to the high-aperture telescope and aimed it at the target. By now, Jack Ballard was out of the Center position and looking over Powell's shoulder.

"Oh my God," was all David could say when the image appeared. It was an enemy ship factory, located on a large asteroid just off their course in the outer part of Alpha Mensae's asteroid belt. The distance was still being calculated, but it was at least several AU away. It was enormous. There were three ships lined up outside the long, cylindrical structure, apparently docked. They could see the forward part of an enemy ship emerging from the factory.

"Well, Powell," Evans said, "that settles whether or not we're in the right place."

Two more alarms followed. One revealed another enemy facility elsewhere in the asteroid belt, this time with a long, connected string of spherical objects.

"They're making fuel, don't you think?" Ballard asked.

"Maybe," David responded.

The other alarm was a planet. They had come in behind it, but their position above the plane of the system gave them just enough reflected light that the computer could recognize a living planet.

"OK, drop the factory and put the large-aperture on the planet," Jack directed.

"In progress," David called back.

Ray Salazar slid *Cobra* sideways to point the Dinner Plate at the new planet, hoping to pick up something useful.

Soon more alarms were sounding on the visual workstation, and David was able to identify six enemy ships near the planet, which they could now see was near the inner edge of the habitable zone for this star.

Margie Nixon pointed her high-resolution IR detector to the planet. As she zoomed in on the nighttime side, she could identify several hot spots scattered about a generally cool surface.

Jack was watching her work. "So, Nixon, what's your interpretation?"

"Not sure yet, Lieutenant. The hot spots are well defined, so, some kind of tech there, but the rest is not well resolved yet. We'll get there."

Rich Evans was now moving from position to position, watching the gradual revelation of data on their opponents. He stood for a long time behind Ray Salazar, watching with him the radio frequency detection scan display. As they watched, the green dots that represented any signal above the noise level began slowly to coalesce. Salazar smiled as he watched three lines pull themselves together over a half hour.

"OK, Center, I have three decent signals. One is the same 180 seen at Enemy Station. There's another at 242 and one at 248."

"All CW?"

"Yes, so far, just the continuous wave carrier."

Evans took a seat across the island from Ballard. "Rotten luck coming in behind the planet."

"Yes, sir, sure is. You thinking about hurrying around to the other side? It'll be a while at this rate."

"Thinking, yes. Deciding, no."

Evans decided to hold course and get a better assessment of the system before pushing in closer.

The IR detectors were busy. There were six large ship arrivals in the first twelve hours of surveillance, all near the planet. Four ships were seen departing.

As the planet rotated, Margie could see new heat sources appearing on the night side. She was beginning to get a picture of the planet, able now to differentiate sea from land as well as populated regions from not-so-populated. She combined her minute-by-minute images to create a pseudo-movie. The rotation of the planet was obvious in this presentation, and she now estimated the length of a day to be twenty hours.

Cobra
Alpha Mensae
Saturday, February 4, 2079, 1330 UTC

After two full days of observations, they could now tell that there were oceans over about 40 percent of the planet, less than Earth and much less than Big Blue. There were two large irregular continents with a long, narrow sea between them. There were only a few small islands in the ocean.

Ships kept arriving, about one every two hours. They all landed in the same flat plain near the coast. Ships left at about the same rate, lifting off the planet then heading off under the Drive.

The RF board remained the same, just the three signals, all believed to be intrusion detectors. David's visual surveillance revealed no other ships on guard duty, no pickets like back home. There were the two ship factories, and plenty of ships on or around the planet. Otherwise, nothing.

Evans brought this topic up for discussion in the next day's status meeting.

"So, no pickets, only very basic detection gear. Anyone have an explanation?"

Jack had one theory. "Well, Captain, Powell and I had a discussion about that before we got here. I wonder if maybe they just haven't ever been competently opposed."

"Meaning?"

"Meaning that it doesn't occur to them that they need to plan for defense."

"That would be a serious weakness, Jack. I mean, a fatal flaw."

"Yes, sir, it would. But that thinking would explain their ship design, even the behavior of their ground forces."

"You mean *Intrepid's* report on how they never move backward?"

"Yes. It's like they don't know how to handle any kind of real opposition."

"If that's true, then how do we handle them?"

David leaned forward. "We strike quickly, sir, before they learn that lesson. They're well organized, with powerful ships and decent weapons. If we let them understand they need to defend themselves, we'll lose a huge advantage."

Evans didn't respond directly but instead moved on to the next question on his mind. "So, what do we think of this parade of incoming ships?"

Ray Salazar spoke for the analysts. "We've talked about that a lot, sir. We need to see more before we can say. I mean, we can't even tell if their delivering, picking up, or some of both."

"OK."

"If they're delivering, I would suspect that there are colonies or subject worlds from which they're bringing some kind of material."

"Right," David agreed, "Why conquer a planet if you can't exploit it in some way for the folks back home."

"Exactly, Lieutenant."

Evans looked around the table. "So, am I hearing that in order to tell what's going on, we need to be on the lighted side of the planet?"

Jack answered. "Yes, sir, we need to get around to where we can see what they're doing. The IR is just insufficient from this distance."

Evans nodded. "OK, I agree. Let's go one more day where we are, then we'll move."

Cobra
Alpha Mensae
Monday, February 6, 2079, 0845 UTC

The difference in perspective after the move to the lighted side of the planet was amazing to Ray Salazar. It was as if he'd taken his sunglasses off. They could now see the long row of ships on the ground, fifteen of the nearly half-mile long ships were lined up for unloading. The first few hours were lost to some unfortunate overcast, but once that moved on, they could watch the operation for several hours until the planet turned it out of their view. One end of the ships opened up, and vehicles moved in and out repeatedly, removing some kind of covered cargo and placing it in a nearby storage yard. From there, other vehicles took the packaged cargo and moved it away.

"It's just like any seaport back home," Salazar said to David as they watched through *Cobra*'s best telescope. "Stuff comes in, you take it off the boat, put it in the marshalling yard, and then someone else comes along and hauls it off to wherever it's needed."

They looked at the large spherical structures on the opposite side of the landing complex.

"Meantime, they're refueling," David pointed out.

"Right, Lieutenant. Get the cargo off, get gassed up, maybe load a fresh crew, and go back for more."

"Simple."

"Yeah, but maybe not so simple for whoever it is that's producing this shit."

"Agreed."

Margie Nixon and Steve Kirby continued to accumulate images in both IR and Visual, and as they did, a clear pattern began to emerge. On one continent, the 'west' as they called it, there was a large city with connected sub-cities. On the 'east' continent there was far less population but many more industrial facilities.

The central city in the west was roughly circular, about fifty kilometers in diameter. From it, spaced equally around the circumference, flowed five large highways that ran straight for 250 kilometers. On each highway, at an equal interval of about fifty kilometers, there was a smaller sub-city about twenty kilometers in diameter. From each sub-city, in turn, ran two highways to yet-smaller cities about twenty-five kilometers away. Each of the five highways from the central city eventually ran through five sub-cities. Around the highways and the cities were large areas of green. They appeared to be forests but were dense enough that neither Nixon or Kirby could say with any confidence whether they were natural or planted.

They presented their findings to the assembled Intel staff the next morning. "There must be millions of them, sir. Millions." Steve sat back down after his presentation to Evans, Ballard, and Powell.

"Do we know what they're bringing in?"

"No, sir. The packages come off the ships and then into a distribution network. We never see what it is."

"Where do they go?"

Margie looked up from her notes. "All over, sir. Smaller vehicles — trucks I guess — pick up the packages and then proceed over the highways."

"To where?"

"We haven't tracked them all the way to a destination yet, Captain. We're working on it."

"David, where are we with the ship population?"

"Well, sir, we've now determined that there are two sets of vessels arriving. There are the cargo ships that Margie and Steve have been tracking, and then there appear to be warships assembling."

"Assembling?"

"Yes, over the last week about twenty cruisers of various types have arrived and taken up station in groups."

"Can you see where they came from?"

"No. I suspect maybe they refueled at that facility we saw in the belt, then came here for some kind of staging."

"Staging for what?"

David shrugged. "There was a report from FleetIntel of a long message from here on January 17. There was a lot of speculation about what that message might mean. If it was some kind of recall, we could be seeing that."

"But truthfully, we don't know," Jack Ballard added, "and I don't see how we could, sir. We don't know what they have in mind."

David nodded. "For all we know, sir, they're just coming home for Christmas."

"Or, they could be putting together a task force for a major attack."

"Or that, yes, sir."

It happened quickly, transforming a watch shift that started off completely routine. David was sitting Center, with Ray Salazar and Gregg Browning monitoring the data feeds. Over the last week, they had watched the enemy cargo ships regularly coming and going, each spending about two days on the ground. Evans dropped the routine staffing to three, with everyone else available should some unusual event occur. As they moved in a wide, lazy orbit, they found several accumulations of enemy ships. All four known types were represented, including five of the enormous Type II's that they thought were invasion ships.

David was watching the visual feed showing him several enemy ships as they seemed to be forming yet another group, as the XO, Communications Officer Elaine DeLeon came into the Intel Operations Center.

David looked up to see DeLeon watching the large visual display where this new group was gathering.

"Fifty ships?"

"In total, yeah. Eleven in this bunch. Unbelievable."

"They've been at this for a long time, don't you think?"

David glanced at the visual, then the IR station, before responding. "Yes, I think so. I just wish we knew the full extent of their empire."

"Empire?"

"I don't know what else you'd call it. They hit Inor and Big Blue with the intent to invade and subjugate, right?"

"I guess, sure."

"So, they were too well prepared to not have done that before, and done it successfully."

"Hmm. Maybe."

"So, somewhere, I think, there have to be other species that these shitheads have conquered."

"Do you think that's what the cargo ships coming and going is all about?"

"Yeah, I do."

Ray Salazar stood up abruptly. "They're leaving."

"What?"

"They're *leaving*." He pointed to his IR display. "First, this group went about three minutes ago, then this one just left."

David slapped the alarm button, and the speakers throughout the ship blasted three loud, deliberately annoying sounds. Evans left the bridge and came into the Operations Center at full speed.

"What?"

Ray turned from his displays and repeated himself. "They're leaving,"

The noise level in the room rose rapidly as more analysts crashed through the doors and took up positions.

David handed them assignments as they arrived. "Ray, you want to stay on the IR?"

"Yes."

"OK, Margie, pick up the RF station. Gregg, stick with the visual." He stood up in the raised center console. "Keep your heads, everyone. Just focus on what data you're working and don't worry about what else is going on."

The phone buzzed, and David picked it up.

"Powell." He listened for a few seconds, his face showing increasing concern. "Where?" He put his hand over the microphone and called to Gregg Browning. "Gregg! Rodgers says there is a group headed almost right at us. 322 minus 15."

David switched his monitor to the regular Surveillance feed, and there they were: eight enemy ships seen head-on.

Rich Evans looked over his shoulder. David looked back at Evans, then the display, then back.

"So, maneuver?"

Evans looked at David, then back to the approaching ships. "Not yet. They're still at least a million klicks away. I doubt they've seen us."

"But, sir, seen us or not, if they go FTL right through us there's going to be a lot of paperwork to do back at Fleet."

Evans grinned. "I always did like your sense of humor, Powell." He looked back at the display, serious again. "I think they're going to pass behind us." Evans reached over the counter and picked up the phone.

"Surveillance...yes, Myra, it's Rich...looks to me like they'll pass behind us a bit, don't you think?" As he spoke, Evans kept his eyes on the approaching ships. "OK, very good, thanks." He hung up and looked over at David.

"She agrees. So, we dodged a bullet here."

"They're going to pass by awfully close, sir."

"Well, Powell, we could rig for silent running, but there's no sound in space."

"Point made, Commander."

Gregg Browning interrupted their banter. "Another group is throttling up, Lieutenant!"

"That's three in less than ten minutes," David said.

Jack Ballard had come into the Operations Center right after the alert and sat with Ray Salazar on the IR data feed.

He stood and came to Center Console.

"Before all this started there were six major groups of enemy ships. Three have already left, and we can see IR changes on the last three. Something is happening, something very big."

David nodded. "There were fifty warships here a few minutes ago, sir. If Jack is right, they'll all be gone shortly."

They all looked at Evans, who was watching the visual of the group approaching them as if he wasn't quite as convinced as he sounded that they were going to move on by. He tapped his fingers nervously on the console's side counter. Finally, he broke his focus and looked at the brain trust around him.

"We're faster than they are. SLIP is faster than they are."

"Neither seems to be quite fast enough when it counts, Commander," Jack said quietly.

Evans looked at him, then back at Powell. "If we leave now, we won't know the full extent of what's happening."

"Sir, even if we stay, we can't see what's at Enemy Station. We still won't know."

"Yes, Powell, I understand, but we're here now. So, we're going to wait until they've all left. Then we'll have a number we can give to Fleet. That should give them enough time to cover Inor and Earth, at least."

"What about Big Blue?"

"The ships there will get the warning, but it might be too far for CINC to send them any help."

"That sucks."

Evans nodded. "So much about this war sucks, to be sure."

Ray Salazar called Ballard back to his position, and they held a fast, animated conversation. Jack turned back to Center. "David, pull up Data Eight."

David displayed the data set.

"Oh, shit," Evans said, looking over his shoulder. Salazar had taken the IR tracking through a reverse navigation process, from which he derived some very uncomfortable conclusions.

"One to Inor, two to Earth," Jack said, saying aloud what they were all reading in the data.

"What types?" Evans asked.

"No Type II's, sir, if that's what you're wondering."

"It is."

Ballard answered, "Those are still here, but from what Ray is saying they're powering up."

David leaned back in his seat. "Why would they go to Earth? They can't possibly win there."

Evans shrugged. "I don't know, but wherever they're going, we need to get there first."

Ballard watched another group of enemy ships depart. "We've been searching for months, and now that we've finally found them..."

David let out a cynical laugh. "Yeah, too bad they seem to have found us, too."

As they watched over the next several minutes, the rest of the enemy task forces set their courses and were gone. One to Beta Hydri which included the Type II invasion ships. One more each to Earth and Inor. There could no longer be any question about what was happening. Evans had a grim look on his face as he left the Operations Room to draft a message to the fleet. Len Davis had seen that same look on the walk back into Inoria a year earlier.

After Evans headed forward, David leaned back in his chair, wondering about Carol, and about *Antares*, but, honestly, mostly about Carol. *Antares* could carry more Marines than other ships, as could *Intrepid*. They might already be at Beta Hydri to provide more security for the Seekers. To David, that meant she'd be much more likely to find real trouble, and soon. Carol could handle a rifle as well as anyone, and as Weapons Officer, she might be one to jump into a fight. He loved that about her, that streak of reckless abandon that would show up from time to time in her normally well-controlled mind. On the one hand, he hoped she would be more cautious, but on the other, he knew that would not be like her. He looked up to see Ray Salazar's eyes on him. He'd clearly been watching David as he wrestled with his feelings about Carol.

"Hansen?"

"Yes, Mr. Salazar. Guilty as charged."

Ray Salazar nodded. "I understand. But, meanwhile, Lieutenant?"

"Meanwhile, Mr. Salazar, meanwhile, we fight."

The screens and data feeds went dark as they slipped into FTL, *Cobra* vibrating as she pulled out at flank speed towards Beta Hydri.

For now, there would be nothing more to watch.

A deadly race was on, and it was a race they could hardly afford to lose.

Silver Search

Acronyms

Acronyms are everywhere these days, and the world of this series is no exception. Some people seem to love to hate acronyms, some just plain hate them. Whichever you might be, here's a handy list of the acronyms used in *Silver Enigma* and *Silver Search,*

Term	Definition
Actual	When used in a message address or sender name, indicates message is to only, or directly from, the commander personally.
ASV	Autonomous Surface Vehicle. A completely self-driving electric car.
AU	Astronomical Unit. Nominally, the average distance from the Earth to the Sun, roughly 93 million miles, or 150 million kilometers.
BOQ	Bachelor's Officers' Quarters. Sort of a permanently temporary motel on base.
CDR	Commander, same as NATO/US rank. Silver oak leaf insignia.
CINC	Commander in Chief
CPT	Captain, same as NATO/US. Silver eagle insignia.
EMR	Electro-Magnetic Radiation, which includes heat, light, and radio waves. Fleet ships are heavily shrouded to keep their heat and other EM radiations low. Stealth is their friend. There are movable EMR covers to insulate the bridge windows when necessary.
ENS	Ensign, same as NATO/US rank. Single gold bar insignia.
ETA	Estimated Time of Arrival
FDR	Flight Data Recorder. All ISC Fleet ships have an FDR which records the last 24 hours of sensor data, communications, and Bridge conversations.
FPI	Forstmann Propulsion, Inc., the company that builds and operates all Forstmann Drive systems.
FTL	Faster-than-Light
GLxx GJ xx	One or the other of the Gliese star catalog designations.
IR	Infra-Red, a wavelength of light longer than red, generally perceived as heat.
ISC	International Space Council, the governing body for the mining companies and sponsor of the Fleet.
KIA	Killed in Action

Lazy Dog	A sharp, dart-like anti-personnel weapon dropped from high altitude. Many were dropped on Inoria in the early moments of the enemy's attack.
LCDR	Lieutenant Commander, same as NATO/US designation. Gold oak leaf insignia.
LT	Lieutenant. NATO/US equivalent is a Lieutenant Junior Grade. Single silver bar insignia.
NetLink	A wrist-worn health monitor, tracking, and communications device.
NLT	Not Later Than
OIC	Officer In Charge
Ops	Operations, usually referring to the Admiral who is the Chief of the Operations Section.
PCH	Pacific Coast Highway. The *Antares* crew nicknamed the coastal highway that ran along the ocean the entire length of the Seekers' territory the 'PCH.'
PIO	Public Information Officer.
RADM	Rear Admiral. One Star.
RFG	Rods From God. These are telephone-pole-sized inert heavy metal projectiles dropped from space. Their mass and speed create their lethality.
RTB	Return To Base
RTG	Per Wikipedia, a radioisotope thermoelectric generator is an electrical generator that converts the heat released by the decay of a suitable radioactive material into electrical energy. Many deep space NASA probes like the New Horizons mission use RTGs because they are too far from the Sun to use solar panels.
Sentinel	A surveillance drone invented in FleetIntel, originally named the 'Info-Mine.'
SFU	Space Fleet University. This is the service academy for Fleet.
SLIP	The FTL communications technology used by the ISC Fleet. A SLIP message traverses a light-year in 90 minutes. This speed has a price: the bandwidth is very low and messages are similar to text, more like a WW II teletype or Morse code message.
SLT	Senior Lieutenant. In the US Navy this would be just a Lieutenant, or earlier, Lieutenant Senior Grade. Two silver bars.
Slug	Fleet slang for a heavy, Cobalt-infused self-contained breathing device, basically a Scuba for walking around on alien planets that might want to kill you with their bacteria.

Sol	A Sol is a solar day on a planet other than Earth. On Mars, a Sol is 24 hours, 39 minutes, 35 seconds. Sols are generally counted from the time a lander arrives. Fleet adopted this convention for measuring the days on Beta Hydri (d) 'Big Blue,' where the planet turns in 47 hours and 15 minutes.
TDOA	Time Difference Of Arrival. This is a method for locating the source of a radio signal by accurate timing of when the signal is received at multiple well-defined locations. Used in reverse, this is how your car GPS works.
UTC	Coordinated Universal Time. This used to be known as Zulu time or GMT.
UV	Ultra-Violet, a wavelength of light given off by the sun (see also sunburn) and some artificial light sources.
WO x	Warrant Officer. The Warrant officer ranks fall between enlisted and commissioned officers. They are typically addressed as 'Mister' or 'Ms.' The insignia is Saturn, with a number of rings corresponding to the grade.
XO	Executive Officer, second in command of a ship or other unit.

Dramatis Personae

Here is a handy list of the most significant characters (less spoilers) from *Silver Enigma and Silver Search*. There is a full crew breakdown by ship or department at iscfleet.com/bonus-material.

Who	Rank	Description
Alonzo Bass	LCDR	XO on *Intrepid* with Joanne Henderson.
Ann Cooper	LT	HQ Intel Analyst. Ann is the main inventor and driving force for the Sentinels.
Anna Nonna	CDR	*Bondarenko's* Captain.
Ben Price	WO4	Worked in Plans at the beginning of the war and is later assigned to *Intrepid* when Henderson takes command.
Carol Hansen	ENS	Our Heroine. Weapons Officer on *Antares*.
Connor Davenport	ADM	Fleet Commander
Dan Smith	LCDR	Dan was a classmate of Carol and David, probably their mutual best friend. As *Silver Search* opens, he is in command of *Columbia*.
David Powell	LT	Our Hero. As this book opens, he is an Intel officer on *Columbia*.
Dean Carpenter	CPT	*Liberty's* Captain when she was destroyed at Inor.
Denise Long	WO1	A new, young warrant officer assigned to *Liberty;* she barely survived the attack at Inor. She continues with Terri Michael on *Antares*.
Donna Wright	CDR	Fleet Chief Public Information Officer.
Elias Peña	LCDR	Deputy Chief of FleetIntel under Harris.
Fiona Collins	CPT	Chief of Plans Division. Ben and Joanne were working for Fiona when the war began.
Frances Wilson		HQ Intel Analyst. Older than most of her co-workers, she worked for years at NSA before joining FleetIntel.
Gabrielle Este	Ph.D.	Gabe is an archeologist who goes back to Beta Hydri on *Antares*.
Gregory Cordero	Ph.D.	Greg's language research in recovering lost languages makes him perfect for the return trip to Beta Hydri.
Jack Ballard	SLT	Intel Officer on *Antares*.
James George	LCDR	XO with Terri Michael on *Antares*.
James Kirkland	SLT	Weapons Officer on *Intrepid*.
Joanne Henderson	CPT	Previously Deputy Chief of Plans Division under Fiona Collins, she now commands *Intrepid*.
Joe Bowles	MD	Joe is a retired US Army pathologist who goes back to Beta Hydri with *Antares*.
Kathy Stewart	LT	HQ Intel Analyst.

Kelly Peterson	CW3	HQ Intel Analyst.
Kieran Barker	CPT	*Dunkirk*'s Captain.
Leah Farley	ENS	Communications Officer on *Sigma*, she was killed in the battle at the end of *Silver Enigma*.
Len Davis	LCDR	Navigation officer on *Liberty*. After Inor, he goes on to command *Sigma*, and is killed in the battle.
Linda Rodriguez	LCDR	XO on *Sigma*, killed in battle.
Lisa Briggs	LT	Weapons Maintenance Officer on *Sigma*. She was a friend to David, and was killed in the battle.
Marcia Soto, MD	SLT	Medical Officer on *Antares* and Carol's roommate.
Mark Rhodes	LDCR	Aide to Operations Chief Patricia Cook, he later commands *Chaffee*.
Melinda Hughes	LT	Surveillance Section Chief on *Columbia*.
Meredith Harris		Ron's wife.
Natalie Hayden	SLT	Weapons Maintenance Officer on *Intrepid*.
Patricia Cook	RADM	Fleet Operations Chief.
Randy Forstmann		Inventor of the Faster-than-Light drive.
Rich Evans	LCDR	Intel Chief on *Liberty*, he survived the attack on Inoria and is now in FleetIntel.
Roger Cox	ENS	HQ Intel Analyst.
Ron Harris	CPT	Chief of Intelligence. He and Fiona were SFU classmates.
Ryan Lewis	LT	Surveillance Officer on *Antares*.
Scott Morgan	CW2	HQ Intel Analyst.
Stanimir Yakovlev	VADM	Deputy Fleet Commander.
Susan Scranton	LCDR	An MD Exobiologist, she leads the mission to the *Sigma* battle site.
Terri Michael	LCDR	Terri was the senior surviving officer from *Liberty* after the attack on Inor. She now commands *Antares*.

Acknowledgements

Thanks for reading *Silver Search*. Please leave a review where you purchased it. If you have questions, suggestions, or comments, please email me at rock@iscfleet.com. I'd be glad to hear from you. *Silver Victory* should be out in the Spring of 2020. After that, who knows?

The origin of the 'fate whispers' quote is unknown. I found several references to it online, including one in a book by Jake Remington. I love the quote and the solemn bravery in the face of danger it radiates.

The character of Joe Bowles is in honor of Joseph Boccia, MD, a former US Army pathologist for whom I worked early in my career. Joe gave me my first break into the clinical lab software business, opening the door to a successful career. I owe him a lot. Beyond the name (boccia is Italian for 'bowl'), Bowles's personality and expertise are much different from his namesake.

Archeologist Gabrielle Este first appeared in a middle school creative writing project by my daughter, Becky. Her appearance, character, and the general outline of her recruitment is derived from that story. So nice to have smart kids you can steal from.

I hatched the idea that the Preeminent species were expatriate evolved dinosaurs soon after I started this story in the late-1990's. I picked Alpha Mensae because it the closest thing I could find to a 'South Star,' analogous to Polaris. But I have to acknowledge the similar concept in paleontologist Dale Russell's Troodon Sapiens, published in 1982. The Preeminent are somewhat different in design, however, and far more evolved.

Many of Greg Cordero's ideas on recovering the Seeker language are based on Dr. Marc Zender's lectures on Writing and Civilization from The Great Courses. (www.thegreatcourses.com) Additional ideas about the Seeker language are derived from Dr. John McWorter's lectures on the History of Human Language and Language Families on that same site. Any potential errors of fact or interpretation from these two very interesting lecturers are mine.

Cordero's translation process was also inspired/informed by two scholarly papers. The first is *Unsupervised Machine Translation Using Monolingual Corpora Only*, by Guillaume Lample, Alexis Conneau, Ludovic Denoyer, and Marc'Aurelio Ranzato. This was presented as a conference paper at ICLR 2018. (See https://research.fb.com/publications/unsupervised-machine-translation-using-monolingual-corpora-only/)

The other paper was *Unsupervised Neural Machine Translation*, by Mikel Artetxe, Gorka Lablaka, Eneko Agurre, and Kyunghyun Cho. This paper was also presented at ICLR 2018. (See https://arxiv.org/abs/1710.11041)

Neither of these papers describe a method quite like Greg Cordero describes, but together they made it seem much less crazy an idea. Again, any misinterpretation of what these papers report is mine.

The scene where Susan Scranton says there was life at Enceladus but not Europa was written several months before NASA announced in April 2017 that the conditions were such that there might be life there. Not that I can take any credit for my insight. We already knew both had sub-surface oceans, so I flipped a coin and Europa lost.

I have again rummaged around the internet for supporting data to inform the places and situations in the story. I used the following extensively and recommend them to anyone interested in the nearby stars, or how to generate names, or spell stuff correctly.

www.solstation.com
https://theskylive.com
https://www.omnicalculator.com/physics/orbital-velocity
https://www.namegeneratorfun.com
behindthename.com
www.dictionary.com

I have some individuals to thank as well.

The support of Dina, Erica, Jan, Kurt, Mike, Steve, daughter Becky, and my wife Carey, who read and gave sometimes blunt feedback on the initial version helped make this a better work. I am in their debt.

Becky's friend Colin McCrone helped me with the math to inform the list of stars that would be on a line from Enemy Station to Earth. The calculation of a given point's distance from a line in 3-D is surprisingly complex, but with Colin's help I was eventually able to beat Excel into submission.

My Lorain County Community College professor Kimberly Greenfield-Karshner provided ongoing support during the writing and took on the unenviable task of editing the first proof version.

Finally, of course, my wife Carey supported this project even while there was a still-growing to-do list and I am grateful for her help and especially her tolerance of my long days in the office, playing with my imaginary friends.